The Mercy Seller

Also by Brenda Rickman Vantrease

❧ ❧

The Illuminator

THE MERCY SELLER

BRENDA RICKMAN VANTREASE

ST. MARTIN'S PRESS
NEW YORK

This is a work of fiction. All of the characters, organizations, and events portrayed in this novel are either products of the author's imagination or are used fictitiously.

www.stmartins.com

LIBRARY OF CONGRESS CATALOGING-IN-PUBLICATION DATA

Vantrease, Brenda Rickman.
The mercy seller / Brenda Rickman Vantrease.—1st ed.
p.   cm.
ISBN-13: 978-0-312-33193-1
ISBN-10: 0-312-33193-2
1. Illuminators—Czech Republic—Prague—Fiction.   2. Illumination of books and manuscripts—Fiction.   3. Prague (Czech Republic)—History—15th century—Fiction.
I. Title.

PS3622.A675M47   2007
813'.6—dc22
2006050970

First Edition: March 2007

10 9 8 7 6 5 4 3 2 1

For Don

ACKNOWLEDGMENTS

n expression of appreciation is due my agent, Harvey Klinger, to whom I shall always be indebted—never was a writer more fortunate in representation. I also wish to express appreciation to my editor, Hope Dellon, for her candor and compassion, for her patience and her relentless pursuit of realized potential. I am grateful to all the wonderful folks at St. Martin's Press for their good work on my behalf.

The support of my friends and family far exceeded my expectations during the first critical weeks of the launch of a new author. Without their enthusiasm this second book would not have been possible. These much loved people are too numerous to name, but I hope they know how much I value them and their contributions.

I am also deeply grateful for the support of my community. Here, I wish to single out for special thanks: Carolyn Wilson and Saralee and Larry Woods for their early professional recognition and belief in my work.

Thanks are also due to Bernice Rothstein for putting me in touch with Miriam Halachmi of the West End Synagogue, and to Miriam for her gracious assistance with the bit of Hebrew translation I needed. As always, thanks to my fellow writers who read portions of this manuscript and through their encouragement helped me to find my story: Meg Clayton, Mac Clayton, and Leslie Lytle.

Most of all, I thank God for blessing my life through these individuals. I thank Him also for giving me words.

THE MERCY SELLER

PROLOGUE

PRAGUE, BOHEMIA
1410

Jan Hus chose an open window high in the left tower of Týn Church from which to watch the burning. This church gave him courage. It was a Hussite church, a Czech church, not built with Roman funds but built by and for the people of Bohemia. Yet even here in this sacred place, he could not stop the grinding in his gut as he watched the scene unfold below. This burning in the town square was Archbishop Zybnek's declaration of war.

Today, it was only books—only holy words consigned to the flames, not the people who copied them—not flesh and blood and bone. But this was prelude to the greater drama.

Hus knew it as surely as he knew that the Church from which he'd been excommunicated oozed corruption. Like a fish, it had rotted from the head down. The papacy preached lies and peddled false redemption to finance its lust for power. John Wycliffe had been the first to point out the abuses of the clergy, the first to translate the Bible into the language of the people, so the people would know that the "truths" the friars preached were lies that served themselves and not the Christ they said they served. Jan Hus was determined to carry on the movement in Bohemia that Wycliffe had begun in England.

So then why wasn't he down there to stop the burning? He who dared to defy Holy Church doctrine by offering the people the wine as well as the bread in celebration of the mass? He who every Sunday from his university pulpit at Bethlehem Chapel harangued against the false teachings of learned friars and Roman prelates? Was he too craven to gather a brigade of Lollard "heretics" to pour a little water on the archbishop's flames?

They'll cook your goose soon enough, Hus, his good sense argued. *Don't be too eager. It is only paper and ink and parchment. The books can be replaced. The hands that copy them cannot. The more the archbishop burns, the more we will copy until the meanest hovel in the Holy Roman Empire has its own gospel in its own language.*

But in spite of his brave thoughts, as Hus peered into the Prague twilight, it was himself he saw tied to a stake in the center of the bonfire. Sweat poured from his armpits as though he stood in the middle of the flames himself, as though the faggots catching fire licked their eager tongues against the hem of his rector's gown. He could smell the stench of his hair singeing, blistering his skin. His gorge rose in his throat. Shutting the window, Hus turned his face away to avoid the imagined heat that scorched the air, burning face, eyes, throat, and deep into his chest.

Give me courage for that day, Lord.

He prayed his Gethsemane prayer in Czech, not in Latin, and he prayed with some hope that for today at least he would not drink from that cup of sorrows. He had more work yet to do.

How cunningly the archbishop had chosen this spot in Staré Město, Old Town. The smoke from his bonfire would taint the air all the way to Betlémská kaple, where each Sunday Hus preached what he had learned from the Englishman John Wycliffe.

He looked again into the square where Archbishop Zybnek postured and strutted. His brocade garments, his gold pectoral cross, his white bishop's miter, forked as a serpent's tongue, glittered in the firelight. With each new parchment hurled upon the flames, the fire hissed and spewed orange sparks against a twilight sky. The crowd howled in protest. So much labor, so much richness, so many holy thoughts heaped upon the fire.

Zybnek raised his crosier in a triumphant salute to the church steeple, as though he knew his quarry watched from a darkened window.

"Hus, take care or you will be next upon my heretic's fire. The burning calf-skin will smell sweet compared to your thin, pale skin." That was the warning written in the smoke and fire.

Hus retreated from the window, but the fire of his own resolve burned as hot as the yellow flames chewing the books. With the backing of King Wenceslas, despite the rancor of the archbishop, the movement would continue. While these books burned, a legion of copyists was already producing their replacements. And come this Sabbath, Hus would preach again in Bethlehem Chapel, where the people would hear the truth proclaimed, not in some dry Latin homily that they could not understand, but in their own Czech tongue, and each one would celebrate the mass at Týn Church by drinking the symbolic blood of Christ from the chalice.

But the image he'd seen of himself tied to the stake in the square below followed Hus home and into his dreams. Jan Hus would be wakened many nights by the illusory smell of singed hair, until the day came when the smell was no longer an illusion.

ONE

PRAGUE, BOHEMIA
JULY 1412

The Avon to the Severn runs,
The Severn to the sea,
And Wycliffe's dust shall spread abroad,
Wide as the waters be.
—FROM AN ADDRESS BY
DANIEL WEBSTER (1849)

nna never went to the *hrad*, the great walled castle on the western hill overlooking Prague. It hunched just across the Vltava River, a world away. Nor did she go to the great cathedral standing guard over the castle lest she encounter the dread archbishop. Zybnek. The burner of books.

Anna attended mass at Týn Church or met with the rest of Prague's dissidents at Bethlehem Chapel. After Zybnek's great bonfire of the Wycliffe tracts and the translated gospels, Lollard texts the Church called them, heretical texts because they charged papal corruption and challenged priestly authority, Hus had warned his growing congregation, "The day will surely come when

Rome's prelates are not content to burn the Word but seek out for their fires those who would bring the Word to the people. We must pray for the strength to stand for our beliefs. We must fasten our courage against such a day."

Her grandfather had warned his little clutch of scholars and translators too, chastising them for their careless zeal.

And wasn't he the one to talk!

After all, it was he, her own grandfather, Finn the Illuminator, Finn the Lollard scribe, who, along with Master Jerome, had started Prague's secret enterprise to disseminate the banned translations. As a young exchange student, Jerome had returned to his Czech homeland from Oxford, bringing with him the Lollard texts. *The Trialogus* and *De Ecclesia* of John Wycliffe. Banned in England, they'd found new life at the new university at Prague. Its rector, Jan Hus, had translated the condemned texts, along with a good portion of the gospels, into Czech. And for years, right under the archbishop's nose, her own grandfather, a refugee from a long-ago brush with English Lollardy, had gathered a wellspring of university dissidents into his little town house, where they copied the banned pages.

Anna glanced at the castle and the cathedral spires of Saint Vitus standing sentinel behind it. She shivered even in the summer heat. But she would not think about the monster on the hill today. Not on a day when the sunlight flung dancing diamonds on the water and no smell of burning tainted the air. Not on a day when the birds wheeled in joyful circles above the river, their wing tips flirting with cloud pillows.

Not on a day when she was meeting Martin.

She turned her back to the castle and looked downriver. In the distance she could make out a camp of some sort, likely pilgrims traversing Christendom to any number of shrines—Jerusalem the holiest—in penance. That was what sinners did, sinners who could not afford to purchase expiation from the Church.

From the town sprawled on her left a familiar figure approached, but not the figure for whom she was looking. "Master Jerome! I thought Martin was coming," she said, feeling her face redden, her disappointment all too obvious.

"Martin is otherwise occupied, it seems," the gray-haired master said wearily. He handed her the bag that held the translated texts to be copied at the next meeting. "Thank you for doing my laundry, mistress," he said loudly.

Who knew the carp in the river had eyes and ears? Or that the woodcutter hauling his cart across the stone bridge might be a spy for the archbishop? But she bit back her sarcasm. She would not belittle him for his excess of caution. She had too much respect for all he had accomplished.

Anna took the university master's "laundry" and was about to bid him good afternoon when she heard rapid footsteps approaching from the other end of the bridge. She turned to see a lone figure running toward them as though the devil gave chase. Seconds later Martin joined them beneath the sheltering shade of the gate tower. He was gasping for breath and his face was flushed and his black hair fell in an unruly wave across his forehead.

"I'm sorry, Master Jerome. I was detained—"

"You didn't have time to put on your cap?" Anna pushed Martin's hair away from his forehead with her hand, a ruse to caress his face.

"I lost it. But in good cause," he said, breathing heavily. Winking at Anna, he sucked in air and lowered his voice to an almost whisper. "I'll show you at the meeting— No. I can't wait. I have to show it to you now." He drew them deeper into the shadowy hollow of the tower gate and pulled from his plain brown student's doublet a black velvet packet. It was marked with a Jerusalem cross.

"Put that away," Jerome hissed. "How did you come by it?"

"Is that what I think it is?" Anna asked, not remembering to lower her voice. "I've never even seen one. May I see it?"

Alarm showed in Jerome's face. "Not here, Martin! You didn't—"

"No, we didn't hurt the pardoner, didn't even scruff him up—well maybe a couple of . . . you know, smallish bruises. He was just setting up shop outside Saint Vitus Cathedral. Stasik kicked him in his shins, and the pardoner dropped his 'grace notes.' While he was nursing his shins—he even curses in Latin—we took off down Crooked Alley. Stasik made for New Town. I headed for Old Town. As easy as taking pennies from a blind beggar."

You'd be more likely to give pennies to a blind beggar, Anna thought, but kept silent, letting him enjoy his moment.

Martin was grinning broadly as he darted glances across the bridge to assure himself he had not been followed. As was usual in the heat of the mid-afternoon, the bridge was deserted except for the woodsman who was exiting on the other end and a beggar who sat at the gate on the other side of the river.

Anna could see from Jerome's scowl that he was not impressed. "Fool, do you want to bring the archbishop down on our heads? Wait till Finn hears what you've done. This is not our way." He snatched the little packet of papal indulgences and hid them quickly in his shirt.

At the mention of her grandfather's name, some of Martin's bravado vanished.

Jerome's gray eyebrows bunched together in a scowl. "I don't think such exploits will weigh in your favor when the illuminator seeks a husband for his granddaughter."

He was nothing if not direct. Not now. Not ever.

Martin's smile vanished quickly.

"I want to see one, Master Jerome," Anna said. "All my life I've heard my grandfather and you ranting about the pope's sale of indulgences to finance his wars, as though they were written by the devil's own hand, and I've never even seen one."

The old man looked at her and shook his head. "You're as stupid as your suitor. You deserve each other," he said. "Just pray I'm not arrested before I can dispose of them."

"Please, Master Jerome. Bring them to the next meeting. Let us all see what it is we are risking so much to rid the world of. Then you can burn them. We'll have a little bonfire of our own."

She smiled at him, her wheedling smile, the same smile she had used from childhood on her grandfather to push him through the occasional cloud of melancholy that sometimes descended upon their little house in the town square. "Please. A wee little bonfire of our own. Sweet revenge. To rally our troops."

"Methinks our troops have a surfeit of rallying." That was his parting jibe, but his scowl had lightened somewhat.

"He'll bring them," Anna said as the old master walked away.

"Of course he will. How could he resist such pretty pouting? I know I couldn't." Martin reached up and touched her lips with the tip of his finger, bent forward as if to kiss her.

She pushed him away. "Not here, Martin. Somebody will see. Besides, we are not betrothed. Not yet. Not until Dědeček gives his consent."

"Aye," he said, letting his arms drop to his side. "Your grandfather. And therein lies the curdle in the coddle."

Now it was his turn to pout. She resisted the urge to kiss the pout away.

"I don't think he likes me overmuch," Martin said.

His lips were full, and round, and cherry ripe.

"Don't be silly. He likes you, Martin. He just thinks you're a little head-strong. He thinks nobody can take care of me the way he does."

"Well, for my coin, putting you in the middle of a twice-weekly meeting of heretics is not taking very good care. Why do you call him Dědeček, any-way? I thought both of you were English?"

She reached for his hand. "Come on. You can walk me back to my door," she said, leading him. "I have called him that since we first came here, when I was a child. Besides, I don't feel English, even though my grandmother was from England too. She was a grand lady and lived in a manor house. But I wouldn't want to live there. I can't imagine living anywhere but here with you and Dědeček."

He glanced up at the castle on the hill, his eyes widening in mock terror. "Don't tell me I'll be taking a blue blood to bed as wife."

"My grandmother was lesser nobility. But we climbed down from that hill long ago. If you take me, you will be taking a humble artisan's granddaugh-ter to wife—with a dowry to match."

"Well, that's a relief. Not the dowry part, maybe." He grinned. "Did you know her?"

"My English grandmother? Only her name, Kathryn. She was not Dědeček's wife. His wife was named Rebekka, and she died giving birth to my mother. Kathryn was my father's mother, but she and Dědeček knew each other. I think they were lovers. Though he seldom speaks of her, I think he loved her very much. She died when I was hardly more than a babe. I have this faint memory—more dream than memory—of her singing to me. She called me 'poppet' or 'moppet' or something. And she took me to see Dědeček. He was shut up in some kind of castle."

Anna looked up at the *hrad* and shivered. The sun had gone behind one of the pillow clouds, turning its underbelly gray. The castle looked even more menacing under the sunless sky. "A castle on a hill like that but more . . . for-tified. 'Castle Prison,' they called it. Whenever I think of England, I think of that awful place."

"Did you know your parents?"

She shook her head. "My mother died when I was born. I was scarcely old enough to walk when my father died."

"In battle?"

She wished he hadn't brought it up. She didn't like thinking about it, but she supposed if he were to be her husband he was entitled to know her history.

"He died in the Lollard cause. Killed by the bishop's soldiers. Kathryn died in a peasant rebellion when they burned her manor house. The Church blamed the Lollards for the uprising and killed everyone they could find. My grandfather and I escaped from England to the Continent."

Martin whistled low. "So you come from a royal line of heretics. And your grandfather continues in the cause. A wonder that he never returned to England. Old Jerome says in England some of the nobility have embraced the idea of reform. It might be easier there."

"He says there is nothing for him there but painful memories. Why should we want to leave Prague? We have been happy here. He has his art and his friends from the university. I have friends here too."

She tried to make her tone teasing, playful, but talk of so much death had spoiled the mood. As they neared the square, he slid his arm around her waist, pulling her back toward the cover of the twisting street. She shook her head and pointed to the great two-faced astronomical clock.

"Hurry, Martin. Look. It's almost three o'clock. My grandfather will be worried, and he gets cross when he's worried. Besides, I still have to prepare his supper. It will have to be fish now; there's no time for anything else."

The sun did not reemerge from behind the cloud, and suddenly it seemed to Anna that the joy—like the sunlight—had drained from the day.

"Don't walk with me the rest of the way. You do not want him to think you're the reason that he must have fish and not a nicely roasted joint for supper."

"No. I want him in a good mood for what I have to ask him," he said. "Why shouldn't I ask him now? Before he finds out about the fish?"

Anna looked across the street at their little town house of baked brick and half-timbers with its pretty carved door standing open to the square. By now her grandfather would have finished his day's work, cleaned his brushes, neatly stacked his paint pots along the window ledge, and would be napping in his chair.

"Not now, Martin. Give me a chance to prepare him."

He frowned. "That's what you said last week, Anna. How much longer do you want me to wait?"

"Just a few days more, I promise." She reached up again and brushed his hair away from his eyes—eyes that flashed his frustration as she turned to leave.

Now I'll have both of them angry. In trying to please both, I've pleased neither. She sighed as she hitched up her skirt so she could make it to the fishmonger before he closed shop for the day.

TWO

CANTERBURY, ENGLAND
12 JULY 1412

*But though his [the pardoner's] conscience was a little
   plastic*
*He was in church a noble ecclesiastic. Well he could
   read the*
*Scripture or saints story, But best of all he sang the
   offertory.*
For he understood that when his song was sung
That he must preach and sharpen up his tongue
To rake in cash, as well he knew the art
   —PROLOGUE TO CHAUCER'S
   THE CANTERBURY TALES

riar Gabriel had set up his indulgence table just outside the portal of Canterbury Cathedral. He was almost hoarse from a day of preaching and bone-weary from witnessing so much misery in the faces of the penitents.

"Find pardon for your sins. All who are contrite and have confessed and made contribution will receive complete remission for all their sins," he cried in his best preacher's voice.

Hands reached toward him from all sides, pulling on his black habit, entreating him to take their ducats and shillings and pennies in exchange for the little pieces of paper he carried in his velvet pouch. The pouch was embroidered with the Jerusalem cross and held bits of parchment tied with ribbon. Receipts of grace dispensed, penance paid. His pouch also held the papal bull that granted him his pardoner's rights. This he displayed on a gold-embroidered banner and—unlike the many counterfeit pardoners—his was real. He'd received it himself from the pope's own hand.

"Listen to the voice of your poor father, your poor mother, who nurtured you and loved you and who now suffer torment, pleading with you for the pittance that will release their souls from purgatory. As soon as the coin in the coffer rings, the soul from purgatory springs."

A well-rehearsed refrain, but his heart was not in it. It was late in the day and the crowd of pilgrims was thinning. The bells tolled vespers. Their peals, muffled by the rising fog, crept across the valley like the ghosts of saints long dead. Something about the bells saddened him. There was a loneliness in the approaching eventide.

For the first time in hours, he sat down on the velvet-cushioned stool he'd borrowed from the chapter house and surveyed the last of the pilgrim line. A bloated sun draped a mantle of light, like a blessing, on the shoulders of the penitents: old men, young men, maids, wives, widows, masters, and vassals, garbed in plain pilgrims' smocks and hooded capes as they crawled on their knees into the great cathedral, into Trinity Chapel, a muddy river of them, oozing up the stairs to worship at the jewel-encrusted shrine of the martyr Thomas à Becket.

The veterans among them sported multiple badges on their cloaks and hoods, small lead pins from Little Walsingham shrine, cleverly contrived, holding tiny receptacles of the virgin's tears, or the image of Saint Peter or Saint Paul from Winchester shrine. Both were stops along the Pilgrim's Way—the penitential way. He noticed with a smile that all the pilgrims wore Canterbury bells and little tin bottles of water from Becket's well. The tiny Latin inscription below the bottles read *"Optimus egrorum medicus fit Thomas bonorum."* Thomas is a good doctor for the worthy sick. Thomas was also a good doctor for the coffers of Church, town, and crown, Gabriel reflected. Like the souvenir sellers in Mercery Lane, his pardoner's collection box was heavy with coin.

The price of mercy was not cheap: six gold florins for a duke or earl, four for lesser nobility, two for a wealthy merchant, and on down the social ladder. He even had an allowance for dispensing free pardons for those who could not afford to pay and who could not perform their penance. But the guidelines were strict and he had already exhausted that. It was time to close up shop, he thought, and rose to do so. He had promised to preside over the Divine Office.

"Please, Brother, how much?"

He turned around to see the pilgrim that matched the voice. A young woman. A very pregnant young woman.

"I cannot climb the steps to the chapel on my knees." She smiled and blushed. "I can't even get on my knees."

She had traveled far. He could tell by the condition of her cloak, not the "pilgrim's cloak" that so many purchased just for the journey, but a too-small mantle well-worn and threadbare. Her scrip was a bundle tied with a rope knotted high over her protruding belly.

"Where are you from, mistress?"

"I come from Charing. This was the closest shrine."

A journey of several days on foot, harsh for a pregnant woman, he thought, cursing in his mind the priest who had given her such a penance. Her eyes were red and shadowed by deep circles. Dust and grime from the road covered her bare feet.

"What was your crime, that your confessor thought such an untimely penance necessary?"

"I desecrated the host."

Oh, he thought. She's one of those. One of the Lollard dissidents, who question the truth of the Eucharist, one who denies that it is the real blood and body of the savior. His sympathy faded.

"That is a grievous sin," he said.

"I know, Brother, but I did not do it on purpose. When the father went to put the wafer in my mouth, his furred sleeve tickled my nose and I sneezed. The wafer fell to the ground." Her eyes grew round and frightened at the recital of her great sin.

Gabriel might have laughed had she looked less pitiable. Instead, he felt a little swell of anger. He could almost see the parish priest who, infuriated at this young woman's interruption of his performance, lashed out at her with this ridiculous penance. He knew the kind: pompous, pulpit-proud. Any compassionate priest would have known it was an accident. Then, of course, many of his brethren denied the possibility of an "accident." Everything was the result of direct intervention by either God or the devil.

She gestured toward the cathedral doors. Her voice was soft and carried a slight tremor. "I thought I could do it. I did not know there would be so many steps. But I'm afraid if I . . . I have money for the indulgence," she said. "My husband sold our cow to pay for my pilgrimage. He would have come with me, but he stayed behind to care for our little girl and gather in the grain. I have two shillings left."

"He sold your cow?"

She looked down at her large belly, meaningfully. "Brother, I cannot go into labor in a state of mortal sin. I might not—"

She couldn't even finish. But she didn't have to. Even from within his insulated cloud of ignorance, he knew how many women died in childbirth. He reached in his pouch and withdrew one of the bits of parchment, untied the ribbon, and handed it to her.

"Is that it?" she asked, peering at it. "What does it say?"

"It says that you have found pardon in the eyes of the Church and God. It says your sin has been forgiven. And it is good for two months. That should get you through."

She closed her eyes and grasped it as though it were made of gold and precious gems rather than paper and a bit of ink. A tear tracked its way from the corner of her eye down her dusty cheek. She rolled the parchment up carefully, retying the ribbon, and put it in her bundle, then withdrew the two shillings and put them on the table. He pushed them back at her.

"You sold the cow. You'll need the shillings to buy milk for your children. You have completed most of your penance anyway by making the journey."

After she had stooped as low as she dared to kiss the ring upon his finger, after he had dismissed her with the admonishment to "go and sin no more," he gathered up his indulgences and went into the great cathedral to say vespers, wondering as he went why God had called him for a job to which he seemed so ill-suited.

Only midafternoon and already the drunkards gathered in the taverns. Friar Gabriel steered his horse through the north gate of London Bridge. He looked forward to enjoying a cool drink himself on the other side of the river. The sun beat down on his tonsured crown and his horse was foaming and restless as he waited for a parade of royal barges to make their slow and splendid progress beneath the bridge. No doubt a cutpurse or three in this crowd, he thought, cursing the mayor of London under his breath that he had not cleared the bridge for the archbishop's conference.

"Make way. Make way," he shouted when finally the bridge was lowered and he spurred his horse to the front of the heavy foot traffic. He ignored the curses and grumbled imprecations from the carter his horse nosed aside. Others in the crowd also muttered their dissatisfaction, but he ignored them. The peasants always nattered against the clergy—until they needed them.

The closeness of the multistoried houses and shops huddled along the bridge fed his claustrophobia. He had almost forgotten the stench of Southwark. It wafted up from Lambeth marsh. Not just the swampy, brackish smell of the Thames south bank in summer, but the smell of squalor and lust boiling out of the stews and brothels of Bankside Street. Open sewers, refuse, rotting offal, even a bloated carcass washed up at the river's edge added to the foulness of the heat-burdened air. Animal or human? It was hard to tell from the south gate of London Bridge. But huddled on the bank of the river he saw a tavern. THE TABARD INN, the sign said. A familiar name, yet he was sure he'd not been there before. It looked a decent enough place to enjoy a cool drink.

The room was long and low and blissfully dim after the hot summer sun. He chose a spot by a window in the corner, away from the midafternoon carousers who were entertaining themselves by flirting with the barmaid. The innkeeper approached him.

"A little surprised to see you here, Friar."

"Oh, how so?"

"Just the reputation of this place. Thought you might not appreciate it. Might take offense."

"I'd like a tankard of beer, please. From your cellar, if you have one. Why would I find your establishment offensive, publican? Do you water your beer? Or fail to give good measure?"

"Best beer this side of the river and poured with generosity. Bailey. My name's Harry Bailey. This be the Tabard Inn." He waited expectantly. "Of the famous *Canterbury Tales*."

That was where he'd heard of the Tabard Inn. The poet Chaucer. With his unflattering portrait of the pardoner.

"And why should that offend me?" Gabriel took a slow, deliberate sip of the beer. It was good and cool to his parched throat.

The publican had the good grace to look embarrassed. He pointed to the velvet pouch with the Jerusalem cross. "I see you carry the indulgences. You're a pardoner as well as a friar."

"An honest pardoner, Master Bailey. My papal indulgences are not counterfeit like those of the poet's pardoner. Every dime I collect goes to Rome to build hospitals and feed the poor. I'm sure there are charlatans in every business, wouldn't you say?" He took another sip. "Even in the tavern business?"

The tavernkeeper only shrugged and moved on with his tray of tankards to the next table. Gabriel swallowed a few sips, relishing the cool liquid. His gaze traveled around the room. Little knots of yeomen, a trio of pilgrims—more literary than holy, judging from the way they nudged each other and pointed to the placard above their table that said GEOFFREY CHAUCER SAT HERE. The publican laughed with them as he gave them their drinks, then pointed to the crudely drawn illustrations, probably by his own hand, of the Canterbury pilgrims along the walls. The portrait of the richly dressed pardoner was the most offensive, charlatan to the core. A clever caricature. That was all. He looked nothing like Gabriel in his black habit.

On the other side of the room, a scarce two tables in breadth, the only other person who sat alone, was another cleric. But there the similarity ended. He looked like one of the self-styled poor priests, as barefoot and threadbare as the Franciscans, though these belonged to no holy order. The priest in his brown cassock sat near the other window, studying a crudely bound book.

Gabriel cleared his throat loudly to draw his gaze. The poor priest raised his head, looked straight at Gabriel, and went back to reading his book.

What had he expected? That the Lollard priest would be so intimidated by Gabriel's Dominican habit that he would rush to hide his book? Maybe. In a world where the Divine Order was not being threatened by rabble-rousers and spiritual dissidents. Or maybe he wasn't reading a Bible at all, but another English book. Perhaps the house copy of *The Canterbury Tales*. The proud innkeeper was sure to have one poor copy for his patrons' enjoyment.

Gabriel motioned for the publican.

"Buy yon priest a tankard and tell him Friar Gabriel would like to discuss with him the book which makes such great claim upon his attention."

The innkeeper raised his eyebrow in surprise, took a mug of beer to the poor priest. Gabriel could see him whispering and gesturing in his direction. He came back shortly. Alone.

"He thanks you for the drink, but says to tell you he has no desire to debate with you. However, if you wish to see the Holy Word in English he will be privileged to share it with you."

How brazen they'd become! No wonder Archbishop Arundel was calling his special council on orthodoxy at Lambeth Palace. Lollardy was a cancer growing in their midst. Their growing following threatened the very foundation of the Church, its teaching, its power.

"Tell him to enjoy his drink in peace, and one day soon he'll perhaps have the opportunity to *share* his English Bible with the archbishop."

Gabriel finished his beer in one gulp and made a great show of withdrawing twopence to pay for it and the Lollard's, not waiting for the innkeeper to offer it to him gratis as he might have. The coins clinked on the wooden deal of the table.

"Perhaps I'll read Mr. Chaucer's poetry sometime. You seem to recommend it so highly," he said as he left.

He mounted his horse and headed for Lambeth. But the experience at the inn had made him ill at ease. He should not have come this way. He should have ridden around to the west and crossed by the ferry closer to the archbishop's residence at Lambeth Palace. Gabriel's mentor, Friar Francis, would not have sullied the hem of his habit with Southwark dust.

By the time Friar Gabriel approached the archbishop's palace, low-hanging gray clouds were humped on the horizon. Lightning crawled through them like glowworms.

The smell of the marsh and the heat were still heavy in the air, but the stench was gone. Across the Thames, the high towers of Westminster Abbey gleamed golden in the lambent light, lifting his spirits. A light breeze cooled both him and his horse. The heat lightning in the distance promised rain. As he approached the gatehouse of Lambeth Palace, two grooms welcomed him, one to take his horse, the other to guide him to his quarters.

"His Excellency will attend you in the chapel in the undercroft, as soon as you are refreshed from your journey. He said that you should know that Prince Harry will be at the meeting."

An archbishop and a prince!

Friar Francis would be very proud of the company his protégé kept.

᠁

"What do you know of a man by name of Sir John Oldcastle?" Archbishop Thomas Arundel belched his question in Gabriel's direction.

Gabriel was the first to arrive and now sat with the archbishop at a large oblong table in the center of the chapel. At one end was a high-backed chair, larger than the rest. That was for the prince, Gabriel conjectured. The support arches that held up Lambeth Palace lent strange shadows to the place. No sunlight spilled upon the candle-banked altar at the far end of the room.

He looks even thinner than when I last saw him, Gabriel thought. He could play the grim reaper in one of the guild plays without darkening the hollows in his face. The heavy torchlight lighting the subterranean chapel lent the archbishop's face an orange pallor. Or maybe that was his natural complexion. Gabriel had heard that he was ill. Perhaps that was the reason Arundel felt so driven to rid England of heresy. Maybe he was looking out for his legacy.

Gabriel rephrased the question. "You mean Lord Cobham?"

"One and the same," Arundel said.

He was always uneasy in the archbishop's presence. Gabriel did not remember ever having seen him smile. He answered carefully. "Only that he is a man of some standing, congenial, his merit and mettle proven on the battlefield."

The archbishop frowned. That was obviously not what he wanted to hear.

Gabriel added, "I hear he is a particular friend of Prince Harry's."

The archbishop's scowl deepened, and he emitted another belch behind his skeletal fingers. "He is a heretic."

"I did not know. I had not heard—" Gabriel stammered.

Those same beringed fingers gestured Gabriel to silence. "We mean to stop him. Even if we have to burn him. He is an enemy of the Church."

Arundel's fierceness almost took Gabriel's breath away. "Stop him from what?"

"He is publishing the English Scriptures abroad and holding secret Lollard meetings where he entertains poor priests, as they call themselves—as if we weren't all sworn to poverty."

Gabriel thought of the poor priest he'd seen at the Tabard, contrasting his worn brown tunic with Arundel's ermined cape—even in this heat—and gem-encrusted pectoral cross. What kind of poverty was that? he wondered, and then immediately rebuked himself for the unworthy thought. But when Arundel prissily crossed his skinny legs, encased in their costly silk hose, his glove-leather shoes pointing sharply upward in the latest silly style, Gabriel suppressed a smile and had to pinch himself to bring his thoughts back to the orthodox view that even the archbishop's riches belonged not to him but to the Church.

The archbishop continued. "Oldcastle speaks openly against papal abuses, spreading the Wycliffe heresy. He has succeeded in getting Parliament to pass a ruling whereby all prisoners of the Holy Church are under the jurisdiction of the king. So we must first gain permission from the king for Oldcastle's prosecution, and since the king is too sick to give it, we must get it from Prince Harry."

"But I thought Oldcastle was a friend of Prince Harry's."

"And I am the Archbishop of Canterbury. Without my approval how can young Prince Harry become King Henry the Fifth? We'll get his permission."

And where do I fit into this scheme of yours? Gabriel wondered, suddenly wishing he were somewhere else.

THREE

We therefore decree and ordain that no man shall hereafter of his own authority translate any text of the Scriptures into English . . . this most wretched John Wycliffe of damnable memory, a child of the old devil and himself a child or pupil of the anti-Christ.

—FROM AN EDICT OF THOMAS ARUNDEL,
ARCHBISHOP OF CANTERBURY

Prince Harry was not looking forward to this meeting. It was his first official ecclesiastical council, and he was going to be late. He'd nodded off after dinner and would still be dreaming had not his chamberlain shaken him awake. And it had been such a pleasant dream! Truth to tell, he'd been most reluctant to waken from it.

In his dream he'd still been Prince Hal, not Harry at all, not soon to be Henry V, and he was back with Merry Jack and the old gang. He and Jack were arm-wrestling mightily across Mistress Quickly's alehouse board while the others gathered round and egged them on, the winner to pay for the next round of ale.

"Get the whippersnapper, Sir John!" came Pistol's guttural growl.

"Nay, my money's on Prince Hal. What 'e lacks in weight, 'e makes up in spirit!" Bardolph punctuated this with a slap to his thigh.

"Be careful! You're going to break the bottle. I'm calling the constable on the lot of you!" That high thin wail belonged to Mistress Quickly.

Back and forth they'd wrestled, leaning first to Jack and then to Hal, then back to Jack until Hal took one deep breath and almost—

"Your Grace, Your Grace, wake up. Lord Beaufort is without. He says you are to be at Lambeth within the hour."

Harry had opened one eye to see the harried chamberlain leaning over him.

Those dear, glad days, swept away in a cloud of garlicky breath.

He opened the other eye and leaped up, drawing on his own boots. "Bid him enter."

By the time Beaufort entered the room, Harry was shrugging into his jerkin. With one hand he buckled on his sidearm while reaching for the cup of wine with his left.

"Your Grace," Lord Beaufort said, "I'm not sure it's such a good idea for me to go with you. Arundel will not be happy to see me."

"All the more reason for you to be there," Harry said after he'd drained the cup. "The archbishop must learn to share power."

❧

Gabriel was about to gently protest to the archbishop his lack of credentials for participating in a hunt for heretics—in spite of the signal honor bestowed upon him to be summoned to the conference—when from beyond the chapel he heard scurrying feet. He recognized the cleric Flemmynge from his fine dress and affected manner. He'd met him only briefly once at Blackfriars Hall, and had not particularly liked him. He had something of the sycophant about him. Red-faced, the newcomer took the seat opposite Gabriel as he muttered about traffic on London Bridge.

Arundel scowled. "I believe you know Friar Gabriel. He crossed the same bridge. He arrived early."

Flushing even deeper at the implied reprimand, Flemmynge nodded perfunctorily in Gabriel's direction. He was stammering an apology when he was interrupted by a short blast from the horn of the king's herald. The sound echoed discordantly in the undercroft. The archbishop and the bishop sprang to their feet as if jerked. Gabriel followed suit.

Two men entered the room.

The prince took his place in the high-backed chair reserved for him at the head of the table. The other stood beside the chair to the prince's right, directly opposite the archbishop.

Gabriel considered the prince from beneath a respectfully lowered gaze. He looked nothing like the scapegrace youth who was the subject of so much tavern gossip. He looked older, more sober. His hair had been shorn high above his ears like a monk's, and he was simply dressed in a studded leather jerkin and hose, the costume of a soldier. He cleared his throat and spoke in a well-modulated—almost practiced—tone.

"Archbishop Arundel, you may introduce us. You are, of course, acquainted with our honorable uncle Henry Beaufort, Bishop of Winchester, who is here at our invitation and whom we will soon see restored to the post of chancellor."

The archbishop's strained look and the pink stain on his sunken cheeks showed his dislike for this decision. As John of Gaunt's bastard, Beaufort was uncle to the king, but his bastardy would be enough to exclude him from the Privy Council, in the archbishop's estimation. Gabriel had heard there was bad blood between them though he didn't know the particulars and didn't want to know. The less one involved oneself with court intrigue, the better. Indeed, the initial glow Gabriel had felt at being summoned to this august assemblage was beginning to wane. He had thought there would be many participants, all discussing orthodoxy, an erudite body representing the finest minds of the Church.

"Chancellor? Ahem. As you wish, Your Grace," Arundel said. But the frown he bestowed upon Beaufort would have withered a cabbage. "Next to Lord Beaufort"—the sour expression on the archbishop's face suggested Lord Beaufort's name tasted of vinegar—"is Richard Flemmynge, of Oxford College, bachelor of divinity and commissioner appointed by His Highness, your father, to examine the writings of the late John Wycliffe for heresy and to act upon their extinction."

Flemmynge stepped forward and dropped to one knee, his elaborate sleeves dusting the floor with their dagged edges. "Your Grace."

Gabriel suddenly wished he were somewhere else.

"And on your right?" Prince Harry looked point-blank at him, taking his measure with his eyes.

"Your Grace, this is a friar by name of Brother Gabriel of the Dominican Order of Friar Preacher. Young in years, but already much advanced in service to the Church. As an envoy to Rome from Battle Abbey, he was given an audience with His Holiness, and now he has a unique opportunity to travel in circles some of us never see. As he preaches, he keeps his eyes and ears open, always alert for heresy."

Anywhere else!

"Brother Gabriel." Prince Harry inclined his head in slight acknowledgment of the introduction.

Gabriel gave an attenuated bow, hoping it would satisfy protocol.

"Have you replaced the archangel Gabriel's horn with that pardoner's velvet scrip tied at your waist?" the prince asked.

The archbishop answered for him. "Brother Gabriel serves his church not only as preacher and ordained priest, Your Grace, but he is that rare jewel, an *honest* pardoner. The crown is also enriched with each and every soul who receives forgiveness from the holy treasury of merit built by Christ and all the saints."

A politic answer, Gabriel thought, reminding the prince that the sale of the disputed indulgences enhanced his own exchequer, thereby giving the crown all the more reason to suppress the Lollards because they railed against the practice.

"Then you do double service, Brother Gabriel. To both your church and king."

"My liege, we all who are gathered in this room—Commissioner Flemmynge, Friar Gabriel, and myself—are committed to stamping out this heresy that your father the king fought so hard against. Except of course for Bishop Beaufort. I do not know where Bishop Beaufort stands on the matter of the Lollards."

It was a direct challenge to Beaufort. But Prince Harry answered in his behalf.

"As chancellor, Lord Beaufort will concern himself with more secular matters. He will advise us on the war with France. But he is here today because as chief adviser to the king he serves *ex officio* on all matters important to England. You may be seated, my lords, and we shall begin the discussion."

Thomas Arundel cleared his throat above the sound of scraping chairs and shoe soles, the rustling of silk stockings.

"Your Grace, it is my thinking that it is not enough to go after the peasants and the so-called poor priests. The Lollard heresy has spread beyond the peasants who are drawn by the heretical notion that God created every man equal. At the universities and in the towns, people meet without fear of retribution to discuss the Wycliffe harangues against Holy Church and read the profane English Bibles. Moreover, we can now say that we have the distinction of having exported this heresy to other lands. The exchange of academic ideas between Oxford and Charles University of Bohemia has carried the Lollard teachings there."

"So far as that!"

Gabriel too was surprised at first but then remembered that an exchange of scholars between Charles University and Oxford had begun during the time of Queen Anne, who was of the royal house of Bohemia. It was logical enough—especially in the early days—that they would have included the texts of John Wycliffe among their exchanged works.

"It is spreading across the Holy Roman Empire like a plague. Two summers ago, Bishop Zybnek of Prague burned Wycliffe's heretical scribblings in the public square and prohibited the teachings. But with little avail. A heretic named Jan Hus still preaches these teachings daily from the pulpit, and the people of Prague are rallying to him in great numbers. If we do not act now, England will become another Bohemia."

The prince looked thoughtful. Arundel looked impatient.

Finally the prince spoke. "Why is the reading of the Bible for oneself so bad? With the renewal of our own interest—under the tutelage of my lord archbishop in matters of faith—I've often thought I'd like to read the Scriptures for myself, but my mastery of Latin renders such a task more burden than joy."

Gabriel heard a sharp intake of breath and hoped it was not his own. Arundel's face turned the color of bile. Gabriel cringed as the archbishop pounded his fist on the table.

"I shall tell you why, Your Grace. Bible reading by the unlearned masses fosters rebellion. You are too young to remember the riots in eighty-one. I remember. Ignorant peasants used their imperfect understanding of the Holy

Scriptures as an excuse to burn and pillage the property of their betters. Your father remembers. Ask him. Ask Henry Bolingbroke how the rebels burned the Savoy Palace, beheaded the archbishop, blackmailed the young King Richard by marching on London. Why do you think your father has spent his effort and his treasure to root out this heresy? If the Lollards would kill an archbishop, Your Grace, do you really think they'd quibble to overthrow a king?"

Arundel paused to let this sink in, then resumed in a more reasonable tone. "And there is the matter of the sale of indulgences, which the Lollards despise. The crown gets a portion of those monies."

The prince held up his hand to indicate that he'd gotten the point. "If these Lollard Bible readings have been forbidden, why don't we just break up the meetings and confiscate the materials?" he asked. "If it is the law of the land—it *is* the law, is it not?"

Thomas Arundel nodded. "The Act of *De Haeretico Comburendo,* on the burning of heretics."

"Well, then, if it is the law, just enforce the law. Have we not soldiers?"

"We've tried that. We even burned a heretic priest named William Sawtry. They call themselves lay priests—who flout the law—and their numbers grow daily. They get away with it because some of your nobles have succumbed to the heresy and protect them. Some who even sit in Parliament. Surely you can see the danger there; if the heresy spreads in Parliament, well . . . Until we prosecute one or more of these, we will make no headway."

"The nobility?" Prince Harry asked. "This is a serious charge. Have you proof?"

"Not enough to stand in court. But we are determined, with your permission, to obtain it."

"You mean spying on my nobles? I would be loath to commit to that, I think."

Gabriel felt a kind of sympathy for him. It was plain he did not want to make the same mistake as his father, Henry Bolingbroke; he did not want half his nobles turning on him. Civil war would not be an auspicious beginning for a new reign.

The lines in Archbishop Arundel's lean face deepened with his frown, then relaxed into a smile. Gabriel knew what was coming.

"Those who commit heresy are in danger of hell," the archbishop said. "You as their prince are responsible for their souls. Surely you must know that. Your father knew it well. He would have no problem spying on the nobles to save their souls. If this heresy is allowed to gain full sway, the whole of England could be placed under papal interdict. Are you prepared to have all those souls on your conscience?"

It was the whip the Church always used to bring a monarch in line. Excommunication. The gates of heaven barred. The king and all his subjects turned away. Gabriel's unease was growing with Prince Harry's. What his own part in this matter was to be he was not sure, but anyone who stood too close to Arundel was bound to have his own soul scorched by so much fiery zeal.

"What of the evidence gained?" the prince asked. "Who would decide on prosecutions?"

"Any evidence gained must be presented to His Majesty, if he recovers, or to Your Grace, if His Majesty remains indisposed, before any punitive action can be taken. That is the law too." He frowned as though this were one law he did not like. "It will probably only take one prosecution from you to bring the rest in line."

Gabriel watched the young prince pursing his petulant lips in concentration. He could almost imagine what was going on in his mind. One prosecution. One nobleman, who would have his own retainers. One nobleman who would spread sedition, gather arms against a king who imprisoned his own nobles. One nobleman with a banner under which all his enemies could unite. Yet the threat of papal interdiction was not to be taken lightly.

Prince Harry exhaled deep and long. "I suppose we may proceed if we are only gathering evidence. Just to see. But no action shall be taken against any of the nobility without the king's assent."

"Your Grace is in accordance, then?"

Prince Harry nodded. "Only for the gathering of evidence. Under the greatest secrecy."

Arundel rubbed his hands together impatiently as though he relished the idea of beginning immediately. "It shall be done, Your Grace. As I told you, Commissioner Flemmynge is in the process of studying all of Wycliffe's written documents and outlining the heresies therein. We will post these heresies, so that none can say they were not informed of the law. In the meantime, we have chosen where to begin. Brother Gabriel will gather evidence by inserting himself as confessor to an abbey within proximity of the household of a known heretic who sits in Parliament. He will begin gathering evidence there, and when he has a sufficient preponderance, we will bring formal charges."

Gathering evidence! So. He had not been summoned for theological consultation. *Stupid fool, to feel flattered by the archbishop's attention! Pride always goeth before a fall.* His was the Judas role. He was to be a spy. He had been right to wish himself well away. He felt as though he'd just been punched in the stomach.

"Does Brother Gabriel have your permission to proceed immediately?" Arundel asked.

Arundel had not even asked him, not given him the opportunity to refuse.

"Brother Gabriel has our permission to begin. But only to gather evidence."

Arundel smiled.

"May I ask who the lord is?" Prince Harry asked.

"An acquaintance of yours, Your Grace. By name of Sir John Oldcastle, Lord Cobham," the archbishop said, unfurling a rolled parchment.

Now it was the prince's turn to receive the fist in the stomach. Gabriel saw the blood drain from his face. He'd not known it was his old comrade of battlefield and tavern haunts. How cleverly Arundel had worked his prey!

"There must be some mistake. The Sir John I know cares not a fig for religion. He is a scoffer, yes. But he's harmless." Prince Harry's alarm showed in the working of his mouth. He chewed on his lip.

"Harmless no more, Your Grace. He has become a Lollard. And he takes no pains to hide it," Flemmynge added, handing the prince a quill. There was a gloating in his tone that Gabriel despised. "Sir John Oldcastle has found religion," he said and snickered. "From what I hear, he could use some. Trouble is, 'tis the wrong religion. And now he's going to burn."

The prince put down the pen and scowled at him.

"In hell, I mean. If he does not repent, of course."

The archbishop scowled at his lackey for the second time that day, then shoved the order in front of Prince Harry.

The prince picked up the quill, laid it down, picked it up again, fiddled with it.

"Your Grace, the soul of England—"

Prince Harry signed it with a flourish, blotting the parchment in his anger. He exchanged glances with none but Beaufort, who made no attempt to hide the sympathy in his eyes as he reluctantly nodded encouragement.

From outside the chamber, thunder grumbled. Gabriel felt the threat of it settle in his soul. With the slash of a pen, the prince had turned a nobleman into a fugitive and a preacher into a spy.

FOUR

I will take you as my people, and I will be your God.
—FROM PSALM 52,
RECITED IN THE PASSOVER SEDER

nna was just outside the walls of Judenstadt when she heard the taunts. She decided to ignore them. Who had appointed her guardian of hurt souls anyway? That was the job of saints and angels, and she was neither.

All Anna wanted was to deliver her book to the rabbi at the Staronová synagóga and get back to prepare for tonight's meeting. Her grandfather had insisted she take the decorated megillah to the rabbi as soon as it was finished, and he'd finished it last night.

"Dědeček, it's the story of Esther! The rabbi will not need it until the next Festival of Purim. You said so yourself. You still have months to finish it."

He had rubbed tired eyes. "What does a little jasmine flower like you know about the urgency that drives an old man? You have plenty of time."

Plenty of time? Try telling that to Martin, she thought.

The taunting grew louder. "Ring around the rosey—silly little Jew boy, silly little Jew boy."

A childish game. Just children in a circle, chanting.

It was hot—even the flag hanging above the walls of Judenstadt could find no breath of air to lift its Star of David bravely on the breeze. The boys would tire soon enough of their games and go home to their mothers to find cool drinks. She glanced away. With her free hand she wiped sweat beads from her hairline, then unbound the kerchief from her hair. It tumbled in a heavy cascade of curls down her back. She wiped her face with the kerchief, inhaling its sour smell—she had washed both hair and kerchief only two days ago. If she hurried maybe she could get back in time to wash it again.

"Ring around the rosey. Plague maker, plague maker."

Of course she knew what Dĕdeček would do if he were here. But she had not his virtue. And there was supper to get yet. Everything had to be just right. Martin was determined to ask for her hand tonight. She rebound her hair in the kerchief. A whisper of a breeze cooled her neck.

"Pocket full of posey. Christ killer, Christ killer." This was accompanied by the sound of a clod of earth breaking against some firmer substance. The child in the center of the circle started to cry. Thin little whimpers.

Oh, Holy Jesu!

How could any Christian woman—how could any woman—not respond to *that*? Sighing, Anna laid down her package and rushed into the huddle of boys. Their shrill voices rose to shrieks as she jerked one of them, the ring-leader, by the arm and pulled him out of the circle.

"Shame on you, Petr. I know your father. Go on home this minute, or I'll tell him what mischief you have been up to."

She wanted to shake him until his teeth rattled in his hateful little skull, but she dropped his arms and turned to the rest of them. "All of you. Go on home. Before I give you the back of my hand." She shooed them with her hands as though she were shooing chickens. "Leave this child alone. He's done nothing to you."

The miscreants scattered.

"Jew lover," one of them called to her over his shoulder as he flung another clod of dirt. This one landed at her feet, spattering her hem with dust.

"Won't do you any good to tell my father," Petr yelled. "He's not a Jew lover, like you."

But they kept on running.

"Now you."

The child cowered, as though he were rooted in the sunbaked soil.

"I know you too. You're Jakob, the rabbi's boy."

Speechless, he stared back at her out of wide, dark eyes rimmed with tears, his black hair plastered to his forehead beneath the silly little conical hat, the *cornutus pileus*, that marked him as a Jew. Marked him as a target for the taunts and jibes of others. Every time she entered the cramped misery of the Jewish quarter, it was always the same. Part of her wanted to raise her fist to heaven and scream at a God who let his chosen people be treated in such a way. Part of her wanted to fall on her knees and thank that God because she was not one of those "chosen" ones.

"You know better than to play outside the walls of Judenstadt," she scolded.

He couldn't be more than six years old. A huge teardrop slid down the boy's cheek, making a track along his dusty face. She gathered him into her arms and hugged him against her, wiping his face with her apron.

"Stop that now," she said, her voice softer. "You are not really hurt, Jakob. Come. I'll take you back to the synagogue. I'm on my way to see your father. I have something very special to show him." She picked up the book and unwrapped it. "See."

The boy smiled when he saw the bright menorah spread across the carpet page. Anna turned the page. He reached out his hand to touch the human figures with heads of animals that decorated the margin: Hamin with a weasel's head; Mordecai, the head of an ox for his steadfastness; and Esther, the body of a beautiful woman bearing the head of a lioness, to display her courage. *Thou shall have no graven image before me.* But her grandfather had rendered the figures so skillfully that there could be no doubt, even for a child, of the characters in this story.

"The queen is beautiful." The boy pointed to the lion's head.

"Yes, she is. My grandfather painted her. But he is old, and sometimes he doesn't see too well. See this funny little ochre mark? It's where he got outside the line. Here, you carry the book for me. If I had to guess, I would guess that you have an old grandfather too. While we go, tell me, do you have a grandfather?"

"*Ano.*" The boy nodded his head, forgetting all about his fright and humiliation, and babbled on about his grandfather. As they entered the Judenstadt gate, Anna listened with only half an ear.

She was wondering what she would do if her grandfather refused Martin.

Finn explored his face gingerly with his hand and then inspected the tip end of his finger. Still bleeding. He pressed hard against the spot. It needed to stop before Anna returned. She would be angry with him for trying to do it himself. And her anger could be a sight to behold. But a man had his dignity to consider. Even an old man with trembling fingers. He touched another spot on his chin. Apparently, he'd let the razor slip more than once. When she came home, she'd find him looking like a pockmarked fool.

Getting old was hell, but the worst part was what it did to his work. The palsied fingers. The bleary eyes. The megillah would probably be his last book. He knew how his granddaughter labored over his manuscripts when she thought he was asleep. More than once, he'd seen her hunched in a corner by the fire, her woolen shawl wrapped around her thin nightdress, her blue eyes straining against the meager light of a nearly spent candle to clean up the ragged edges and to color in the missed spots.

He would have liked to paint her in that light. He should have. Before he had grown so old. Now, all he could do was watch her from the shadows, regretting and yet not regretting—for there was some private pride in the savoring of such beauty reserved for him alone, even while his artist's heart wished to share that picture framed in his artist's eye with the world. She'd got the wide almond shape of her eyes from her mother, but not the blue color. She'd not got that chaos of red curls from her mother either. Those had come from Kathryn's side. As had the stubborn set of her chin. But the wide mouth and noble brow, those had been gifts from his daughter, Rose.

From outside, in the busy square, he heard shouting, curses, but paid scant attention. The peace was often marred by the noise of traffic and commerce. They lived in a small house diagonally across from the Staroměstská radnice, the Town Hall, at the corner of the Old Town Square. Their little town house had one common room that served for cooking, eating, working, and entertaining downstairs and two small bedchambers and a garderobe upstairs. It was clean—thanks to Anna—and comfortable and decently appointed with two chairs, a table, a wooden settle with feather pillows, good pewter, a silver salt cellar, and even a well-placed tapestry on the wall facing his workbench and table. Two beds made of ropes strung on wooden frames supported fine feather mattresses, and two chests with real drawers furnished the small bedrooms at the top of the narrow winding stairway just off the entrance. And from all the windows, upstairs and down, windows with real glass, Finn could see the great astronomical clock with its two faces and golden hand.

When he and his young granddaughter had first come to Prague from Ghent he had located them halfway between the Jewish quarter and the university, planning to support them by illuminating manuscripts for both communities. It had been a good plan.

He opened the door to let in a fresh breeze. No breeze. Only noise poured in. Wasn't this Sunday? Yes, he was sure it was Sunday. He'd wanted to go to mass at Týn Church to take the Holy Eucharist, but there had been the manuscript to finish. The square was usually quiet on Sundays after the Hussite mass had finished and the celebrants gone home.

Finn stepped outside to find the source of the commotion. Across the square, a small knot of noisy onlookers gathered in front of Týn Church, and they did not sound like worshippers. But whatever it was, it was none of his concern. He'd long ago decided which side he was on. He was too old and tired to worry about churches and their politics. Lately he had a new worry, pains in his chest and sometimes trouble getting his breath after he climbed the stairs to his bed. And his conscience pricked like a burr in his breeches, robbing him of sleep and paining him almost as much as his worn-out old knees. He worried about Anna.

It was time to give his granddaughter up—past time. He knew that. She should long ago have been building her own nest, not tidying his. And Finn knew Martin had more on his mind than flirtation. He could see it in the way his stare followed Anna's every move. As she sharpened the quills they used for transcribing or bent to ladle the broth from the kettle hanging on the fire, Martin's gaze never left her, and there was more than a young man's lust-filled yearning there. Finn could see that too in the way he rushed to help her lift a log onto the fire or relieve her from a tray of drinking tankards as she served the other students.

There had been others before Martin. Equally worthy. There had been that student from Oxford, a proper Englishman. Finn would have liked to see his granddaughter with an English husband, but when he went home he would have taken his new wife with him. And Finn knew he could never return there.

He could not dig that close to the root of all his pain.

Then there had been the burgher who lived in a fine house in Malá Strana, the Little Quarter just below Hradčany in the shadow of the great castle. Why had he not nudged Anna long ago in that direction? By now she should be sweeping her own hearth, scolding a brood of children, tending her husband's prosperous business. He had told himself she had too good a mind to waste on women's drudgery.

He knew in his heart he had not encouraged her to marry because to give her up would kill him. Anna was the incarnation of all the women he had loved and lost. And now it was time to lose her too. But at least this one would not be taken from him. He would give her up of his own free will.

The shouts and commotion from the cathedral steps rose to a crescendo. Time was when he would have gone across to investigate to see what it was that drew such an uncommon crowd, what it was that disturbed the Sabbath peace. But today he stepped back inside and shut the heavy oaken door, sealing in the quiet, bloated air of the common room.

He was suddenly very tired. And it hurt him to breathe deeply. He'd just take a little rest before Anna returned.

FIVE

[An indulgence is] the remission of the temporal
penalty due to forgiven sin, in virtue of the merits of
Christ and the saints.
—OXFORD *DICTIONARY OF THE CHRISTIAN CHURCH*

rother Gabriel surveyed the hunched tenements languishing
along Bankside Street. After the conference at Lambeth Palace was ended, he
had not meant to return this way, back through Southwark and Bankside.
And yet memory drew him to it. Memory or his dissatisfaction at the way the
conference had gone. He needed a reminder of where he'd come from, what
he'd been before Brother Francis saved him.

He had thought his future settled. Father, Brother: those callings he embraced. When he'd received the commission to sell the papal indulgences,
he'd been less enthusiastic, especially when it seemed this service to his
church preempted the other two. Now his archbishop had decreed he was to
add spy to his calling. But whence came that calling? Yet to question that
would be to question the very institution that had brought him the means of
salvation. It was still the only means as far as he could tell.

He left his reverie of self-doubt—for that must surely be its name; he
could never doubt his church—to consider his surroundings from astride the

horse that same church provided. It was as though this place, these smells, these sounds of cursing and bear-baiting and bargaining, echoed some half-forgotten dream rather than his own childhood memories. He'd been six years old when Brother Francis rescued him from the cesspit that was Southwark.

Was it still there? The brothel? Where his mother, little more than a girl herself, had plied her trade? A whore's apprentice at twelve, whore at fourteen, mother at sixteen. He'd proved a stubborn fetus that would not turn loose even with the scraping of a knotted rope. "Marked by God," Brother Francis had said, "a child protected in the womb to do His work."

Yet he hung on to the thinnest thread of belief that she had loved him. The brothel that kept her was more generous than some, giving her a half-day every month for herself. Every month she had made the five-mile trek to the priory to visit him. Every month she had brought him sweets and together they had played at toss the ball in the abbey gardens. And every month at leaving time, she had crushed him to her, his face pressed between the cleavage in her breasts, suffocating him with her musky sweat and woman smells, overlaid with stale perfume, attar of roses, provided by the house, the cost deducted from her wages.

"My pretty blond cherub," she'd called him. "My sweet Gabriel." Every month. For two years. The last time—he had not known it would be the last, how different might have been his demeanor if he had—her eyes had glittered with wetness, her arms resting on her high round belly. He'd known what that meant. And he'd been ashamed for her. Ashamed for himself. And when she'd tried to hug him good-bye, he'd pulled away, refusing to look at her.

She had not come again.

Now, as he looked down the street, he tried to pick out the house he remembered.

There. The one with the rotting gable—no, it was too narrow. The one leaning into the street? No, it had no wide window. He remembered a wide window seat where he'd been allowed to play as a child. But only in the daytime. At night, he'd had to sleep in a small closet. From that tight, dark place, he sometimes heard his mother moan or cry out, and he'd been afraid for her. Afraid for himself. But she had told him never to leave the closet until she opened the door. He never did.

The day Brother Francis had taken him away his mother had cried, but that occasion for her grief had proved his salvation and his singular good fortune. He, the bastard son of a harlot, had been to Rome, had kissed the ring of the pope. Brother Gabriel was a man marked for greatness. Brother Francis had said so. More than once. So it must be true.

His horse picked its way gingerly. The whole of Southwark was a field of stinking mud. Never mind that it had not rained for days and the heat wave lingered long past its welcome. Dead fish and the rotting carcass on the quayside added pungency to the air.

He was thinking he should definitely have taken the ferry when he saw the house.

A surge of recognition. A flash of memory. His heart beat the tat-tat rhythm of that small boy shut up in the closet. He should leave, right now, and let this place stay forever buried in its slag heap of regret and shame.

He got down from his horse.

A youth of about twelve leaned against the portal, picking at scabs on his arm, an employee, perhaps, or a product of the house, some knight's son or even the by-blow of the lord mayor himself—who would ever know? Certainly not the boy who reached for the reins. Himself at twelve, Brother Gabriel thought, except for the grace of God. And Brother Francis.

"This way, Father." The boy opened the door and stepped away with a smirk on his face that only half registered. "Just ring the bell to let 'er know yer here."

Brother Gabriel lifted his hand to clang the little bell. Its clapper hung beneath the bell-shaped skirt of a woman painted obscenely in the costume of a whore. Its tinny sound echoed pitifully in the empty hallway. A familiar sound. A familiar place.

The narrow entry, the low ceiling that opened on the left into the crowded little sitting room, closed in around him. He'd played in that sitting room in the daytime, with his hands galloping a toy horse across the cold floor. It still looked the same. Watery light filtered through the large grimy window fronting on the street. And it still smelled the same: some yeasty, musty odor he could not name, and stale wine, and dead coals—for no matter how cold and gloomy the day, they only lit the fire and the lamps at night.

The closeness was too much. His heart skittered against his chest wall. Hearing the sound of a door opening abovestairs, he turned to flee. Then the fragrance of attar of roses came back to him as though memory had materialized at his side. But it was no memory that flounced down the stairs to greet him.

"Come in, Father. My name is Mary. After our Lord's mother."

The profanity of it nearly took his breath.

"I can take away that frown," the woman said.

The fading bruise on her neck, he wondered, was that a souvenir left by her last customer? Her gaze traveled down his clerics' robes and back up. She offered him a smirk in welcome and ran her fingers self-consciously through her hair, tossing her head, arching her back. Her nipples showed through her thin bodice.

"The younger ones are all still abed." A little half-laugh. "Sleeping. It is early for us. Most of our customers come at night."

Her gap-toothed smile might once have been pretty. Hard to tell.

"What I lack in youth, I can make up in experience. I've learned a trick or two that is certain sure to give ye pleasure." Then she added, dropping her eyelids, reaching for his hand, "And I can be discreet."

Had experience taught her that his Dominican robes rendered no protection from her flesh-peddling? They rendered him little protection either, he thought, as he felt an unwelcome tightening in his loins. He clasped his hands together to stop her from touching him—and to stop their trembling. His body's treacherous response to the woman's lewd promise sickened him.

"You misunderstand," he said.

It was hard to tell her age, but for all her worn-out appearance, he guessed her to be no older than he was. A woman still in her thirties. Not old enough to be his mother.

"I've come on another matter altogether," he said, sounding pompous, self-righteous even to his own ears. "I'm inquiring—for a parishioner— whether you have a girl . . . a woman . . . who lives here by the name of Jane. Jane Paul."

"Jane, is it? Well, I'll be Jane, Father, if ye're partial to Janes."

This time, it was his heart that betrayed him. The desperation in her sunken eyes, the longing, touched him, evoking more compassion than he should probably feel for one who embraced sin so willingly.

"Another time, perhaps," he said, cursing himself for a coward because he'd let compassion overrule the reputation of the clergy. He tried to smile at the woman. And then let it fade. She would only take it for encouragement, not compassion. "Today, I need to find a woman named Jane Paul," he said, clearing his throat.

"There's no one here by that name." Her face went hard, her tone flat.

She turned her back on him and retreated up the stairs, her posture rigid, her steps careful as though she could summon dignity with her will. A flood of relief washed over him, weakening him in the knees. What foolishness had prompted him to inquire here? He heard the sharp slam of a door. What would he have said, what have done, if the woman had said she knew his mother, given him an address? Or worse yet, said Jane Paul was sleeping abovestairs at that very moment?

The boy handed him the reins to his horse. "Are you all right, Father? You look poorly."

Unable to speak for the tightness of his throat, he shunted the boy off with a nod, and mounting his horse, rode away hastily lest he embarrass himself by vomiting in the street.

Only after he'd made good his escape, did he think about the boy. He should have given him something, still could. He hesitated. But he could not bring himself to go back.

~⚡~

From the open door, Anna kept one eye on the astronomical clock as she laid the table with pewter plates and bread and cheese and grapes. The pigeon stew in the earthenware pot buried in the embers should be falling off the bone by now. She had put it to bake before leaving for Judenstadt. Fifteen more minutes and the students would be here. The inkwells were filled, blank paper laid out for the copying, fresh quills, the Wycliffe Bible laid out for her grandfather to read from. As scholars from the university, most of them would pay close attention to the English, and then Jerome would read Jan Hus's translation. She should wake Dědeček, see that he was alert, then maybe she'd have time enough left to brush her hair and change her apron.

"Dědeček, are you up from your nap? It's almost time," she shouted up the stairs.

"Let him sleep." The familiar voice came from a figure silhouetted in the doorway.

Jerome was early. There would be no time to refresh her hair and change her apron.

"Come in. I was just going to wake my grandfather."

Jerome ducked under the lintel post, stepped just inside the door. "Let him sleep. Time enough for bad tidings when he wakes. I came to tell you there will be no meeting tonight." His face looked grim.

"No meeting? Is Martin not coming either?"

She felt her face color at the transparency of her question. Of course Martin would not be coming if the others weren't. But the old man did not notice. Or he let it pass.

"No, Anna. Martin's not coming. He's been arrested along with Stasek and Jan."

"Arrested! Why?" But she knew why and her mind was whirling. *Please, God, let him keep his mouth shut. Please, please let him not mention Finn the Illuminator.* "Jan Hus too?" she asked. If they'd taken Jan Hus, they must have damning evidence indeed!

"No. Jan from the trivium. I fear all his learning in rhetoric and dialectic has gotten him in trouble. But Jan Hus will be next. The bishops are going after the small fry first. I blame myself for this." He had taken off his hat in the heat and was twisting it in his hands. "I should never have brought the Wycliffe works from Oxford."

"No, Master Jerome. It's not your fault. You were only doing what you thought was right. And you weren't the only one who brought them."

Her mind was whirling as she tried to reassure him. Would her grandfather be next? Surely they would not disturb an old man who only studied the Bible in his own home. There was the prohibition, surely enough, but everybody read the vernacular Bible. The edict was openly defied. But the Lollard texts, the Wycliffe translations, these would be harder to explain away.

"What did they do to give the bishop cause? Has he found out about the meetings?"

Jerome shook his head in exasperation. "The brash young fools attended Sunday mass at Týn Church and burned the indulgences on the altar! The archbishop's spies were there. As always."

"The indulgences! But I thought you took them."

"Martin talked me into giving them back to him. He said that I should not endanger my family by having them, that I was watched by the archbishop's men. He promised to burn them." He laughed bitterly. "Well, he burned them, all right."

Anna felt her heart rise into her throat. She could see Martin with his reckless, flashing eyes, haranguing. She'd heard him on the subject before. *"The holy fathers peddle pardons as though they were the gatekeepers of hell itself. And that would make them the devil's henchmen, then. Wouldn't it?"* Foolishness to take his argument to such a public place. Why did they not let well enough alone! The people were going to Bethlehem Chapel anyway. Such rashness would give the Church the excuse they needed to act. Sweet, impatient Martin! He needed her almost as much as Dĕdeček. One too old to listen to reason and one too young to understand it. And she was caught between them.

"Jan Hus is trying to get them out," Jerome said. "He's facing off with Zybnek now. But it will end badly. Even King Wenceslas is under pressure. He's always been tolerant, but it's hard when the crown gets a portion of the license money from the sale of the indulgences."

Shuffling footfalls on the stair caused her to signal Jerome, a finger against her lips to shush him. If Hus could get the students released, Dĕdeček might never have to know. Her grandfather appeared at the bottom of the narrow wooden staircase, leaning against the casement for support. He looked frail, and his skin had a grayish cast.

Anna had resolutely refused to think of her future without him, but as he leaned on the carved wooden balustrade of the stair, the specter of the little town house in Staroměstké náměstí after he was gone flashed across her consciousness. The sweat trickling at her hairline turned icy. He'd been all she'd ever known. Father. Mother. Sister. Brother. This old man and his passion for his work had illumined her life.

"Dĕdeček. Jerome has come to tell us we must postpone tonight's meeting."

She went over to him, offered him her arm. He shook it off gently but with a frown.

"What will end badly?" he asked.

"Nothing. Just the usual. The archbishop and his threats." She shook her head very slightly, catching Jerome's gaze with her own, then busied herself with taking up the stew, her face hidden from her grandfather lest he read the lie in her eyes.

"Your supper is ready. Master Jerome, your wife won't mind if you eat with us, will she? To keep us company?" she implored him with a lift of her eyebrow.

Her grandfather held the edge of the table for support as he lowered himself to the bench. "What about Martin? Is he not coming?"

Anna ladled the fragrant stew onto the plates.

"No, Dědeček, Martin will not be coming tonight."

⌁

Anna slept fitfully. After Jerome left, her grandfather had been seized with a paroxysm of coughing. He sometimes had a spell after working long hours with his paints and inks, but this time the phlegm he finally hawked from his wheezing lungs was the color of ditch water. Anna had dosed him with tincture of horehound and honey and distilled spirits, and finally, after assuring herself that his brow was cool, she banked the cook fire and went off to bed.

But it was a hot night. She lay awake, listening to night sounds drifting through her open window: the occasional creak of wooden wheels on cobblestone, the call of an owl to its mate, the distant sound of the cloister bells calling the cathedral monks to vigils. Listening too for the rattling cough. She threw off her coverlet, wondering if Martin was shut in some airless cell, wondering if he was afraid—or worse, being tortured in the castle dungeon. Just before dawn, she drifted off to troubled sleep.

When she woke to the sound of the church bells tolling prime, the sun had already laid a saber of light across her counterpane. She hurriedly ran a comb through her tangled hair and bound it into its kerchief, then laced her bodice over yesterday's shirt—no time to find a clean one—and threw on her kirtle. She rushed to Dědeček's room, knocked softly, pushed open his door. His bed was empty. She smiled to see how neatly he had made it up. As always. His chamber so spare and tidy it made her own seem a riot of disorder.

Her world was back in place with the morning light. She would probably hear soon that Martin and the others had been released with a warning.

Dědeček should not have let her sleep so late. He was probably making his porridge for himself. But when she reached the bottom of the steps she found him standing at the door, hot sunlight pouring in around him. He was talking to the girl who sold them milk and eggs.

"You should have called me," Anna said.

"Anna," he said, frowning. "The milkmaid says they have arrested some students for breaking up Sunday services."

"I know, but it will be all right. That was yesterday. Master Hus has probably already gotten them released by now."

"You should have told me," he said over his shoulder as he counted out pennies to the woman. He shut the door behind her, turned to Anna, frowning. "Did you know Martin was among them?"

She reached for her apron hanging on a peg beside the hearth, swung the water pot around, avoiding his gaze. "Master Jerome told me last night. I wanted you to sleep well. I was going to tell you this morning. Don't fret. This is not the first time they've gotten themselves in hot ashes."

He slumped down at his workbench, idly fingered the brushes neatly arranged in the drying rack he'd made for them. Anna watched him anxiously. This was just the kind of worry an old man didn't need.

"Never mind the porridge," he said. "I have no appetite this morning. I want you to go across the square to the town hall and find out what you can. And if they've already been released, then go to the university and find Martin. I want to talk to him." He was suddenly seized with a fit of coughing that rattled his whole body.

"I don't want to leave you." She put the back of her hand to his brow. "You have a fever. Come. Let me help you back to bed."

He shook off her hand. "Anna, do as I say!"

The only time he had used that gruff tone with her, even as a child, was when she played too close to the fire or dabbled with his paints without permission.

She had never directly disobeyed him. Not as a child. Not as a woman. Was this the time to start?

He motioned impatiently with one hand for her to go, supporting his ribs with the other, the way he always did when he coughed—a habit born of his sojourn in Castle Prison. His body might be weak, but his spirit and his mind were as strong as ever. To defy him now would undermine that spirit, and then he would be truly old. The town hall was just across the square. She could at least go there and see if the men were still being held. Maybe see Martin.

"All right, Dědeček, I will go, but first let me help you back to bed."

He shook his head. "It's cooler down here." The coughing had left his voice raspy. "I'll just sit in my chair and wait. Leave the door open so I can watch you go." He motioned to the deep cushioned chair that he'd tied together out of bent willow and leather strips.

She retrieved a feather pillow for his head, cracked an egg and stirred it with a stick of cinnamon into a glass of milk and honey.

"Drink this and I'll go."

When he was settled into the chair, she handed him the drink. He frowned down at it then took a swallow or two.

"Drink it all. You need it. Besides, the milk will sour quickly in this heat."

"I will drink it," he said. "Now go."

Anna stepped out into the sunlit square. The air was thick. She could feel the hot cobblestones through her thin leather soles.

The hand of the great clock showed half past seven and already the heat was rising.

SIX

An old woman can be more expert in the love of God . . . than your theologian with his useless studying.

—RICHARD ROLLE, 14TH-CENTURY HERMIT

everend Mother, come quickly to the scriptorium. It's Sister Agatha and Sister Matilde. They are—"

"You do not have to say it. They are quarreling again."

The abbess of the newest abbey in Rochester, England, laid down her quill hastily then covered up the stacks of lined parchment spread across her desk. Kathryn did this unconsciously, a habit born of prudence. She stood up slowly. Lately she'd felt as creaky as an old wooden stair.

"No, Sister. I will not come. This time they shall come to me. You tell the sisters I wish to see them in my chamber. Now!"

"Yes, Reverend Mother."

The novice scurried away. Kathryn listened with dread to the sound of shuffling footfalls and angry voices in the corridor. The two old warring nuns set a sorry example for the younger ones, she thought as the quarreling voices grew louder. The two combatants must have been waiting nearby and now each hurried to press suit before her sister could avail herself of the opportunity.

The door burst open as the two, both ample hipped—with their flying headdresses like two boats under full sail—tried to breach the opening at the same time.

Any other time Kathryn might have laughed at the spectacle. But not today. She raised the thin gauze of veil that usually covered her scarred face, so that the two women could see the displeasure in her countenance.

Sister Matilde's mouth froze on the complaint she was about to utter, her lips pursing in a perfect *O*. Sister Agatha's mouth clamped down into a thin line, her bottom lip protruding slightly, pushed up by her heavy jowls. Sister Matilde's eyes sparked blue fire. Sister Agatha's squinted into little pinpoints of pure anger in a face the color of a boiled ham.

Kathryn sat back down, grateful for the barrier of the wide oak desk between her and the storm. She motioned for them to sit also.

Matilde squeezed her wide posterior into an opposing chair.

The abbess reflected idly that both women might need to be rotated to garden duty. Their sedentary occupations were not serving them well.

Agatha remained standing, tapping her foot. "Reverend Mother, it's disgraceful. It's unbecoming. It's . . . it's heresy!"

"Your intemperance, Sister, is likewise unbecoming. Tell me, calmly, what it is that has you so overwrought."

Matilde answered for her. "Overwrought seems to be Sister's natural state. Maybe she requires a draught to improve her bowel function."

Kathryn favored Sister Matilde with a disapproving look. The nun ducked her head to hide the smirk at her well-delivered barb, but Kathryn knew she would later relate it to her sisters to their great amusement. While Sister Matilde, because of her humor and her kindness and her wit, was well loved in their little cloistered community, Sister Agatha's self-righteous piety did not make her popular among the nuns. They should have left her behind at Saint Faith when they split off into their new abbey. But Agatha was an excellent amanuensis. Her script was flawless, her hand flowing.

"Sister Agatha's bowels are not your concern, Sister Matilde."

Emboldened by the rebuke, Sister Agatha scolded Matilde, "You'd better save your concern for the state of your immortal soul."

Sister Matilde looked up, no longer smiling. "It's the English Bible, Reverend Mother. Sister Agatha takes it upon herself to chastise me for reading it."

"It is only out of concern for Sister Matilde's soul." Agatha's round little eyes bulged in righteous indignation.

Matilde's usual tender visage hardened. "Look to your own soul, Sister. Leave mine alone. Our Lord said to get the beam out of your own eye before—"

Kathryn raised her hand. "Enough! Sister Agatha, you know the rule here. You know that we serve as amanuenses for all manner of literature. Copied pages are what we produce. As other houses produce bread or wine or cheese, we make books. Making books provides us with a roof over our own heads and allows us to minister to the poor of Rochester."

"But Reverend Mother, Sister Matilde was not merely *copying* it. She was reading it." Her voice shrilled in outrage. "I saw her lips moving!"

Kathryn lowered her own voice to counter Agatha's shrillness. "It might do us all good to read it. The words of our Lord in any language are instructive to our souls."

Sister Agatha's face flushed as red as the scarlet cloth covering the Holy Virgin's shrine behind her. "Profanity. That's what it is—"

"We have had this discussion before. Many times, Sister." Kathryn lowered her veil to indicate dismissal. "If you don't wish to copy the Wycliffe Bible, you may work on *The Life of Saint Margaret*. We have several orders for that. Or *Julian's Divine Revelations*, or *Saint Bride's*."

"*Saint Bridget's?* I shall not touch that either. There's another woman with too much learning for her own good."

The abbess felt her spine stiffen of its own accord. "Perhaps you need to work in the garden for a while. A little tilling of the soil, a little gathering of the fruits, might give your scribe's hands a necessary rest."

Sister Agatha's face betrayed her shock. "But I'm the best—"

"Pride is a deadly sin, Sister. And spiritual pride is the most damning of all."

In the moment before Agatha lowered her head and murmured, "As you wish, Reverend Mother," Kathryn saw the resentment in her eyes and knew that it would fester.

But she would not deal with that today. Not on a day when she had to reconcile the abbey's flagging accounts. Not on a day after she had slept so badly, her dreams haunted with old memories, old yearnings.

After the two women departed, this time progressing through the door in single file—one sober, one scarcely concealing her animosity—Kathryn covered her right eye with her hand, looked out into the room. This was a test she performed periodically. Lately, her vision in her damaged eye seemed to be improving. She could now tell light from dark, sometimes even shapes and shadows, insubstantial as ghosts.

Today, through the haze of light she saw such a form, an old ghost. He was so real she could see the faintest smudge of azure paint clinging to the edge of the sable-tipped brush he held in his hand, the azure that matched the blue of his eyes. Her old heart almost stopped its beating. She reached out to touch him. But where his hand had been, her hand encountered only the cool metal bar of the door left open by the departing nuns.

A trick of the mind. Nothing more.

But the seeing of it had left her with a feeling of unease, a wrinkle in the peace she had worn like a mantle for these many years. It was probably just disquiet brought on by the warring nuns whose souls were in her care. But disquiet it was. And more. A kind of aching loneliness and impending loss as one might feel at the deathbed of a loved one.

Foolishness. An old woman's fancy. Best to work through it; experience had taught her that. Whenever her spirit sagged, she picked up her quill and dipped it in a pot of ink. She did that now.

But she did not apply it immediately to the parchment over which the nib was poised. Instead her mind was snared by the image of a child pretend-painting with the light from a sunbeam. The image brought tears. She wondered—not for the first time over a span of years—what had become of Colin's little daughter. Her granddaughter would be a woman grown now. Probably with children of her own. And Finn? No. She would not think of that. She'd long ago made peace with her choice. She would not gainsay it this late in her life.

She didn't know how long she sat thus before her reverie was interrupted by a gentle knock.

"Mother, there is a friar to see you. A Brother Gabriel. He says he's been sent by the archbishop."

"I shall attend him in the parlor," she said.

A friar? What business would the learned preacher have here? She hoped he was only seeking hospitality for the night. The friars with their "pure" doctrine made her nervous. When she read of the Pharisees who challenged Christ, she pictured them in Dominican robes.

She covered up the manuscript she'd been copying and checked to see her face was covered.

With an unquiet soul she went out to meet the friar, closing the door firmly behind her.

SEVEN

Do not fear those who kill the body . . . everyone
whether priest or layman who knows the truth ought to
defend it to the death; otherwise he is a traitor of the
truth and of Christ as well.
—JAN HUS IN A LETTER TO THE PEOPLE OF
PILSEN, OCTOBER 1411

s Anna hurried across Old Town Square, the light was bouncing up from the cobblestones in waffling waves of heat. Týn Church, with its
twin irregular towers bristling with spires and pinnacles, shimmered in the
Prague summer sun.

It was eerily quiet. Not even the pigeons strutted on its steps.

She went up to the great doors. No notice of public punishments or ecclesiastical censure posted there. None posted on the town hall doors either.

This feeling of foreboding was silliness. The church was quiet because of
the heat. Her imagination was running away with her. Martin and the others
had probably been threatened and then released. She had determined to go
back and tell her grandfather that he need not worry, that this was obviously
a fool's errand and her time was better spent washing their dirty linen, when
she heard faraway shouting coming from the direction of the Vltava River.
More specifically from the stone bridge. Angry shouts. Catcalls.

As she moved toward the crowd, her anxiety increased. A public whipping? She did not want to see the poor unfortunate. She'd seen a public whipping once. She should go instead to the university and see if the students had been released.

The crowd noise increased.

The whipping she'd witnessed had been a poacher caught in Hradčany while killing the king's deer. They'd brought him to the Old Town Square to make a lesson for the people there. A mercy, a boon granted by King Wenceslas, the burghers agreed, to whip the villain instead of hanging him as the law decreed.

It had not looked like mercy to Anna. They'd stripped him to the waist, this man whose crime had been to find meat for his family in the dead of winter. The king's guard had tied him to a pole while his wife watched them turn his back to raw meat. The soldiers had held her back as she'd struggled and cried out her husband's name. Karl. His name had been Karl. He'd been about Martin's age.

Martin! But no whippings were carried out by the king's men, and the king was a supporter of the Hussites. Wasn't he?

Besides, she reasoned, they would not hold a whipping on the bridge.

A dunking, then! The bishop's public warning for them all. The bishop would not need the king's permission for that. Martin hated the water. He would not even grapple for fish in the shallows.

She picked up her skirts and ran.

As she approached the castellated tower entrance to the bridge, she encountered students running the other way. One pushed her roughly aside. "Watch where you're—"

"Anna." Someone, an older man, grabbed her arm. It was Jerome. "No. Anna, don't. You don't want to see—"

"I have to go to him. Whatever his punishment is, he needs to know I'm there to give him courage." She wrenched free, her heart pounding, started to push through the crowd.

Past the tower gate.

"Anna, they will see you there, and you—"

Past the great bronze crucifix that decorated it.

She was vaguely aware of Jerome tugging at her skirt. Then it pulled free.

"Anna, please. Think of your grandfather, please. You'll endanger us all."

She pushed on, not knowing if he was still behind her. Not caring. She broke to the front of the crowd, suddenly grown silent.

All eyes gazed upward. Hers followed.

There, beside the great bronze crucifix of Jesus, stood three poles. Like the three crosses on Golgotha, she would later think when, in the heart of the night, again and again, her mind replayed the grisly images.

On the top of each pole was a human head.

Jan from the trivium on the left. And Stasik on the right.

And impaled on the middle pole was the once beautiful head of Martin, his curly black hair dripping blood onto the stone of the bridge.

⁓⁂⁓

Finn watched for Anna's return. He had seen her cross the square, then seen her disappear in the direction of the river. His anxiety and the bright light spilling through the open door made his head throb. Little shallow breaths were all he could manage, and he knew he had a fever. He could tell from the parched skin on his lips and the way his tongue cleaved to the roof of his mouth. And he was cold. Despite the waves of heat dancing in the sunlight, he shivered beneath a blanket, longing to close his eyes against the brightness. But he did not. He watched for Anna.

She appeared at last in the doorway.

She did not cross the threshold, just leaned into the post. Her face was bleached white and her skin drawn tight against the bones.

Fear clutched at his heart. It had finally come. And for all the archbishop's threats and Hus's warnings, it had caught him unprepared.

He got up and moved as rapidly as he could to the door to catch her before she fell.

Her eyes were wide and staring. "Dědeček, they have killed Martin. They . . . they cut off his head." Her voice broke on the last word, filled with disbelief, and so low he could not have heard her had he not been holding her in his arms. "All their heads."

Beheaded? Had he heard aright? He had to stay calm for her sake.

"It will be all right, Anna." He thought, even as he said those same words he always used whenever she'd cried, how foolish he sounded. This was not some child's skinned knee, some favorite toy broken. The man she was to marry was killed almost in front of her. He should not have sent her. He should have gone himself. But he'd not thought it would come to this. Please, dear God, let her have been spared the actual execution. "Tell me, child."

"On the bridge. Their heads on pikes . . . on the bridge."

He guided her to the wooden bench beneath the window, feeling the weight of her in his arms, on his heart. "Tell me all of it," he said as he stroked her head. "I am here."

"They are dead," she said, her voice a hoarse whisper. "Their heads on poles on the bridge. All three. Jan, Stasik. And Martin. Martin is in the middle. Like Christ."

He closed his eyes and drew a pained breath at the vision her words conjured. He had known the persecution was coming, but he had not thought it would burst like a summer storm over their heads. He had thought they would have more warning. What thunder they had heard had been distant, far on the horizon. He'd thought there would be time to protect her, if not himself. What a selfish, blind fool he had been!

"Martin was going to ask you. I made him wait. I should not have made him . . . He would not have been so careless. It is my fault . . . my fault . . . for making him wait." She started to sob, great ragged breaths tearing at her chest, stealing both her breath and his.

"Shush, child. Of course it's not your fault. If anyone besides the bishop is to blame, it is I. Not you. I should have seen it coming."

She started to stand up but sank to the floor, hugging his feet, hiding her face against his knees. He could feel the quivering of her shoulders through the cloth of his breeches as she struggled to gain control.

When Anna was a child, he'd never taken her to look at the heads of the criminals on pikes as other parents did—the object lesson: behave or your head might wind up here someday. Or if you can't behave at least be smart. He should have, he thought. It would not be so hard for her now. It would be a common thing. It was a common thing. *And yet this time it's lads you know and love, lads you helped lead into danger,* a voice inside his head insisted.

Stasik and Jan. And Martin. Their young lives snuffed out like candle flames. And what of Anna now?

His old heart hammered erratically. He sucked air to fill lungs that felt as though they were leaking. Time! There was not enough time!

"Hush, Anna. Pull yourself together." The words came out in a wheeze. "You must be strong. We can mourn for Martin and the others later. Right now we must act to save ourselves. Get up and go fetch Jerome."

"Jerome was there, Dĕdeček. Jerome was at the bridge, where they . . . where I saw . . ."

"I know, child, I know what you saw. But we have not much time." He gathered more breath, felt the wheezing in his chest. "Jerome will go back to the university to warn the others. Tell him I need to see him right away. I must give him instructions." He touched her cheek. It felt cool against the palm of his hand.

She lifted her face from his knees and looked up at him, rubbing the tears from her eyes with her sleeve. Now, she held the back of her hand to his forehead. It was as cool against his face as her face had been against his hand.

"Dĕdeček, you're burning up! I must get you to bed. Find you a doctor." But she did not move. "I must . . . find a doctor . . ."

"Anna—"

She moved like a sleepwalker as she put his arm around her neck, and standing up, half lifted, half dragged him from the chair. As they struggled up the stairs together, the room swirled around him.

"Find a doctor. That's the next thing . . ." She had stopped crying, but her voice sounded strange and far away.

"No, Anna . . . Jerome—"

"Do not worry about Martin," she said, wiping her face with the back of her hand. "He has no need of Jerome now. The angels will bear his soul to heaven. But you and I are still here, and we must fend for ourselves. I have to take care of you now. I should have taken care of Martin. I still have you. I will take care of you."

He opened his mouth to answer her, but there was not enough breath. He felt the bed rush up to meet him.

~ ※ ~

When Finn woke hours later, Anna was leaning over him, bathing his forehead.

"Dědeček, you're awake. Thank God." She smiled bravely, as though the horror she had witnessed had only been a bad dream.

She looked like his beautiful bride, like Rebekka the day he had pledged to protect her—but he'd been unable to protect her from death—and like their daughter too, their Rose, who had died giving birth to Anna. And when she touched his face so gently, he saw Kathryn. The day Kathryn had come to him, in the prison at Norwich, with his tiny granddaughter in her hands and offered her up like a sacrifice.

"Jerome came while you were sleeping, Dědeček. He brought you this." She spooned some vile-tasting liquid the color of squid ink into his mouth. He almost choked swallowing it. "Jerome says he thinks we will be safe enough for a while. The authorities will wait to see how this works out. If it shuts Hus up. They will not risk the anger of the crowd again so soon."

Finn tried to prop himself up, but when he was too weak to speak above a whisper, he motioned for her to lean over him.

"You must leave, Anna. You must go to England. Get a paper and a quill. Write down the name I'm going to give you."

"Shush, Dědeček. *We*," she pleaded. "*We* must go. I will not leave you."

He could see fear and grief and disbelief in her eyes, but he had no time to assuage it.

"Do as I say, Anna. The paper." His voice was hoarse. He closed his eyes to gather his strength, listening to the sound of shuffling papers, the clatter of a jar of ink. When he opened his eyes, she was hovering over him, the quill poised in her hands. *She is humoring me*, he thought. But no matter. She would do as he asked. She would remember his instructions.

"Sir John Oldcastle. Lord Cobham."

"No, Dědeček. This is foolish. I will not—"

"Write it, Anna. Cooling Castle, Kent, England." He croaked out the last syllables over the scratching of the nib. "That's where you are to go, if anything happens to me."

"Nothing is—"

He ignored the pleading in her voice.

"Sir John is a powerful man. And a good man. He will protect you for the cause we share. Did you write his name? Repeat it back to me."

"Sir John Oldcastle." Her voice quivered with emotion.

"Jerome will arrange for your passage. Sell the household goods. There's some coin in my purse and some in the chest beneath the Bible. Our lease is paid up, but Mistress Kremensky is a fair woman. She will refund any balance you don't use. Do not sell the Bible. Take it with you. Show it to Sir John. It will be proof of who you say you are."

"Dědeček, please. You are frightening me. Do not talk so. Jerome has gone for the doctor."

She was crying openly now, her tears spilling onto his chest. But he was too tired to respond. He closed his eyes and slept fitfully. Each time he opened them, she was there, holding his hand, wetting his parched lips with her fingertips dipped in cool water. They smelled of jasmine. His little jasmine flower. A tiny child playing among his empty paint shells on the floor, "painting" with a broken quill from the light of an errant sunbeam.

"The paper?" he tried to ask her. Had she written it down? But it came out of his mouth a jumble of words even he couldn't understand.

"It's here, Dědeček. I have it right here. Sir John Oldcastle."

The last time Finn woke, Anna's head was lying on his chest as though she were listening for his heartbeat. He could feel the imprint of the cross she wore around her neck engraving itself into his chest. The cross he'd given her. The cross he'd made for her grandmother Rebekka. The cross that was all she'd ever had from her mother, Rose. "It would please me if you'd wear it always," he'd said when he gave it to her, "to remind you of your heritage." Though God knew he'd told her little enough about that heritage. Though God knew, he'd meant to. One day.

The room was darker. It must be late in the day. The light was filtered through the red of her hair, making the room all rosy like the afterglow of a sunset.

He closed his eyes, but the light remained, grew even brighter at its center. He thought he saw his grandmother standing in the light, holding out her hand to him. And Rebekka, his young bride, beside her. And their daughter, Rose, was there too. They smiled at him, beckoning him. They were beautiful women, more beautiful even than in memory.

The whole room filled with the scent of jasmine. He inhaled deeply, the heady fragrance making him dizzy with delight. The pain that had been so long his companion, so that he'd forgotten what it felt like to be without it, was gone. And in its place was a feeling of extreme well-being, so intense it almost gave him back his breath.

Then he noticed that of the women standing in the light, one was missing. Kathryn was not there. Kathryn was not standing in the light.

He heard again the words the prioress had spoken to him. That Kathryn had signed a corrody before she went to sleep. "To sleep," she'd said. Not "died." And later, "her lands are sufficient to see to her needs." In his grief, he thought she'd meant for praying masses for her soul. "We've done all that we can do," she'd said. The prioress had not lied to him, but she'd let him believe that Kathryn had died.

It was suddenly as clear as the light around him, and his old heart laughed with the understanding of it. Kathryn was not there among the souls of the dead because she had tricked him. All those years they'd spent apart when they might have been together! But no, that was not true. There had been no other way. And in the purity of that light around him, anger could not take hold. Nor regret. It was enough that Kathryn lived.

And Kathryn lived in England.

He was not leaving Anna to make her way in the world alone.

Find Kathryn. He tried to breathe the words into Anna's ear. But the only sound in the room was her quiet sobbing, which, strangely enough, did not disturb his peace as it once would have. For in that tear in the fabric of time when the passing soul brushes against the fibers of the curtain separating us from paradise, Finn's soul whispered to Kathryn's.

Then he was swallowed by the light, and could no longer hear Anna's unquiet sobbing.

EIGHT

It is no pampered glutton we present
Nor aged counselor to youthful sin
But one whose virtue shone above the rest
A valiant martyr and a virtuous peer
—PROLOGUE TO *SIR JOHN OLDCASTLE* (1600)

It was late in the afternoon of the next day when Lady Cobham found her favorite peregrine falcon with its neck wrung. It had strangled itself with the twisted strings of the little hooded bonnet covering its head. She would have cursed when she saw it had not the stable boy been present. What was worse, Sir John's favorite mare had gone off its feed. And she'd been informed that very morning that the broody hens refused to lay. Lady Joan was not a superstitious woman, not given to star watching and casting lots for lucky numbers—she sought her prophets in Holy Writ—but she knew such happenings were not auspicious. Of course, with Sir John gone how could it be a good day, even if the stars were perfectly aligned? Which obviously they were not, because her portents had augured aright.

It had not been a good day.

Now to add to this catalogue of aggravations her chamberlain was telling her that an emissary from Canterbury was seeking an audience with his lordship. Her first inclination was to send him away, saying Lord Cobham was not at home and Lady Cobham was indisposed. But good sense warned against such an action. If the legate had come from Thomas Arundel, she should not turn him away. Sir John was already crosswise with the archbishop for ignoring an earlier summons demanding his attendance at Canterbury. In place of giving these worthies the benefit of his hearty personality and rotund person, Sir John had sent an equally substantive statement in writing designed not to anger the archbishop, while at the same time not compromising his beliefs.

"Tell the friar I shall attend him in the solar," she said, thinking that the afternoon sun would have heated up the air in there so that the monk would be less likely to linger.

No. It had not been a good day. And not likely to be a good night either. She would be sleeping alone again tonight, nesting against her husband's comforting girth only in her dreams. Dreams she could not get to until after she'd dealt with this interloper.

❧

Gabriel followed the red and silver liveried servant into the solar of Cooling Castle. He should have waited until the morning, when it was cooler, but better to get it behind him than to dread it. He disliked pretense. But the archbishop's instructions were clear. "Don't challenge Oldcastle outright. Give him enough rope to hang himself. You are only there to gather evidence of his heresy." Gabriel felt the moisture beads pop out on his forehead at the very thought of his being the means whereby someone might be burned. Even a heretic.

"I will bring you a basin of water and a cloth to refresh yourself, Brother. Would you like a cool drink?" the servant asked.

"Yes, please."

The servant moved away on silent feet, leaving Gabriel to wipe the dust and sweat from his face.

Gabriel had been told that Sir John had married well. He had earned a knighthood for his service in the French wars, an annual stipend of 40 pounds, and a wealthy royal wife as well. The widow Cobham had brought him a seat in Parliament and Cobham lands. The tapestries in this room alone were worth a king's ransom. Not to mention the books lying on the table. Some were richly bound in tooled, jewel-encrusted leather, others plain and unadorned. He opened one of the plainer ones.

By all the saints! The fellow was nothing if not bold. Here, right in plain view, was a Wycliffe Bible. Brother Gabriel shut it quickly. *Fool! Do you think some taint of heresy will float off its pages and infect your soul through your eyes?* But one thing he did know. Spying out evidence of heresy here would be child's play—for one who liked that sort of game.

The servant returned with a ewer of water. "My lady will attend you presently," he said, pouring water into a basin in which a few bits of dried lavender floated. He handed Gabriel a scrap of linen.

The cool rag felt good to his face. The servant poured a cup of cider and left. Gabriel dabbed at his underarms with the scented water. He would not want to offend a lady—even a lady against whose husband he was gathering damning evidence.

Both basin and ewer sat on a small table beneath a narrow window that looked out over a lonely marsh. A sea breeze wafted in and refreshed him. Cooling Castle, splendid in its isolation, stood sentinel on a peninsula that jutted out into the North Sea—one of those castles granted license to protect England's shores from French marauders. It was an easy enough place from which a man could plot the overthrow of his church. The archbishop had said Oldcastle held clandestine meetings here, where artisans, peasants, even some nobility mixed together to read the Wycliffe Bible. A kind of adulteration of the holy mass.

"Brother, I am afraid I must tell you that Sir John is away. He is in Herefordshire, seeing to his holdings there. But Cooling Castle will be honored to offer you hospitality against your return to Canterbury." The voice was low for a woman's voice, throaty and full of breath.

Gabriel had not heard her enter the room. He looked up, his hands still holding the cloth with which he had recently bathed. He felt his fair complexion burning as though his thoughts hung in the air for her to read. He knew Lord Cobham was away. The abbess had told him, but he thought his initial foray into the enemy camp might be easier under such circumstances. He could sound out the wife. Being the weaker sex, she would be easier to read.

"I see my servant has already given you a modicum of hospitality. May I offer you food before you begin your return journey?"

"You are kind, Lady Cobham. But I am fine. The sisters at the abbey refectory fed me dinner. With so much light left in the day and vespers already done, I thought to call on Lord Cobham."

Her pretty heart-shaped face screwed itself into a frown. Fine lines fanned out from the corners of her mouth. A chestnut-colored strand of hair snaked out of its snood and framed her face. He noticed too the way her cleavage pushed above its tight bodice. He quickly averted his eyes. This temptation of the flesh was another of the demons he fought, and this demon always ambushed him when he was weak in his spiritual resolve—as now. He was here to catch Sir John out—not to ogle his pretty, plump wife. He laid the rag down on the table, withdrew his hands into the full sleeves of his habit.

"I fear, Brother, you have wasted your trip. Lord Cobham may be away for weeks, surely your duties—"

"Then I will serve his household in his absence. The archbishop has sent me to serve as confessor to a nearby abbey. Perhaps I can serve your ladyship in that capacity as well. If you have no resident priest, that is."

Her face hardened into a mask of disapproval, making her lips less full, less tempting, a little half-smile that curved at one corner of her mouth.

"Brother—"

"Gabriel. Brother Gabriel."

"Brother Gabriel, you may tell His Excellency that Cooling Castle and its inhabitants require no confessor. We confess our sins directly to our Lord and Savior Jesus Christ."

Her boldness almost took his breath away. It seemed there were two Cobham heretics to be rousted out.

"I am somewhat in sympathy with that feeling, myself," he said. He would do penance later for the lie, a light penance for a lie told in the service of his Church. "I fully understand. I have often wondered what it would be like to preach to those who brought a . . . personal understanding to the Word."

Was it his imagination or did the lines of her face relax a little? But her amber-colored eyes remained wary. The late-afternoon sun was drifting in a haze in front of the glazed window, picking out dust motes floating between them. One or two settled on the wide window casement. The air was very close, as was she. She fiddled with the petals of a rose on the window casement, brushing away the dust, pinching away a withered petal, bruising its wine-red skin, releasing the heady smell into the overheated room. Gabriel was sweating beneath his cassock.

"You said the archbishop sent you?"

"Only as confessor to the abbey. I merely thought . . . of course if you have no need of a priest . . ."

"We have no need of the services of a priest of Rome." She said it firmly, and then to soften it, "But we would not be inhospitable to a neighbor. It grows late, and it is six miles back to Rochester. You are welcome to stay here tonight and return to the abbey tomorrow. Unless of course the sisters need you for the prime office."

"It is a kind offer, my lady, and truth to tell, I do not welcome the ride back at such a late hour. As to prime, the old priest to whom I am offering respite is an early riser."

The answering nod of ascent was just a split second too delayed. It did not cover her disappointment.

"My needs are simple," he said. "Just a cot in a very small chamber is sufficient."

"Cooling Castle will see that you are comfortable, Brother Gabriel," she said, avoiding his gaze. She rang a tiny bell to summon the servant. Her full hips swayed gently as she turned to go. "We are known for our Christian hospitality."

"My lady. There is one more thing. I have heard that Sir John has a Bible that gives the words of our Lord in the English tongue. I wonder if I might trouble you to see it."

He made a tent with his hands. A nervous habit he was trying to break. He let his hands fall to his side. Her gaze glanced off the Bible on the table behind him, appeared to come to rest on the windowsill.

"But you read the Word in Latin. Why—"

"It has long been a dream of mine to see it as it might appear to humbler men. To divine there some truth for all."

A little of the suspicion left her face, softening it. She looked like a woman trying to make up her mind.

"There is such a Bible on the table behind you," she said. "I cannot deny access to any who ask with pure intent. Your intent is pure, is it not, Brother Gabriel?"

The scent of the bruised rose petals mingled with the heat, squeezing his breath. "I assure you, my lady. My intent is very pure."

♦

Sir John Oldcastle rode his horse hard from Rochester. He was determined to make it home tonight. His ample belly heaved a sigh of relief when he saw the white rock face of Cooling Castle ahead. He could smell the sweat of the foam-flecked horse. Could smell too the brine and the marsh grass and the evening mist rolling in from the sea. It smelled like home.

He whispered in the horse's ear as he leaned low in the saddle. "Just a little farther, Jack. There'll be a bag of fresh oats for you, old boy." He dug his heels in hard to the hunter's side.

The wind on his face felt good after the heat of the day. A fresh bag of oats for the horse. A cellar-cooled tankard of beer for the rider. And tonight he would sleep in his own bed with his loving wife beside him. Ah, it was going to be good to be home!

As the horse clattered to a stop in the courtyard, Sir John flung the reins to the gatekeeper.

"Welcome home, milord. We've missed you," the old man called.

"Glad to be home, Tim. Tell the ostler to give old Jack an extra bag tonight. And see that he's properly cooled. He bore a heavy burden well and fast." A heavy burden just to carry his rider from Herefordshire. Heavier still, with what he carried in his saddlebags from the abbey in Rochester.

"Aye, milord. Will do. Her ladyship was not expecting you afore tomorrow. Shall I send for her?"

"Nay, Tim. I'll sneak up on her." He winked at the servant.

But first he secured the contents of his saddlebags in their hiding place below the entry stairs. A psalter and two Gospels of John, one Gospel of Saint Matthew, and one Acts of the Apostles. It was a good haul. And one he'd had to collect himself. He could not risk compromising the secrets of the abbess by sending even his most trustworthy aides.

He stowed the books carefully, making sure no sign clung to their wrappings to link them with the abbey. Then he hesitated just a moment. God's wounds, he was hungry!

But he was hungrier for the sight of his Joan.

He went first to the solar. That's where she would probably be. Having a bit of supper by herself. More fun to share hers, anyway.

He heard the mellow tone of her low laughter before he got to the door. How he had missed that laugh! The fact that she was not alone, not pining away, registered with him at about the same time he crossed the threshold of the solar.

His lady was with a man—though they seemed engaged in an innocent enough activity. With their backs to the door, they were sharing a repast of what looked like a roasted capon and peas. The succulent smell hung in the air. Definitely a roasted capon. Two cups and a bottle of his cellar's best stood on the table between them. He surveyed the situation in a hare's leap, before they were even aware of his presence. They were that engrossed in conversation. It was with considerable relief Sir John noticed the cleric's cassock, though truth to tell, a cleric's garb was not something he usually relished seeing.

"I'm away only a fortnight, and already my lady has taken a lover." A joke for her, a barb for the friar, a slur on the reputation of his order.

Joan gave a delighted gasp and was on her feet and in his arms before he could say anything else. She planted a kiss full on his lips.

"John, what a shameful thing to say! Though the way you smell, your lady would probably be well enough justified. This is Brother Gabriel. He is a legate from Canterbury."

"From Canterbury, you say?" His guard was instantly up. What was the woman thinking?

"The archbishop has sent us a confessor." Her eyes glinted mischievously.

Suddenly the weariness of the long ride home swept over him in a wave. His good humor evaporated as he considered this spoiler of his homecoming.

"I am surprised that you did not tell the legate from Canterbury, good wife, that we have no need of a confessor."

"I did, my lord, be sure, I did. But he has really come to preach at the abbey, and his visit and offer to us are merely a *courtesy*."

That part at least rang true. The abbess had mentioned the newcomer to him and expressed some concern that his presence might slow down the abbey's output. But why was he here at Cooling Castle?

His lady leaned into him and whispered in his ear, or made a pretense of whispering, for she said it loud enough for the friar to hear. "Brother Gabriel has Lollard sympathies. Isn't that shocking!"

Sir John disentangled his wife's arms from around his neck and looked more closely at the interloper. He was certainly a fine-looking specimen for a monk. He remembered Joan's laugh and felt the tiniest pang of jealousy.

"And specifically with what aspect of Lollardy does this emissary from His Excellency agree?"

Brother Gabriel looked him straight in the eye, his manner forthright, honest. "I cannot say I totally agree, nor can I say I totally disagree, with Master Wycliffe's teachings. Let us just say, Sir John, that I am a seeker after truth. Your lady was kind enough to show me your copy of the Wycliffe Bible. I found it very impressive."

"And do you think the archbishop would find it 'impressive'?"

The friar smiled. "I daresay not. But the archbishop does not speak for me in all matters." The visitor took another drink of John's wine then stood up and wiped his mouth. "I see, Sir John, that you are weary from your travels. I will bid you good night. Tomorrow or the next day perhaps we can discuss theology." He gave a little half-bow and moved toward the door. "Thank you, Lady Cobham, for your kind hospitality. No need to ring for a servant. I can find my way back to my chamber."

"And what was that about?" Sir John asked when the priest was gone.

"Now, my love, before you go and get all bothered, have a little faith in me. I told him nothing of our endeavors. He saw the Wycliffe Bible on the table and asked to examine it. That's all. I thought by not pretending to hide anything, he would lose interest and go away. Sometimes a little bit of truth bluntly spoken hides what is unspoken. Besides, if Arundel went after everybody who owns a Wycliffe Bible, he'd have to put half of England in chains. And don't forget, my husband, the young king has always held you in high favor."

"He's not king yet."

"In all but coronation." She pulled him into a chair and sat on his lap. "You must be starved. Here." And she broke off a sliver of meat and put it between his teeth, then raised her goblet to his mouth, and after he had drunk, she kissed away the drops that lingered there. "Don't worry about the monk, John. He's harmless enough. Who knows, we may convert him. And wouldn't that put a wrinkle in old Arundel's breeches."

Sir John patted his wife on her plump behind and stood up. He couldn't help but laugh. God's wounds, it was good to be home.

~ ~

Alone in the chamber to which the servant had shown him, Brother Gabriel tried not to enjoy overmuch the gracious furnishings and convenient appointments of his surroundings. A man could become fond of luxuries like the feather mattress and the beeswax candles glowing softly in the darkness. To his way of thinking, too many among his fellows already had succumbed to the love of luxury, forgetting their vows of poverty. It was a weakness he would not allow himself. Still, he was grateful for the candle. By the glow of its light, he could examine the Wycliffe Bible.

It was a crudely copied affair. No decorated capitals. No color in the margins. Just line after line of English written in a cribbed hand. Written as though paper were very dear to the scribe. It was, he decided after his cursory examination, a profane document, just by the appearance of it. Imagine the Holy Scriptures, deserving of all the beauty that could be lavished upon them, written in such a common hand! In such a common language! Think of the dirty and callused hands that would touch it, turn its ugly pages. But the worst part was that the words themselves would fall from the lips of ignorant peasants not worthy to mouth such holy words.

It was truly casting pearls before swine. That was the established position of the Church he served, and who was he to disavow it?

He should put the profane text aside. He opened it, instead, to the Acts of the Apostles. At first he was caught up in the translation itself. And he was forced to admit, except for a word here and there, the translation was correct. Gabriel prided himself on his Latin. He would certainly spot a mistranslated word, an aborted phrase—had there been such. But then, nobody ever accused Wycliffe of being ignorant. The thing that surprised him most was that long after Wycliffe's death, when the translations were completed by other minds, copied by amanuenses of varying levels of education, the translation was readable and reasonably accurate.

But it was still a profane document. The Church had condemned it. History had proven it worthy of condemnation, for had not these very words in the minds of ignorant and unlearned men incited riot and murder? Without John Wycliffe's heretical teachings about every man his own priest, without his sermons on the abuses of clergy, would Wat Tyler and John Ball ever have dared lead a raid against the the nobility and the clergy, killing even the archbishop? And yet it looked so innocent.

The candle guttered. Where had the night gone? Of course there would be no bells to toll the hours in such a profligate house—that would be too much to expect. But it must be nigh unto matins judging by the spent candle.

He knelt on the floor among the rushes and recited the Divine Office: *Domine labia mea aperies.* The image of Lord Cobham's plump, pretty wife intruded. *Et os meum annuntiabit laudem tuam.* Trying not to think of what they might be doing now in the hovering darkness of their chamber. But the carnal thoughts interrupted his devotions with surprising force—the glow on Lady Joan's cleavage, the smell of the bruised roses in the heat of the afternoon. He'd thought that struggle behind him, with his youth, after that first carnal straying, after the crofter's daughter from the village. She'd been older than he and not a virgin, but he'd thought he loved her. He'd cried when she ran off with a traveling tinker, confessed his sins, done his penance, and vowed to put women behind him. They always left anyway, Brother Francis had said. Only the Holy Virgin was faithful. He tried to think now of the Virgin's face, but Lady Cobham's smile—the coquette's smile reserved for her husband—intruded there too.

When his prayers were complete—some words repeated several times to chase away the English words from the profane text that he'd just read; how quickly the devil worked, first the carnal images and now the heretical text— Brother Gabriel did not avail himself of the feather bed. A sinner who could not control his thoughts deserved to spend the night on the stone floor in mortification of his flesh. He had not brought his *flagellum* with him. It had been a long time since he had felt the need for such an instrument of contrition. False pride. False spiritual pride—and lingering too long with the profane text—had weakened his control, and now these lustful thoughts had entered his mind, sullying his contemplation. Brother Gabriel reached inside his cassock and pinched his thigh until he felt it throb with pain.

When he awoke for lauds, he was satisfied that the bruise was sufficient to keep his thoughts pure. It ached when he walked. He recited the office of lauds—his mind not once straying from the Latin words he mouthed—and then lay fully clothed across the feather bed, where he fell into a deep but troubled sleep.

NINE

Ne'er do well fortunetellers, ventriloquists and wizards . . . who are inspired satanically to pretend to predict the unknown . . .
—FROM AN EARLY 13TH-CENTURY
BYZANTINE RECORD

It was not the approaching Prague twilight that chased the old Gypsy woman from the stone bridge spanning the river Vltava—not the advent of eventide but the soldiers.

"Begone, hag, lest you want a fagot lit under your filthy skirts."

Jetta knew why the soldiers were at the bridge. They had come to take down the death's heads. Jetta had come to watch. She retreated just out of reach, yet close enough to appease the voices in her head.

Three skulls gleamed in the slanted sunlight like ivory globes. Picked clean. It hadn't taken long—she'd watched the daily gleanings—less than a week in the summer sun, with sharp beaks pecking at skin and sinew and carrion flesh. Even the twittering little birds came at the end to feast on the leavings of the black-winged crows. But it was the way of all things. The way of predator and prey, and the birds didn't know they picked at flesh that had once pulsed with life, or care, any more than people cared who ate the flesh of birds. It was nature's way.

Though Jetta ate no meat. And she gave scarce meat to her Little Bek, because what she gave to Little Bek she had to chew first. He could not keep rough food on his stomach. But he was getting stronger every day. One day soon, he would be able to chew his own food. He might never walk. Or talk. But that was all right. Her head was filled with too much talking anyway.

Jetta put her hands over her ears, tangling scrawny fingers in the dirty gray strings of hair that hung beneath her kerchief, and shook her head from side to side. Nothing, not even this violent shaking, could rid her of the demon voices.

"Jetta will look, Jetta will look," she muttered in reply to their incessant nagging.

One of the soldiers pointed in her direction the long pike he was using to take down the skulls. "Look," he said. "She's a witch. She's talking to her familiar. Let's take her in, chain her to the altar of Saint Vitus Cathedral so her witch's ears will hear the mass."

"Nay. She's no witch. That's just old Jetta. She's harmless, one of the vagabond Egyptian pilgrims camping downriver." Then he raised his voice. "Off with ye. Go back to your vagabond camp. There's no one here to *dukker* with your fortune-telling."

But still Jetta did not flee. The voices in her head wouldn't let her. She skittered to the edge of the bridge, still within eyesight, still within earshot. She had not come to tell fortunes. She came today same as every day to the stone bridge, driven by the whispering in her head, whispering that turned to shrieking when she did not obey. In the beginning she had resisted, humming plainsong like the monks or wailing like the violins around the Gypsy campfires, but the voices would not be ignored. They would torment her until she tied little Bek in his chair and went in search of the red-haired girl.

The soldiers were lowering the pikes now. One of them removed the skull from the center pole, hefted its weight in his hand. "A well-made brain pan, that."

He made to toss it into the river, but his fellow, the one who'd spoken up for Jetta, stopped him. "Shouldn't they have a Christian burial?"

"This is a fit enough burial for a heretic, I'd say," and the soldier threw back his hand, hurling the smooth, round dome into the river.

Jetta watched as it arced high and skipped once before catching in the swirl of the current. A flash of bleached bone, a flash of sunlight on the water, and the skull disappeared. Its pole mates dropped after, plopping without ceremony into the black waters beneath the shadow of the bridge.

Then the soldier stopped and picked up a fresh nosegay of flowers resting at the base of the pike: pink and purple coneflowers tied with a blue ribbon. "Send these after," he said, flinging them into the river.

"Gone. All gone. Swallowed by the river spirits. She'll not come anymore." Jetta whined to her voices. "Now let Jetta rest. Let Jetta go back and tend to Little Bek. Little Bek needs Jetta."

But she knew the demon voices would torment her until their purpose was accomplished. As before. When she'd found Little Bek on a bed of rags, abandoned at the edge of the bridge, flailing with his hands against the hard stones, flopping on his twisted legs like a discarded trash fish precariously close to the water's edge. She'd named him Bek because that was the only sound he made, screaming like a wounded bird, *bek, bek, bek,* his screams growing louder as she carried him on her bent back, his stringy legs dangling almost to the ground, to her camp.

The soldiers were gone now, but they'd left the naked, upright pikes on the bridge to await their next adornments.

The slipping sun was turning the river the color of blood. The young woman would not be coming today. Jetta knew she'd already come and gone, because the flowers floating on the current were fresh. The voices were mostly silent when the red-haired woman came tentatively across the bridge and laid her offering beneath the pike.

Jetta had watched her at other times, wondering what demons drove the woman to the bridge. Sometimes the woman cried and threw stones at the birds. Sometimes she just stared with large, sunken eyes in a face that would have been beautiful if not distorted with grief. At such times, Jetta could read her mind, and she trembled for her and would have approached her.

Wait, the voices would say. *Not now.*

And Jetta would wonder why they drove her to be a silent witness to another's grief.

The soldiers had gone. The voices were silent now. Jetta walked to the end of the bridge, looked back at the great bronze crucifix at its opening on the other side of the river. It too had caught the reflection of the dying sun and was the color of blood.

She ventured a few steps. Quiet, still. She hiked up her ragged hem and ran as though distance between herself and the bridge could keep them silent. By now, Bek would have pounded his poor wrists against the sides of his chair until they were blue, and he would be hungry. It would have been a mercy to let him fall into the river. But the voices would not let her.

The rind of an orange sun floated on the surface of the water. It would be dark soon, and she did not like to be on the streets after dark, but she still had to go to Celetná, the street of the baker, to buy *calty*. And she had not enough coin even for the smallest loaf. She looked around hurriedly for her *gorgios* mark. There. Just entering the street. A wealthy merchant.

"Dukkeripen," she whispered hoarsely, offering to say his future. Then before he could turn away, "You have been three times in danger of death," she said, making her voice low and heavy with warning.

This always got their attention, for it was true. What soul did not live with death all around?

The merchant looked furtively about, before giving her the silver penny and extending his palm to her. She quickly pocketed the penny in her begging apron, glancing askance at one of the soldiers who had driven her from the bridge. She muttered the familiar litany: a long journey undertaken to escape danger, a fortuitous encounter with a beautiful woman. The *gorgios* saw the soldier too. He had paused in the doorway of the chandler and appeared to be watching them.

The merchant's palm, whose lifeline she traced with a ragged nail, twitched nervously, then tried to retract, but Jetta held on for a second longer just for the sport of it, as she muttered, "Danger surrounds you."

The pudgy hand with its beringed fingers, the largest ring, a signet ring, circled his fat sausage finger—no chance to steal that one; it clung too tight, biting into the flesh—jerked free. Jetta chortled to watch him wipe his palm against his fine cloak, casting furtive glances in the direction of the soldier as he pretended to saunter away. He could be fined or worse for his attempts to divine the future with soothsayers and Gypsies. The priests laid all divination and magic at the devil's door.

But never mind, she thought, fingering the silver penny. The *gorgios* in protecting themselves protected the Gypsies too. She waved a bangled wrist at the soldier and hurried into the baker's. She had her penny, and little Bek would have his bread, and his eyes would light with pleasure when he saw her.

And for now, the voices were quiet.

The voices stayed quiet until the next day at noontime. Jetta was singing to Little Bek, delighting in the way he singsonged back to her—still the *bek bek*, but he carried the melody in his high, sweet tone even when she varied it.

He was learning to chew his own food too. He would hold a bit of bread in his mouth until it softened with his slobber, sometimes mulling it with his teeth, watching her, copying the way she moved her own jaws as she chewed, and then he would swallow it. He had only choked once and then but lightly. He was coughing his way through that spell when the whispers began in her head.

Go to the bridge. The red-haired girl is coming. Go now. Now. Now. Now.

"Not now," Jetta muttered, "not now." Little Bek looked at her with startled eyes and beat his bruised fists against the floor of the wagon. He knew what was coming, and she hated it. But the longer she resisted the worse the voices would become, until the shrillness gave her a headache, and she would still have to go.

"Just a little while, Bek. Be still. You can sing while I'm gone," she said, tying him to the chair. He flailed his arms against the sides in protest, *bek, bek, bek,* no sweet tones now, but shrieks. He beat the sides of the chair so furiously—more than once she had to duck his flying fists—that she feared his fragile wrist bones would snap. She could have wept for his terror and hatred of being tied, but she had no choice. The one time she had not strapped him in, he had scooted to the edge of the camp wagon and fallen out. It had been during the heat of the day, when the camp was deserted. He was exhausted and coated with dust when she found him, his poor bottom scraped raw with his scooting.

She dodged a flying fist and handed him a small doll. "Here, sing to the doll while Jetta is gone." She began the singsong tune she had taught him earlier. To her amazement, he ceased his screaming and pounding and began to singsong, clutching his doll to his chest.

Go now, while the boy is quiet, the voices said. *Go now, gonow gonow gonow gonow gown ow n O W N   O W N   O W.*

Covering her ears, Jetta rushed from the camp in the direction of the great stone bridge.

Anna always waited until the double-faced clock across Staroměstké radnice said midday, when the heat from the cobblestone, baking in the sun, drove the inhabitants into the shadows of their houses and alleyways. Every day for a week she'd forced herself from bed, too often forgetting to comb her unkempt curls. Sometimes she would dress, but more often she'd fallen asleep in her clothes and would change only when she noticed how smelly and rumpled she'd become.

At such times, she would rouse herself as from a dream, remembering how fastidious her grandfather had been in his personal habits, remembering too her childhood, when he'd struggled to braid her hair into a coronet of neat coils. They had lived in Ghent, then, in Flanders. But that was before that city fell on hard times, before the English started weaving the cloth that Flanders had been famous for, before the great cloth merchants became too poor to buy books.

She'd been only six years old when they left, but she remembered the name of the street they lived on. Sint Veerleplein. Sometimes she dreamed about it, mostly in the mornings, when her mind had had its fill of sleep, but her will would not let go. When, at midday, the sun heated up the east face of her bedroom, forcing her from sleep's oblivion, pushing her from her bed, she would expect to wake in that childhood place.

Then she would remember.

Her marrow would congeal to lead, leaving her limbs too heavy to move. Dědeček was not here. He was sleeping in the churchyard behind Týn Church. She was completely alone. And Martin. When she thought of Martin, with his teasing grin, his flashing eyes, she would be so overcome with grief that she would cry out and beat her fists upon the walls of her bedroom. But all she ever got were hands as bruised as her heart.

Even Master Jerome was gone. They'd arrested him three days after they'd buried her grandfather. Jan Hus had come to tell her. He had warned her to sell her belongings, to go away and live with relatives, even offered to send a deacon from Bethlehem Chapel to assist her. She thanked him politely and sent him away.

Then, she'd trimmed her lamp and gone to bed.

How could she leave? Not with Dědeček sleeping all alone in Týn Churchyard. She had promised him she would go to Sir John Oldcastle. The name was written on her brain, but surely he would not have wanted her to make her way alone. It would not be safe. And now there was no one to take her.

Infrequently, shamed by the memory of her grandfather's fastidiousness, Anna combed her hair, changed her smock and blouse, and swept the ashes from the cold hearth where no cook fire bloomed. Sometimes, she even choked down a cold biscuit. Then, she would venture into her grandfather's room to seek his presence, walking as quietly as any ghost, not wanting to disturb the air. Perhaps, if she sat perfectly still in his chair, he would feel her grief and come to her. But he never did.

She always left the room as silently as she had come into it, tiptoeing so as not to leave even the sound of footprints on the floor. Then she would go to the flower sellers in the square and buy two nosegays.

One for the churchyard.

One for the bridge.

Every day it was the same.

The old flower seller pitied her. She could see it in his eyes, though she never told him what the flowers were for.

"Two for the cost of one," he would say. "They will wilt soon enough anyway."

Anna always tried to thank him, but the words clotted in her throat.

Today, like each day, the sun was low when Anna left the churchyard to go to the bridge. The shadows were already creeping onto the hard-baked earth of the new grave. By the time she reached the bridge, the shadows of the *hrad* on the hill leaned into the river.

In her left hand she carried her little nosegay of remembrance. And in her right a handful of stones plucked from the riverbank. That first day she'd come, she'd tried to frighten away the feasting birds with shrieks and hurled stones, and it had worked. They had scattered in a great fluttering of wings and raucous cries, circling high in the bright blue sky until they settled like gargoyles upon the balustrade of the bridge's entrance. But she knew they only awaited her departure so they could return. That first time she thought only of protecting the skulls, like Rizpah in the Hebrew Bible Dĕdeček illuminated, the woman who had camped for months beneath the hanging bodies of her dead sons to guard them from desecration. Anna had lingered for hours, huddled beneath the poles, shrieking and throwing stones at the birds.

But she'd not looked at Martin's head.

She could not bear to think that the grotesque thing affixed to the pole had once been Martin's beautiful head. She'd watched instead the other two, for a sign of the birds returning. They always did. Then she would shake the poles, and scream, hurling her stones at the ravens until the soldiers had come and made her leave. Every day she left, trembling with relief when they chased her away, but she cried hot tears and cursed herself for lacking Rizpah's courage.

Today, as she approached the bridge, she forced her gaze upward, dreading what she would see. But today there were no birds—not even one—perched upon the smooth skull.

The bridge was empty.

The riverbanks were empty too except for one old woman who huddled beneath a weeping willow at the water's edge. She was shaking her head and muttering to herself. The heat shivered up in waves of light from the stone pavement of the bridge. At the midpoint of the bridge the poles stood sentinel—was that a trick of light? Were the poles empty? Had some scavenger eaten away even the hard bone, some devil bird sent from hell to devour this last remnant with its iron beak?

She looked from the pole hard into the low-angled sun as if to find an answer written on its bloody face. A large black-winged bird floated across the swollen orb, circling lazily. She looked back at the poles. Three black spikes in silhouette, each unadorned at its apex.

Anna dropped her stones. Clutching her skirt in one hand, the bouquet in the other, she ran toward the center of the bridge. The sound of the old woman's muttering had stopped. Anna was alone on the bridge, running in a world suspended in heat and silence. The heads of the flowers in her hand bobbed with each footfall, spilling feathers of color onto the gray paving stones.

In the center of the bridge she jerked to a stop. Looked up. It had not been a trick of light. The poles were empty, the skulls gone.

She stood transfixed, gazing upward. The muscles in her neck cramped, and in that instant her wounded mind conjured not Martin's head on the center pole, but another. Her own bright curls, her own gaping mouth, a home to wasps and flies. She gave a little cry and blinked hard against the light, closed her eyes, but the image painted itself on her eyelids as well.

She shook her head hard to dispel the horrible sight and opened her eyes.

The poles were once again empty, but they seemed to sway slightly. Or was it she who swayed? She lowered her head.

The bridge was strangely silent for the end of the day. As though Christ had returned to claim his saints and taken them all away and she alone had been abandoned to this loneliness upon the bridge. She, alone in a world where even the sun had turned to blood—she and one other, the old woman huddling beneath the bridge on the verge of the river, watching Anna as though she were a mummer in a play.

I should cry for Martin, she thought. One last flood of tears. For the man who would have been her husband. A good man. A man of fair countenance and fairer disposition. A man who had loved her. A man who would have been the father of her children.

But the sockets of her eyes felt as dry as the hot stones burning through the leather of her shoe soles. How then to mourn this final parting when she had no more tears? She gathered up the stones, smooth and warm, that she had dropped crossing the bridge and formed them into a cross beneath the pole. Stepped back to view her memorial. Only slightly more substantial in form than the fair flesh now gone to make food for birds. But the cruciform would mark this spot a while. Travelers crossing the bridge would be wary of dismantling a cross.

She looked down at the wilted bouquet in her hands, the fragile stems broken by the clutching of her fist. At last her vigil was over. There would be no more birds to chase away. No more birds—except in her dreams. And now what was she to do? She leaned against the bridge balustrade for support and looked down at the water beneath. It looked so cool.

Where had they taken them—the heads of the three young men? She looked hard into the water, dark ripples in the shadow of the bridge. Would it be so bad to be there? she thought. It was cool. Dark. Deep. She could envy Martin such a peaceful place. No need to flee. No need to hide. These waters would quench an angry bishop's fire. A final baptism.

Was that a gleam of bleached bone in the water?

No, only a sunlit fish, flashing in a deep pool. She felt light-headed as she leaned forward and dropped her flowers one by one into the water. The heat from the bridge rose in ghost waves. She could smell the baking stones of the pavement. What was she to do now? *Sir John Oldcastle, Lord Cobham.* The name repeated itself in her head. But how could she get across the sea to England? She could not fly like the great gull soaring in silhouette against the sun.

She watched the flowers drift on the wind then float down to the surface of the rippling water, mesmerized, feeling as though she were floating with them.

And then she was.

Anna would never know if she jumped, or if she fell. If the heat and her grief and the effort expended on the bridge pushed her past fatigue. Or if her soul's wish worked its will upon her body like some unseen puppet master.

All she knew was that the moment she sank into the cool water she felt a sudden great lightness as if some terrible burden had been lifted from her. The water lifted up her skirts, bearing her up, buoyant, a petal, a leaf, a dragonfly floating on the face of the water.

Free. Free from her grief. Free from her promise.

A spirit no longer bound in flesh. Then as her clothing became more sodden, she began to sink. She did not flail about. She simply sank into the cool darkness, embracing death as though it were the lover of her imagination.

Is this the way it would have been with Martin? Or was this Martin who embraced her, not the river, and she was only dreaming of the river, and the head on the pole had all been some terrible nightmare? She relaxed, sinking slowly below the rippling surface. The water closed over her eyes and seeped into her mouth, sealing her in, accepting her as it had earlier accepted the other offerings falling from the bridge.

On the surface of the water a coneflower petal snagged upon a drifting bird feather and floated gently to shore, where the old woman waited.

TEN

Which is the villain now and which the knight,
That worms have gnawed their carcasses so bare?
Christians, Jews, and heathens serve Him all,
And God has all creation in his care.
— WALTER VON DER VOGELWEIDE IN
MY BROTHER MAN (13TH CENTURY)

nna woke. Panic stirring.

Were those shrieks, that *bek, bek, bek,* the cries of damned souls in torment?

She opened her eyes slowly. That light, glowing crimson overhead in this cavelike space, was that a reflection from the devil's furnace? Had they been right all along, those black-robed priests who preached perdition for unshriven souls? Were they even now hanging her body and dragging it through the streets as punishment for self-murder as her soul awoke in hell?

No. More than her soul. She could feel her corporeal body. It ached. But then it would, wouldn't it, in eternal torment? At least that's what the learned friars would say.

But if this was hell, there was an absence of the smell of sulphur, not a hint of brimstone—they'd got that part wrong. Instead, the scent of something frying and the hiss of sizzling fat. Not an unpleasant odor. It smelled like . . . like *bacon*? The incongruous picture of a horned devil dangling his pitchfork over the flames like a toasting fork might have made her laugh, if she had had air for laughing. Or she might have cried out in fright, if she had had air for crying out.

She opened her mouth, tried to inhale deeply, and strangled, coughing, sputtering, choking on the overheated air. She sat upright. Panic rising. The crimson light danced and shimmered at one end of the tight little space, glowing like a fiery curtain of coals. A tiny gasp of air, and her quivering lungs strangled her again. The curtain parted. Embers, sparking fire, shivered with the movement.

An old woman with a lined brown face and stringy gray hair emerged. The devil's minion come to torment her? To gnaw at her liver? Or squeeze her flesh with hot pincers, like the images carved on cathedral doors?

"Drink, missy."

Strange eyes darted quick as fireflies above a clawlike hand offering her a metal cup. A cup of water in hell? Not unless the creature had come, like Tantalus, to tease.

Anna took the metal beaker and held it with both hands, but she did not drink. She coughed again but with less vigor, the spasms in her chest gentler now. She was beginning to remember.

Panic falling.

She lifted her head gingerly, feeling its stuffed heaviness, but was able to assess her surroundings with calm. She lay on a pile of blankets on a wooden floor. A barrel ceiling curved overhead. Windows on each side, hung with cheap red cloth curtains, filtered a blaze of sunlight through their coarse weave, and the curtain of coals at the end of the room was made up of strings of brightly colored beads. The old woman holding the cup, the clawlike hands—it was the old woman from beneath the bridge.

A dreamlike memory struggled to free itself, a memory of being pulled from the water's edge, pummeled and pounded, half carried, half dragged, and finally lifted by many hands under curious, peering, black-eyed faces up into the place where she now lay. She was in some kind of wagon, not unlike the elaborate carriages the nobility traveled in, but smaller, and of meaner substance.

Anna tried to hand back the tin cup. "I think I've swallowed enough water for one day."

But the old woman refused it, shaking her head. "Not water. Medicine. *Tate shilalyi.* Hot-cold. It will ward off fever and ague from the river. Drink it."

Anna thought she should pretend to drink it to spare the old woman's feelings. After all, she had pulled her from the river. Anna lifted the beaker to her lips. The smell made her nose wrinkle. "What's in it?"

"Powder of frog's lungs and livers," the old woman said. But she wasn't looking at the cup as she spoke. Her darting gaze had come to rest on Anna's head with an expression that looked almost hungry.

Maybe this was hell after all.

"Then I shouldn't drink it," Anna said, grasping for a reason that wouldn't offend. "I once drank something with . . . frog parts in it, and it made my . . . tongue swell. I'm feeling much better. Truly."

Anna held the cup out again, suppressing the cough that threatened, and this time the woman took it. Without even a glance at the cup, the old woman set it down on the floor, and reached out to touch Anna's hair, never unlocking her gaze. Anna could feel the gnarly fingers trying to comb through her hair. She tried not to cringe. After all, this strange-looking creature had saved her life. And she supposed that was a blessing. A ragged fingernail caught and pulled against the matted curls. In spite of herself Anna cried out. Her wet hair had dried into a frizzled mass. She probably looked like a wild woman. It was a wonder the woman wasn't afraid of her.

"*Rawnie bal,*" the woman whispered, fingering Anna's hair as though it were gold.

"What did you say?"

Not the language of Bohemia, not even German, Anna was sure.

"Lady hair. Red hair. Much good fortune." The woman let go, sighing as though she were letting go of some treasure. Was this the reason her benefactress had pulled her from the river? Because of her red hair?

"Well, it certainly hasn't brought me much good fortune. Where am I?" Anna asked, trying to distract the woman, who looked as though she might at any moment take scissors to Anna's locks. Unruly though they were, she was a little reluctant to part with them under the circumstances. "And who are you?"

"I am Jetta," the crone said, unlocking her gaze, removing her fingers from Anna's mop of hair. "I am Roma. You are with the Romani. You are safe."

"Roma?" Anna had never heard that word before either, though Martin had told her about a strange band of pilgrims he'd encountered passing through Hradčany on the high spur above the river Vltava. They had finally camped downriver. She'd seen their camp from the bridge.

"We are Christian pilgrims. 'Gyptians who did not fight the Saracens when they came into Egypt. Now as our penance we must roam the earth for seven years to please our Lord." She said it as though it were some memorized litany.

But this Jetta, as she called herself, was the oddest-looking pilgrim Anna had ever seen. No pilgrim's staff, or cloak, or scrip. Her head was tied with a ragged kerchief and she wore large colored hoops of string and metal around her neck and a long ragged skirt and loose shirt. The barrel-topped caravan looked as though it were some sort of permanent home, with its thin curtains, and beads, and bright colors. Nowhere did she see an altar or a statue of the Virgin. The bottom and sides that were not covered with bright cloth looked to be made of wood, penny farthing boards, exactly the width of a penny and a farthing.

Anna had not imagined that strange shrieking noise either. It was even louder now.

"Do you keep birds in your camp?" Anna asked, trying not to shiver, remembering the winged scavengers on the bridge, remembering too how she came to be in the river.

"No birds. Little Bek. My boy. He cannot talk, so when he wants something he makes that sound. He is impatient. He smells the bacon that Bera brought for you."

"Bera?"

"The Romani king."

"But why would he bring bacon for me?"

"Because he likes pretty women. Or because of the red hair. It is good luck for birthing women to wear an amulet of red hair against their bellies. Bera's wife, Lela, is almost full to the brim."

"He can have a lock of hair for his wife. I have plenty to spare. It is the least I can do to repay him." The smell of the bacon was stronger. And Anna was hungry. "The meat might burn, if you don't tend it. I am feeling much better. I will get up and come with you. I can entertain your child while you cook." Anna pushed back the bright coverlet that covered her, then as quickly snatched it back up.

She was totally naked underneath the blanket.

"My clothes! Where are my clothes?"

"We washed them. They are still drying. We washed you too so that you would not be *mahrime*. Polluted. By the unclean water from the river."

She had a vision of the peering eyes that had hovered over her, felt her face flame with sudden heat. "Who undressed me?"

"Me. And Lela helped." Jetta removed a red blouson and skirt from a peg. "Bera brought these for you to wear until your clothes are dry."

Anna took the strange garments. They looked new and—it wasn't a matter of fit—loose with a silk girdle of knotted rope to belt the waist, though the skirt exposed her ankles. It was either put them on or remain here under the counterpane, naked. Holding the coverlet in front of her chest with one hand, Anna reached for the shirt with the other. She was thinking that apparently there were to be no undergarments when Jetta produced a shift from a cupboard. It was unbleached linen, wider than Anna needed and too short, but she took it gratefully and slipped it over her head.

⚓

When Anna emerged from the back of the tent, strong arms covered with fine black hairs reached up to help her down. The arms were attached to a torso garbed in a scarlet blouse, not unlike the one she wore. But his was silk, not linen, which she encountered first at eye level, taking in also the red silk sash holding up his breeches. A man of about Martin's age, though at least five inches shorter, flashed large white teeth. He set her down with a flourish and a sweeping bow.

"Welcome to our humble camp," he said. "I am Bera, King of Roma, leader of this band of pilgrims."

In spite of his short stature, he was the most striking man she had ever seen: broad in the chest, narrow waist, and eyes as black as his hair, and that as black as any coal.

"We have come to offer you our hospitality and to celebrate that we saved you from the river."

With a graceful sweep, more dance than simple gesture, he indicated a small crowd of men and women gathered around a fire of white ash charcoal. On this fire sat a frying pan of monstrous size. Other barrel-shaped, colorful caravans were clustered in a circle surrounding the cook fire. But a quick survey showed Anna that not everybody in the assemblage wanted to celebrate her presence. One woman, younger than Anna, also short and a little squat looking, though it was really unfair to judge her so because of her slightly protruding belly, eyed Anna suspiciously. She sat a little apart from the others, who wore friendlier but openly curious faces.

Lela, Bera's wife, Anna thought, and she was obviously not happy about something. Her stare made Anna aware of the ill-fitting clothes she wore. They were probably Lela's clothes, her best clothes that she had put away until she could fit in them again. No wonder she looked so resentful. Anna tried to smile at her, but the young woman's hard-set scowl never changed.

Bera took Anna's hand and pulled her into the circle where the others sat cross-legged a cool distance from the fire.

"We have prepared a feast in your honor." The broad sweep of his hand indicated not only the sizzling bacon, but also a table with loaves of dark bread and hunks of cheese and onions and a fresh-cut melon with its green rind sweating and its pink flesh oozing juice in the hot midafternoon.

"You are too kind," Anna stammered. "How can I—"

"Good deeds are their own reward," Bera smiled. "Of course, we are always grateful when kindness is returned with kindness."

His meaning was clear. Some token of gratitude was expected. She thought of her own meager resources, the few florins hidden away at home, her little hoard already less than what Dĕdeček left her. And when it was gone, there would be no more. Then suddenly her heart lurched. Surely they did not think to hold her for ransom!

"Alas, I am not a wealthy woman, but an orphan with no husband and little more than a few furnishings." A circle of eyes stared at her, waiting. "I have only a bed, a couple of chairs, and the clothes you see spread out to dry on the bushes behind you." Though that last was a lie and she blushed when she said it. Dĕdeček had always clothed her in the best the sumptuary laws would allow.

Bera shrugged. His disappointment was palpable. The whole little band of them seemed to wilt. Except for Lela. Somehow the fact that they had not netted a rich man's wife or widow pleased her.

Bera recovered gracefully. "We expect no payment," he said. "But perhaps you have some talent that you would like to contribute to our celebration. Do you sing?"

At the word "sing," a boy of about seven or eight years—it was hard to guess his age because he was malformed—scooted forward on spindly legs too small for his body and began to hum in a high, sweet voice, a sort of half-melody.

Bera laughed. "Not you, Bek. We hear enough of your squawking."

There was no malice in the tone with which he addressed the boy, and the child nodded his large head as if he understood. The boy and the other faces in the circle turned toward her expectantly.

"I'm sorry," she said, embarrassed. "I have no talent for singing, and my voice is hoarse from coughing."

Bera smiled and did a little half-twirl and a leap, scissoring his well-shaped legs.

"Or dancing either, I'm afraid," she said. "And I can't play an instrument," Anna said, eyeing a stringed dulcimer lying next to the bread and cheese.

From the corner of her eye, she saw Lela smile for the first time. It was not a smile that warmed. Anna cast about for some way to please them, some way to thank them. Then she remembered.

"You said you were Christian pilgrims. I have something you might want to see."

"A holy relic?" Bera smiled politely, revealing startling white teeth, but the twitching at the corner of his mouth showed the smile was forced.

She suspected he'd seen enough of relics and knew how easily they were manufactured. Perhaps he'd even hawked a few false ones himself. Martin had said they were a strange group who lived by their wits.

"It is not exactly a relic," she said. "It's better. It is a book."

He laughed. "But the Romani does not read. We do not value—a book, you say?"

Too late, she could almost see his mind whirling.

"It is not a book I could ever sell," she added hastily. "But it is a very special book. It is the written Word of our Lord, and it is very beautiful. The next time I come, I will bring it, and you can see it."

"But if you have such a book, why can't you sell it? Then you would no longer be poor."

Because my grandfather told me not to. It is all of him I have left.

"It is very precious to me. Besides, if the authorities knew of its existence, it would be confiscated and burned. It is against the law to have such a book."

Those words coming out of her mouth reminded her of how foolish she had been to mention it in the first place. But her grandfather had never kept it a secret. He had shown it to anybody who asked to see it. *Anybody who could read the words, you stupid girl,* she chided herself.

Jetta had lifted the pan off the fire and set it on the table. The others were already lining up, dipping chunks of bread in the grease drippings, cutting bites of bacon and cheese. Jetta got a small piece of bacon and crunched it between her fingers until it was broken in tiny bits and began to feed it to Little Bek. Bera broke off a piece of bread and handed it to the boy, who nodded, smiling. His head bobbed like a heavy blossom on a too-fragile stem.

"When we have finished with our feast," Bera said, "I will take you to your home, and you can show me this book that has the words of the Lord Jesus."

"Now that I think about it, it probably is not something you would care about. It is written in English, not in the language of Bohemia."

"Since I do not read, the language is of no importance." He said it proudly. "It is the Word of the Lord. You can read it to me. I can touch it. It will bring good fortune."

Anna heard a noise behind her, some Roma expression that sounded like *gadje*. Whatever it meant, she knew it was spat in her direction, and it was not a compliment. She turned to see Lela stalk from the circle and heave herself into the gaudiest of the wagons, then draw the curtain across the entrance with a swish.

It sounded to Anna like a slamming door.

⸻

Anna went no more to the Vltava River, but she still went every day to the grave in Týn Churchyard, where she talked aloud as though her grandfather listened. *I remember the name. I do. Sir John Oldcastle. And I know I promised. But how can I go alone? It would not be safe.*

There was never any answer.

It was mid-August and two weeks had passed since her encounter with the river. She'd not let Bera escort her home but left word with Jetta that she would visit again soon, and truly she'd thought each day she might make the excursion to the little camp downriver to return Lela's red skirt and blouse, which were already freshly laundered and neatly folded. She had planned for sure to do it today. But during the night it had rained enough to moisten the earth and cool the air and that circumstance suggested another more pressing task.

Now as she flung more grass seed onto the new grave and glanced at the angle of the sun, she thought it was probably too late to go. This was more important. If she could not keep her promise to him, she could at least tend his grave. The dirt was already less mounded—one day it would sink like the older graves around it, the neglected ones with nobody left to care. She scattered some wildflower seeds and watered them from the little tin pitcher she had brought.

A month ago I could have watered them with my tears, she thought, but ever since the old Gypsy crone had pulled her from the river, her heart hurt less, as though the waters of the Vltava had indeed offered her a kind of baptism. The ache was still there, a wound knitting, but some of the rage was seeping away, replaced with a duller kind of anger, a simmering deep in the bone.

Lately she had noticed that whenever she visited her grandfather's grave, in place of the simmering anger a strange peace settled over her. As though he were still close. And on some days, the peace walked home with her, remaining with her until she ate her solitary meal and readied herself for bed by removing her tunic and folding it neatly the way Dědeček would have liked. Sometimes, she even caught herself talking to him as she brushed and braided her chaos of curls, once laughing out loud as she gleaned bits of hair from the bristles and laid the silver-backed brush he'd given her as a birthday present facedown, exactly as he'd arranged it whenever he came into her room. *See, Dědeček. I do remember. All of them. All the lessons that you taught me.*

But today was different. Today, after she had watered the new-sown grass and pulled the weeds from around the stone cross that she had used some of her precious florins to purchase, peace did not walk home with her. And peace was not waiting for her in her little town house.

A wide-hipped, square-jawed woman with an unsmiling face framed in a white lace cap met her at the door.

"Mistress Kremensky! Is . . . is something wrong?" Anna asked, trying to remember if she'd straightened the downstairs rooms before she left for the cemetery.

The door was open, but Mistress Kremensky's bulk filled it. She just stood there barring the door, wringing her hands in agitation. "There's something I . . ."

Anna raised herself on tiptoe, to peer over her landlady's shoulder into the front room, but all she could see was a goose feather floating in the air.

"Wait . . . don't—"

"I'm afraid I'm not as good a housekeeper since . . . I promise, I'll do better."

Anna tried to go around her, but Mistress Kremensky continued to block her way. She'd stopped wringing her hands but was shaking her head to deny that Anna's housekeeping was the issue. Anna had never seen her in such a state of frustration. Finally she spoke.

"I'm sorry, Anna. I could not stop them. They threatened me. They said . . ." She looked down at her feet, avoiding Anna's eyes, her voice trailing off.

Anna touched her landlady's shoulder, gave it a gentle shake, as if she could shake the words from her lips. "Stop who, Mistress Kremensky? Who did you try to stop? What has you so upset?"

It was the Gypsies. She should have returned the red skirt, not given them an excuse to come here, and wondering at the same time how they had found her.

"It was the soldiers. They have just left."

"Soldiers!"

Anna pushed past her into the chaos of the downstairs room.

She sucked in her breath. Papers were strewn everywhere, the willow chair overturned, its cushion split open. The cushions on her grandfather's workbench were likewise split. An overturned glass of milk lay on the kitchen table. But it was the sight of her grandfather's worktable—the worktable she'd tended like a shrine—with her grandfather's paints, and brushes, and quills all spilled and scattered and broken that made her eyelids sting.

They had no right.

A smear of red paint clotted on one of the ruined cushions. Anna dabbed at it with her hand. It had the consistency of blood. Anna just stared at it, then wiped it on her skirt already stained with mud from her grandfather's grave.

They had no right!

She felt the simmering rage pushing its way up from the marrow through the bone, threatening to erupt into that all-consuming flash of anger that Dědeček had spent a lifetime teaching her to control.

"They shall not get away with this. I will go to the authorities." She was shouting, unable to control herself, shaking so she feared she would fall. She hugged her arms around her body to stop the trembling. "I will petition the alderman. I will—"

Her landlady drew her into her arms, half restraining, half supporting her, the flush of her own distress forgotten in the heat of such a great conflagration.

"Hush, girl. The walls may have ears. Get control of yourself."

"I'll go to the authorities—"

"Anna, don't you understand? It's the authorities who did this. The soldiers were searching for something. They showed me a writ. Else I'd not have let them in."

"But there is some mistake. I have nothing—"

"They said they were searching for the banned writings of the heretic Wycliffe."

"But all I have is—"

Mistress Kremensky laid her hand gently over Anna's mouth. "I don't want to know what you have, Anna. I always told your grandfather, I don't want to know. It was none of my business. But now people have been executed for this offense and the authorities suspect you. Things will have to change. I don't think they found anything today, so you are safe for the time being. But they will be back. They will keep coming back until they find what they are looking for."

Anna was hardly listening to her. Her gaze was quickly searching the room. The lock had been broken on the small chest she kept in the kitchen. Table linens were strewn helter-skelter around it, but the false bottom looked to be still intact. That was the place where her grandfather always kept the Wycliffe Bible.

Mistress Kremensky's mouth worked with emotion, but she leaned away from Anna as one leans away from a blaze in a gust of wind. "For your own safety, as well as for ours, you must leave. I can no longer afford to have you here," she said.

The words had the effect of a slap in the face.

No. She must have misunderstood. Mistress Kremensky had always been so kind to her, ever since she was a little girl, businesslike in some ways, but always kind. And since her grandfather's death, she had been especially generous, bringing her food, urging her to rest, even going with her once to visit the grave.

"What do you mean, I have to leave? Are you putting me out of my home?"

Anna was not shouting now. The blaze had died as quickly as it flared, leaving a numbing cold behind. Little beads of perspiration were lining Mrs. Kremensky's forehead. But Anna shivered.

"You must understand my position, Anna."

There was pleading in her voice, in the little gray eyes that had always reminded Anna of shiny little buttons sewn into the cloth face of an overstuffed doll.

"You must understand. I have no choice. I thought that they would not bother you, now that your grandfather was gone. A woman alone—what danger could you be? But now it seems you have, for some reason, come to their attention, even though the . . . meetings are no longer held here."

Mistress Kremensky was wringing her hands again. She couldn't look Anna in the face, but looked instead over her shoulder.

Anna moved to force the woman to face her, trying to control the fear rising inside her. "Mistress Kremensky. If you force me out, I have no place to go."

"Surely you have some friend, some relative who can take you in."

"My grandfather was my only living relative. And the Church has taken away my friends."

Fed their flesh to the birds and burned their bones to ashes. How could she make this woman understand that she could not be separated from this place, this last link to the only family she had ever known?

The landlady put her hand to her forehead, its wide square palm covering her button eyes, pushing her mobcap absurdly askew.

"I am sorry, Anna. I have my husband to think of. He's not well. This house provides our only living, and if I allow you to stay, it could be forfeit."

She turned to leave. Anna was too stunned to try to stop her.

"Your grandfather had paid the rent through the end of the year. I will refund your money. You can change your name, find a place in a new town. None of us is safe as long as you are here. You must understand."

But Anna understood nothing. Except that now she was alone. And she was soon to be homeless as well.

"Please try to leave by tomorrow, Anna. You need to be gone when the soldiers come back, and I don't want to know where you are going. I am sorry."

Anna didn't turn around. She heard the door close behind her. She just stood there, frozen, among the strewn papers and rumpled linens. A goose feather, disturbed by the waft of breeze from the closing door, floated down and settled on Lela's fanned red skirt.

⁓⋇⋋

A whirlwind of anger and fastened rage, Anna started with her grandfather's worktable and restored it to its original orderly status. The soldiers had not disturbed the upstairs rooms. Either they didn't notice the recessed door leading to the stairway or they were only interested in this one room because that was where the Bible study meetings were held, and Anna almost had this room back to order. She had to do that first, before she could even think about leaving. She had righted the chair, cleaned up the spilled milk, thrown out the ruined cushions, all with tears streaming down her cheeks, muttering to herself angrily, a behavior she had thought she left behind with her childhood. She was straightening the contents of the chest when she heard a knock on the door.

Mistress Kremensky come to say she had reconsidered? Or even to beg her to stay? Well, at least, to give her more time. Anna tried to straighten her face, wiped her eyes and her dripping nose, and going to the door, she lifted the heavy bar. Anna spoke above the sound of the creaking hinge to the crack in the wooden door.

"I'm so glad you've come—"

But it was not her repentant landlady who stood silhouetted against the late afternoon light in her doorway.

"Jetta was right! We have found you at last," the king of the Gypsies said. "I have come to see the holy book."

And he said it in a whisper, conveying to her with his smile and his wink that he knew it was not a secret to broadcast in the street.

When the soldiers came again at the beginning of the following week, the little house in Staroměstké náměstí was swept clean. Not even a paint pot remained in testimony of its former inhabitants.

"My tenant left in the middle of the night. I don't know where she has gone." Mistress Kremensky stood in the middle of the room mustering a look of indignation. Tiny dust motes floated in a sunbeam around her. "If you find her, she owes me rent for the month of August."

Satisfied, the soldiers left.

Anna left nothing behind in the city of Prague except a woven wreath encircling the little stone cross in Týn Churchyard. Its flowers had already begun to fade by the time the little band of Romani pilgrims entered the dark forest on their way west.

ELEVEN

The man who is wise and earnestly intent on guarding his salvation watches always with such great solicitude to repress his vices that with the belt of perfect mortification he girds his loins.
—FROM *THE MONASTIC IDEAL* (11TH CENTURY)

ut I've already been baptized, husband," Lady Joan Cobham said to her husband. "Proper. With a priest."

It was a warm September day at Cooling Castle as Sir John led her by the hand across the courtyard. Past the gatehouse. Past the stables. Through the hedge lining the garden boundary and into the woods where acorns and last year's dry oak leaves crunched underfoot, down, down, until the leaves gave way to a cushioned carpet of moss.

"It's not baptism I'm thinking on, wife. It's another of the Holy Sacraments."

He drew her into the circle of his arms as they emerged into a small clearing where the sun shot an arrow of light into the dark green forest walls. "I want to show you to what other use we can put this holy pool." His breath came in little huffs from the steep descent.

Lady Cobham looked down from the outcropping of rock on which they stood. A pool of clear water sparkled sapphire bright beneath the shaft of light. Now it was her turn to gasp.

She had watched throughout the summer, wondering, as he'd scooped out the earth, dammed up a spring, moved more earth, planted rocks, planted trees, until he'd transformed the only hollow between Gravesend and Cooling Castle into a hidden sylvan glen. "A secret baptismal pool," he had said. Like the one in which he'd been baptized just six years ago in the Olchon Valley deep in the heart of the Welsh Black Mountains. Now here, spread out before her, was the proof of his labor.

A trickle of water from the overhead rock tantalized. Huffing, John shifted a couple of rocks, angled a log, and the trickle became a cascade of water spilling and splashing from the outcrop into the pool below.

"Oh, John!" It was all she could say.

"Come on. Let's cool off."

"Dare we? I mean, it was made for a holy place."

"So was Eden. Come on." And taking her hand, he led her down through a curving path, stripping off his jerkin as he went.

She could feel him watching her as she unlaced her own chemise. She, a widow who had buried two husbands, felt like a maid when he looked at her that way. She resisted the urge to cover her breasts with her arms.

"You first," John said.

She waded into the pool, feeling the shock of the cool stream swirling around her ankles, glad for even the warmth of her unbound hair falling over her neck and shoulders.

"Go on. You'll get used to it. Stand under the spray," he urged.

She felt the water first on the top of her head and the curve of her back, then turned, face up, watching, as droplets played in a stray sunbeam, scattering pink and green and yellow before landing on her skin. I'm playing in a rainbow, she thought. She heard him splash into the pool, not tiptoeing as she did, then she felt his arms around her.

A shadow crossed above her. Some movement among the trees. A rustle in the undergrowth above them. And then the stillness returned.

"I brought soap," he whispered into her ear. "The kind you like." And he began to wash her, releasing the sweet lavender smell of it into the fragrance of moss and wet earth and sunbaked rock. His hands slid in a froth of bubbles against her skin.

"My turn," she said, laughing, and taking the soap from him, began to bathe his large shoulders, the whole broad expanse of his chest and belly.

"That's enough." He laughed. " 'Tis not fit that a man should smell over-much of flowers."

He tossed the soap beneath the cascade. Little bubbles floated in the water, popping around her feet in tiny bursts of color and light. But he drew her closer, warming her with the warmth of his own body. She felt his lips in the hollow of her neck.

"Oh, John," was all she had breath enough to say.

·⇥⇤·

As Sir John crossed the courtyard early the next morning, he recognized the familiar regalia of the Roman Church on the horse carrying its black-cassocked rider. Since attaching himself to the nearby abbey as confessor to the sisters, the friar was always around on some pretext or other.

Sir John stifled a sigh. He was no fool. Brother Gabriel was spying for the archbishop. Why else was he always underfoot uninvited? In the kitchen, chatting up the cook whenever Sir John went for his wife-rationed allotment of small beer—no strong sack in buckets now, just enough to keep his throat from parching—or in the solar laughing with Joan, pretending a holy inter-est in the Wycliffe text, pumping his wily wife for information.

So this morning, Sir John was neither surprised nor pleased to hear him-self hailed in his own courtyard. He wondered on what pretext Brother Gabriel came today. Today, of all days! Two Lollard priests were visiting, and there was to be a meeting later this week of all the lay priests in Kent and Suffolk counties. Sir John had planned to pass out the new Wycliffe tracts the abbess had promised would be ready.

"Brother Gabriel, to what do we owe the honor of this visit?" He tried to keep the edge from his voice.

As the friar leaned down from his horse, he looked oddly dispossessed of his usual ease. His gaze was directed away, like a man catching another in a state of undress.

Sir John stroked his little pointed beard, to make sure it was not coated with grease from his morning repast, then, satisfied, glanced down to make sure the lacings in his breeches were secure. No, everything seemed to be in order. Odd how the man's discomfort was catching. He'd never noticed that unease in the friar before. Usually he was an affable, hail-fellow-well-met sort.

Finally, the monk's gaze met his. "I am on my way south to the ports to bring the Grace of our Lord to sinners there. I wished to say my fare-thee-wells to you and Lady Cobham."

Well. Here was good news. They were to be rid of the spying Dominican. Sir John should have guessed it from the way the pardoner was dressed in rich black robes and from the large velvet pouch carrying the "Grace" of which he spoke, the papal bulls and indulgences to be exchanged for coin. *Time to refurbish Arundel's coffers?* he wanted to ask.

But what he said was, "What about the sisters at the abbey? Who will administer the sacrament while you are away?" Even though he knew the abbey had its own resident priest, knew the pardoner's presence there was a mere pretext. Though Sir John wasn't worried about the sisters. The abbess was a woman of intelligence and faith. She would not give away more than she should. And in truth, he worried less for all those who pushed the Lollard cause since he'd helped move the law through Parliament whereby all accused heretics were to become prisoners of the crown rather than the Church. This was important to Sir John because he had friends in high places at court. Very high places. Though there had been recent talk that Prince Hal had laid claim to piety.

But he couldn't quarrel with that. He'd got a hefty dose of religion himself. He and the soon-to-be king might be on opposite sides, but with Christ in the center—Christ, and the good times Prince Hal and Merry Jack had shared—how far apart could they be? Let Arundel and his spy do their worst. The old archbishop would be giving his own reckoning before his maker soon enough, if appearances could be believed. And wouldn't Sir John like to be around for that accounting! Still, he was glad to see the backside of the priest. Things would be easier both at Cooling Castle and at the abbey near Rochester without the archbishop's lackey poking his head out from every corner.

"The old curate at the abbey can provide while I'm away. His infirmities still allow for a simple mass, though they say he sleeps in the confessional."

But not you, I'll wager, Sir John thought. *Your ears are as perked as a hound's on the scent of a fox.*

"Then the sisters will miss you. How long will you be away?"

"I'll be back before the roads turn bad with winter rains. I plan to spend some time with my own father confessor. He is very old and almost blind. I fear he might not make it another year."

"Is he in Canterbury?"

"No, in the South Downs. Battle Abbey."

"I'll call Lady Cobham, then," he said, feeling suddenly generous and lighthearted as a schoolboy granted recess. "She will want to bid you good journey."

This sentiment was true. Joan was fond of the fellow in spite of both his vocation and his avocation.

But Brother Gabriel uncharacteristically demurred. "No. Please." His skin flushed to the roots of his hair. "I would not want to disturb her."

What was this sudden shyness? He'd never seen the priest reluctant to engage his lady before. Indeed, their discourse was often quite lively, with Joan poking gentle fun at his orthodoxy, toying with him, teasing him with information but never really giving anything away.

"Please convey my fare-thee-well to her."

The pardoner's horse tossed its head, jingling the gold bells on its scarlet harness, as if in agreement.

"Tell your lady I shall call on her upon my return. I really must be away."

The fellow seemed as flustered as a schoolboy.

Sir John watched as the friar trotted the elegantly outfitted horse back across the courtyard, past the gatehouse, and through the barbican. The sun polished the blond rim of his tonsured head. The skin inside it was as pink as a new spring berry. Could it be? Now it was Sir John's turn to blush, for he also had heard the rustle in the bushes as his wife undressed to enter the sylvan waterfall. He had put it down to the bolting of a curious hare, not pursued it, not wanting to break the moment, not wanting to alarm his wife. Could it be that the serpent was voluntarily quitting Eden? he wondered.

Not bloody likely, he thought.

But at least they were to have a respite. He could meet with the Lollard priests in peace.

⚜

Within the priory garden the abbess sweated beneath her veil and wimple. It was early afternoon, just past sext, and the sunlight pressed the fragrance of sage and rosemary into the air. The floating gauze of her face veil trapped her breath. Tiny beads of moisture gathered in the creases of her cheeks, but it never occurred to her to remove the veil—not even in the privacy of the cloistered garden. The semitransparent veil was like a skin covering her face, and she felt raw and exposed without it, though she sometimes, as now in private, lifted the right side of the veil so that she could see unobstructed by the thin black gauze.

As she hunched over, gathering the berries of the shrub *Vitex agnuscastus* that grew in the right quadrant of the garden, she became aware of footsteps above the plopping of the water drops in the center fountain. They were heavier than the footfalls of the sisters and they were accompanied by a masculine voice.

"Sister Agatha said I would find you here." A resonant voice. Familiar and jolly. The abbess straightened up, lowering the veil fully before turning to greet her visitor.

"Sir John. I expected you earlier. How is Lady Joan?"

"My lady is well. She sends her warm regards. She would have come with me, but she is preparing for tonight's prayer meeting. We are expecting upward of fivescore, and after prayers and Bible reading, she plans to feed them all."

"Will they overnight?"

"Some of them. They'll spread their bedrolls. Some in the hall. Some in the courtyard."

"Sounds like a grand encampment."

"That's the plan. To send them back out well fed and well fired. Preachers of the Word."

She smiled, her spirit buoyed by his enthusiasm. The Lollard cause—her cause these twenty-seven years—was enhanced by such a man.

She lowered herself onto one of the stone benches inside the colonnade that squared the garden, inviting him with a gesture to sit on the opposing bench across the cloistered walkway. The sisters often sat thus in the late afternoons after dinner and before vespers, the one time of the day when they could chatter together as women were wont to do. But the cloister walk was empty now at midday, the nuns all busily at work in the scriptorium. The only other occupant was a butterfly that hovered. It flapped its butter-colored wings and disappeared, disdaining the company of human intruders.

The abbess quickly surveyed the garden, making sure they were alone, their conversation witnessed only by the carved saints circling the capitals of the columns.

"I would have been here earlier, but your monk delayed me," Sir John said as he arranged his bulk on the seat. "It seems you are to be without his company for a while."

She laughed. "And you are to be likewise deprived of his fellowship. Though I think we both will survive. But I must say that Brother Gabriel is popular in our little cloister of women."

"A bit of a fox in a henhouse, aye?"

This time, her laughter was full throated, echoing in the garden. "My nuns are all devoted. It does no harm to them to look upon a comely face. But Brother Gabriel is very careful never to be alone with any of them. He hears confessions only from the safety of the enclosed confessional. I suspect celibacy is his particular cross. For his journey he took the last of the monk's pepper from the infirmary."

She held out a gloved hand to show a handful of round little berries that she had taken from the chaste tree. "That's why you found me in the herb garden. Replenishing our supply."

"If I'm not making too bold to ask, Abbess, why does a company of women need monk's pepper?"

Sir John's question was accompanied by a flash of strong white teeth above his pointy little beard. If he hoped by his blunt sexual innuendo to have a bit of sport at her expense—well, two could play that game.

"The chaste berries help with female problems too. At certain times of the lunar cycle, some in our community of women become irascible and can-tankerous. Surely a man of the world such as you must have noticed that phenomenon."

Her guest's rotund belly heaved with a chuckle, causing the wooden bench on which they sat to shudder. She had a momentary concern for its stability. But it was of good English oak. Surely it would hold one frail old woman and one sturdy knight.

Sir John leaned forward, picked a sprig of peppermint. "Good for the stomach," he said as he began to chew. "You'd best give some of your chaste berries to Sister Agatha, then," he said. "She was cross as an old broody hen. Pointed a turnip at me like it was a dagger."

The abbess sighed. "Ah, Sister Agatha, she's—I'm afraid her ill temper is not of the kind that waxes and wanes with the moon. Sister Agatha has been sowing wild tares for weeks. She doesn't want us to copy the Wycliffe papers or the English Gospels." She weighed the chaste berries in her hand, their juice staining the glove that covered the scars on her arms. "I don't know what to do with her. She's one of my best scribes, but I've banished her to the vegetable garden. I thought working with God's growing things might improve her temper."

"I do not think your plan is working." A deep chuckle gurgled up with the words.

"I'm glad you find it so amusing," she said archly. "But Sister Agatha is really no laughing matter for either of us. I suspect she has already complained to Brother Gabriel about the heretical documents we copy. He seemed uncommonly attentive to her confession—or complaint."

His tone turned serious. "I'll wager the truth of that. Take care around him. He may be here to listen for more than confessions. He could be spying for the archbishop."

"I thought of that possibility. I told him we no longer provided copies of the English Bible—a lie for which I've already begged forgiveness, pleading the service of a greater good."

"For a holy woman, Mother, you have a surprisingly practical nature."

She ignored his comment and the admiring tone in which it was delivered. "Brother Gabriel is charming company, but I'm glad to be shed of him for a while. At least until I can think what to do about Agatha."

She stood up. "Come, I'll get you the copies for tonight's meeting, but I urge you to keep them well hidden. I sense a hardening of the Roman will, and the archbishop is overly mindful of his legacy."

"I'm going to give the gospels to the congregants."

"Well, be cautious to whom you give them, old friend. Brother Gabriel says even the mere possession of an English Bible will soon be sufficient for a charge of heresy."

"I've heard that too. The law is close in Parliament, though I'm working just as hard against it. And I have some insight that the new king will lean toward tolerance. I know him. He is a man of reason. And rumor says that old Arundel is dying. Without the fuel the flame will die."

Here was good news. She was surprised to hear that Henry IV's heir would be kinder to their cause, but she knew Sir John, as a member of Parliament, was a man whose information could be relied upon.

"So. We are soon to have a new king and a new archbishop? And you are hopeful for religious tolerance?"

"I am hopeful, Abbess. I am hopeful, but I am cautious too. One can never be certain of tolerance when Rome is concerned."

"No, never certain," she said. "Not if one is prudent." A tenor bell tolled three times, calling the sisters to prayer.

"We must hurry. We do not want Sister Agatha to see your arms loaded with texts."

She led him from the sunlit garden, through the shadowy interior of the chapel, and into her visitor's room.

"Wait here," she instructed and went into her chamber and then into her garderobe. From the deepest corner of her wardrobe, where not even the chambermaid went, she brought out an armload of copied scripts.

When she reentered the visitor's parlor carrying her load, he rushed forward to help her. "That's a goodly haul! How are you able to copy so many?" he asked. "Especially if your nuns are reluctant?"

"Not all are reluctant. Some are very devoted to the cause. And each thinks the others are at work on other things. I sprinkle enough of the other—poetry, Latin texts, song sheets, husbandry pamphlets—to give us the look of legitimacy."

She carefully checked to see that a few pages of "the other" were on top, then held open a large sack in which to place the lot.

"The bill of sale is tucked inside the last copy. You know we—at least some among us—would gladly copy them for nothing, but without your generous custom we could not continue. We are just a company of poor nuns. Not a decent corrody or endowment among us. We are extremely grateful for your patronage."

"And I for your effort. If you and the sisters did not have to spend so much time filling my orders, you would produce enough of *the other* to keep your refectory provisioned. Just concentrate on keeping them coming. Don't worry about the cost."

She was grateful for the easy way he brushed off the expense, grateful too for the depth of his purse.

"How do you disseminate so many?" she asked.

"I send the Wycliffe sermons to Prague University by way of Oxford exchange students. The movement is ripe to bursting there. They translate Wycliffe texts into the language of Bohemia as fast as Rome can burn them. The lay priests can use as many of the Gospels, and more, as your industrious scribes can provide. The people are hungry for the truth of the Word."

"It is a great risk, Sir John. Why do you do it?" She rubbed her left arm where the weight of the manuscripts had stressed it.

"You ask why? That's an easy answer, Abbess. Once a man has seen the light of truth he cannot turn his back on it. Not and call himself a man. I could ask the same of you," he said. "You could easily maintain your enclosure without copying contraband texts. This is a dangerous enterprise for you. Especially if Parliament bans possession."

"Oh, I do it for him," she said.

"For our Lord."

"Him too," she said, surprised by her own words. Surprised that she had given voice to some secret buried deep, so deep she'd never really acknowledged it to herself.

He smiled. "I'll not chase that rabbit," he said. "A lady is entitled to her secrets of the heart."

She watched him out the door, carrying the heavy sack in one arm as though it were of no more consequence than a sack of turnips. She feared for him: trembled for his confidence in his power, in his ability, in his cause. He would not be the first strong man she'd seen brought down because he trusted too much in the power of truth.

"Secrets of the heart," he'd said.

It was cool in her chamber. From the window that overlooked the cloistered garden, she could see that the yellow butterfly had returned and lit upon a marigold. Its wings pulsed in the stillness, barely moving, hovering in the heat. The nuns were all in chapel. Their plainsong chants answered the murmurs of the old priest as he read the Office. It sounded like the droning of summer bees. She would allow herself that most exquisite of all luxuries—to sit quietly in her shaded chamber. As the afternoon sun ripened the light-filled garden outside her window, and the cloistered creatures, human and nonhuman, went about their ordered work, she would linger over her memories, a happy miser examining each jewel in her chest of memory.

She drew back her veil, feeling a rush of air against her left cheek. For the first time in a very long time, she felt the wetness of a tear slide down her ruined face. That *is* why I do it, she thought. Not that she didn't believe with her whole heart in the people's right to address God directly, in the people's right to read the wondrous truth of the Gospel in a language they understood. She likewise acknowledged the truths of the other doctrines the Church condemned in the Lollard heresy. So Sir John's misinterpretation of her answer had not been wrong. She indeed did it for the divine Him.

But she could have served Him in any number of ways, all less dangerous. She willingly took the risk, laboring long past what her years should allow, for that other "him," because with each stroke of her pen, each smuggled transcript, she felt his remembered presence. And she knew he would be pleased. Copying the Word was an occupation she shared with a lover long gone.

She tried to remember the shape of his hand cradling the pen, the lift of his brow, the touch of his hand on her skin. His face. But she couldn't. All that had fled long ago. But for all these years, whenever her fingers cramped with fatigue and her eyes ached from strain, she had felt as though he were with her in the very room where she labored. She closed her eyes, willing that presence to come to her now.

Sometime later, she heard the sisters begin their silent shuffle back from the chapel, then the sound of voices in the refectory as they laid the table for the evening meal. She lowered her veil, lit her lamp, and took up her pen, waiting for the knock on her door that would summon her to a simple supper in the company of women.

⚜

Will Jaggers hated to steal from a priest. It was bad luck, and this one looked as though bad luck followed him, if his threadbare cassock told a true tale. Still, the priest probably had bread, maybe a rind of cheese, in his scrip, and Will Jaggers had not eaten since yesterday, when he had begged a paltry crust from the kitchens of Rochester Castle, known more for the white lady that haunted its battlement than for its charity.

Though the morning was well on, the priest was still sleeping in front of his campfire, so it'd be easy pickings. But Will would have to roll him over. He approached the sleeping priest carefully, pulled gently on the strap of the scrip. The priest didn't move. There was a flask inside the scrip—Will could see by the outline—and judging by how soundly the man slept, it held more than water. Less gently, he rolled the priest onto his side to free the scrip, then swore under his breath, making the sign of the cross.

Will Jaggers had seen enough corpses in his life to know one. And if he hadn't, the knife buried to its crude hilt in the dead man's chest would have been clue enough. Poor sod. Probably never even had a chance to defend himself. Strange, though, he'd not looked to be robbed. More like he'd come crosswise with a band of zealots who disagreed with his particular brand of religion and thought to rid the world of one more heretic. He was one of them poor priests, one of them Lollards, not known for rich living. Just my luck, Will thought, to stumble upon a dead, poor priest instead of a rich friar. But it was not a total loss. With cold nights coming on, at least the cassock would be warm, and a poor priest could get better alms than a common beggar.

Will looked around to see that no one was watching, then dragged the priest behind the bushes and quickly stripped him down to his braies, which he left—a man should keep some shred of dignity even in death. He donned the brown cassock, posed momentarily with his arms crossed, hands hidden in the opposing wide sleeves. He tried the hood—yes, just the thing for a cold night, but not now, not with the bright afternoon sun shining down. He pulled it back, picked up the scrip, and turned it inside out. Only a scrap of paper fluttered to the ground. No food, not even a moldy crust, and the flask contained only water. He flung it to the ground in disgust and picked up the paper.

It was a map.

Will couldn't read the words but it had a crude drawing of a castle with a hulking round keep that looked a lot like Rochester Castle. A line curved northeast and ended in an *X*, another crude drawing of a smaller keep, and the letters *C O O L I N G C*. It didn't take a smart man to figure out that the priest was on his way from Rochester to some other destination. Will knew of one other castle in the area. Just north of Gravesend. Lord Cobham's castle. He'd stopped there once. The cook had given him a pasty, a pot of ale, and some bread for the road. It was off the main road, out on a jut of land in the marshlands. A bit of a trek but maybe worth it. He'd likely find a good meal there.

As he covered the dead man's body with brush—at least he would not lie exposed—he tried to remember the Paternoster but failed. In the end he just crossed himself and mumbled, "Good day to ye, Father."

Then, feeling much less like a beggar, he headed west toward Gravesend. He walked sedately, arms tucked into sleeves.

Brother William. It had a good ring to it.

"Bless you, my son," he said to a spindly bush. And Will smiled, thinking how convenient it was that he could give his blessing in English. He didn't even have to worry about mumbling some Latin mumbo jumbo.

A wiser man might have considered that an English blessing just might have been what spurred the purloined cassock's original owner to his death.

~⚓~

As Brother Gabriel rode the five miles back from Cooling Castle, he chided himself. He should have seen Lady Cobham. Sir John must have wondered about the purpose of his visit—five miles north when the priest's destination was south, and all on the flimsy pretext of saying farewell to two people whose acquaintance he'd so recently made, a clumsy ruse made clumsier by his adolescent embarrassment. He knew Lord and Lady Cobham suspected him of spying. A visit planned to put them off their guard had instead incited suspicion because of his stupid behavior.

He was just now nearing Rochester, this time bypassing the lane leading to the abbey. The abbey. Now, there was a place Brother Gabriel would be missed. He'd ingratiated himself with the sisters and found one in particular who was flattered by his company. Sister Agatha had a very loose tongue. She had said enough to let him know the abbey was hip deep in heresy. Though the abbess claimed to no longer fill orders for the English Scriptures, he knew she had at least one good customer. But how to prove it? Possession of a single copy, like the one Cobham kept boldly on display in his solar, was not enough to charge a nobleman with heresy—a peasant or even a merchant perhaps, but not an English lord who sat in Parliament, and not the abbess he protected either. Though truth be told, Brother Gabriel doubted that one small abbey could produce enough for export. He'd told the archbishop as much in his last report.

Arundel had suggested a brief time away from the abbey and the Cobhams to ease suspicions. Take a two-week hiatus, sell a few indulgences on the Pilgrim's Way before the season ended. Perhaps Lord and Lady Cobham, even the abbess, would become accustomed to his comings and goings, be more accepting of him as a semipermanent fixture in their community. Be less careful in his presence.

Gabriel was glad enough for the respite. He hated spying on the Cobhams. He rather liked them—even envied the obvious comfort each found in the other, their easy intimacy, their wordless communication. But being in their presence had made him feel his loneliness keenly and he was glad to be leaving. He could not get the vision of what he had almost seen in the woods out of his mind—no matter how enthusiastically he pinched his thigh or tightened his hair shirt. He had been on his way out of the wood after watching Sir John scooping out the earth beneath the diverted waterfall and guessed its purpose when he'd seen the pair, innocent as children, enter the wood. He'd turned and bolted when he realized their intent.

But he'd seen enough to set his imagination to mischief.

The old lust he'd thought conquered long ago was roused. And the monk's pepper he'd taken from the abbey's infirmary was not helping.

As Gabriel neared Rochester, he steered his horse off High Street toward Boley Hill and into the hub of ecclesiastical buildings, past the great cathedral, the monastery, and the bishop's palace. Here was his first stop: the narrow Pilgrim's Passage leading to the tomb of Saint William of Perth, a shrine that rivaled the tomb of Thomas à Becket on the pilgrim road.

He dismounted and handed his horse off to an ostler, then reached into his velvet pouch and withdrew the bull bearing the seal of Pope Gregory XII; not the counterfeit seal of one of the antipopes in Avignon or Pisa, but the original imprint of Rome, the stamp of the true descendent of the Fisherman, given to Brother Gabriel in person. The imprint designated him as an official purveyor of Divine Grace from the treasury of forgiveness built up by the deeds of the saints.

As he unfurled the document and spread it carefully on a table provided for his use at the opening of the Pilgrim's Passage, he did not feel the sharp thrill of exhilaration that the mere handling of it usually gave him. Nor did he look forward to this day's preaching and dispensation of Grace to the long line of pilgrims pressing into the entrance of the narrow passageway. They waited patiently. Like customers outside a stall at the fair, and he just another merchant. More devil's mischief in his mind, he thought, and set to work.

"With your gift to rebuild the basilica in Rome you will find pardon for your sins," he intoned.

But shouldn't Grace by its very nature be free? some Lollard's voice inside his head insisted. He shrugged his shoulders as if to slough off that heretical thought and to get some momentary relief from the chafing on his back, but the movement accomplished neither.

"If you cannot go to Rome, your ducats and your marks will make pilgrimage for you to the Holy City. His Holiness himself assures your penance will be heard."

But didn't Christ assure that already with his death and resurrection? If all it takes to secure forgiveness is a bribe, then why are you wearing the hair shirt that's rubbing your skin to one great open sore?

Here was the devil's argument indeed, and inside his head! Gabriel could name the sin that let the devil in, but how to rid himself of it?

As a youth in the first flush of sexual hunger, he'd gone to Brother Francis for advice. "Discipline," his mentor had said when he gave him the small corded and knotted whip, taught him how to wield it until the stripes on his back burned with fire. "Think of our Lord, think of his stripes," Brother Francis had said. "Your celibacy is your gift to Him. As you grow older the blood will grow calmer, your animal lust will lessen."

The pilgrim at the front of the line reached into her scrip and pulled out a coin.

"Pence for penance," he offered her. She had a female companion, and he could ascertain, with the help of his accursed imagination, their provocative female forms beneath their pilgrim cloaks.

How many pence for peace? he wondered. How many stripes would it take to chase the devil from his head?

※

Sir John listened to the preacher who stood in front of his congregation of brothers. They sat on hewn log benches, arranged in rows from trees Sir John and his grooms had felled, all ears and eyes attuned to the brother who spoke to them. But Sir John's eyes and ears were attuned to a different sound. The sound of hoofbeats, the archbishop's men, soldiers flushing out their quarry.

"We meet here beneath this canopy of blue sky in this cathedral made by

God's own hand to celebrate the great love and sacrifice made for us by God's only Son," the priest, in his simple brown cassock, proclaimed in a voice loud enough to disturb the rooks roosting high overhead.

"Rome calls what we do here heresy, gainsays our truth for their falseness. It is the pope and his minions who worship as the pagans worship. It is the pope and his minions who kneel before relics in golden caskets, encrusted with jewels, to practice their idolatry. It is the pope and his minions who kneel in great stone cathedrals built with money from the poor. They sell the devil's lies and peddle false forgiveness. You, my brethren, will go forth to preach the Truth. Grace is free. Grace demands no coin except obedience. We do not worship a cross of gold. We worship the Lord who died upon that cross. And it was not made of gold but of wood. And He is no longer hanging on that tree but is risen."

Sir John's most trusted retainers stood well armed, facing outward in a circle, to protect the congregation of worshippers. If any party from crown or Church came to Cooling Castle seeking him, Joan was instructed to tell them that he and his men had ridden to Herefordshire to a convocation. They would be sure to follow, thinking to catch him out. He knew she could be trusted to get rid of them. As a last resort, she'd said she would plead illness, hint of plague, while pretending to offer hospitality, in order to speed them on their way. Or, she'd said with a gleam in her eye as she inspected the blood puddings and pasties to feed his guests, she'd just tell them that she was "feeding the local lepers as a penance," and invite them to stay.

After the service, if all was clear, she would send a groom to summon them to the hall, where they would feast on roast capon and custards, and maybe there would be apple tartlets coddled beneath great lumps of clotted cream—

He really should be listening to the sermon.

"We confess, each man of us, our sins directly to God. We mumble no Latin prayers that we don't understand. We read his Word for ourselves in our own language, and we will go forth from this place to free the people of the calumny of an apostate pope who endangers the souls of God's people with chains made of superstition and forged in the fire of greed."

One of the priests led a couple of converts, a yeoman and his wife of about the same age as Sir John, to the baptismal pool. They shivered in the twilight breeze. The waterfall had been dammed up and the pool reflected the indigo of the sky overhead. The first evening star had appeared beside a pale quarter moon.

He said his own private prayers of thanks as the community of brothers intoned the "Our Father." Said it in plain language—a man's language that a God in whose image he was made would understand. Sir John's God was not still hanging, bloody and defeated, imprisoned like a dead idol above some altar. He sighed in the wind and shouted in the thunder and laughed in the ocean's roar. And Sir John hoped He was watching them now, with approval. Let it be so, he prayed silently. They all had a lot riding on His approval. Leaves rustled in the canopy overhead. The voice of God whispering? "Free my Church," it said.

Or was that just his imagination? Would he have to listen harder, longer, on his knees for that still, small voice?

⁓≍⁓

The next day, after the last lay brother had received his parcel of food for the road from the generous kitchen of Cooling Castle, after Sir John and his lady had retired to her chamber, Sir John watched his wife as she stood in front of her pier glass, brushing her chestnut hair.

"You are satisfied then, my lord, with the convocation?" she asked.

"Very satisfied, my lady. All went as planned. It was a goodly meeting. We gave out every last one of the translations."

"Give me the bill of lading for the abbess, and I will see that she is promptly paid. The abbey runs on a tight resource."

Too late, Sir John remembered. He groaned.

She laid down her brush and turned to him. "What is it, husband? I told you not to eat that last portion of—"

"Every last one. We gave out every last one. The bill was in the last one."

Now it was Lady Joan's turn to groan. "Does the abbess put your name on the bills?"

"Always. I insist on it for her protection. She just writes 'Gospels copied.' She does not say 'English Gospels.' "

"But John, if it is found with the book—"

"It is too late to worry about it now. Anyway, the brother who has that book will see the bill and destroy it. And if he doesn't, well, it's not like our efforts here are secret. Brother Gabriel has already seen the Wycliffe Bible in our solar."

"But owning it might be tolerated," she said. "Whereas disseminating it would not be." She paused, her hand on the brush, but she did not take it up again. "At the least, it means you must make another trip to the abbey to ask the abbess what she is owed."

He nodded. "We'll probably hear no more about it. It has probably already been lost or thrown away. Unless it is found with the book, it can be of no importance." But he didn't sound convincing even to his own ears.

She leaned forward and kissed him lightly on the cheek. "What's done is done and cannot be undone. We will think no more about it," she said, taking up the brush again.

As Sir John felt the smooth touch of her lips against his skin, he winced at the memory of one ill-at-ease brother who dozed through the Bible reading and devoured his food like a wolf. Oh, bugger it! It was just a piece of paper.

"Did we have any of those apple tartlets left?" he asked.

"You are a man of insatiable appetites, husband." She laughed and made a clucking noise with her tongue as she dragged the brush through her unbound hair.

"I know," he said, and putting his arms around her waist, he guided her hands to lay down the brush.

TWELVE

*Let him [a monk] confine himself within the walls
of his cloister . . . for the world is . . . polluted by
the contamination of so many crimes that any holy
mind is corrupted by the mere consideration of it . . .*
—PETER DAMIAN IN *THE MONASTIC IDEAL*
(11TH CENTURY)

abriel was weary from his travels: two weeks of castle yards,
country markets, churches, town crosses from Maidstone to Bodiam Castle,
all in need of "Grace." More than once it had occurred to him that he was
hardly more than a tinker with a pack, and then he would remind himself
that in his pack he carried the Grace of God, and it was profane to even think
thus.

By the time he finally reached Hastings, it was late September. A cold rain
was falling, and he thought of seeking shelter, but knew he was nearing his
destination at Hastings Field. Senlac. The old Norman name meant a lake of
blood, and the sodden earth truly did look as though it were sweating blood.
The locals spoke of hauntings from the old Norman battle where William
killed King Harold. He could almost believe it on such a shrouded afternoon
when the mists rolled in from the sea, mingling their salt smell with the
smells of earth and moss.

He could see the gray stone dormitory of Saint Martin's Abbey looming on the hill in the distance. He knew Brother Francis was there. Gabriel would find comfort in the old man's company. And absolution. It had been too long since his last confession. His soul was burdened, heavy with longing for something so elusive he couldn't even name it. He tugged on his cowl, shielding his face from the rain, and spurred his horse to pick its way up the hill among the red puddles that bubbled up like blood.

⸙

"Have ye finished, Brother Francis?"

Mistress Clare could feel irritation pulling her angular face tighter, disapproval pursing her mouth to a thin line. The old man didn't eat enough to keep a cuckoo alive. Never mind that she'd stood on swollen ankles to chip the beef into tiny bites—after she'd cleaned his chamber pot and swept his hearth, after she'd ironed his shirt and scraped the muck from his boots, after she'd bathed his crepey skin oh so careful like lest she tear it. Since gentleness had long ago fled Mistress Clare's nature, it was a testament to her pure determination that the skin on Brother Francis's arms remained unmarked by the dark purple discolorations he was prone to. Next she'd be chewing his food for him, like a mother—or grandmother, for she was long past the age for one of her own. But Brother Francis was not her child.

He had not touched the beer either. Time was when he would have had a second, and even a third, serving of both. She looked at him in amazement, never ceasing to be surprised, as though somewhere inside the puckered cheeks and sunken eyes that constantly searched the shadows around him, she could find lurking the vital hulk of a man she had once known.

"Shall I call one of the novices to read to you?"

She had never learned to read. "What use does a charwoman have for letters?" he'd said whenever she mentioned it to him. And he'd looked at her blankly, not meaning to be unkind, but genuinely puzzled, as though he were surprised by the inappropriateness of her request.

He did not answer her now, just shrank down inside his woolly blanket, shivering.

"Are you cold? Shall I add more peat to the fire?"

He closed watery eyes and shook his head, reminding her of a terrapin hunched inside his shell.

"It will only smoke," he said. "Smoke makes me cough." And he coughed, as though to speak of it made it happen, a wet, phlegmatic cough that left his skinny frame shivering and weak. She reached for the horn spoon, dripped a decoction of comfrey leaves down his throat, and, catching the excess drool with the spoon, tipped it back in.

Outside, the rain ran in silent rivulets down a black-paned window. Inside, the old man coughed.

By all the saints, how could she endure it! Both. Or either. Her ears hurt with the sound of his hacking, and she ached in her bones from the dampness seeping through the bare stone walls.

She shared the small apartment with Brother Francis, if sharing it could be called. The old priest lived more in his head than in the real world. That much, at least, had not changed. Most of the time, he hardly acknowledged she was there. She was, like the candles and the chair on which he rested and the bed on which he slept, just another furnishing, old and worn with too much use. A woolen curtain separated their two rooms, which were attached to the end of the monks' dormitory but with a separate entrance. Her room served as a small larder/cupboard from which she prepared the meals he ate. At one time he had taken his meals in the refectory with the monks. Now he seldom ventured away from the tiny brazier over which he huddled. Some times the monks, and other visitors, for he was well respected, came to him. At such times, she was pressed to serve them too.

He had not always been thus. Time was when he'd been a strong barrel of a man. Heavy bearded, muscular in mind and body. Now, sometimes, he looked at her as though he hardly knew her, studying her face with half-blind eyes, cocking his head so as to see her from the outside rim of his failing eyesight.

"You are Mistress Clare," he said, as though she had just dropped in to visit him, as though she had not served him every day and every night for nigh onto twelve years.

"No, Brother Francis. I am lady-in-waiting to Her Majesty the Queen of England." And then, instantly repentant, trying to soften the harsh edge of her voice, patting his shoulder, "Of course I'm Mistress Clare, Father, and that's the hard luck of it for both of us, I reckon."

She removed the bowl of soup, the untouched beer, and opening the door, flung the contents out into the rain, narrowly missing the rider who was preparing to dismount. His face was hidden by his cleric's cowl, pulled low, but she would recognize his comely form anywhere.

"Ye'd best wait until the morning. I was just about to put Brother to bed. Like as not, he'd not even know ye, tonight."

The rider nodded and turned toward the guesthouse.

Mistress Clare stood in the doorway, heedless of the driving rain as it blew under the lintel, wetting her skirt and her stained apron. She clenched the empty beaker and the bowl so tightly that her big bare knuckles turned from red to white. The utensils would surely have shattered had they been made of finer stuff.

Only when she heard the old priest call her did she close the door, shutting out the rain and the wind, and enter the cluttered emptiness of the old priest's quarters. For a long time she lay on her cot in the dark watching the rain crawl down the dark window like widows' tears. Just before the cock crowed dawn, she entered into a murky half-sleep.

⊰⊱

Brother Gabriel woke to the peal of predawn bells tolling vigils. *Opus Dei.* God's work. He listened for the shuffling of feet down the dormitory stairs, and when the sound had been replaced with the first faint notes of plainsong, he stirred from his own bed, thinking to join his brothers in the choir. He was slipping through the cloister, since it was closest to his guest cell, when he heard a faint rustling. At first he thought it some small nocturnal creature on its perpetual quest for sustenance, but the rustling grew to a shuffle and was accompanied by a faint sniffling. Nocturnal creatures did not sniffle.

There it was again. Unmistakable this time.

At the intersection of bench and wall, Gabriel thought he saw a patch of darkness, a mere thickening in the weave of night. It shivered and drew in toward the wall. With head bowed and folded arms, the posture of the contemplative monk on his way to prayers, Gabriel proceeded through the night corridor. The sniffling stopped as he neared the corner of the bench.

Gabriel slowed.

He could almost feel the creature lurking there, holding its breath. Probably one of the *infantes*, the oblates, shirking the praying of the hours. But why would the child huddle here in the cold and the damp? Unless he was a runaway. This would make some lord who'd paid the Church handsomely for his child's education and subsequent vocation very unhappy, but Gabriel had a moment's sympathy for the boy's need for freedom. He had felt the same need often as a child. Only he'd had no place to run.

When Gabriel's foot was adjacent to the bench, he thrust his leg out, pinning whoever it was against the wall. Bending down, he pulled the quivering boy to his feet and across the quadrangle to a flickering lantern hanging outside the chapter house. The shadows danced. The cloister promenade at night was a frightening place to a boy. Gabriel remembered it well. Perhaps it was that memory that caused the gruffness in his voice as he addressed the child.

"Let's get a look at you," he said, holding the squirming boy under the light. He was only about six, around the age Gabriel had been when Father Francis had first brought him to live with the brothers.

"Are you going to beat me?" The voice was small yet brave, almost defiant, demanding to know the worst. Defiance was not a good trait in a boy in a monastery. Gabriel remembered that as well.

"Should I beat you? Does somebody beat you?"

"Brother Bartholomew."

"And why does Brother Bartholomew beat you?"

"Because I don't go to choir."

"Why don't you go to choir? You're not a sleepyhead, are you?" Gabriel tousled the boy's mop of curls. The guttering lantern light fell across the child's face, highlighting the heavy eyelashes, pointing downward. The child's voice was no longer defiant when he answered.

"I'm afraid."

"Of what are you afraid?"

Gabriel suddenly remembered the large carved crucifix hanging overhead in the chapel, and how when the brothers sang the *kyrie* he'd been afraid the wooden Christ would be awakened from his agony and start to bleed, dropping great crimson drops on his head. He would sing softly, afraid to add his voice, and then afterward he would be ashamed because he had been afraid of the blood. The saving blood. He'd never told anybody that he was afraid. Surely it was a mortal sin to be afraid of the Savior's blood.

He'd learned not to look at the crucifix whenever he entered the choir.

"I'm afraid of the devils that are there," the small voice answered in a whisper.

"Devils? What devils?"

"The devils carved in the misericords."

Misericordia, from *miserere,* to be merciful. As a boy, before he'd learned his Latin, he'd thought the name for the carvings was from *miseria,* for misery. Perhaps the carver had thought so too, for there was little mercy depicted there. He remembered tracing the horned devils and the grotesque gargoyles carved in the hinges of the choir seats.

Gabriel held the boy out at arm's length, forcing him to look up so he could see his face. "You're not running away, are you?"

"No. I was just hiding from Brother Bartholomew. He won't think to look for me out here at night." A note of hope, even bravado, crept into his voice. "By morning he will have forgotten."

Gabriel made a mental note to speak to Brother Bartholomew.

"Well—what's your name?"

"Andrew."

Gabriel could hear the soft plainsong from the chapel. Vigils would be ending soon. "Well, Andrew, you come back to the refectory with me. We'll forage for a bit of bread and cheese, and I'll teach you how not to be afraid of a figure carved in wood. I'll show you how to carve one for yourself."

The child slipped his small hand in his. Gabriel felt his heart squeeze.

"What about the night shadows? I'm afraid of those too."

"The shadows, Andrew, we all have to live with. We all have to learn to deal with them in our own way. But you have a brave heart, and you can do it. That's how brave hearts are made stronger."

"Is that how you get to be a man?"

"Yes, I suppose it is, Andrew. I suppose it is."

THIRTEEN

nna hated being beholden to Bera and his sullen, pregnant wife. She had tried to give back the red skirt, but Lela refused it.

"It is *mahrime*," Jetta explained when they were alone in the wagon—the *vardo* the Gypsies called it—except for Little Bek, who was sleeping on his mat.

"But I washed it," Anna said, hearing the indignation in her own voice.

The old woman shrugged. "It has been worn by *gadje*. To Lela it is unclean. You might as well keep it. She will not wear it again. You should not be offended. It is the way of the Romani."

Anna bit back her reply as she looked around the dusty, cluttered confines of the wagon. She longed for the polished floors and neat, sunlit rooms of the little town house she'd left behind in Prague. She was like the little Jewish boy outside the walls of Judenstadt, standing alone and frightened in his silly peaked hat. How she had pitied him in his otherness. But even he had his

Jewish tribe. His Jewish family. What did she have? She was *gadje* in a Romani world.

Her eyelids pricked, but she would not cry. What was the point? Who was there to care about her tears? Not Jetta. She would just look at her new charge out of empty gray eyes and mumble to herself. And Little Bek would cry with her, *bek, bek, bek,* reminding her that others had worse crosses to bear.

The tinkling of the beads in the curtain at the end of the wagon, a shift of light, and then a soft thump: Jetta leaping from the moving wagon onto the carpet of pine needles. She would be on her way to another wagon filled with Romani women, women with whom she could gossip, maybe even about the red-haired *gadje* who added more burdens to their daily lives. As they scolded Jetta for pulling the strange woman from the river, they would laugh. Anna had heard their laughter, though they were always somber when she was around.

As the caravan snaked its way through heavy evergreen forests where it seemed they traveled in perpetual twilight, Anna blinked hard and, closing her eyes against the jarring of the wagon, tried to escape the boredom of her loneliness through napping. But her thoughts made sleep impossible. She wondered why she had come with them. But she knew why. The very night she'd been put out of her home, Bera had showed up at her door and offered escape. He'd said they were going west.

"To England?" she had asked, thinking perhaps here was some savior God had sent her—or even her grandfather from beyond the grave.

"Is England west of Prague?" he'd asked.

"It is a great distance, but it lies west," had been her reply. His gaze had traveled around the room and then he'd flashed his glistening smile.

"Then we go to England. And you are welcome to come. But bring with you the holy book."

She wondered now if she had made a mistake. But what choice did she have?

She wondered too when they would stop for camp, wondered why the women would not let her help with the laundry and the cooking, wondered why they insisted on bathing her, dressing her, preparing her food and serving it as though she were some princess even though these reluctant ministrations added to their endless chores.

But she'd given up asking why.

"It is the Romani way," Jetta would say, shrugging, "If you want to help, you can wash Little Bek. He is *gadje* too."

Little Bek stirred on his mat and opened his eyes, blinked at her as if he understood her sadness. He offered her his crooked, slobbering smile in consolation.

"Let's sing, Little Bek," she said.

And as she pitched the tune, he joined her with a wordless harmony. Their plaintive melody drifted from the wagon and melted into the heavy green canopy shutting out the sky.

❧

By Michaelmas, Anna and her Romani companions were camped in the shadow of Strasbourg Cathedral. The band had grown so that, by the time they crossed the Rhine River, they were five wagons and several single travelers on horseback, numbering a group of, more or less, forty pilgrims on any given day. But Anna noticed that when nightfall came, the group divided into two separate communities. The little clutch of painted wagons always found shelter in the nearest wood while the others, the "real" pilgrims—as Anna had come to think of them spread their bedrolls in a nearby clearing around a communal campfire. If they were close to an inn or a town, the pilgrims sought out the comfort of straw mattresses beneath real roofs. Anna, alone of the *gorgios,* the outsiders, was allowed to camp within the bosom of the community. Only Anna—and Little Bek.

For that inclusion Anna was grateful, though she sometimes wondered why. True, she paid for her passage with the little horde of shillings and nobles and florins hidden in her wooden chest, but she suspected that the "pilgrims," whose faces changed with each new town, also paid Bera for the right to travel under the Holy Roman Emperor's writ of safe conduct. This document Bera often bragged about. If they were challenged on the road or denied entry to a walled town, he would take the rolled-up document from his pocket, presenting it with a grand flourish. "See," he would say, sometimes in Czech or German, even mixing in a few English words that Anna had taught him. "Right of free passage." Then he would point to the seal of Emperor Sigismund as though he could read every word of it.

Anna never knew how he had obtained it, though it certainly looked official. And it always worked. Even the most reluctant mayor or alderman would relent, letting them enter the town or castle yard, even allowing them to set up their little booths close to the cathedrals and pilgrim shrines so they could sell crude tin copies of the "official" pilgrim badges sanctioned by the Church. Anna suspected Bera charged the pilgrims for such free and easy movement among territories, hence the way the Gypsies' numbers—and their fortunes—ebbed and flowed.

Today, they were set up at the Strasbourg Michaelmas Fair, and it showed every sign of being a good day. Late September sunshine poured down. The roads were clogged with pilgrims journeying to the several shrines scattered around Strasbourg.

Anna hoped it would be a good day. They needed a good day. Bera said the provender for the horses that pulled the wagons had just about dried up in the late summer drought. They had been forced to buy hay. Last week he had even come to her for a few extra shillings and outright asked, a thing that he had never done before. Before, he had always merely hinted that the company was in need of this or that. And she would contribute a few coins. Mistress Kremensky had been generous in her refund of the rent, and had paid Anna for the furnishings she abandoned, but by now Anna had only a few gold coins left and none of the silver. This little horde she was determined to hold on to. At least until she got to England.

Anna didn't think the Gypsies would put her out; at least, she hoped they were superstitious enough to think that they bore some responsibility for her because one of them had saved her life. Though there was certainly one among their number who was ready enough to send her packing. The bigger Lela's belly grew, the more hostile toward Anna she became, and the more uncomfortable Anna became with Bera's openly appreciative stare. Anna had heard them arguing last night, with Lela crying and saying she would go crazy cooped up in the wagon, unable to enjoy the fair, and him shouting back at her that she should keep herself hidden away until after the child came. It was the Romani way.

And now Anna had taken Lela's job behind the table at the fair, another item to add to the list of Anna's imagined injuries and insults that Lela kept in her head. Though Anna had to admit she was happy to have something to do at last. She liked arranging the little tin badges for sale, lining them up in neat rows, trying to place those that represented nearby shrines closest to the front, placing a tiny bouquet of wildflowers in the center of the display table to draw customers. Even the Romani women could not object to her labor here, since it didn't involve touching *their* food or *their* water, or even their dirty clothing.

Anna placed the medal with the picture of Madonna cradling the infant Jesus in front of the wildflowers. This badge was her favorite. The expression on the Madonna's face, even in this crude tin copy, evoked in Anna a longing that was so intense it was almost a physical hurt. She didn't know how to interpret the longing. Was it for the mother she never knew? Or was it for the child she would probably never have?

She looked up and saw Bera watching her, his expression thoughtful, calculating. She'd seen that look on his face before—whenever he was making, or about to make, one of the shrewd horse trades he often bragged about. She pitied his victim.

Then she realized there was nobody else around. That cunning look was for her.

She pretended not to see him, pretended to be absorbed in laying out her merchandise.

She'd been thinking about how she could earn her way, maybe make a better pilgrim's badge, something less obviously a copy, an embroidered cross that looked like the cross hanging from a silver chain inside her shirt, the one that Dědeček had given her, the one that had belonged to her mother. She could make the pearls encrusted on the cross arm with little French knots of silk thread. She had one blue silk bodice that she could cut up into little square pillows. She had seen some cream-colored silk thread at a nearby booth. A ha'penny's worth would do. Though the look on Bera's face as he approached told her, if she was not careful, she'd not have a ha'penny left.

She watched him from below lowered lids. The collar of his red silk shirt was frayed, and he had a split in the seam of his blouson sleeve. She knew he would wear it until it was in tatters—that was something else she'd noticed about the Romani way; they did not mend—and then discard it for another one just like it. She'd never seen him wear anything else.

He was close enough now that she could smell the strong scent of sandalwood, his trademark scent. His eyes narrowed. He appeared to be squinting against the sun. But she knew better. It was a look of concentration. At first he did not speak to her but leaned against her tent pole, picking his teeth with a piece of straw in a pose of studied casualness.

She pretended busyness with the icons. Finally he spoke.

"The horses need hay," he said.

"I know." She felt herself flush but was determined that she too should be direct. "Unfortunately I have no money left. I cannot help this time."

She took a deep breath to hide the lie, flicked an imaginary speck of dust from one of the tin badges. Now he would tell her she had to leave if she could no longer pay. What would she do? Where would she go? But that was why she could not spend her gold coins down to the last farthing. She had to keep a reserve, so she would not be totally destitute should he decide to turn her out.

"A shame," he said. But he appeared to be waiting.

"I have a plan to earn some, though," she said. "A pilgrim badge, not metal but made of fabric. An embroidered cross. I—"

"I have a plan too. I know how we can get enough hay to get us to France."

We. He had said *we.* Not a good sign. "But don't you want to hear—"

"Do you still have the English book?"

So. That was his plan. He knew she had brought "the book" with her. Knew it was in her traveler's chest, had helped her load it the day she escaped from Prague. But he had never mentioned it.

Until now.

He could steal it from her, but somehow she did not think he would. He would have already done it. Though she knew the Roma pilfered small things: mostly food, pies left in an unwatched window to cool, melons growing in the field. Anna had watched Bera steal a chicken once right out of a cottage yard. He'd attached a string to a bit of grain, then flung the grain into the yard as he sauntered by. When the chicken swallowed the grain, Bera drew the chicken by his gullet into a nearby wood. Anna figured she'd eaten hearty chicken stew, thus procured, on more than one occasion. And she'd been grateful for it.

The men of the company considered such paltry crimes payment for their cunning. Indeed they bragged about them, as though whatever the earth produced should be equitably dispersed, and they were just righting a wrong. They were proud of their shrewdness too. Bera might sell the same old horse over and over, putting tar in the worn-down hollows of a tired old nag's teeth so they looked like the black centers of a young horse's teeth. When the trick was discovered, another of their company would commiserate—"Tsk, tsk. Don't the world hold too many scoundrels?"—and offer to buy the old horse back for a cheaper price. "Just to take it off'n your hands."

This was just part and parcel of the horse trader's skill as far as they were concerned. But she had never known them to outright steal money or valuable goods, and certainly not from one to whom they were offering hospitality.

"The English book," Bera said, scarcely hiding the impatience in his tone. "The Bible that you showed me in Prague. Do you have it?"

"Yes," she answered because she knew it would avail her nothing to lie about it. Indeed, in his skewed moral world, he might consider her denial as giving him some kind of just grounds to steal it. "I have it. But as I told you once before, I will not sell it." She said this as firmly as she could, so there could be no mistaking her resolve. "Not while I have a breath in my body."

He laughed. "Easy, little mare."

She'd heard him say that exact same thing to Lela when she berated him for his inattentiveness. Anna despised it and was about to open her mouth to tell him that, king or not, he could not talk to her that way. She would not be compared to a horse.

"I'm not asking you to sell it," he said. "We only have to take it out and open it. That man over there, the yeoman waiting beside our smithy's booth"—the Gypsies had set up a booth to shoe horses, another of the many ways in which they earned a few pennies as they passed through towns—"he has promised us a load of hay just to spend some time with the book."

"But surely he speaks German or French. He could not read it."

Bera picked a ragged cuticle, frowning. "It does not matter. He probably can't read in any tongue. He will pay just to see it. He has heard about it, says he wants to see it. Wants to touch it."

Some stranger touching the pages her grandfather had copied, laboring for years in snatched moments by candlelight, moments left over from the long hours of decorating manuscripts. She could still see him, rubbing his gnarled fingers to relieve the cramps and then going back to the page, time and time again.

"All the Scripture we have copied over the years, Anna. This one is for us. This one we will not sell. This one we will not give away."

"No. The book is not some cheap tin badge or saint's fake finger bone. There's no Roman magic in it. Touching it will not heal the body or give a sinner a pass out of purgatory."

Bera shrugged. "As you wish. But without hay, we will not be able to leave Strasbourg. You said you wanted to go to England. If we have to sell the horses, we will have to stay here."

"I cannot let the book out of my sight," she said.

"The yeoman understands. You may sit with him while he looks at it. You may even read it to him. I know you like to read the book. I have seen you with it."

He had been watching her when she did not know he was there! What else had he seen? She would need to be more careful of her privacy in the future.

"Besides, you should not be so free to mock others who treat the book as though it were magic, when you yourself treat it as though it is some great holy thing." He waved his hands about in exasperation. "It is only made of paper and ink."

He was right, of course. Dědeček would certainly have agreed with him there. The book was not holy in itself. It was the meaning, the words that were important, the truth of the words, not the paper upon which they were scratched. And yet that paper, that ink, was sacred to her because it was her grandfather's legacy to her.

But his last words to her had been "go to England." She could not stay with these Gypsies forever. She looked nervously at the yeoman, who was watching their conversation intently. He looked harmless enough, a man of medium build; his clothes were clean and respectable, and his hair and beard had had some acquaintance with a comb, albeit a passing acquaintance.

"No more than two hours," she said. "And he must come to Jetta's wagon and Jetta must be present."

Bera flashed his smile at her, approving, arrogant in the success of his persuasion. He was a cunning, conniving scamp, and she knew it. And he knew she knew it.

"He will be pleased. I had only promised him one hour," Bera said, motioning for the yeoman to come forward, which he did with such haste that he rushed too close to the smithy's hammer and a spark from the anvil caught in his hair. He had to beat it out with his hands in a fool's gesture that made Bera laugh out loud.

"Tonight our horses will have hay," he said. "Tomorrow, we will leave for Rheims."

"But what about the booth?"

"I will watch the booth, Anna from Prague," he said as his hands busily rearranged the badges in a helter-skelter fashion. Apparently he had no liking for her well-ordered merchandising technique. "You have more important things to do. After you have finished reading from your magic book, you must scour the market for the materials for your special pilgrim badge."

She had not even known he was listening.

FOURTEEN

*If priesthood were perfect, all the people would be
    converted
Who are contrary to Christ's law and who hold Chris-
    tendom in dishonour.*
    —WILLIAM LANGLAND IN
        PIERS PLOWMAN'S PROTEST (14TH CENTURY)

It was well past prime by the time Brother Gabriel had finished with his own private devotions, donned his hair shirt, and sought out Brother Bartholomew. He'd confronted the stern-faced disciplinarian with the truth of Christ's gentleness for children and reminded him of the fragile nature of a small boy. This had at least gained the boy a reprieve from one beating. By the time he'd finished, the rain had ceased and a weak sun was threatening to tear away the gauzy film of morning fog. The same austere woman who had turned him away the night before answered his knock, unsmiling, nodding only a curt welcome.

"He is eating, but he is expecting ye," she said. "I will be in the herbarium when ye've finished. I left some bread and goat cheese for ye as well."

"Thank you, Mistress Clare. That was kind."

Her visage seemed to soften, but it was so fleeting that he must have imagined it.

"He tires easily," she said, pausing as though she wanted to say more. She looked at him so intently that it made him uncomfortable. Then she lifted the latch and walked out.

"I never know how to fathom that woman," he said, kneeling beside the elderly friar, taking his hand, kissing it. "She has the countenance and tone of a harpy, and I think she bears a special antipathy for me."

"She is a bitter woman, but she serves me well. God will reward her for her service. Life rewards her for her bitterness."

"I would like to hear her story sometime, Brother."

"It does not concern you, Brother. Move around to my side so I can better see you. With these old eyes I can't see what's in front of me."

Brother Gabriel pulled his stool up to the old man's knee so as to face him at an angle. The old man tilted his head.

"Now tell me about how you do Christ's work," he said, his voice as thin and raspy as his skin.

They talked as clerics do of church matters, church polity, church politics. Finally, Brother Gabriel told Brother Francis about his latest venture for the archbishop.

"So the archbishop has singled you out for special work. I knew you would go far."

"It's not an assignment I relish. I find myself becoming fond of Lord and Lady Cobham. I do not wish them ill."

"Then fight to save their souls. What harm can you do by restoring them to the bosom of the Church?"

"Yes," Brother Gabriel mused. "What harm?" That was a question he'd asked himself over and over, and he did not like the answer. But he did not want to have such a debate with his mentor. He could not argue against centuries of established doctrine. He was sure to lose. And worse, he would prove a disappointment to an old man who deserved better.

The morning sun had finally broken through and laid a strip of light beneath the door, which Mistress Clare had left ajar. It came through the unshuttered windows too, lighting the gray stubble on the old man's face. When had he become so old? Gabriel wondered. Where was I when his cheek began to wither and his eyesight began to fade? A deep sadness settled over him.

"Father, will you hear my confession?" Like Brother Gabriel, Brother Francis was an ordained priest as well as a friar.

"Of course, my son." But the old man was seized with a paroxysm of coughing.

Brother Gabriel looked on anxiously. "Shall I call Mistress Clare?"

The old priest shook his head. "It will pass," he said, motioning for his amice.

Brother Gabriel handed the soft linen vestment with its silk fringe to the old priest, who fumbled for the embroidered cross, bringing it to his lips reverently, before placing the garment around his neck.

Gabriel began. "Forgive me, Father, for I have sinned. I have committed lust in my heart."

And then Gabriel told his confessor about the carnal images that haunted his dreams and the lascivious thoughts that plagued his days. He confessed too of the loneliness he felt and the fresh new doubts concerning his clerical duties.

Brother Francis listened in silence. When Brother Gabriel had spit it all out, he pronounced his penance, light enough under the circumstances, much lighter than he himself would have given. Perhaps the old priest had not understood.

"Is that sufficient? For such sinful thoughts as these?"

There was a long silence. Had he nodded off? Had he not heard?

Then slowly, with shaking hands, Father Francis took Gabriel's two hands in his own brown-spotted ones. "We talked about this before, in your youth, remember? When you strayed from the Rule?"

Brother Gabriel remembered it well. And felt great shame both at the memory and the stirring in his loins the memory prompted. He'd been heartbroken when the girl, for whom he thought to sacrifice his vocation, ran off with another. The bitterness of that heartbreak had made it easier to accept the Rule of celibacy. Easier to be alone. Until now.

"You prayed for strength and you received it. Did you not?"

"Yes, but the temptation has returned, and, like the demon returning to the possessed man in the Scriptures, has brought his fellows with him. I cannot fulfill my vow of celibacy. Not and stay sane."

"Have you used all the methods I taught you, distracted yourself with studying Holy Scriptures? Have you fasted? Prayed? Have you tried mortification of the flesh?"

"Yes, yes, I have done it all. I can recite the Psalms and the Acts of the

Apostles verbatim. The flesh beneath my cassock is raw from my camel's hair shirt. I fear I may have misunderstood my calling. Else why . . . ?" Brother Gabriel raised his hands to his face and rubbed it as if to scrub off the skin of the flesh that tormented him so. "Perhaps I should renounce my vows, leave the Church."

"Nobody ever told you it would be easy." The old priest removed his amice, kissed the cross stitched on it, folded it carefully, and handed it to Gabriel. "I would give you this advice," he said. "A greater sin is to let this come between you and the work of the Church. It has already driven you from your duties. If you go back without some relief, I fear the object of your current fixation will interfere with the fulfillment of your calling."

"Relief? How can I obtain relief and stay faithful to my vows?" Then, thinking what Brother Francis might be hinting at, he said, "I've tried that too."

The old priest coughed, cleared his throat, and spit into the bowl Mistress Clare had left by his chair. He tilted his head back at an angle so that he could see his young charge from the periphery of his vision. Gabriel remembered the former directness of his gaze and was saddened.

"I have known some good men, good priests, who in your place gained release through discreet intercourse . . . with an . . . appropriate woman."

Had he heard right? Was his confessor, his mentor, advising fornication? Was the old priest losing his moral vision with his sight?

"Are you saying I should break my vows of celibacy?"

The old man wheezed. It sounded like the sighing of a bellows. "It would be the lesser sin. After all, Saint Paul did say 'it is better to marry than to burn.' You cannot, of course, marry and retain your position. Though Saint Peter himself was married. And in earlier times the Church allowed us to marry." The old man's voice was so hoarse this last remark was almost a growl. "Surely you know you would not be the first. None of us is perfect. We are all flawed. A priest, even a good priest, can avail himself of some female company. As long as he is discreet." The words came out intermittently with little rasps and coughs.

Brother Gabriel could hardly believe his ears. He wanted to ask, "Is that what you did?" But he could not bring himself to ask this of the man who had been both Brother, Father, and father to him. The man he'd thought a saint.

"There are two problems with such a solution, however," Brother Francis said. "One would not want to despoil a virgin, of course. Yet some of the women of the brothels carry disease. A woman of the common sort but with some limited experience—perhaps a widow."

It wasn't that Brother Gabriel was not aware that this went on among some in the Church. This and more. He'd heard the rumors among the boys as he was coming into puberty in the monastery, the jokes about unnatural relations among some of the monks. He'd heard of alliances with promiscuous nuns as well. But for the man whom he most admired to counsel fornication was almost sufficient to drive the lascivious thoughts away.

"Of course, she would need to have no sign of the pox, and she should be . . . compensated. Else she might sow scandal. We have too much scandal as it is."

"But—"

"*Opus Dei* is more important than your personal weakness. If you cannot destroy your lust, then you must control it through careful indulgence. Else the devil will use it to drive you from His work. The archbishop is right. All heresy must be stamped out. Nothing should interfere with your work. You are marked by God for greatness, maybe even a cardinal's hat." He paused and drew a ragged breath. "I am an old man and I must rest now. We will talk again later."

"Of course," Gabriel said. For what else was there to talk about? Unless it was Gabriel's desire for more than carnal release. But how to give voice to that longing for more than physical intimacy? Dare he say that he wanted a woman to look at him the way Lady Cobham looked at Lord Cobham, to have her eyes light up the way hers did when Sir John entered the room? Dare he ask, if marriage is a sacrament then why are we denied it? How could Father Francis, who had lived all his life alone, understand such a need?

"Call Mistress Clare," the old priest said. "The mornings are growing chilly. She's probably freezing outside. That will not improve her temper."

Gabriel heard a rustling outside the door and suspected that Mistress Clare was not that far away. But when he opened the door, she was sitting on the turf bench of the herb garden, so still and erect she might have been a stone statue.

"Brother Francis calls for you, Mistress Clare." He could see his breath.

She stood up. She was a tall woman, almost as tall as he. The sunlight picked out the gray of her hair, where the hood of her mantle only half covered it.

"The first frost will come soon," she said, looking at him directly. "Brother Francis will likely not make it through another winter."

He was taken aback by the flatness in her voice. "That's a hard thing to hear," he said.

"I'm telling you only what is true. He is old and frail and weak." She moved past him, the hem of her cloak brushing across his feet. "I am warning you because I know of your special bond. I want you to know that I will send for you when it is over, so that you may see to his burial. Leave the place where you can be reached with the prior."

She hesitated as though about to say something else, then turned and walked away. When she had shut the door, he sat down on the turf bench that she had vacated. The dew was still on the grass, but the spot where she sat was dry and warm from her body. He sat there for a long time pondering the advice that Brother Francis had given him. It was hard to know which gave him more unease: his father confessor's advice or Mistress Clare's warning.

He tried to imagine his world without the old priest in it, the man who had been his spiritual touchstone in a world that made no sense to him. *What would Brother Francis do?* That had always been the question he asked whenever he was confronted with a problem.

It had been a long time since he'd felt such uncertainty. He closed his eyes and the sunlit garden disappeared. He was once again a small boy shut in the closet in a house on Bankside Street, his hands over his ears, trying to shut out the sounds on the other side of the door. His heart hammering in his chest, he opened his eyes to still the panic.

"A cardinal's hat," Brother Francis had said. That was what his mentor wanted for him. Was that what he wanted for himself? A bishop's miter or even a cardinal's hat? He tried to envision it, but all he could see was Arundel. Himself as Arundel. The image did not appeal. And yet, he reminded himself, the head that wore a bishop's miter or cardinal's hat would be so far removed from Bankside Street that he would never have to think of it again. The head that wore a bishop's miter would have no time for lustful thoughts.

But what thoughts would fill a bishop's miter to crowd the unworthy thoughts out? Holy thoughts? Again his mind conjured Arundel's worn and hollowed visage beneath his glittering white miter, and he knew what he was thinking. He was thinking how to trap and burn a man whose only crime was spreading the Gospel.

A Gospel of heresy, Gabriel, a Gospel of heresy, he reminded himself. *And if your calling is to rout out heretics in the service of your Church, then you'd best be about it.*

But he lingered just a little longer. The sun felt good on his tonsured head. He reached up to feel the bald cap of skin, the mark of Saint Peter that showed he was a slave to Christ. He'd been so proud the day the bishop had shaved his head, so proud to look like Brother Francis. It had been the first part of his ordination ritual; he was hardly more than a child, an altar boy, given to the brothers to serve God through serving them. And after the ceremony, after the final prayer, Gabriel had walked beside Brother Francis, thinking now they were alike, now they were brothers.

He rubbed his hand over the stubble on his head. He shaved it once a month, and not as widely as some of his brothers—he thought that prideful and ostentatious, though he was always careful to preserve the heavy rim above his ears, his "crown of thorns." But he'd neglected that too in his distraction. Soon that crown of thorns would disappear, if he did not shave it.

As Gabriel got up from the turf bench, he pulled the hood up on his cope to hide his growing hair and tried to remember if he had packed his razor. He was still a slave of Christ. Or a slave of the Church. And that was the same thing. That's what Brother Francis had always taught him. And like it or not, it was time to be about his business.

FIFTEEN

For childbirth red hair is sewed in a small bag and carried on the belly next to the skin during pregnancy . . .
—A GYPSY GOOD-LUCK CHARM

or the last two weeks, the little train of Gypsy *vardos* had made good time. At last they were out of the deep forests. Just outside Strasbourg they had joined with another Romani band, swelling their numbers to eight wagons. They had left some pilgrims behind in Strasbourg but picked up others who wished to travel through France under the Holy Roman Emperor's safe conduct pass. On any given day they numbered about thirty souls.

"We will make France before All Saints' Day," Bera boasted each night, "if the weather holds."

And the weather held. Warm, sunlit autumn days and crisp, clear, starlit nights made the Romani life more pleasant for Anna. But at night, when they gathered around the campfires for their dancing and singing, Anna mourned her loss of connectedness in a world that no longer made sense. The women left her to her own company. Even the children, whenever she made overtures to them, just stared at her with their big black eyes and ran away to hide behind their mothers' skirts. Once or twice, after Bera had danced as light-footed as though he were dancing on eggs and was pleased with the shower of coins from the delighted pilgrims who traveled with them, the dark-skinned king squatted beside her for a moment or two, offering a flashing smile and a wink.

On this night; they'd all come together around a great bonfire—even the traveling pilgrims who usually kept to their own campfires. The flames leaped as high and fierce as Bera's flashing pirouettes. This night, when he squatted beside Anna, he tried to pull her into the circle of dance, but she, ever mindful of Lela's watchful gaze, stepped back into the shadows. Though tonight she had not seen Lela sitting in her usual place at the end of her *vardo,* door open and curtain drawn back to watch the campfire rituals from her sheltered distance, because pregnant women were not allowed in the company of men.

An overhanging branch stirred in a light breeze. Above the hiss and pop of the fire, Anna heard the dry crunch of pine needles and dead leaves underfoot. She looked up to see Bera. He had followed her away from the fire. She glanced apprehensively at Lela's *vardo.* Lela still did not appear in the doorway. Though Anna and Bera weren't strictly alone, they might as well be. The forest shadows separated them from the firelight circle.

"Anna of Prague, you must come with me," he said. "It is time." He wasn't smiling, and there was urgency in his voice.

"Time for what?" she asked, her heart beating faster. He'd never sought her out except to ask for money. She steeled herself against his request.

"It is time for my son to be born. Lela is calling for you."

"Lela! Calling for me?"

He reached for her hand.

"But I—"

From the other side of the trees, Jetta emerged. "Hurry. Lela is birthing. We need you."

But there had to be some mistake, Anna thought. Why would they want her help now—these women who wouldn't even let her touch their food! She knew so little of women's things. She'd been raised in the company of men.

Ignoring her protests as though they were of no more importance than the smoke that blew from the bonfire, Bera and Jetta drew her toward the wagon.

As she approached Bera's wagon, the most colorful *vardo* of them all, painted bright green, the gold leaf on its carved doors visible even in the fire-light, a woman's scream reverberated from inside. Bera immediately let go of Anna's hand and beat a hasty retreat back to the warmth and comradery of the fire.

"Come," Jetta insisted, pulling on Anna. Some part of Anna, uncon-scious as she had been when Jetta pulled her from the river, remembered that tug. Jetta was always saving things. And now she was expecting Anna to help.

But Jetta stepped aside.

"You're not going in with me?" Anna asked.

"There is not enough room in the wagon."

Wherever had they gotten the notion she knew anything of childbirth!

"But I'm no midwife. I've never even seen—"

"Rawnie bal," Jetta said, reaching up to remove the kerchief from Anna's hair. "Just touch her belly with your hair." The old woman showed a gap-toothed grin. Anna had hardly ever seen her smile. "Just give her your luck."

"My luck?"

Who would want my luck? Anna thought. But she was too flustered to linger long on that irony. Another ear-splitting scream hurtled from the car-avan, like the high-pitched wail of a banshee. This bloodcurdling sound was followed by a stream of curses in Romani with a couple of Bohemian words thrown in for seasoning.

"Lela hates me," Anna hissed. "She will not let me near her. Or her babe."

"She will not hate you if she bears a healthy child. Go, Anna of Prague," and she gave Anna a little push toward the back door. "The midwife is al-ready there. You will have to do nothing but watch and learn."

Another scream and Anna, half pushed by Jetta, hoisted herself up the wooden steps and into the wagon.

Lela lay on a mat on the floor—no birthing chair like the ones Anna had seen in some of the practical texts she copied for the women of Prague, texts with rudimentary illustrations she'd executed in the margins. When she was passing into womanhood, Dědeček had first given her such a text to work on, saying the illustrations were simple enough that she could do them. Just draw what the text describes, he'd said. And even as a green girl, she'd known why he gave them to her to illustrate. He had guessed how avidly she would pore over them, filling in all the information that no mother or sister would pass on to her, information that he could not bring himself to discuss with the grandchild who was on the threshold of becoming a woman. As Gilbert the Englishman's *The Sickness of Women* had passed through her hands, Anna had copied out large portions of it in English to keep for herself. She had consulted it often over a span of years. How she wished she had it now.

Observing Lela's obvious discomfort and the crescendo of her labor pains, her spread-eagled legs bent at the knee like two towers guarding the entrance to her great mountain of a belly and the midwife crouched between, Anna remembered her crude drawing and realized she'd got it right in the main part. The midwife, an ancient crone Anna recognized from the last wagon, rose up from between Lela's legs and jerked her head sideways, with a jingle of the bangles in her ears, motioning for Anna to kneel beside Lela's great belly.

"Like this," the midwife said, throwing her head forward, as though what she was asking Anna to do were so ordinary.

"Like this?" Anna asked, feeling her unbound hair cascade over her head, making a bright auburn curtain in front of her eyes.

"No. Closer. On the belly." As she said this, she pushed Anna's head down until her cheek rested on Lela's belly, covering it with her hair.

Lela's skin was smooth and warm, pulsing with life. Anna could feel the pulsing, and then she realized that what she was feeling against her cheek was the pulsing of not one life but two. The mound beneath her cheek quivered. Lela started to groan and whimper, grabbing double handfuls of Anna's hair. She screamed. She pulled on Anna's hair. Hard. But Anna, suddenly realizing that she was so close to this miracle that was about to happen, hardly felt the pain, indeed welcomed it. It was as though she too, in some strange way that made no sense, were a part of the birthing miracle.

"The babe is crowning," the old midwife said. "One more push. One more big push."

Lela hurled a curse at the midwife in Romani that even Anna could understand, some universal female language that had originated with the birth of Cain. Anna stiffened herself for the hard pull on her hair she knew was coming. Lela grasped a fistful of Anna's hair in one hand. In the other she grabbed the necklace that had fallen out from the inside of Anna's shirt. As Lela pushed in response to the next great wave of pain, Anna felt the silver chain of the necklace break and fall from her neck. Then Lela gave one last shrill cry, rising high and lusty before falling away into a descending wail. Seconds later it was answered by a thin, small cry.

"He's here. Jetta. He's here," the old midwife called, loud enough for the woman waiting outside to hear. "Call Bera. Tell him he has a son. A healthy son." Lela let go of Anna's hair. Anna lifted her head and smoothed her hair back.

Lela's face was covered with sweat and there was blood everywhere. Anna had not known there would be so much blood, but the midwife seemed not to think it unusual. Jetta had crowded in with hot water and rags and was busy cleaning first the babe and then Lela. The babe was crying in earnest now. The old midwife laughed at him, delighting in the healthy sound, and placed him on his mother with the cord still attached.

Anna watched in wonder as Lela's whole demeanor was transformed. She seemed to have forgotten the pain completely. She stroked the babe's wet head, struggling to lift her own. "Cover him. He might get cold," she said. "Is he all right? You're sure he's all right?"

Here was another miracle. Fiery Lela with her stormy ways, her strong spirit totally conquered by this infant that had just moments ago caused her so much pain.

After being reassured by Jetta and the midwife that the boy was as pretty a babe as they'd ever seen, not once but twice, the new mother closed her eyes and sighed. She would probably sleep now, Anna thought. She should leave. But she was reluctant to leave the little circle of women where, for the briefest moment, she had belonged. She stirred slightly in preparation for getting up from her place on the floor, where she still sat so close she could see the rise and fall of Lela's chest. The baby lay as still as a doll except for the little sucking motions of his tiny mouth against his balled fist. Anna would have liked to touch him. But she did not dare. She was *gadje*.

She was on her knees, trying to get up as quietly as possible, when Lela reached out and took her arm. "Anna of Prague, I am grateful."

Anna was taken aback. Here was a miracle indeed.

"I did nothing," Anna said, tossing back her mass of tangled hair.

Lela laughed. "I was afraid you wouldn't have any left," she said. "But you have plenty. I am sorry I broke your necklace. Here, give it to Bera. He will fix it for you. He can fix anything."

Anna reached out and took the necklace, slipped it silently into her pocket. She would not risk it with Bera.

"Today, you have brought good fortune to the *vardo* of Bera, King of Gypsies," Lela said, as though she were a queen conferring some great honor on Anna.

Anna didn't know what to say, just murmured that she was glad enough to do it. It did not seem to be the moment to lecture Lela about silly superstition. She turned to go.

"You want to hold him?" Lela asked.

Had she heard right? No. Lela would not let a *gadje*, especially this *gadje*, touch her new prize, not Lela who wouldn't even wear a favorite dress that had once been worn by a *gorgio*.

"Go on. Take him. He won't bite. He has no teeth."

Anna wanted to hold him, more than anything she wanted to hold him, but she had never held an infant before, was not sure she would know how.

Lela was propped up on colorful pillows, her dark, wet hair spread out on the bright fabric. The midwife had cut the cord, but still attended to Lela in her woman's parts. Lela ignored her but nodded to Jetta, who placed the little boy in Anna's arms.

Anna held her arms out as though she were accepting a stack of wood. The babe started to whimper.

"Like this." Jetta made a slanted cradle with her arms, rocking her upper body back and forth.

Anna tried to follow her example, bringing the child's face close to her breast. He rooted around against her blouse, then found his fist and resumed sucking.

"He's a greedy one," the midwife said as she placed a bracelet of red beads on the child's arm.

Some sort of good-luck charm, Anna supposed. She had noticed that all the Romani children—at least all the babes in arms—wore similar amulets. Anna rocked the baby gently back and forth, dreading the time she would have to give him back. She watched his working mouth. How did he come into the world knowing how to suck? Who taught him that? Who taught him how to snuggle so in the crook of a woman's arm, making her heart ache with longing? Here was something no book had ever explained to her, she thought, and then she remembered a bit of verse from the Hebrew prophet Jeremiah: "Before I formed thee in the belly I knew thee; and before thou camest forth out of the womb." She could still see the brilliant aquamarine color of the capital of her grandfather's illumination on the letter *B*.

Lela reached out and taking a strand of Anna's hair, which fell almost to her waist, gently brushed it across the baby's body, even his face. As it touched his cheek, he stopped sucking on his fist and smiled as though he were dreaming—or remembering—some vision of paradise.

Anna thought her heart would break with the beauty of it.

"Leave us now," Lela said as imperiously as any queen. "Take the infant and show him to his father."

Anna reluctantly handed him over, then stood up in the slightly bent posture to which she'd become accustomed.

"No, Anna of Prague, you stay. I wish to talk to you."

Surprised, Anna sat back down beside Lela. A clean cushion had been placed on the wooden floor. All the bloody linen had been taken away. And the afterbirth. Anna wondered if they had some ritual way of disposing of it, but she did not ask.

Lela lay back and closed her eyes; gray smudged circles had appeared beneath them. Was she sleeping? No wonder, Anna thought, after the ordeal she'd been through. But if the books—and that was the only rule of comparison Anna had—if the books could be believed, Lela had had an easy enough time for a first birth. "Twenty pangs or less," Gilbert of England had said. And Lela, judging from the screams, had suffered much less. Still, she had earned her rest.

"Are you comfortable, Lela? Can I get anything for you?"

"You have already given me enough."

Anna opened her mouth to try to explain to her that the business of red hair bringing good fortune was superstitious foolishness, that she should place her faith in God, but she did not.

"I have one more thing to ask of you, Anna of Prague. But first I must confess something to you."

The wagon was stuffy. Jetta and the midwife had closed the door behind them when they left, trapping the air still thick with the herbs the women had burned for the birth, unfamiliar, heady smells.

"Shall I open the door?" Anna asked.

"No. What is to be said between us should stay between us. Will you promise me that?"

It seemed a rash thing to promise an unknown, and yet Anna did not want to see Lela agitated in her weakened state. Besides, to whom would she tell whatever secret Lela was going to confide to her? She had no one with whom to swap gossip. She nodded her head.

Lela closed her eyes, took a deep breath. "I turned you over to the authorities in Prague. It was I who told them to search your house for the Bible. I see that you are a good woman, and I am sorry."

She said it so casually, as though she were asking to be excused for some trifling offense. The memory of the little town house crowded in, with all its loss and longing. The woman's words, the smells swirling in the room, the bits of smoke and dust floating in the sunlight all converged to choke Anna. She could not breathe.

Because of this woman, she had been forced to leave the home of her childhood. Because of this silly woman, she had abandoned her grandfather's bones, left him rotting in a churchyard in another country, a country to which she would likely never return. She tried to get up, but she was trembling.

"Don't you want to know why?"

"It doesn't matter why, you filthy little witch. I don't care why!" Anna screeched, alarmed at the high, angry sound coming out of her.

Get control, Anna. Calm yourself, she heard her grandfather say in the steady, quiet voice he had used whenever her temper erupted.

"All right then, suppose you tell me why."

"I hated the way my husband looked at you. I wanted to hurt you."

"I cannot help the way Bera looks at me!" But she remembered the flashing smiles, the winks, the way he leaned into her face when he talked to her, enough to bother any wife. "He only helped me out of the perilous situation you created. If it were not for you I would not even be here for him to look at in any way whatsoever. I'd still be back in Prague, safe in my own home."

Lela sighed wearily. "I know," she said, "but he wanted you from the beginning. I saw it in his eyes. And now the fact remains that you are here. But I have given him a son, and that will bind him to me. My husband will not be unfaithful. It is not the Romani way. But he will still look at you with wanting in his eyes, and I cannot bear it. So, Anna of Prague—" She scrunched her hand into a half-fist, unscrunched it, scrunched it again.

"So I am asking you for two things."

The quiet, sincere way in which she said this last calmed Anna's temper somewhat. It was clear the girl felt some remorse. They had shared something with the birth of the child. More than their skins had touched as Lela's child pushed his way into the world. It was as though their souls had fused long enough for each to see into the other's. And each had sensed a self in the other.

"Two things?" Anna said. Calmer, but still wary.

"First your forgiveness. It was a cowardly, evil thing for me to do. But you must forgive me. You are a Christian. That's what Christians do." She said it so assuredly, as though there could be no doubt of it.

As if forgiveness were a commodity to be gained or given easily.

"You said two things."

"I want you to leave the caravan when we get to the next place on the pilgrim journey. The pilgrims say there is a great cathedral there. There will be many people. Many men who will give a beautiful woman protection."

Leave the caravan! She had feared banishment would come when her silver coins ran out. When it had not, she had gained new hope. But it was not the money. It had never been the money. It had been her hair all along: the stupid, silly superstition that her red hair could give Lela a healthy delivery. And now that that fact had been accomplished, she was being cast aside like a ragged Roma garment. Maybe she could appeal to Bera. But now more than ever his wife would have a hold on him. Frantically, she tried to calculate the value of the gold left in her traveling chest.

Lela put out her hand and stroked Anna's head as though she were a child rather than the older of the two women. "Don't look so fearful, Anna of Prague. I will help you find a man. Somebody better than my Bera." She lowered her voice to a whisper as though she were about to vouchsafe some choice morsel of gossip to one of the other Gypsy women. "You know he is not really a king. There is no Romani king. He just calls himself that because he wants to be boss." Then she added proudly, "But he is a good boss."

Some of Anna's anger turned inward. *Fool, what did you expect? You should not have spent the shillings for the thread for sewing the badges. You knew that sooner or later these pilgrims who are not really pilgrims but vagabonds would abandon you when you were no longer of use to them. You should have trusted that instinct and been prepared.*

"Don't frown so, Anna of Prague. It will make crones' wrinkles in your brow. A woman who looks like you will have no trouble finding a husband of her own. And then you will have no need of mine." Again, the conspiratorial voice, "I know a love philter we can work. Now leave me to rest. We will talk again later. Now that we are friends. You can come back tomorrow and hold the baby again. You'll need the practice. Now go."

She dismissed Anna with the same regal ease with which she pronounced Anna's forgiveness. Dazed, Anna stumbled down the steps of the wagon toward the glowing bonfire. *"Christians must forgive. That is what they do."* Dědeček had once told her the very same thing. In almost the exact same words. Forgive maybe. But trust? That was an altogether different thing. Next time, Anna would trust only her instincts.

SIXTEEN

*Thirty foreigners from the country of Egypt who
arrived led by a count bearing letters from the
emperor . . . women wore low-cut chemises . . .
women and children had rings in their ears.*
—FROM THE 15TH-CENTURY PAPER OF AN
ALDERMAN IN BURGUNDY

nna was relieved when the midwife held up three stubby fingers, so close to Bera's face he could have bitten them, and said, "Three
weeks." She waved her fingers three times so he could not mistake her meaning. "Three weeks before the mother can ride. Your son tore her. She bled
like a stuck pig. She has to have time to heal." The accompanying frown
seemed to say she regarded all men as beasts. Those three weeks at least
bought Anna a little more time.

Bera left the camp grumbling but came back a few hours later, wreathed
in smiles. He'd struck a "brilliant" bargain. All of Bera's bargains were
"brilliant." It was an English word that he'd learned from Anna. And when
he said it, he rolled the double *l* and raised his shoulders, adding almost an
inch to his stature. He'd concluded this deal, he pronounced, with the lord of
a nearby manor. They could camp in his fields, would be given a daily ration
of hay for the horses, ewe's milk for the children, and fresh eggs in return for

shoeing the manor lord's horses and mending his metal pots.

"He also has a smokehouse and a root cellar. Full to bursting. He'll not miss a bit of bacon or a few wrinkled apples."

The real pilgrims, who traveled with them, went on ahead. The ease of Bera's safe conduct pass was no longer worth the delay, especially now that the rainy season was approaching and no official had demanded traveling papers of them since they'd crossed the Rhine. But one of the pilgrims, a wealthy burgher from Flanders, left behind something of great importance, bartering it to Anna in exchange for a look at the Wycliffe Bible. The small, much-thumbed, crumbling leather-bound book called the *Pilgrim's Guide* gave Anna a new idea.

Its Latin text outlined all the stops along the way from Paris to the ultimate pilgrim's destination of the shrine of Saint James in Santiago de Compostela, Spain. Anna had been fascinated by the book. She wondered about the "Gascons" who talked "much trivia," were "verbose" and "mocking," "short in stature"—they sounded a lot like the Roma. And even though her grandfather and her education in Wycliffe's theology had bequeathed her a healthy disdain for both relics and shrines, the "brightness of the celestial candles" and "angelic adoration" the guidebook promised intrigued her. But the little map sketched inside the *Pilgrim's Guide* showed the route lay far south and then west and Anna knew, even if the Gypsy *vardos* traveled that way, she would not go with them. Lela would see to it.

It was just as well. Anna had planned to leave the band somewhere in France, anyway, to find her way to England. But it would have been hard to leave the known for the greater uncertain wilderness that lay before her. The burgher from Flanders had told her there was a river, a body of water that separated England from France.

"Bigger than the Rhine?" Anna had asked, remembering with what difficulty they had forded that expanse. Had it not been for Bera's ingenuity they would have lost a horse and wagon.

"Oh, much bigger. More like a small sea. England is an island. You will have to take a boat."

So when Bera proudly announced that once they got to Rheims he was leading the Roma to Spain to visit the holy shrine at Santiago de Compostela, where they could see the sarcophagus containing the body of Saint James, Anna knew that Lela would get her wish sooner rather than later.

The little band would turn south, Bera said, pointing toward a crude map marked with *X*'s and circles that one of the pilgrims had drawn for him, toward Paris and Chartres.

And Anna?

Anna would head west toward England across a small sea. Her heart hammered in her chest, just thinking about trying to make such a journey alone. But it was what her grandfather had wanted. There she would find Lord Cobham. There she would find protection.

What was more, she finally had a plan. And thank heaven and all the saints, it did not include the sewing of pilgrim badges. She had given up on the intricate stitches of the cross, settling for an embroidered scallop shell for the pilgrim followers of Saint James. But she pricked her finger so that it bled all over the blue silk pillow. Apparently, the handling of a needle required a very different skill from the handling of a quill. Nor did Anna's new plan include Lela's elaborate schemes and spells for finding her a husband. Walking stark naked by the light of a full moon around a field, casting behind her at every step a handful of salt, would bring her someone other than the lover of her dreams, Anna was sure.

Her new plan—why had she not thought of it first?—involved doing the one thing she could do well: the making of books. There were paper and quills in her traveling chest. Even a small bottle of ink, and when she ran out she knew how to make more. So while Lela healed, and Bera played his dulcimer and schemed, and Jetta washed and cooked and tended the cook fires, and Little Bek sang in his high, plaintive voice, Anna copied the *Pilgrim's Guide* by candlelight and torchlight until her fingers were stiff with cold and fatigue.

But at night as she worried about her future and listened to the drumming of the rain upon the barrel-vaulted roof of the Romani wagon, more than once she dreamed about the town house in Staroměstké náměstí and wondered if she would ever again find a place that felt like home.

⁓⟫⟪⁓

Gabriel was rummaging in his valise for his razor and sharpening stone when one of the novices knocked on his cell door. Gabriel recognized Arundel's seal on the rolled-up parchment the boy handed him. He dismissed the messenger and opened it apprehensively. But perhaps this is good news after all, he thought, as he read Arundel's instructions. A long trip at the onset of winter would ordinarily have been most unwelcome. But surely the hand of God was here—divine intervention, providing him time for his spiritual sickness to heal before returning to Cooling Castle.

The archbishop's instructions were clear. Brother Gabriel was to leave Hastings immediately for France to investigate the possibility of French suppliers of the banned texts to Sir John Oldcastle, the good Lord Cobham. A great rebellion had erupted in Bohemia. Pope Gregory had excommunicated Jan Hus and threatened to put the whole city of Prague under interdiction. A cleric by the name of Jerome, who traveled between Prague University and Oxford University, had given evidence, under torture, that many of the texts brought to Prague were supplied by a member of the British Parliament. If the Church could find proof that he had purchased quantities of the transcribed heretical texts from the Paris Guild, or even from booksellers in Rheims or Cologne, then that would be proof enough to send a man of Oldcastle's power and influence to the stake.

Rome would be grateful for such an effort. Arundel had hinted that there might even be a cardinal's hat for someone who performed well—though Gabriel was sure he meant for himself. The archbishop had warned that it would not be easy. The wars with the French, not to mention the existence of the rival papal throne in Avignon, would not make the French disposed to aid the English in any such investigation. Arundel had said he would go himself, but he was afflicted with bad humors. He was sure that Brother Gabriel could ferret out the necessary information on his own and bring favor upon both himself and his archbishop.

Since he would need to travel in the guise of a rich merchant, he should not wear his friar's garb—he was being granted special dispensation to set it aside for this mission. He also had permission to cease the shaving of his tonsure until the mission was accomplished. The antipope's spies were everywhere, and if he should be arrested, the Holy See would have to pay his ransom. He was further authorized to use whatever monies he had collected from the sale of his most recent indulgences to pay his expenses, bearing in mind the needs of his Church in the shepherding of such funds.

Gabriel ran his hand over his no longer bald pate. It appeared he wasn't going to need his razor after all. The monthlong stubble would stand him in good stead.

On a fogbound autumn day, Brother Gabriel headed up the coast to Dover, where he embarked for Calais. Instead of his priestly garb, he wore a merchant's scarlet cloak and square cap to hide the shadow of his tonsure. On the day that he had donned his habit as a novice, Brother Francis had told him, "This holy garment will keep the devil and his temptation off your back." The cloth had been rough and so coarsely woven that Brother Gabriel thought any devil who sought to sit upon his shoulders would find it a mighty uncomfortable ride. But he had grown accustomed to it, and now the finely woven red merchant's cloak left him feeling almost naked.

Was it his imagination or did the other passengers on the boat that ferried him across the Channel treat him differently when he was dressed like this? One woman actually flirted with him! He felt himself flush remembering Brother Francis's advice, but he had resolved he would not take that path. He would stay true to his vows or he would not stay a friar. So he turned away in consternation and pretended to be gazing out on the gray vista of a veiled sea. She moved on. The Channel was smooth.

In Calais he hired a carriage to take him over the rutted, muddy roads to Rheims. He was deep within the French countryside, listening to the drumming of the rain on the roof, the pounding of hoofbeats, and the occasional sound of the coachman's horn, when he remembered. He had left his hair shirt behind in Battle Abbey. His back and shoulders would prove a comfortable perch for whatever devil might want to hitch a ride.

SEVENTEEN

In a place named Lorca, east of Puenta la Reina,
  flows a river called the Salty Brook; . . .
Beware of drinking . . . for this river causes
  death . . . On its banks two Navarrais
Sharpen their knives . . . to skin the mounts of the
  pilgrims who drink this water and die.
        —FROM *LIBRI SANCTI JACOBI*, BOOK V
        (12TH CENTURY)

abriel had been in Rheims a week and had learned enough to know the burghers of that city were too distracted by violent political struggles between the powerful dukes of Burgundy and Orléans to worry about the less immediate danger of hellfire. In the guildhalls, where his scarlet costume gained him admittance, there was talk of the king's levies but none of heresy.

He sat, chatting, with the resplendent cloth merchants on benches lining the walls of the hall. The mercers welcomed Gabriel so completely that he had to remind himself to keep his mouth shut, to be on his guard. To the question of his origin he mumbled, *"Je suis de la Flandre. Un négociant en tissu."* From Flanders. A cloth merchant. They merely nodded, handed him a cup of dark red wine, and went on complaining about the high taxes the mad king imposed for arms to fend off the English raids.

"Sacrés chiens Anglaises." Gabriel's understanding of the French language was good enough, close enough to the Norman French still spoken among the older nobility in England. Of his accent he was less confident, so he spoke carefully lest he be discovered as one of the "damned English dogs" against whom the merchants railed for ruining their economy. His merchant's disguise earned him more candor than his priest's cassock would have done. When he asked about the Church, one of the guildsmen rolled his eyes and complained about the corruption, the vice, even the Council of Pisa that was supposed to rid them of the extra pope and instead had imposed a second Italian. Since the first Italian refused to give up his See and the Avignon pope refused to abdicate his, now the schism had calved a third pope.

When Gabriel made a casual inquiry regarding the proliferation of Wycliffe or Hussite heresies, a tapestry weaver from Paris shrugged and told him if he was interested in religion he should go to Avignon. But he'd be more likely to find a fine-feathered nest of splendid plumed birds than black-robed rooks and poor priests.

"Are you overtaxed to provide luxuries for the papal courts? Do not the people complain?" Gabriel had asked in his careful French, thinking to flush out dissenters.

"They complain more about the dauphin's upkeep than the pope's. And the king's arms against the English. At least the Church spends money to keep its cardinals and bishops in finery." The tapestry weaver winked. "Better French fur on His Holiness's cope than Italian leather on his slippers. As for the poorer lot, I guess they feel closer to heaven with having the pope at their own back gate."

But he's not the pope—he's a pretender. Gabriel bit back the retort just in time. He lifted his glass in a false toast to his companion's sentiment, then sipped, enjoying the fine French wine in his mouth. This comes too easily, he thought, as he drained his glass. For the sake of his soul he needed to make quick work of this mission. He was becoming altogether too used to the taste of French wine on his tongue and the feel of fine silk next to his skin. Even the blisters on his back were healing.

After leaving the guildhall, Gabriel inquired about a coach for Paris.

"Demain à une heure de l'après-midi." The coachman wiped down the foam-flecked horses as he repeated, *"Demain."*

Tomorrow it would have to be, then. Unless he hired a private coach. But that would be expensive. He already felt as though too much was being spent on this mission for so little return. Though he had high hopes that when he got to Paris, where the largest guild of bookmakers and scribes resided, he would find some evidence. Lord Cobham had to get his copies somewhere.

But with no coach leaving until tomorrow, he had the remains of the day to kill. The afternoon was well on, a bright, sunny afternoon with the golden autumn light pouring into the square outside Notre Dame Cathedral of Rheims. The cathedral itself looked cold and forlorn, stiff in its peaked collar of stone lace. The first time he'd seen it, he'd been moved by its beauty, but today he found the sunlit square, alive with people and color and noise, more welcoming. A street sweeper, wearing raised wooden clogs on his feet to protect himself from the offal he sluiced into the gutter, bumped against Gabriel, almost treading on his fine leather shoes. Even that did not dampen his spirits. The autumn sun warmed his skin. The mercers' wine warmed his belly. And he was becoming acutely aware of the interested glances darted in his direction from the ladies in their fine-furred mantles who picked their way daintily among the cleaner stones of the pavement.

Voices collided around him: French, German, a smattering of English now and again, all hawking their wares in the marketplace. With time to kill and no place to go, Gabriel considered. There was the cavelike darkness of the cathedral, where he would kneel before a candle-banked altar and offer his prayers. But he would learn more by visiting some of the stalls operating in the square. And wasn't that why he was here?

He was weighing these choices when he saw her.

It was the hair he noticed first. A gleaming nimbus of copper, a sun-sparked mass surrounding a face that was a flawless oval set with eyes as clear as Murano glass. His eyes drifted downward from her hair to her full-bosomed figure. Not a girl's figure. A woman's figure, but well shaped, with a waist a man could enjoy measuring with his hands. No, he would not let his mind stray to that forbidden place.

He was about to turn back toward the cathedral when he noticed that the woman looked to be selling something. She turned the pages of a codex in her hand. She was a bookseller. He should investigate. That's why he'd come, wasn't it? To investigate? To listen in the marketplace?

She tossed her head. Her bright fringe of curls rebelled against a faded velvet caplet that adorned rather than confined them. She leaned toward the customer, pointing to something in the book, then smiling as the customer exchanged his ducats for the small, crudely bound codex. As she leaned forward, her breasts strained against the lawn of her bodice, the cleavage deepening. *The book, Gabriel, you are interested in the book, not the woman.*

Her attention was fastened on her customer. She scarcely seemed to notice as Gabriel approached. A child with spindly limbs and a blond head too big for his thin body—too big also for his elfin face and reedy wrists that flailed about, beating empty air—sat on a bed of rags immediately behind her, his eyes trained on the woman. The boy's eyes were quiet pools, the only stillness in his frenetic body. The boom of the cathedral bells startled him. He blinked large gray eyes and began to whimper. The sound of it was disconcerting. It took Gabriel a minute to realize why—the child's whimpers marked the precise tone of the cathedral bell, perfectly pitched, though two octaves higher than the bell tones. It was as though the bells with their doleful toll had suddenly been made flesh in the thin, pitiful voice of the boy. It made Gabriel's skin creep.

The woman, without breaking her conversation with her customer—a pilgrim, judging from his cloak and staff, and German, judging from his heavily accented French—reached behind her with one hand and gently stroked the child's blond hair until the bell ceased its tolling. The gesture, for some reason that he couldn't fathom, precipitated a pricking behind Gabriel's eyelids. It also quieted the child.

"The book's title is *Libri Sancti Jacobi*. If you are on the Pilgrim's Way, it is a perfect guide," the bookseller said. Her voice was pleasant, well modulated, the voice of an educated woman. "It is in Latin, but I've provided a translation beside it in English and an appendix summary in French, though my French is probably crude. I'm not fluent in that." She apologized. "I'm sorry I have no German text. Though I know a little, I would not attempt a translation."

"I can read the English as well as the French," her customer said, this time in English. "But I confess that though I recite the Latin prayers, the words have little meaning for me."

Gabriel's ears perked. Familiar with the English? How familiar? From whence came that familiarity? An English Bible perhaps? Such a knowledge of languages could put both bookseller and customer under suspicion. But it was not a Bible she was selling, just a pilgrim guide, he reminded himself.

The child had ceased his whimpering. The woman removed her hand from his head and used it to turn the pages of the book. "Pay special attention to Book Five," she said. "It is a warning to be well heeded. If you are headed south, you must cross a stream that can be deadly if you drink from it."

She paused and looked out over the crowded plaza as the customer examined the page she'd indicated. Her face lost some of its animation, became more sober in aspect. "I wish I could post a sign at the river's edge," she said, "in *every* language of the world, a sign to warn the travelers of the perils there." Her bosom heaved as she sighed. Gabriel could almost feel the breath of that sigh against his skin. "But I suspect the evil men who bide there would only tear it down."

The weariness in these last words bespoke experience with evil. Gabriel wondered what her story was. The pilgrim thanked her for the warning and slipped his purchase into his scrip. She slid the coins into the reticule hanging from her belt but hidden in the folds of her skirt. The German completed his purchase and wandered off, inspecting the pages of his find. Gabriel moved closer, appeared to inspect her wares.

"*Bonjour, monsieur.*"

He looked up at her across the table that separated them.

His throat constricted. Eyes of clearest Murano blue looked even bluer against pale skin and bright hair. She reminded him of a picture of the Magdalene he'd seen in Rome. But more innocent. More wise. If only for the suffering honesty of her gaze. If he were a painter, he would paint her thus, surrounded by her books. But he was not. He was a cleric posing as a merchant, he reminded himself.

"Hello," he said in English, fearful that her knowledge of both French and German would far exceed his and find him out as an imposter. "I'm glad you speak in English. I do much commerce with the English and am grateful for a chance to practice it."

She looked suddenly wary. "Are you an alderman, sir? If you've come to inspect my license, I have it right here." She bent to rummage in the basket at her feet. He could see the shapely curve of her hips. He averted his gaze to a gargoyle on an ell of the cathedral overhang behind her. "My husband, Martin, was a stationer in Prague. As his widow I have inherited his guild right and gained permission to sell within this city." She unfurled a rolled parchment, handed it to him.

Gabriel glanced at the official-looking seal beneath the words *femme sole* and the name Anna Bookman of Prague.

Prague. The seat of heresy. The ultimate destination for Lord Cobham's train of heresy.

"You are Anna?"

She nodded, drawing in her breath sharply. Her bosom strained against the lacings of her bodice with the extra breath. He fastened his gaze on the boy behind her, who returned his look with a vacant, unblinking stare. The rest of the boy's body twitched and jerked restlessly. A widow, she'd said.

"I am sorry for your loss," he said. "Was it recent?"

"Are my papers not in order? You will see I have permission to sell in the marketplace as long as I don't set up a permanent stationer's shop." Anxiety pressed her full mouth into a sharp line and deepened the fine furrows etching her brow.

He felt immediate remorse for causing her anxiety—whether her license was fake or real was no concern of his. He rolled the paper up and bound it with the silken thread she'd loosened, handed it back to her. Just because she was from Prague should not make her suspect. Still, she might be a source of some information.

"Your papers look in perfect order to me. But I would not be in any position to say. I too am a visitor in the city. I just came over to your stall to purchase a book." He fingered two of the five books she had on display. Pilgrim guides, simply bound with an awl-punch tool and strips of leather, but transcribed in a fine hand. "Do you do the translations yourself? Or are they your husband's work?"

"They are mine," she answered, pride in her voice. Then quickly added, "I've sold all of . . . all of Martin's."

"You are a remarkable scribe," he said, and meant it. Some of the copies were even illustrated with sketches of pilgrims, the opening capital on the first page sketched in startling detail. "I would like to purchase this." And then he asked idly, as if it were of only casual interest, "I have also some interest in other English translations. Of a religious nature. Do you have any such? The writings of a master by name of John Wycliffe perhaps, or even the earlier works of William of Ockham?"

"I do not sell those. They have been banned by the Church," she said quickly.

Perhaps too quickly.

"The English Scriptures, then?"

"I have only the Gospel of John. In the Vulgate Latin." He could see her mind working, taking in the fineness of his garments, weighing the risk against the needs of her child. "I could transcribe a rough translation for you myself, perhaps, but I should warn you that possession of it is, or might be, against the law in France. I'm not sure. It was harshly dealt with in Bohemia."

A shadow crossed her face; her mouth twitched with some remembered pain. Heretics had been dealt with harshly in Prague. Some even executed. Perhaps she herself was a fugitive. He could let it lie. He could walk away. Get his information elsewhere. If such was indeed the case, she had suffered enough. God had punished her with the loss of her husband, punished her too with the idiot child.

But he did not turn and walk away.

"This is not Bohemia," he said. "This is France. The French care more about fashion and good burgundy than heresy. I don't need the whole book. Just a chapter or two. The first three chapters, I think."

"How long do you plan to stay?"

Demain, the coachman had said.

"The length of my stay depends upon many factors. Would you have time to do one or two chapters for me in a week's time?"

The cathedral bells tolled again. The child resumed his tonal whimpering. The bookseller turned to the child to hug him to her. "I shall think about it," she said over her shoulder.

"Then I shall return tomorrow for your answer," he said.

He walked away with his blood rushing in his head, wondering just what seeds he had sown for some future harvest. He did not think to consider whether it was the spying friar in his black cassock or the worldly mercer in his scarlet cloak who would reap that harvest.

The boy hated the cathedral bells. The bells—other bells, yet the same bells—loud, thunderous clanging in his head, had been tolling the day his uncle left him on the edge of the bridge. He had known his uncle was not coming back. He knew it by the scraping sounds in his throat. By the shuffling of his footfalls as they faded. At first slow then fast fast fast thump thump thump.

The clamor of the bells fear fear fear. Feeling again the sensation of his body edging ever closer ever closer skin scraping on the hot cobblestones feet dangling over empty air. Scooting beyond the lip of the bridge. With each bell tone ever closer to the river. Ever closer. He could not stop. Could not stop the jerking motions of his body. Could not stop the bells.

His uncle was not coming back.

Other footfalls on the bridge. Slowing. Pause. Then thump thump thump. Another bell tone clanging.

Stop. Help me. The cries coming out of his straining throat. *Bek bek bek.* The more he'd tried to still his twitching limbs the closer they jerked to the edge of the bridge. *Bek bek help me.*

Ripples in the water count the ripples one two three. Count the bells one two three. Ever closer.

A clawlike hand had plucked him from the brink.

Another hand, a soft hand, stroked his hair now, muting the echo of the bells.

Now there were two to care for him. A one and a two. One. Two. Like the first two fingers on his hand. One. Two. Like the smooth stones in his pocket. The claw hand had taken his stones away. *No. No. Bek. Bek.* And Anna—he knew her name. A beat on the last—An na, An na had given them back. His stones. Two stones. He was looking for a third.

Two stones. One flat. One round. Two hands. One gentle. Her touch light and smooth. Powdered river mud in summer. One gritty as coarse sand.

Two voices. One voice guttural and low. The sound of the nighttime croaking of the river frogs. His uncle left him on the bridge to grapple under fallen logs for eels and fish. One voice like birdsong pitched low. Tones up and down a melody of half-tones. He sang with this voice.

The old one her oldness in the loose skin of her hands left him behind.

Tied him to the chair. Clung to her crying. *Bek bek bek*. His skin rubbing it-self raw against the bindings. The red seeping out of his skin. Seep. Ooze. Seep. Ooze. And he could not stop it.

But the young one carried him with her. He sat behind her in the little market stall. Her wide blue skirt his blurred horizon. Sometimes he peered past that horizon, watching people shift before his dim eyes like sticks wide thin short tall a parade of color a hidden melody of notes in their hushed and shouted talk. Picking out the tones from the voices he liked. Stringing them like beads singing their tunes in his head. He tried to hold his arms and legs still for her—An na the beat on the last An na An na—he sang her name over and over in half-tones to calm his flailing body. He could do it except for the twitching in his legs. Even when dogs barked and doors slammed he could do it. An na. An na. But not when the bells clanged.

Too weak now to sing the An na in his head. All the music scattered. Falling beads. He listened trying to gather the notes again. There. A bass note. A beginning. He'd heard the same voice the same note a bass note—a base note—to build his melody on. He'd heard it for the last five days. Five days. Like the fingers on one hand if he counted the short one. Or was it six? Sometimes the short one twitched meanly counting itself twice.

The bass note spoke again. He strained around the blue cloth of his hori-zon to see the singer. A tall stick garbed in cloth the color of the blood beneath his skin. Inside seeping outside. He sang to himself then paused to listen.

A new melody in his head. An na's medium tones playing against the low notes. He liked the sound of the notes together.

The tones were perfectly matched.

⁊⁊⁊

Anna's heart beat faster as she showed the merchant from Flanders the first chapter of his commissioned work. He'd strolled by her booth every day, pausing to inquire about progress on the manuscript and to practice his En-glish. That's what he'd said, even though his English was perfect. After his second visit, she'd found herself looking for him, her eyes scanning the square for the scarlet cloak and admitting a flush of disappointment when she'd spotted one that turned out not to be his.

Scarlet tunics seemed almost as popular among wealthy merchants as among Roman cardinals.

At first, she had been wary of the merchant from Flanders—VanCleve was the name he'd given her that first day. His queries about the heretical texts had seemed too studiedly offhand, but with each visit she'd become more friendly with him. Heaven knew she needed a friend. The Gypsies would be leaving soon, and she would be alone. If this man from Flanders wished to be her friend even for a little while, what harm could come to her here in the marketplace? She enjoyed his company.

And if she had any shard of distrust for him left, he dispelled it on the occasion of his sixth visit to her stall.

The late autumn sunshine had given way to low-hanging clouds and a cold drizzle threatened. Anna spotted him across the square. He appeared to be watching her. She looked away, embarrassed, and when she looked back he was gone. But about an hour later by the town crier, just as Anna was thinking she would have to take Little Bek back to Jetta's wagon before the drizzle penetrated the blankets his restless limbs threw off, Anna spotted the merchant again. He was making for her booth in a sort of half-run. Behind him a youth carried two tent poles and an awning.

When she protested she couldn't afford such a luxury, he'd held up his hand to silence her and paid the youth out of his own purse.

"It's a pittance if it will keep you here so that I can enjoy your company for half an hour," he said.

Her instinct was to refuse.

"It will keep the boy dry on rainy days," he said, "and protect him from the sun on fine days. And think of my fancy tunic. You know a man of my standing can't strut about the square in rain-spotted silk. It would not be good for the cloth trade."

He'd laughed when he said this last, as though he were making fun of himself. What he was really doing was making it easier for her to accept his gift. And how could she not? For the sake of Little Bek, if not her merchandise, which she constantly had to protect with oilcloths, wrapping and unwrapping whenever a prospective customer came by.

"I shall consider it only a loan then," she said as the youth pounded the tent poles into the earthen verge of the cobblestone square. "Until the gospel is finished. Do you want to see how it progresses?"

He shrugged. "If you're ready to show it." She brought out the loose pages from a basket at her feet, grateful for the awning that protected them.

"I'm sorry if the work is slow. But the days are getting shorter and the stationers' guild has a rule about working by candlelight. They say it makes inferior work."

"Nothing inferior here," he said, giving the pages a cursory thumbing.

She was disappointed. He paid but scant attention to her careful work.

"Little Bek is quiet today," he said, handing the pages back to her.

"He's listening to us."

"Does he understand what we're saying?"

"It's hard to know. He can't talk. I think he just likes the sound of our voices. He likes music too. He is happiest when the organ grinder comes by. I have spent all my ha'pennies for a few tunes, but afterward he will hum them for hours, happily occupied. The words he sings are gibberish, like some fairy language. But he makes the most perfect little melodies from the notes he steals from the organ grinder."

"But he doesn't like the bells."

"I think it's because they're so loud. Loud noises frighten him. Probably because he doesn't see well. He doesn't know where they're coming from."

VanCleve reached into the pocket of his tunic.

"I've brought him something," he said. "May I give it to him?"

He didn't wait for an answer. He was already moving behind the table on which Anna's books were displayed. He squatted down beside the boy and opened his palm, then put Little Bek's hand over the smooth elliptical stone about the size, shape, and color of a robin's egg.

A broad smile spread over the boy's face. Anna's heart almost broke with the joy in that smile. Little Bek took the stone in his hand and beat it three times against the cloth of his pallet. A string of slobber fell from his grinning lips onto the cloth of VanCleve's sleeve.

"I'm so sorry," Anna said, dabbing at the spot with a clean rag from her basket. "All over your fine robe."

"It matters not a pipkin's worth. It's just cloth. It's been wet before." And taking the cloth from Anna's hand, he gently wiped the boy's face. "Can't wipe away that grin," he said, satisfaction in his voice. He stood up, handed her back the cloth.

"But how did you know?"

"I've seen him playing with the stones. I thought he might like another. Three is a more perfect number." He paused, watching the child for a moment, then looked up at her. "He can count, you know?"

"Why do you think that?"

"Didn't you see the way he beat against the floor? Three times. And see, he's laid them out in a row."

There was something about the mercer's quiet compassion, or perhaps his dual powers of observation and reason, that reminded her of her grandfather. She blinked back unexpected tears, hoping he wouldn't notice.

"There's some intelligence there," he said. "I've read about others like him who have capabilities far beyond what the rest of us have. Some gift from God to compensate them."

Anna could have hugged him. Not only for his kindness but for his confirmation of something she had long suspected. She might have hugged him, if they'd been standing in her grandfather's little town house in Prague and not in the square of a city in a foreign land. If he'd been one of the students who came to study and translate the Wycliffe texts. But they were not. And he was not. He was a stranger in a strange land, and she'd seen enough of the world since leaving Prague to be wary of strangers.

They stood close together beneath the sheltering awning with the cloud and mist closing them in, narrowing the place into an intimate room. She had to resist the urge to reach out and touch VanCleve's scarlet sleeve, to feel the arm beneath it. Unconsciously, she arched her back, smoothed her hair with her hands as if trying to tame it. Something stirred in her woman's part, something sharp and quick as a lightning surge, almost like a pain. She could not look at him. She turned her flaming face away, pretended to straighten the books and pamphlets on her table.

"Do you have children, Monsieur VanCleve?" A man such as he must surely have a wife and children, strong sons to carry on his business.

"No, I am . . . alone . . . I am unmarried."

"A pity," she murmured, trying to quiet the fluttering of her pulse. "I mean, you seem to have a fondness for children."

"Suffer the little children, our Lord said." He smiled. "He had a fondness for them too."

Behind her Little Bek beat his stones against the floor. One, two, three, muted beats against his pallet. The mist changed to rain and dripped from the edge of the awning.

"I hope you live nearby," she said. Then felt her skin flush lest he mistake her meaning. "I mean only that I would not want your fine clothes to be twice wet in one day."

He laughed. "I have a room on the other side of the cathedral. In Rue de Saint Luc. Do you live close by?"

"I am staying with a band of . . . pilgrims, but they will be moving on soon. I plan to stay in Rheims through the winter. The custom is good here."

"There may be rooms in the place where I am lodging."

"I'm only a widow and a poor bookseller. I could not afford the same as a wealthy merchant."

"The house is simple, but clean. And reasonably priced. I shall be happy to inquire of the landlord if you like."

While she was hesitating, groping for an answer, he added, "Let me help you gather your books and we'll go now. You and the child will both be soaked if you try to manage alone."

And before she could protest, he had packed her books into the basket at her feet and lifted Little Bek into his arms. "Here," he said, handing her the basket. "We'll make a run for it. The second house on the other side of the cathedral."

He had hardly gotten the words out of his mouth before he darted off across the square, carrying Little Bek wrapped in his furred cape.

There was nothing Anna could do but wrap her shawl around her frizzing hair and follow.

EIGHTEEN

s it turned out, the landlord of the little daub-and-wattle house in Rue de Saint Luc did have an extra room to let. Anna looked at it at the urging of VanCleve—at the urging too of the pounding rain that had set in. The room was clean and cozy. It boasted a wooden bed with a mattress of real down, a settle with a chest beneath it and a bright embroidered throw over its back, a dresser topped with a pewter bowl and pitcher for washing and a small polished bronze mirror poised above. A glazed window leaded in small squares leaned out slightly over a bit of garden. A charcoal brazier warmed the room.

She looked at the little chamber longingly, fighting a sudden wash of regret. It was so like her pleasant room at the head of the twisting stairs, the room she'd left behind in the little town house in Prague. "I can't afford such luxury," she said, shaking her head.

VanCleve laughed. "You haven't even asked how much it is. How do you know you can't afford it? It's close by. You'd probably do enough business in the extra hours spent walking—you said what, six, eight furlongs?—to pay the rent. I'm sure the landlord would make the best possible deal to a young widow with a child." His glance included this rotund little man who squinted at Little Bek through nearsighted eyes.

Anna scolded herself for not telling VanCleve on that first day that Little Bek did not belong to her. But his false perception had served at the time to reinforce her story of widowhood, a story she had made up along with the forged documents to gain license to sell her books in the marketplace. Now it would be awkward to explain. And though the stranger from Flanders had shown them kindness, how did she know he would not turn her in for being other than what she said, a widow carrying on her husband's lawful trade? Anyway, he would be leaving soon. A week or so, he'd said.

"Quel est le prix de cette chambre?"

The rotund little man squinted, held up one chubby finger. *"Un ecu par semaine."*

Half a crown. Five shillings a week. She could make that on Thursday market days alone. But there was also the cost of food and linens and laundry. And candles—despite the guild master's prohibition, she had to work by candlelight to make enough money to live. Yet she was going to have to find a place soon. Bera was talking incessantly of pilgrimage to Spain. It was just a matter of days until the Gypsies left, and she could not go on to England alone with winter coming on.

VanCleve reached into his purse and pressed the silver coins into the landlord's hand. *"Nous prenons cette chambre,"* he said.

"Non—"

"It is but an advance for the work you are doing on the book. You can't walk home in such a downpour. You can't possibly carry the child that far. You can stay here tonight, and tomorrow we'll send around for your belongings."

Outside, the rain beat against the windowpane. Inside, the warmth beckoned. Little Bek grinned at them with a wide, wet smile, his big head cocked to one side, bobbing on its slender stem like some pop-up jester in the box. Anna sat down on the mattress, its feathers sighing with her weight. The boy likes it here, she thought. And he likes being with a man.

VanCleve reached into his purse and produced a silver groat for the innkeeper. *"De la viande, du pain, du fromage, s'il vous plaît."*

Five more shillings for meat and bread and cheese. Her stomach growled just thinking about food. She had not eaten since leaving the Romani wagon that morning, though she'd purchased a farthing's worth of biscuit and dripping for the child. The innkeeper nodded and left, closing the door behind him. Anna was suddenly uncomfortably aware of the intimacy of her surroundings. But what reputation did she, a strange woman in a strange city, have to lose? Distant thunder rolled over the drumming rain.

VanCleve took off his scarlet cloak and spread it on the floor. He sat down beside Little Bek. "We'll have a picnic when the landlord returns," he said, grinning at the boy as if he thought the idiot child understood every word. "We'll pretend this floor is a flower-strewn meadow and the raindrops are stray sunbeams."

"Your cloak—"

"It'll brush off," he said, reaching into Anna's basket and pulling out the robin's egg stone. He scrambled it around with flashing fingers, then held out his fists to the boy. "Which one?" he asked.

To Anna's surprise the boy slapped haphazardly at the hand that held the stone. A lucky guess? Even she had not been sure and she had keen eyesight. But again and again the boy slapped at the correct hand. Over and over. Never missing. Not once. Finally, Anna wearied of trying to second-guess the flashing hands; she watched instead the way VanCleve's eyes crinkled at the corners when he laughed and the way his short blond hair curled beneath his square, flat cap. It reminded her of the silk scarves, liquid as cream, in which the rabbi in Judenstadt had wrapped his Torah scrolls lest the holy words be defiled by impure hands. Now why had she thought of that tonight? For the second time, she felt a wave of homesickness rise inside her.

What would Dĕdeček have thought of VanCleve? she wondered. Another roll of thunder. A knock at the door.

"*Entrez,*" VanCleve called.

The door opened and the smell of roasted meat and yeasty bread filled the room.

Minutes later, after the landlord had laid the feast on the makeshift picnic cloth, he paused outside the door just to listen to the sound of laughter. A strange trio. But it was good to have happy people in his house, he thought. It was good for business.

And it was none of his concern what went on behind closed doors. None of his concern at all.

—☙❧—

Jetta worried when Anna and Little Bek did not come back to the camp. She thought of going in search of them. She knew where Anna had set up her book table in the shadow of the great cathedral, but she had gone there only once and been chased away by the bailiff when she tried to *dukker* the *gorgios* in the square. The bailiff had called her an ugly name. She did not understand his language, but she understood the threat. She did not want to go there again.

When she went to Bera to ask if someone else should go in search of Anna and Little Bek, Bera said Anna had probably taken cover from the rain, not to worry, and he went back to bouncing his son on his shoulder, grinning heartily when the infant let out a loud burp. Lela, lacing up her blouse and looking for all the world like a satisfied cat who had just finished a bowl of cream, told Jetta not to worry too.

Easy enough for them to say. They had not rescued the child and the woman from the river. Easy enough for them; they were not driven by the voices.

But Jetta didn't need the voices to tell her she was not part of this intimate family scene. She returned to her own damp *vardo,* where she chewed on a rind of cheese and stale bread. The rains had doused the campfires so there would be no hot food for supper. No dancing. No music. No laughter.

She hoped the red-haired woman and the boy fared better. The wagon felt empty without them. Lonely. Like the desolate sky that spilled its tears on the barrel-vaulted roof of the wagon. She lay on her back in the thickening darkness and stared at the ceiling, listening for the sound of the voices in her head. The voices that would tell her what to do. When they did not speak, she pulled a scratchy wool horse blanket over her body and drifted off to sleep.

Only the sound of the drumming rain disturbed the heavy silence.

—☙❧—

Anna woke to sunlight streaming through the thick leaded panes. Her heart leaped. For a moment she thought herself back in the little bedchamber at the top of the winding wooden stair in Prague. But Little Bek's whimpers summoned her to full consciousness.

He was probably wet, needing to be changed. She hoped the wetness had not leaked through the oiled canvas braies that Jetta had sewn for him. It had never occurred to either of them that he might be taught not to wet himself, even when they had remarked upon his strong bladder control. A blessing in one who seemed to have so little bodily control. He hated being wet and always cried when he soiled himself, but he had never once waked them during the night.

She checked him quickly. His padding was soaked through, but he'd not wet his breeches or his blankets. She was rummaging through her basket, sure she'd used the last clean rags for clearing up from last night's feast, wondering what she would use, trying to reassure him, when she heard a tentative tap at the door.

She recognized the landlord's voice. *"Pardon, madame, s'il vous plaît,"* then in a halting English, "From Monsieur VanCleve. For le boy." The portly landlord stood there holding a stack of clean linen in one hand, balancing a bucket of water and a basket in the other.

Anna opened the door and watched with relief as the little man replenished the water in the washing bowl and deposited the stack of linen.

"Monsieur VanCleve. Has he gone out?" Anna asked in her adequate French.

He smiled with relief. *"Oui,"* and handed her a note and a basket of apples. *"Bonjour, madame. Avez-vous besoin de quelque chose d'autre?"*

"Non, merci. Merci beaucoup."

As she closed the door on the landlord, she hurriedly scanned the note. It merely said that VanCleve hoped she found everything to her liking and that she had slept well, and that he would return shortly and help her transfer her belongings.

But Anna had no intention of letting VanCleve accompany her to the Gypsy camp. She couldn't put a name to it, but there was still something about him in the clear light of day that she didn't quite trust. Though all heaven knew she wanted to. But why should this stranger, by all accounts a prosperous merchant, take such a sudden interest in the welfare of a woman whom he did not know?

Except for one thing. Sheltered though she might have been, she knew what that might be, though she had to admit he'd thus far made no improper advances and had treated her with respect. After their shared meal, he'd merely helped her to clean up and gone to his own quarters, telling her to knock on his door should she require anything. And she was grateful for his help, grateful more for the kindness he'd shown the boy. But that was strangest of all. Why would he be drawn to the idiot child so many others avoided, their lightning gazes either staring in rude curiosity or glancing off him as though he were not even there?

No, she would not let her guard down, lest he find out that she was not really a widow carrying on her deceased husband's business and entitled to the protection of the stationer's guild. But now that she'd had a night to sleep on it, she was not sorry she'd made the move. It was good to have that decision behind her. Good to know that when the Roma left she would have a roof over her head. And with only herself to support, she should be able to put enough aside to make the trip to England in the spring.

Sir John Oldcastle. She'd said the name often in the last months to remind her of her promise. Sir John Oldcastle, Lord Cobham. Her grandfather had said, "Go to Lord Cobham, and you will be safe." Feeling safe was what Anna wanted most in the world, and the closest she had come to feeling safe since Martin's execution was last night in the little room off Rue de Saint Luc. It was so tempting to trust the merchant from Flanders. She had almost told him the truth as they laughed together over their little supper in the intimacy of the cozy little room. A shared confidence. What could it hurt? He would go home in a few days and she'd never see him again. But something held her back. And now with the harsh sunlight of a winter day pouring through her window she was glad she had not.

"Here, Little Bek. Eat your apple," she said, cutting it in little bites. "Then I'll take you back to Jetta. There will be no bells there to frighten you."

But Little Bek didn't want his apple. He spit it out and started to sing. She wasn't sure, but it sounded like he was singing her name.

"Don't worry. You'll be safe with Jetta. The Roma will take care of you.

And you'll get to go to Spain. You'll like Spain. The book says the sun always shines there. And it's warm. Not like here."

Last night's rain had ushered in a bright day, but it had the hard cold edge of winter.

Anna shivered just thinking of the long, dark nights ahead.

~·~·~

"We will miss you, Anna of Prague," Bera said when she told the Gypsy king she was leaving.

"But if you cannot go with us to Santiago de Compostela in Spain, it is good you have found a place. Our departure is imminent."

Bera flashed his bright smile. "Imminent." That was a new word for him. Bera collected new words as he collected cunning tricks, displaying both at every opportunity.

"You have found a man! I knew it," Lela squealed. "Soon you'll be bouncing your own babe." She bounced hers enthusiastically against her shoulder as if to show Anna how it should be done. She then passed the baby to Bera, who bounced him harder. With so much jiggling about it was a wonder the child did not spit up butter.

"No, Lela. I have not found a man! VanCleve is just a kind stranger who took pity on us in the storm. He'll be leaving soon."

"Van Clef. Ooah. A fancy name. This Van Clef will fall madly in love with you. I made a lover's spell for you a week ago. He will not be able to resist you, Anna of Prague. You'll see. But you don't have to thank me. You have been my friend, and I will also miss you."

Lela leaped up from her pile of cushions and hugged Anna enthusiastically. Anna tried to hug her back, chiding herself for her lack of forgiveness, remembering, even though she wanted to forget, how Lela had betrayed her to the Prague authorities. She smelled of the sour, sweet, milky smell of her infant, a smell that set off such an inexplicable longing in Anna it almost made her dizzy.

Lela, who was shorter than Anna by half a head, reached up and as fast as an adder's strike pulled a long red hair from Anna's head.

Anna gasped in protest, but Lela only laughed. *"Rawnie bal,"* she said. "You'll not miss it. You have so much left."

Lela wound the hair into a bracelet and put it on the baby's arm. Anna looked at the circle of her hair sliding into the crease of the baby's wrist, a rusty stain beside the crimson ribbon bracelet. Anna sincerely wished that was all that it would take to ensure this child a happy life, but the world was a cruel and dangerous place for children. No charm or spell could stand against the kind of evil she had seen.

I will miss these people and their silly superstitions, Anna thought. She turned to Jetta, who was sitting on the floor in the corner of the wagon. Little Bek sat in the lap of her crossed legs, beating the blue stone in syncopated beats against the penny-farthing boards of the floor. The old woman had said nothing since Anna's announcement that she was leaving them for good.

"I will miss you most, Jetta," Anna said.

Bera handed the baby back to Lela and picked up Anna's traveling chest, groaning as he hefted it onto his shoulders.

"It's the English Bible that makes it so heavy," she said, anxious lest he suspect that her little horde of ducats and nobles had grown, and try to squeeze some last farthing from her.

Jetta pushed Little Bek gently from her lap and stood up. She did not hug Anna as Lela had, but reached for her hand and turned it palm up.

"What does it say, Jetta?" Lela said. "The man in her life will stay, right? Marriage? Children?"

Anna jerked her hand away. "I don't believe in divination, Jetta. You know that. I believe that our fate is determined by our own actions and by the will of God when we ask for His intervention in our affairs. And He does not write our future in our palms."

What harm would it have been for Jetta to read her palm if it pleased her? Was it that she was afraid to hear what the old woman might say?

Jetta narrowed her eyes to a slit and gave Anna her sly smile. "You are about to go on a long journey. I saw it in your palm. Before you snatched it away."

Anna laughed. "That's what you tell everybody that you *dukker.*"

Jetta shrugged, the bangles in her ears bobbing with the motion. "That doesn't mean it's not the truth. Life is a long journey. Wouldn't you agree, Anna of Prague?"

"I suppose it is, Jetta. I suppose it is."

Lela pouted. "But I wanted to hear about her lover."

Jetta's wry half-smile vanished. "Take care, Anna. Whether you believe it is written in your palm or not, there is danger ahead for you. Tread with care this journey of yours."

That was the longest speech Anna had ever heard the taciturn Jetta make except when she was muttering to herself. "And you tread carefully as well, Jetta. You know I will always be grateful to you."

"It was nothing. It was not your fate to die in the river that day."

Anna remembered again the kiss of the water on her face, the peace of it as it closed over her. Her life's journey would have ended there had it not been for this old woman. Perhaps it should have ended there, she thought, ended in the cool, clear waters of the Vltava River, moved by the current into eternity. Journey's end. Safe harbor. With Dĕdeček and Martin. But in the light of this bright day when the air was crisp and clean, and she was surrounded by this unlikely band of friends, she was glad that it had not.

Bera was already stepping down out of the wagon. Anna stooped and kissed Little Bek on the top of his fine, blond hair, then, blinking back unshed tears, turned to follow Bera. Behind her, Little Bek began to wail, "An na An na."

"Hush, child," Jetta said. "You will see Anna again. Soon. You will see her. Soon."

An empty promise to soothe a child, Anna thought, hoping he would forget her quickly and not be distressed. He had few enough friends in this world.

As do I, Anna thought as she followed the King of the Gypsies from the camp that had been her home for months. *As do I.*

⁓⛧⛧⁓

It was late in the day by the time Bera deposited Anna's traveling chest with the landlord and left. She was glad that VanCleve was nowhere around. She would not want him to see the Gypsy and get the wrong idea. Then she immediately repented for that sentiment. What did she care what he thought? He was only a customer who had been kind to her. He would move on and she would never see him again.

"I will walk back with you to the town center, Bera. Maybe buy some bread and cheese from one of the vendors for my supper. Now that I'm to be on my own."

He looked at her evenly, no hint of that smile he used to charm and con his *gorgios* marks. She'd never seen him so serious. "It is not too late to change your mind, Anna of Prague. You can go with us to Spain."

"No, Bera. I thank you. Truly, I do. I don't know what I would have done without you and Jetta . . . and Lela. But it is best this way. My pilgrimage lies west."

But as he walked away, she had a sudden feeling of panic, stifled the urge to call him back.

Who knew what lay ahead for her in England? What if this Lord Cobham refused to receive her? She thought of the *hrad* on the hill above the Vltava River and shuddered inwardly at the thought of approaching such a castle. What if . . . ? *Well, then, you will have kept your promise at the very least. You can earn your bread with your quill in England. Just be grateful that God has given you that ability.*

Apparently Jetta wasn't the only one who heard voices in her head, Anna thought wryly.

≈≈

The day had grown somber with the fading light. The bells tolled vespers. Anna had bought her bread and cheese and was crossing in front of the great doors of the cathedral when she saw a flash of scarlet from the corner of her eye. She recognized the familiar figure going in. Even though his back was to her. Yes, she was sure. Something in the walk, the way he carried himself.

So. He was devout. And he practiced the Roman religion. That was a disappointment. She'd thought them kindred spirits. After all, he had asked for an English gospel. Why would he have commissioned one, if he were not a seeker after a greater truth than the Church taught? But as she'd already reminded herself, VanCleve was really of no importance to her.

By the time Anna had eaten her supper and copied a page, most of her carefully hoarded candle was spent. The darkness hovered outside her circle of yellow light, making the room seem lonelier. She had heard no tread in the hallway. VanCleve must have lingered long over his devotions. His door was close to hers and she'd have heard him return. But what business was it of hers, anyway? Why was she even listening?

She was thinking she should just go to bed—it would be an extravagance to light another candle—when she heard a gentle tap at her door. She opened it warily at first, only a crack, then wider.

VanCleve filled up the narrow doorway, his short, blond hair gleaming in the torchlight of the flickering wall sconce.

"I hope you were not already abed. I did not want to waken you. But I thought I saw a glow from beneath your door."

"No, I was—"

His glance over her shoulder took in the quills, the paper, the open book on her bed. "You are working. May I come in? I promise not to waken your son," he said softly, glancing at the pile of blankets on the little pallet beside Anna's bed. She'd not yet removed them, and the way the coverlet lay, in the dim shadow of the room, it looked as though there might be a child huddled beneath. She started to explain, but what would she say? She was too tired to explain her circumstances to him now, too tired to think how much to trust him.

"It is late. And the landlord—"

He laughed. "The landlord is French. He pays no attention."

This made her blush. She hoped he would not notice in the dim light.

He held out a small, neatly wrapped package. "I brought you candles."

His wheedling voice reminded her of Martin. Were all men the same? She had loved it when Martin flirted with her, but Martin had loved her. She hardly knew this man.

"Please, sir. You are generous in the extreme. But I am—"

She had only half stepped aside, but he pushed his way into the room.

"I see what you are doing. You are reading from the English Bible." His harsh tone and cocked eyebrow suggested disapproval.

"Not reading it. Copying it. For you. The Gospel of Saint John, remember?" Her voice was soft, complicit in his presumption of the sleeping child.

"I remember. May I see the Bible?"

But he did not wait for permission. He was already picking up the book, turning its pages. His manner irritated her. She supposed as a prosperous merchant he was used to having his way.

"I thought you said you were a poor widow. This is very impressive work. And it is a very expensive book."

That irritated her more. His visit to the cathedral had done nothing for his demeanor. He seemed less agreeable, more authoritarian. Or maybe it was just her imagination, and she was looking for something to pick at because she had seen him enter the cathedral. She could hardly order him out of her room when his generosity had paid for it—unless of course his behavior was dishonorable in some way. She should have known better than to accept gifts from a stranger.

"I *am* a poor widow," she said, chagrined at having to repeat the lie. "The book belonged to my grandfather. It is his work. He was a scribe and a renowned illuminator."

He was frowning at the book as though it were something different than the "impressive work" he had pronounced it. As though it offended him. But that was probably her imagination also. After all, he had asked her to copy one for him.

"I wonder that you do not fear for your grandfather's safety. You should be more careful. It is unlawful to own such a Bible."

"My grandfather is dead. Where I come from there are many who read the Word for themselves."

The candle guttered. He opened the package and lit another one. Replaced the spent end. Then he sat on her bed, as easily as if she had invited him. Anna remained standing.

"Having this in your possession is very dangerous, Anna. The Church condemns it."

"But you—"

"That's different. I am a man of some influence. You are a woman alone."

Anna felt her temper rising. "Do you know why the Church condemns it? I'll tell you why. Those who read it for themselves might find that what the friars preach is nothing more than a pack of lies perpetrated out of greed and lust for power."

She could tell by the way his jaw worked she was offending him, but she could not stop herself. Others had died for this truth. She could not keep quiet to please a man who had been kind to her. Not when what she said was true.

She pointed to the Bible. "The doctrine of Purgatory. Tell me! Where in the Bible is there any mention of such a place? You cannot, sir. Because it is a fiction! And the sale of indulgences?" She laughed at his gullibility. A man smart enough to be a successful tradesman, and he could not see beyond the end of his nose. "If the people found out that the grace of God and salvation was free for the asking, then why would they pay?"

Her remark must have hit home for now he raised his voice in turn. "You think every peasant is learned enough to interpret the Scripture for himself?" He gave a little scornful laugh. "Most are not learned enough to cipher a bill of fare, let alone Holy Writ."

He slapped the Bible with his fist. Anna cringed at the sound of it. How could she have thought him such a gentle man?

"I know whereof I speak, Anna. I have traveled among them. I have seen—" He interrupted himself. Paused as if reconsidering his words. "A merchant sees many who are ignorant."

She would not back down. Nor would she be intimidated by his claim to superior insights because of his social position.

"Then give those ignorant peasants the right to choose who shall interpret Holy Writ for them. You might be surprised by how much wisdom resides in the most unlearned among them."

"I see that you are firmly entrenched in this belief," he said softly.

"And I know that, in spite of your curiosity about the English Bible, you are not. I saw you entering the cathedral at evensong."

He stood up. Closed the Bible with a thump. "Be careful, Anna. This is not Bohemia. Heresy is a dangerous charge and the Church—I have heard the Church is mounting a campaign to stamp it out. You have the child to think of." He glanced at the bundle on the floor. "I shall bid you good night before we disturb him with our argument."

"Yes, you should go. Thank you for the warning. I will be careful," she said stiffly. "And thank you for the candles."

"You are welcome on both counts," he said. But his easy affability had vanished.

As she shut the door, Anna wondered if he would acknowledge her with aught but a cursory greeting when next they met.

NINETEEN

*[Our] humble author will continue the story with Sir
 John in it,
. . . where (for any thing I know) Falstaff shall die of
 a sweat,
. . . for Oldcastle died a martyr and this is not the
 man.*
                    —EPILOGUE, *HENRY IV, PART II*,
                        BY WILLIAM SHAKESPEARE

h, Sir John! 'Tis honey balm ye be for these old sore eyes.
Come in, come in."

Sir John held up his arms, laughing, holding off the blowsy, full-hipped
tavern hostess who was about to wrap him in her full embrace.

"Now, Nell. None o' that. My lady would scarce approve. You do know
I've taken a wife since last we met?"

She slapped his arm, only half playfully, before tucking graying strings
of hair back into her rag bonnet. "I heard. Doll came round with the news.
In deep mourning she was. Along with half the whores of Eastcheap. Ye'd
have thought somebody died."

She held him out at arm's length, surveying him with her gaze. "But what
brings ye here? Not tiring of that fancy new wife so soon? Though it's right

glad I be to see ye. It's not like the old times, Jack. Not like the old times at all."

"We move on, Nell. The world changes. How's Pistol?"

"Worthless as allus."

"I remember you didn't think him worthless when you were chasing him."

"Aye, but that was afore I caught him."

Her face sagged with her sigh. He noticed new crow's-feet tracking the corners of her eyes. Her hand flitted self-consciously over her smeared apron.

"Trade has fallen off since ye left," she said. "Pistol's got some cockeyed notion in his pox brain to take up ragpicking. He's got hisself a splintered barrow cart and is out wheeling through the alleys, pickin' through the gentry's flea-filled throwaways." She averted her gaze. "We get by. At least the neighbors don't complain about the rowdiness the way they used to." She grinned, trying to recapture some of her good humor. "The way you, and Prince Hal, and Pistol, and Bardolph could swagger. I scarce ever have to call the constable now. And he doesn't come when I do."

Sir John looked around the familiar public room of the Boar's Head. It was more disreputable-looking than he remembered. The rushes on the floor needed freshening, and the cracked windows were grimed with streaks of dirt and slops from the emptied upstairs chamber pots whose contents missed the targeted street gutters. Filtered through the mess, the afternoon light took on a greenish hue. Mistress Quickly had always kept a clean alehouse. He wondered what Joan would think of such a place as this. No. He didn't really wonder. He knew.

In one corner a couple of ne'er-do-wells plotted some nefarious scheme over an empty tankard. Sir John patted the pockets of his surcoat to make sure his purse was still there. In the corner by the ash-strewn hearth, where a dying fire choked in its own residue, an old drunk slumped in a stupor.

"I remember the last time you called the constable on me. Did I ever pay you that debt of ten pounds you were pressing suit for?" He groped for his purse, aware as he did so that the pair of miscreants on the other side of the room had ceased talking and were watching him. He moved sideways so as to hide the transaction with his girth without turning his back on them.

"Aw, Jack. You don't have——"

"Then there's the interest on the debt. Probably grown another pound in these five years." He removed the eleven gold sovereigns, considerably lightening his purse.

She looked hungrily at the coin in her hand.

"Now that my credit is restored, how about a mug of your best sack?"

Avoiding his gaze, she stuffed the coins into a pouch beneath her apron and smiled up at him. "I've still got yer favorite tankard. The one formed in the shape of a woman with big—" She made a weighing motion beneath her own full breasts.

He settled his bulk onto a nearby bench as she pulled the draught from a keg into the obscene mug. "Ye'll stay till Pistol's come home?"

"If he doesn't come too late. I'm to meet someone here. A parchment maker from Smithfield by the name of William Fisher. Has he been asking for me?"

The two miscreants at the corner table finished their plotting, and, throwing one last furtive glance at him, as if assessing whether or not they dared take on such a mountain of a man, they decided against it and skulked toward the door. They ducked past a newcomer trying to come in.

"What does Master Fisher look like?"

Sir John let the sack slide down his throat, smiling in satisfaction. "Don't know," he said, wiping the foam from his mustache. "Never met him. But the messenger said it was urgent."

The newcomer stood silhouetted in the open door with the sun behind him.

"Seems you've a new customer, Mistress Quickly," Sir John said to the silhouette.

The man stepped forward out of the light and threw back his hood. "What does a man have to do to get a drink in this house?" he said.

"Your Highness," the hostess mumbled, dropping a clumsy curtsy even as Sir John's memory registered the shock of recognition.

"You're mistaken, mistress. My name is William Fisher of Smithfield. And I'm here to meet with Lord Cobham." The voice was low and measured. And familiar.

Nell's smile melted into a frown of chagrin. She looked askance at Sir John, a look that inquired if this was yet another of the elaborate tricks the pair had been known for in prior years. Sir John answered her look with a shrug and she, dropping another uncertain half-curtsy, shuffled off to draw the drinks.

"Master Fisher, is it?" Sir John said as the two men took a table beneath the cracked pane. Nell put the mugs down in front of them, quizzing Sir John with a lift of her eyebrow before waddling away unsatisfied.

"You bear a remarkable resemblance to an old friend I once shared many a merry jest with. His name was Hal, but now I think on it, he was more a callow youth than a man. Though I recollect he had a man's capacity for drink." Sir John grinned, hoping with those words to set a spark in the familiar eyes of the man sitting across from him. None appeared.

"My name is William, not Hal, Lord Cobham. I am, as I said, a parchment maker from Smithfield."

Well! If that was the game his young friend was playing, then Sir John would go along.

"From Smithfield, you say? What can I do for you Mr. . . . Fisher?"

"It's what I can do for you."

"And what possible need could I have for a parchment maker?"

"Rumor says you are a great consumer of parchment, my lord. And a frequent buyer of quills and ink. Rumor says that you are engaged in the exporting of books."

Sir John considered how best to answer. "So then, this is a business call, William. You have come to sell me parchment," Sir John said archly, wondering what was coming next but willing to go wherever the game would lead.

The lad was good. He'd have to give him that. But then Hal had always been able to feign a disguise. He remembered how the pair of them would devise some gaming scheme, more for sport than gain, to separate some lout of a fellow from his purse for the price of the night's drinks. Hal would use his wits as a bow, playing the poor fool like a fiddle. Then Sir John, as accomplice, would close for the "kill." Ofttimes they reversed the roles just out of sheer boredom. Whatever the jest was now, Sir John would play for old time's sake. He chose to bluff, a play he'd often used at cards.

"Well, Master Fisher. Rumors are sometimes true. Sometimes not. Your informant has told you wrong. I am no scholar. Neither am I a book man. I have no need of parchment. You have made the trip from Smithfield for nothing." He picked up his obscene tankard with both hands, rubbing its pink protrusions with his thumbs, waiting for his companion to make some ribald remark in recognition of it. From the corner of his eye, he saw their hostess behind the long bar watching them as she wiped mugs with her dirty apron, imparting even more grime to the already greasy vessels.

"I've not come to sell you parchment."

This Hal who was not Hal leaned forward conspiratorially, placing both hands on the table, palms down, half rising from his seat. It was a posture Sir John remembered well. He'd seen it often enough when Hal's quick temper and surfeit of sack had overpowered his reason. "I have come with a message from Prince Harry, who bade me give it to you out of the good regard in which he once held you."

"Once held?"

There was something in the hard steel glint of the man's eye, in the set of his jaw, that Sir John did not remember in the boy.

Here was no jest.

Sir John set down his cup. He suddenly wanted to be away from here. The filth and smell of stale beer and moldering ash bore little resemblance to the tavern where he'd once thought himself so merry. By this time, in the late afternoon, Joan would be in the rose garden working her embroidery or reading her English Bible. He wished he were sitting beside her on the turf bench, smelling the perfume of the rose she would have plucked and tucked in the neckline of her bodice.

"And prithee tell me, just what might that message be?" he asked this stranger seated across from him. "Your note spoke of urgency."

"Urgent for one who holds his life dear."

The same deep-set eyes, the same mouth slightly petulant in the lower lip, the same brown hair, once worn fashionably curled at the shoulder, now shorn round and high above the ears like some clerics', only without the tonsure.

"The prince would have you know that the king and the archbishop are set to burn out any taint of heresy wherever they may find it. And they are looking with all diligence."

Each word punctuated with a pause, the tone husky, low, menacing.

The same arched brows, the same prominent cheekbones. The same and yet not the same.

"*They* are ever looking for such," Sir John said, matching the prince's measured tones. "And their diligence is equaled only by their calumny. But what has that to do with me?"

"They are turning over every stone. Even in the castles of the nobility. They are not looking blindly. They have informants. They are building a case against all who disseminate the heretical writings both in England and abroad."

There was no news here. Not really. Knowing was one thing. Proving quite another. And proof they must have to charge a member of Parliament, proof they must have to charge a friend of the king.

"And what of Prince Harry?" Sir John asked. "Rumor says that Henry Bolingbroke is on his deathbed. Prince Harry will soon be sovereign ruler of all England. Has this prince no loyalty to the former friend he once called 'brother'?"

There was a pause as if the answer were being worked out deliberately in the man's head before he replied. This was certainly unlike Hal, who had always been ready with the quick answer, the rapier wit honed to a fine edge. Finally, this William answered.

"The prince bade me warn you that his duty lies with England and with his Church. Such a debt of loyalty as he might owe you is herewith discharged by this warning."

Sir John's answer came more quickly, rising in a flush of anger. He could not keep the edge from his voice. "Convey to the young Prince Harry my gratitude for his concern and assure him his fears are unfounded. But tell him too that Sir John also knows where his allegiance lies, and he shall be faithful to it. At whatever cost."

William Fisher dropped his head. With one finger he traced the interlocking moisture rings etched into the wood of the table by countless tankards, in countless drinking sessions in years past. When he looked up, the mask had slipped and Sir John saw Prince Hal's face staring at him.

The prince pushed his untouched drink to the center of the table and stood up, leaning over Sir John. He'd grown taller in the last years. Sir John felt the weight of those years pressing against his heart. Hal touched his shoulder. His touch was light, tender as a woman's.

"Jack, a fat man burns hotter than most."

But the jest was voiced low, if jest it was, in a hoarse whisper, delivered without mirth, but delivered also without malice.

Without even a nod to the hostess, who was wiping at the counter as she feigned disinterest, William Fisher drew his hood back over his head and started for the door.

The sun no longer struck a beam through the dirty window. The tavern room was in deep shadow.

"Master Fisher, I may have some future need of parchment after all. Perhaps we can meet again," Sir John called to the slice of sunlight cutting into the gloom through the open door. But there was no answer except the snoring of the drunk slumped in the corner.

Sir John took a sixpence from his purse and put it on the table. "You're right, Nell. It's not like the old days."

"Pistol'll be sorry he missed ye," he heard Nell call as he shut the door behind him. But he did not look back.

⁓ ⁑ ⁓

Will Jaggers had only been in London two nights before he decided being a poor priest was not a lucrative business. It had been good enough in the byways and open road, where the peasantry called him "father" and gave him free bread and ale, but it might prove more dangerous in the city than even his former trade of pickpocket. For that a man would only be whipped or put in the stocks. But since coming to London, he'd heard tales of poor priests who were accused of heresy and shut up in the White Tower, never to be heard of again. So when he found a warm pair of breeches and a wool tunic airing on a bush behind a house in Merchant's Row, he partook of this unexpected largesse.

Since he was reluctant to part with the good warm wool of the cassock—the nights were getting cold and if he were sleeping in the open in a hayrick, a priest's cassock could keep him warm—he wadded it up and stuffed it into the scrip in which he still carried the book he'd received at Sir John's gathering. But it wouldn't fit. No two ways about it. The wool cloth could keep him warm on those winter nights. He couldn't even read the book. He remembered passing a bookshop in Paternoster Row. 'Twas Holy Writ. It should at least be worth the price of a pot of ale.

⁓ ⁑ ⁓

As eventide approached and Sir John had not appeared, Lady Cobham ordered extra rush lights lit in the courtyard to welcome him. The clopping of hoofbeats sent her to her chamber window to peer out in anticipation. She could see a horse fractured into diamond bits of wavy glass, and even in the dim torchlight there was no mistaking the horse's rider.

The droop of his shoulders and the scowl on his face told her his day had not gone well. The abrupt way he dismounted and pitched the reins to his groom warned of ill tidings, tidings he would probably not share with his wife. That was her husband's one failing. This desire to protect her from bad news, as though not to tell her would in some way protect her from the inevitable consequences. Foolish thinking on the part of an otherwise brilliant man. Not telling her merely robbed her of the means to protect not only herself, but maybe him as well. But she knew it would do no good to confront him. She would have to worm the cause of his obvious distress from him in more subtle ways.

She didn't think it was the estate accounts. She no longer bothered with them herself, leaving that to the stewards and to John, but she knew enough to be aware when things were going poorly. Cooling Castle and its environs wore an air of prosperity. The harvest had been good. The pantries, larders, and breweries were full to bursting with winter stores, and the crofters and serfs seemed happy enough. Neither had there been any report of disaster or difficulty from John's holdings in Hereford—he'd been in a fine mood when he'd set off that morning to meet a parchment maker in London. That left only one thing.

The Lollard enterprise was not going well.

Sometimes she wished she'd never involved her husband in Cooling Castle's troubles with the archbishop. Her lands had been placed under interdiction for harboring Lollard priests before she and John were married, a censure that had not bothered her overmuch, though she'd mouthed appropriate—if insincere—words of penance at the time, buying time and space to practice her faith in secret as she wished. She held no belief in the pope's power to deny or grant the right to the Holy Eucharist. That was a right granted by God. Neither pope, nor priest, nor bishop could deprive her of that grace which her Savior had bestowed upon her freely. The English Bible told her that.

"It doesn't matter, husband. Just ignore it," she had said when she first explained the interdiction to him.

He'd looked at her with alarm, the expression on his face destroying the afterglow of their lovemaking, nestled as they were like two spoons in the small bed made for one. They had been on the second day of their honeymoon in the little cottage in Wales. He'd taken her there to the Olchon Valley to show her the place where he'd won preferment with the prince for fighting the Welsh border lords. To show her the place too where he'd been converted from the Roman way of bought indulgences and forced pilgrimages, to show her the place where he'd been baptized in the pool beneath the waterfall that nestled in a hidden wooded glen much like the one he'd re-created on the grounds of Cooling Castle.

"It matters to the simple folk who will look to me, their lord, for protection," he had said indignantly. "Each time they are denied the Eucharist because of their attachment to Cobham lands they think they are going to hell."

"Then provide them a Lollard priest to give communion. That's what I have always done. That satisfies them. Some of them, more every day, see it as we do anyway. When enough of them see it thus, it will cease to matter at all."

His eyes had flashed with a determination that frightened her. "And what of the others? It is an abomination for them to live in fear that some dissolute Roman priest can deny their rights to heaven because he does not prefer the language in which their masters pray. Or worse, because they do not have the price of a prayer."

He had waved his arms about angrily, nearly smashing a pitcher on the table beside their bed. It was filled with daffodils and pussy willows. They had been married in the spring, and every spring when she saw the swelling of the first soft gray-green buds she was taken back to the bliss of that brief honeymoon in the verdant Welsh valley. Bliss that was soon to be broken with worry, for John had returned with her to Cooling Castle and begun his campaign for the Lollard cause as diligently as he had once conducted his military campaigns for Prince Harry. The prince had rewarded him for his military service by allowing him to marry into a noble house. He would not likely reward him for this campaign.

From below her chamber now she heard his grumbled response to the gatekeeper's greeting, and, smoothing her linen cap and pinching her cheeks, she rushed down to greet him. She met him at the door and planted a kiss on his lips.

"Good e'en, husband. I'm glad you're home," she said, taking him by the hand, leading him into the solar. "The days are growing shorter, and when the sun goes down a man should be by his own hearth."

"Aye, and right welcome it is," he said, slumping onto the settle closest to the hearth. But there was no teasing, no flirtation, in the tone with which he greeted her.

She helped him off with his surcoat, tugged at his boots to remove them, then handed him a cup of honeyed mead she'd kept warming on the hearth for his return. These were all things his chamberlain could be doing, but he preferred his wife to do them for him. She didn't mind. It was little enough to act the role of servant if it made him happy. She stood behind him, massaging the road from his shoulders.

"Did the parchment maker give you a good price?"

"Nay. The cost, I fear, is exorbitant." This answer came after some hesitation.

"Then we will just go elsewhere. Surely he's not the only parchment supplier," she said, running her thumb up his backbone into his neck.

He rolled his head, accepting the pressure of her thumb against tendon and bone. "But he's the one I was counting on," he said flatly.

There was something in his tone that told her they were talking about more than the simple cost of parchment. Beneath her kneading fingers, the muscles of his shoulders remained knotted and tense. She bit back more probing questions. Now was not the time.

"Did you stop for supper?" she asked.

"I had a bite at the pub where I met Master Fisher. It'll suffice."

When did a bite ever suffice her bear of a man? And what had this Master Fisher done to put her husband in such an ill humor? She removed his cap and ran her fingers through his thinning hair, then bent and kissed the top of his head.

"Don't worry, John. Whatever you decide, it will be right. About the parchment maker, I mean. Unless there's something else you want to tell me.

Something else that weighs heavy on you—besides the price of parchment."

He pulled her around and into his lap. But still no teasing, no flirting. He touched her face, running his forefinger over her nose and her chin.

"Nay, my love. There's nothing else. It's just the cost, that's all." He lifted his hand to the back of his neck, his big hand covering hers. "I may have to reconsider the cost."

"Whatever it is, we will pay the cost together," she said, knowing that they were not speaking about the cost of parchment.

"That's my greatest fear," he said. And he kissed her, a long, lingering kiss filled with more tenderness than passion. Then he pushed her gently from his lap.

"Come. Let's to bed. After such a day as this, I've a need to sleep under a feather counterpane with my wife's warm body to chase away the chill. Riding home, I felt the nip of winter at my heels. I fear the summer has been put to rout."

TWENTY

Thou shalt not suffer a witch to live.
—EXODUS 22:18

Gabriel inhaled deeply, filling his lungs with the cold morning air. Bracing. The open sewers running at the edge of the cobblestones had been washed clean by last night's rain. A light breeze fluttered the leaves piled by the dawn sweepers at the corner of the square, scattering them like silver pennies at his feet. A glorious day.

He could not account logically for this feeling of exhilaration. He had certainly not slept well. After a night of restless tossing, thinking about the bookseller and her child sleeping beneath the same roof, he'd risen from an uncomfortable bed—a bed that had heretofore been quite satisfactory—and taken himself out into the early morning sunshine, only to find he had never felt so alive in his life. Or so awake. If he could freeze time here he would. Now. No. Not here in the sunlit square. But last night in the soft candlelight of that intimate space where for the first time in his adult life he felt his soul enlivened by the presence of a woman.

He should be on his way to Paris to finish the archbishop's business— should have already been to Paris. Completed his inquiry and returned to England to report to Arundel what damaging evidence he'd found against

Lord Cobham. So far he'd found none. But even if Gabriel had to go back empty-handed, he'd decided he would not present evidence gained from Anna Bookman. He would not implicate her in the conspiracy to commit heresy. He would take the translation she made for him, warn her against making it for others, and then burn it. Last night he'd frightened her with his talk of heresy. He'd seen it in her eyes. He just hoped he'd frightened her enough so that she would not go about spouting such Lollard nonsense.

He surveyed the sun-polished plaza, shading his eyes with his hand on his forehead, trying to remember. Yes. There it was. Just down the narrow winding street leading to Rue de Vesle. An exquisitely carved woodworker's sign creaked on its hinge next to the barber's blood-striped pole, and the door was open. If he hurried, he could be back at the little town house before Anna left. It was early yet. Her stall was empty still. The square was almost empty too, except for a few grocers heaping great piles of produce in their stands and some stragglers going to mass at Notre Dame. The sight of them pricked at his conscience—on waking, his first thought had not been of saying the Divine Office but of this errand. It seemed he'd discarded his priest's identity with his priestly garb. But he promised himself that he would confess the neglect and do his penance later.

As he entered the woodworker's shop, Gabriel ducked under the giant squared log that served as lintel, then hesitated as his eyes adjusted to the dim light. The shop smelled of fresh pine resin and the floor beneath his leather slippers was already thick with the morning's woodshavings. The woodcarver, an older man wearing a thick leather apron, looked up from the apprentice he was instructing in the use of the lathe and greeted his customer with a grunt.

"I need a special kind of wheelbarrow. A wagon small enough for a child of about six to ride in." Gabriel said this in his deliberate French, gesturing with his hands just what size and shape the wagon should take.

"*Oui, oui.*" The woodcarver fumbled in the pocket of his apron for a bit of charcoal and a scrap of paper and sketched a miniature version of a two-wheeled dray cart.

"*Quatre roues petites,*" Gabriel countered, pointing to the wheels and indicating with space between his hands that the cart should be lower to the ground and the four wheels, instead of two, smaller.

He pointed to the handle and, unable to remember the word for rudder, indicated that the handle should be made so that it could be pulled by Anna or folded back over the cart and attached to the front wheels so that Little Bek could—Gabriel was sure he could learn—steer himself along with one hand while pushing with the other. The boy's limbs were weak from misuse, but with use the muscles in his back and arms would thicken. He certainly had strength enough and energy the way he flailed about with his arms, beating at whatever they encountered. But he had some control too. Gabriel had noticed that he did not beat at Anna's chest when he sat in her lap. He was as still as a child half his size would be when coddled by his mother. An intelligence was locked inside the boy's head. He was sure of it. An intelligence that might be freed with care and diligence.

The woodworker scratched his head in consternation.

"*S'il vous plaît,*" Gabriel said, snatching the paper from the old man and proceeding to sketch out the design himself.

The woodworker left off scratching his head and squinted his eyes. "*Oui. Je vois,*" he said. "*Après-demain.*"

Day after tomorrow.

"*Après-demain,*" Gabriel repeated. "*Merci.*"

It wasn't until after he'd left the woodworker's shop that Gabriel remembered. He hadn't even asked the cost. But blast the cost. After all, the wagon was an act of charity for an afflicted child. God had placed that child in his path.

And what of Anna Bookman, Friar Gabriel? Did God place her in your path as well? To save her from heresy? Or maybe to test your resolve? But Gabriel had determined, in spite of his talk with Father Francis, that he would not be like too many of his brothers. He would not succumb to the devil's fleshpot temptations. He had taken a sacred vow. He meant to keep it. He had resisted others. There had been the woman on the boat from England who flirted with him, and the women of Rheims who sidled glances toward his scarlet merchant's robes. Anna Bookman was a beautiful woman. But Rheims was full of beautiful women. No. If God had placed Anna Bookman in his path, he was sure it was to save her from the heretical path she'd chosen. He might not be able to change her theology, but he could at least protect her from a heretic's fire. For the sake of her child if no other.

⚜

Anna was just thinking about packing up her merchandise and going home to her new lodgings when she heard the commotion, shouts and yelps coming from the general direction of the river. She'd had only one customer since her arrival at midmorning. The market was almost deserted. The grocers who always came early and left early had long ago departed. The cathedral shadow was creeping onto the second mark past the apex on the sundial. But in spite of the slow business Anna had lingered, hoping that VanCleve would come by her stall. She was going to tell him that Little Bek was not her son, that she only cared for him for one of the pilgrims who would be leaving soon. She'd lain awake long after he'd gone, thinking how to tell him. It was simple and it was the truth.

The shouts came from far away, in the direction of Mars Gate, the old Roman ruin where on pretty afternoons children played tag. Anna squinted into the distance. Only a few dead leaves played tag there now, chased by the same light wind that sent a shiver up the sleeves of her thin cloak. In the heat of August her heavy wool cloak had not seemed worthy of its weight, and so she had left it behind in Prague with the rest of her possessions. But she would not think of that now. She thought instead of the little room in Rue de Saint Luc—her room now—with its welcoming brazier. If she left right away, there would still be bright daylight pouring through the window, enough light to translate more of VanCleve's English Gospel—if he still wanted it. If he did not, well, there would be another buyer.

On the way she would stop by the fuller's shop. She remembered passing it down by the Vesle River when she'd first got to town, the day she'd gone to Abbey Saint Remi to ask if the abbot needed the work of an extra scribe. It was what her grandfather would have done. But the prior had sent her away with a scowl, telling her that the abbey's work was done by the monks in the scriptorium.

The trip had not been wasted, however. She'd found a shop close by the scriptorium that sold inexpensive parchment and papers, the very papers she'd used that night to forge her guild license. And she'd found something else besides—a fuller's shop. It was only about half a mile or so beyond the cathedral near Rue de Vesle. She was sure to find a cheap but respectable cloak left by some pilgrim to be sheared and brushed for cleaning and never redeemed. The fuller would sell it to her cheap. It might not have a pretty fur-lined hood or be the quality that she was—had been—accustomed to, but it would keep her warm during the winter, and she would not have to rob her small horde of traveling money.

But as Anna turned down Rue de Vesle, she couldn't see the storefronts for the people. This was where all the shouting was coming from. A crowd had gathered by the banks of the river, a crowd of excited people. From the clamor of voices, a crowd of angry people.

Anna looked about for the entrance to the fuller's shop, but all the shop entrances were obscured. She recognized this mob. She had seen its ugly face before, heard its angry catcalls. This was a scene all too familiar. This was a scene to be avoided.

Beyond the knot of people on its bank, the Vesle River snaked tranquilly into the vine-clad hills. The sun sparked its waters, just as the sun had sparked the waters of the Vltava River, where Anna had first encountered such a crowd as this. An image of Martin's head impaled against a blue sky flashed before her eyelids. She blinked it away, determined to run back to the safety of her little chamber in Rue de Saint Luc, oblivious now of her errand. But her legs, as though they operated independently of her will, carried her instead toward the crowd of people.

Closer.

Close.

Onto the verge of the crowd that sucked at her, drawing her into its heart. The smell of garlicky breath and sweat stifled her.

Behind her a man's voice shouted in her ear. *"C'est une vieille sorcière."*

The crowd took up the chant. *"Sorcière. Sorcière."* Witch. Witch.

All around her, upraised fists pumped the air, hot breath on her neck, on her face. Anna could not breathe amid so much furor and anger. She could not breathe so close to the river.

"Faites flotter la sorcière!" Float the witch. *"Faites flotter la sorcière!"*

She pushed on through the chanting, pulsing crowd until somehow she gained the cleared space between the mob and the riverbank. Two big men, broad shouldered and meanly dressed, laborers by the look of them, shoved an old woman between them as they wound a hemp cord around her body, binding her arms to her sides. Others in the crowd, men, women, even some children, pelted her with handfuls of mud.

The chants grew even louder, faster, more demanding. A chorus. *"Le fleuve. Le fleuve!"* The river! The river!

Anna could not see the woman's face, but the brightly clad figure, the kerchief on her straggled gray hair, the bangles in her ears: all were achingly familiar.

Anna moved closer until the mob was in front of her, the river behind her, a circumstance that frightened her almost as much as the flash of recognition.

Jetta stood between the two men, staring into the middle distance, mumbling to the voices in her head, apparently oblivious to the threatening voices all around her. And clutching at Jetta's skirt was Little Bek, shrieking in his high, shrill tones.

A man in the crowd pointed to Little Bek and yelled, *"Il est le familier de son diable."*

Little Bek! A devil's familiar! Never was there a human being with less devil in him!

Anna ran forward, turned to face the crowd, shouting, *"Non, non, "* as she tried to remember the French words to tell them, to say something, anything, to make them understand that the woman they thought was a witch was just a harmless old woman. Little Bek spotted Anna rushing toward them and turned his cries to the more familiar, yet still terror-laden, "An na, An na."

Anna pulled him away, wiping mud from his face. Jetta was mumbling to herself the way she sometimes did, harmless gibberish, some trick her mind played on her. The more she mumbled, the more inflamed the crowd became.

"No. No," Anna cried, forgetting the French. "She's no witch. She's a Christian. Like you. She's just a Christian pilgrim! Jetta, show them. Say the Lord's Prayer for them! Say the *Paternoster*. Say it in Latin."

But Jetta just kept on mumbling the same gibberish as though she didn't hear, as though Anna were not even there.

"Faites flotter la sorcière! Jetez les trois dans le fleuve."

All three? They were going to throw them all in!

Hush, Anna. Save the child, she scolded herself, and reached down to clutch him to her. Scanning the crowd for some friendly face, some avenue of escape, she spied the sought-after fuller's shop, its open door abandoned. Holding on to Little Bek, she inched toward it.

Anna would remember later that her eye had registered what her mind did not. If her mind had registered VanCleve's presence standing apart from the crowd, she would have called out to him for help. But it did not, and she did not. All her senses were fastened on Jetta and clinging to Little Bek, stroking his head to calm him, trying to stay calm enough to think as the two men hoisted Jetta into the air. They lifted the old woman, still mumbling to herself, and hurled her like a log headfirst into the river.

The crowd sucked air as the old woman's body twisted in the air like a diving gull, then broke the surface of the water.

She sank like a stone into the frigid November water.

The crowd held its collective breath, waiting to see if a witch would float or an innocent woman would drown. They are hoping for the witch, Anna thought. That way their drama will be extended. She heard her own voice calling out Jetta's name, Jetta who had saved her from the river.

The river smelled of death, of the dank logs washed up on its bank and piles of rotting debris. This was mixed with the pungent aroma of her fear.

Seconds passed. Hours.

Anna prayed that by some miracle Jetta would survive, that God would send down an angel to the drowning woman as he had sent Jetta to her. Don't let it be me, she prayed, remembering the weight of the water on her skin, the way it had sealed her breath inside her body. Her cowardice shamed her. She peeled Little Bek from her skirts and moved closer to the river's edge.

With the others in the crowd she watched the unbroken surface of the water.

Not a ripple stirred it.

Behind her now was only one voice and it rose in a high, sweet hymn, marred with trembling: "An na. An na. An na."

Anna took a step forward.

"A shame." The man closest to Anna, one of the men who had thrown the old woman in, shrugged and mumbled, "Don't go after her. If she was innocent, so are you." Arms reached out to hold her back—the same arms that had hurled Jetta into the Vesle. "The current is swift and the water freezing. You'll drown too. It is the will of God."

The same voices who only moments ago had shouted "witch, witch," burdened now with concern lest they compound the guilt of their wrongful prosecution. Trial by ordeal. Trial by the devil, not of the devil.

Anna struggled against the arms, straining to see Jetta come to the surface, but she never emerged. Not once. Proof of innocence, innocence that awarded her death by water instead of fire.

Her mind only dully registered the man standing downstream, apart from the crowd, as he stripped to his braies, leaving his scarlet tunic and cloak behind him in a pile on the bank. Her mind jolted with recognition only when he leaped into the frigid current.

VanCleve!

Her heart stopped beating at the shock of the cold water against his skin.

He swam toward the center of the river.

Her muscles tightened as his strained against the current.

His blond head disappeared beneath the water once, twice, three times, and her breath froze in her chest. An eternity passed. Airless. Empty.

The surface of the water broke. VanCleve reemerged, this time dragging something with him. She breathed again, then started to run downriver to meet him, her feet sliding in mud, catching, sliding again. Her heart pounded, threatening the bars of its bone cage. Short, ragged breaths choked in her throat.

VanCleve struggled toward the shore, dragging Jetta behind him. Anna was close enough now to see him start to pull the body from the water onto the bank. It was as limp as if it had no bones within it. And still. The only movement was the water that streamed from the fringes of Jetta's shawl and from the long gray hair trailing to the hard ground.

"An na, An na," the high sweet voice behind her purer now, calm. She glanced behind her to see that the child was all right. When she looked back, VanCleve was still struggling to free his burden from the river. It was as though the river grasped at her with its clutching fingers, reluctant to give her up.

One by one the crowd drifted away until there was no one left to help the merchant from Flanders pull the dead woman's body from the river. Nobody except Anna. No angel had come this time; the river had claimed the life it was owed.

~ ~

Anna cried that night. She cried for the first time in a long time. After she'd sent VanCleve to the Romani camp. After Bera had come to claim the body. After she'd bathed and fed Little Bek and put him in her own bed to sleep. Sleeping beneath the feather counterpane of Anna's bed, he looked like an angel with his blond hair and pale lashes, long and shiny against his milk-white cheek.

He had clung to her when Bera came to take Jetta's body away, and she had not the heart to send him back to the camp. Only she and Jetta had ever cared for the child. To the others he was *gadje*. He was *mahrime*. So much innocence in the world. So much pain.

But that was not when the tears came down.

"Who are those people?" VanCleve had asked when he returned from the camp with Bera, after the Gypsies took Jetta's body away on a stretcher contrived of saplings and silk cloth. A dozen or so mourners, the *familia*, both men and women from the camp, followed behind, honoring the dead with loud lamentations and a great show of mourning lest the deceased come back to haunt them for some slight of grief.

"They are my friends," Anna had said simply. And then she had started to cry.

The tears began with a trickle and soon became a torrent. It was as though the rivers of the Vesle and the Vltava had sprung a fountain inside her.

"Hush, you'll make yourself sick," VanCleve had said. But still she could not stop.

He had wrapped her in his arms and quietly led her from the room where the sleeping child lay, so she would not wake him with her sobs. He'd taken her to his room and they'd sat together on his bed until darkness came. He did not get up to light a candle but held her cradled in his arms as the river inside her overflowed its banks, else she would surely have fallen apart and floated away like bits of flotsam on a current.

He did not try to stop her crying, only held her, a kind of consternation on his face that she should mourn the passing of such strangeness.

"She was a good, kind woman. She didn't traffic with the devil. She only told fortunes to make a living. There were always *Christians* enough to hear her silly divinations." But the words erupted in little gasps and choked her.

VanCleve gave her a cup of wine, warmed and spiced with cloves and valerian. "This will help to calm you," he said.

She drank the wine and, exhausted, laid her head on his chest and closed her eyes.

She felt the touch of his lips on the top of her head, and she was a child again, sick with a fever, coddled in the cradle of Dědeček's arms.

⁓ ⁂ ⁔

Sometime during the night Anna woke from her troubled sleep, startled at first, not knowing where she was. They lay together now, on VanCleve's narrow bed, her head resting in the crook of his arm, his hand beneath her shirt. His breath, warm and moist against her neck, whispered her name. A three-quarter moon sweat a sheen of light across his bed—a bed only big enough for one—picking out the outline of his body beneath the coverlet. His hand gently caressed her breast.

I should stop him, she thought. *He is not my husband.* But she did not. Her head was thick with the fog of grief and wine. She could not will her arms to push him away. The protest she should have made died on her lips, and came out in a sigh.

"Anna," he said, "Anna," his breath against her throat. There was such need, such urgency in his voice. She loved the sound of her name on his lips, filled with his breath. His hands tugged urgently, pushing at her skirt, bunching it around her. He shifted his body slightly, gently, moving his body against hers, caressing her, covering her throat with his kisses. She had thought her body surely depleted of all moisture by her tears, as dry as a husk.

She had thought wrong.

She closed her eyes, giving in to the heat and fog of her mind, waiting as though her spirit watched her body's betrayal from a distance. Then she felt a sudden shifting of his weight, a stirring of the air around her, and where there had been warmth, there was now an absence of warmth. She opened her eyes to look at him.

He sat on the side of the bed, holding his head in his hands. She shivered and tried to say his name, to call him back. When he did not respond, her arm reached out, independent of her will, to pull back the warmth of his body.

"Shh, Anna, go back to sleep." His voice was low, almost gruff. He smoothed her skirts and covered her with a blanket. She closed her eyes.

She woke at first light to see VanCleve sleeping in the chair beside the bed. The gray dawn made his face look haggard and wan. She got up and tiptoed gingerly from the room, so as not to disturb him or the throbbing in her head. She wondered as she went if she had dreamed he lay beside her in some wine-induced, fevered dream. Her face grew hot at the very thought of it. She felt again his breath upon her neck, and she was sure it was more memory than dream.

— ❦ —

"You are a good man, VanCleve," Anna said when he brought the little wagon.

They both knew she was talking about something besides his charity for the child. And then she added, to lighten the moment, "For a papist," laughing as she said it to mitigate the criticism.

He did not laugh, did not even smile. "Because I did not debauch a woman drunk with grief and wine does not make me a good man." His gaze did not meet hers but settled upon the child as he bent to lift him into the wagon.

"And what about the fact that you risked your life to save an old woman and—" She pointed to the boy, who was laughing as he rocked back and forth inside the wagon, moving it first forward then back, first forward then back, with the motion of his body. "You are a good man because your heart is good. 'Suffer the little children.' "

"Do you quote English Scripture for every occasion?" he asked, rancor creeping into his tone.

"Would it be more true, more comforting to me and less discomforting to you, if I quoted it in Latin?"

"Indeed it would."

She disliked the frown on his face. "Why do you not like being called a good man?"

"You don't know how close I came to not being a good man, Anna."

It was her turn to avert her gaze. She felt the heat creeping up her neck. "Do you think he can learn to ride it?" Anna asked, pointing to the wagon.

"I do." Was that a sigh of relief that she had changed the subject? "If God wills it," he said.

"And why would a loving God not will it? Why would He not want his children to be happy?"

"Why not indeed?" he said. But she had the feeling he was talking about something else entirely.

Anna put Little Bek to bed early. He was worn out from playing with his new wagon, and since he had not yet mastered it, he had more than a few bruises from bumping into things. She was worn out too and her first thought was to decline when VanCleve showed up at her door with a meat pie and cider.

"Bek's already asleep," she whispered.

"Then come to my chamber."

"I don't know if that's a good idea—"

"You need to eat. I have to eat. We might as well eat together. We need to talk about how you can keep yourself and your child safe."

"No wine this time?"

"No wine, just cider." He held up the jug as proof.

"We'll leave your chamber door open?"

"We shall leave my chamber door open so that all the world can see how innocent is our discourse."

They were arguing over the doctrine of transubstantiation—hers the heretic's assertion that the bread and wine were only symbolic, not the literal blood, not the literal body of Christ—when her hand flew angrily into the air and collided with his. She was so close he could smell her hair. The same exotic fragrance he'd come to associate with her, the scent of jasmine flowers. The smell of it, the touch of her skin against his, the passion in her voice, all overwhelmed his senses, rendering his mind inadequate. He could not counter her reasoned argument. He could no longer think. He could only feel.

What an arrogant, pride-filled fool he had been to think he could resist such a temptation. He should ask her to leave. And that he could not bear to do. For if she left, she would take the world with her.

He kissed her.

When she did not resist, he reached with one hand to unlace her bodice. With the other he closed the door.

The plump little landlord, upon hearing the abrupt cessation of their strident voices, peeked into the hall. He noticed the closed door and gave a little shrug before returning to his game of chess. Soon enough they'll move in together, he thought, and I'll have another room to rent. But the thought of the couple together made him smile. He'd known from the first time he'd seen them together that it was inevitable. They belonged together. It was as it should be.

❧

Anna felt one sudden stab of pain, a shock, until she remembered. Gilbert's book, *The Sickness of Women*, had said the first time would hurt and there would be blood. The landlord would see it when he changed the linens. He would know what VanCleve—what they—had done. She felt her face burning with shame. *You should have stopped him, Anna. You should have stopped him. You should have left when he kissed you.* And then he said her name again, but this time it sounded like a prayer and carried so much sadness in it.

He rolled onto his side, still close, pinning her against the wall. He whispered her name again, a mere sigh of breath against her cheek. A sting of burning tears pricked her eyelids. What would she say to him now? How could she look into his eyes and see the reflection of her shame? She could not even plead drunkenness for her sluttish behavior. She could not plead that he had taken advantage of her. She had not even resisted him!

When she heard him snoring—rhythmic, gentle snores—she thought to push him from her, but that would only wake him, and she would have to confront her embarrassment. The solidness of his body pinning hers against the wall was also oddly comforting, she thought as she lay there wondering what she should do.

Is this the way it would have been with Martin? she wondered, and felt a wash of guilt as though she had betrayed him somehow. And not just with her body. For she felt more bonded to this man she hardly knew than she'd ever felt with Martin. *But I do know him*, she thought. *I know his soul because I've seen his kindness. I've watched him with Little Bek. I watched him risk his life for Jetta.*

She looked at his body beside her, memorizing the line of his shoulders, his waist, his hips. His hair looked more silver than gold in the moonlight, and at the crown there was a spot, a perfect circle, where the hair was shorter than the rest, hardly more than stubble. She wondered about that idly. She would ask him when he woke. *How can he be lying here beside me, naked? How did this come to be!*

She held her breath, unconsciously matching it to her lover's. Her lover. She, an unmarried woman, had taken a lover. A grievous sin. She heard some sound from outside, the call of a nightbird? Or Little Bek, awake and frightened. She listened again. No, it was only an owl.

A bad omen, Jetta would have said. Jetta. She closed her eyes, waiting for the tears to come again. None came.

She listened again, hoping she would not have to go to the sleeping child, knowing that she would if he called out to her. But the only sound she heard was VanCleve's gentle snoring, a kind of lullaby.

When Anna awoke again, the sun was pouring through the open window and she was alone in VanCleve's bed. She got carefully out of bed and pulled back the coverlet. A small red stain, hardly bigger than a teardrop, lay on the sheet. She pulled her chemise around to inspect the back of it—a larger spot there, already dried and stiff.

Here was the proof that she was no longer a maid. Proof that might be required from any future husband, proof too that she was at last a woman, no longer a maid—a woman heavy with regret.

How could she have given her maidenhead away so casually? And to a man she hardly knew! Maybe even a man with a wife. A man with children. Foolish, stupid girl. She hoped desperately that VanCleve did not return before she could clean herself up. Embarrassing enough to face him at all—at least she should be dressed. She bolted the door, took off the soiled chemise, and rolled it into a ball. Good. There was fresh water in the bowl and more in the bucket on the floor beside it.

She wet a rag and ran it quickly, more briskly than warranted, over her face and body—it smelled of the tiny bits of lavender floating on the surface—then employed it between her legs. Carefully at first—*why, Anna? That which should be unbroken has already been broken*—then more thoroughly, squeezing the water up inside, washing away what she could of the life force that had spilled inside her.

What had Gilbert's book said about the first time? Wasn't it harder to conceive the first time? Please, God, let it be so.

Wetting the rag again, she dabbed at the small stain on the sheet, widening it, lightening the evidence of her spoiled maidenhead to the brownish tinge of spilled ale.

She poured the dirty water from the basin into the chamber pot beneath the bed, ignoring her own full bladder, anxious to leave before VanCleve returned. When next she saw him, she wanted it to be under more commonplace circumstances and more neutral territory. Perhaps he had guessed that. Or maybe he regretted what had passed between them too and was already confessing his sin to a priest. At the very least fornication. Or, God forbid, even adultery. No. She could not think that. He'd said he was not married. But what if he had lied? Was she an adultress if she didn't know he was married? The very thought of VanCleve in a confessional, her name forming on his lips—the same lips that had whispered her name last night, breathing it into her hair, into her neck—made her feel ill. Soiled, that the priest should hear her name and envision them together. *God saw you, Anna*. But he would understand. He would forgive. The priest would not understand and he could not forgive. And yet VanCleve would think he left his sin behind him in the confessional. She almost envied him that.

As she stepped into the hallway, she listened for the sound of Little Bek. He would be awake now and wanting her to help him onto the chamber pot. Another stick of guilt heaped upon her already heavy bundle. It bothered him when he soiled himself.

By Heaven and All the Saints! How her life had changed in the blink of an eye. Two short days ago she had been a maid—albeit on her way to spinsterhood and her with no sibling's hearth on which to spin—but she'd only had to worry about herself. Now, she was maid no longer, but a fallen woman with a child to care for, and no ordinary child either. But what else could she have done? God had given her the child. Given him to her because with Jetta's death there was no one else to care for him. Truly, even when Jetta was alive, it had been Anna who cared for the boy most. She knew when the Romani moved on they would abandon the boy in Rheims, where he would join the crowd of beggars—leperous, filthy cripples and divers wounded souls—who languished at the alms gate of the priory, howling their misery at passersby.

She paused at the door, listening. No whimper. Not even the restless movement of his limbs brushing against the bed, the sound she'd become so used to she no longer heard. "Little Bek," she called softly, opening the door.

The sunlight filled the pretty little chamber with warm light, cutting across her empty bed. She should have known not to leave him on the bed, should have known he'd fall off. "Where are you, Little Bek? Answer me. This is not a game."

A quick inspection of the room showed his pallet empty and the floor as well. A half-empty cup of milk and the remnants of a washing-up were in the bowl on the stand in the corner. There was only one possible answer. The child had set up a great clamor and the landlord had come to his aid, maybe even taken him out into the garden. A glance out the window showed only a lone scarlet leaf, a last hanger-on of autumn, floating down onto a carpet of brown. Well, one thing was sure. He hadn't got up and walked out by himself, and surely he was with a kind soul. Who else would trouble with such a child? Unless the angel Gabriel had come down and spirited him away. But she could not go looking for him until she took care of her own nature's call and found a clean chemise.

She was fumbling with the ribbons on her shirt when she heard a commotion outside. Little Bek's high voice squealing in delight. She whirled around as the door opened and there stood VanCleve, bearing the child upon his shoulders, stooping like a clown to try to enter the low lintel without bumping the squealing child off.

"I hope you don't mind, Anna," he said with a big wide grin, as though it were the most natural thing in the world, as though last night had never been, as though her world had not been turned upside down. "But you were still asleep. And Bek needed to make water. So I took him outside and showed him how to be a boy."

"Boy!" Little Bek's big head bobbed on his slender neck affirmatively. "Boy!"

"Now, let's go see if we can find some food. I'm starved," VanCleve said.

TWENTY-ONE

> *. . . a monk outside his discipline and rule*
> *is like a fish outside his pool.*
> —GEOFFREY CHAUCER, PROLOGUE TO
> *THE CANTERBURY TALES*

or Anna those first days after Jetta's death wore the heavy twilight color of pain and grief—and guilt. So much guilt. Why had she hesitated at the river's edge? Why had she not gone into the water to repay the debt she owed? For Little Bek, she told herself. She did it for Little Bek. But it lacked the ring of truth. Anna knew she hesitated because she was afraid. Her craven soul had remembered the weight of the water and turned from it.

And then there was the other. She had promised herself it would not happen again. Just because one slips into the mud doesn't mean one must wallow in it. Had VanCleve not been always underfoot she might have kept that promise. But she could not deny Little Bek VanCleve's company when the boy delighted in it so. Could she?

The time Anna spent with VanCleve was opiate to her pain and balm to her spirit. His smile, his touch, replaced sorrow with gladness and pain with joy. At first, she'd made it a condition of their time together that there should be no more passion between them, told him it was the influence of her grief, that she was not that kind of woman. He'd agreed and begged her pardon for taking advantage of their shared grief, for indeed he did seem deeply troubled by the injustice of Jetta's death even though he hadn't known her.

But all of Anna's senses were heightened in VanCleve's presence. Even the hues of autumn set her senses quivering; the golden brown and dusty reds, like spices freshly sealed in a glass jar, waiting to unleash their heady scent. Whenever her mind summoned his face, his voice, a whirlwind danced inside her, quickening her beating heart and stealing her breath away.

Her resolve tore easily. It had only taken three days and hers had been the first move. She had felt wanton and ashamed as she reached for his hand and raised the smooth palm to her lips, the palm that had just handed the blue stone to the laughing child, but she could not stop herself. She kissed the palm. He tried to withdraw his hand, his frustration evident, his glance darting at the boy, but she did not stop until she'd brushed her lips against each fingertip. And that night, after Bek had gone to sleep, Anna had appeared at VanCleve's door.

"No, Anna. It's best if we are not alone. I—"

I love him. How can this be wrong? she thought as she stopped his protest with her mouth. She was to ask that same question of herself many times. But he only spoke of love in the heat of passion and never of marriage—and she never asked. He was always careful to withdraw before he spilled his seed inside her. For that she was grateful.

How could this be the same girl who'd made poor dead Martin wait when he'd spoken to her of love, begged for marriage? But it wasn't. That girl had died with Dědeček and Martin.

Anna knew nothing of VanCleve's past and longed to know, but was afraid to know. Yet she knew enough to love him. He had stood on the bank like a hero from romantic courtly legend to save Jetta. He had taken the afflicted child to his bosom as though he were a much sought-after lost lamb, laughing with each new thing the boy learned, even rigging crutches for him out of sturdy sticks, crossed and padded. The boy had actually learned to drag himself from bed to wagon—the wagon that VanCleve had also provided, making Anne's life much easier, and more melodic. For Little Bek sang incessantly.

Anna wondered at the complexity of tones that came from the child's mouth. And sometimes there were words. The boy almost never spoke, but

Anna heard meaning in the gibberish he sang in his own language: it was a mixture of Roma, and Bohemian, and English sounds all melded together, yet she could understand him.

"Anna, interpret. Tell me what the whelp is saying. He's too smart for me. I can't understand this language he makes up in his head." VanCleve would wink and Little Bek would grin, showing he had understood every word.

Only once did she and VanCleve argue after they lay together. Only once—when Anna spoke about her grief for Jetta. They were in their leaf-strewn bit of garden, playing in the autumn sunshine. She was standing over him as he knelt beside Little Bek, teaching him how to maneuver his new wagon. "I wish Jetta were here to see how he progresses," she said, and suddenly the tears she'd thought had gone away welled up.

VanCleve stood up and wrapped her in his arms, wiped her cheek with his silken cuff. "We will buy an indulgence for her soul."

Choking on her tears, she only shook her head in protest.

"I'll pay," he said. He stroked her hair, smoothing its wildness.

"No. No indulgence." She sniffed. "You know I—"

He waved her objection aside with an abrupt gesture and a quick shake of his head. "I have money to pay for remittance of her sins. You should do this for your friend."

"No! I will not pay some pope's lackey to do that which we can do ourselves. And you will not pay either."

She felt his body grow rigid with tension. He removed his arms from around her. When she looked up at him, his face had set into the same hard lines she'd seen when they had first argued about the English Bible. She'd not seen that look again till now. Yet she could not let his disapproval stop her. "If there's any praying to be done for Jetta's soul, I shall do it myself! I don't need some money-grubbing priest. I am surprised you would suggest it. I would have thought the good people of Flanders more enlightened than that."

His face flushed dark and anger sparked in his eyes, but he made no rejoinder, just gave Little Bek's wagon a push. "Turn the handle! Turn the handle!"

When Little Bek didn't turn the handle, the wagon thudded against a tree. Little Bek squealed and VanCleve reached out to pull it back, moving the handle to show the child. "Anna, there's—"

"I'm sorry," she said. "That sounded insulting. I know you are devout. My tongue is too loose sometimes, but I was always encouraged to speak my mind. I've been told that is not always a desirable trait in a woman." She tried to laugh to lighten the mood.

He was kneeling now beside the boy in the wagon, his back to her. "We've had this discussion before, Anna, remember. These are dangerous times for loose tongues," he said. "Be more careful of what you say and to whom you say it."

The harshness of his tone unsettled her. It was almost as though Van-Cleve had disappeared and in his place some austere stranger had appeared. It was her fault. She had offended him personally by suggesting he was ignorant. She bent to kiss the top of his head where the hair had grown out in a fine blond layer, kissed it gently so as not to disturb the wound for which he said he'd shaved the spot, though she saw no sign of a scar.

"Let's not quarrel over such silliness as pardoners and priests," she said. "They have nothing to do with us. You were right to remind me that Jetta is in the hands of a merciful God. It is a glorious day. The landlord is bringing us a picnic. We shall take it here in the garden. These golden days are a gift this late in November. We should enjoy them while we can. You shall play my knight and I shall play your lady." She took his hands and pulled him gently toward her.

"And Little Bek? Who will he be?"

At least he was smiling again.

"Why, he shall be the court musician," she said. "And we will have wine and bread and cheese and celebrate his beautiful singing."

The boy began to sing as though he'd understood every word and was entering into the spirit of play. Anna thought that even the angel Gabriel would have laughed to hear him.

VanCleve did.

⤧⤙

Gabriel opened the door to the confessional, settled his scarlet mercer's robes onto the polished wood of the narrow seat, fumbling clumsily to open the little wooden door. The confessional was a rare experience for him: Brother Francis had always been his confessor, and he'd knelt before him to receive both penance and blessing. As he waited for the door on the other side of the confessional to open, waited for the priest's shadowy profile to show itself, he thought about how reluctantly Anna would have entered that little wooden closet with its smell of human sweat and old wood. How she would scoff at him if she knew.

He could almost hear her voice, its melody strident with indignation. *He is just a black-robed Roman lackey, just a man like any other, she would say. No different from you.* No. No different at all, he'd thought and cringed at the scorn she had heaped upon the Roman clergy. He had bit back his own anger at her profanity, his righteous protest silenced by the shame of his deceit. But he had determined then and there that she would never know Brother Gabriel. She would only know VanCleve.

The door slid open. A silhouette settled on the other side, emitted a phlegmatic cough. He could smell the priest's garlicky breath. A man just like any other. No, not like any other. Like himself, ordained by God, called of God. He must remember that. It had been too easy for Gabriel to pretend that he was like any other man, pretend that he was entitled to the love of a woman, pretend that Anna and Little Bek were the only responsibilities he had in the world. He was in danger of believing his own pretense.

"Father, forgive me, for I have sinned."

He made his confession in Latin, but not confessing all, not confessing that his allegiance was to the pope in Rome and not in Avignon—that bit of Church politics the French priest did not have to know. It was enough to confess his sins. But the priest seemed not as interested in Brother Gabriel's sins of the flesh as in the fact that he was using Church funds to support his dalliance and that Brother Gabriel was neglecting his ecclesiastical duties.

"You're not serving the Church, Father."

Notice he says nothing about serving God, just serving the Church. But that was Anna talking in his head. To serve the Church *is* to serve God. That's what Brother Francis would have said.

The priest lapsed into French, harder for Gabriel to follow, accustomed as he had become to the king's English that he and Anna spoke at home. Gabriel could see the silhouette of his confessor's profile. His double chin quivered whenever he talked. His voice was raspy, not pleasant.

"You're wasting the Church's resources, Brother, on this unholy dalliance. You should be in Paris, fulfilling your bishop's orders. If heretical teachings are being copied you will learn of it in Paris, where the largest guild of scribes and illuminators operates. You will find the proof you seek in Paris—not in Rheims. The people of Rheims are devout." A flutter of the priest's hands as he made the sign of the cross. "Receive your penance."

And then the priest told Gabriel he must not touch "the woman" again. Must leave her immediately. Must spend the night in prayer, praying for forgiveness.

"Abstinence, Brother, is the bread of piety. Celibacy its wine."

There was a rustle of cloth sliding on wood and then the slamming of the little wooden door. Justice dispensed. Grace departed. As easy as that, Gabriel thought. Not easy at all.

Of course he had always known it. Known that at least he would have to leave her for a season. Until he could make arrangements for her to follow. He had it all worked out in his head. He'd lain awake at night watching her sleeping, the moonlight lining the sweep of her lashes against the curve of her cheek, the wild bloom of hair spread across her pillow, his mind spinning a web of intrigue for a half-life together with her.

A small cottage in Kent—no, that was too close to Brother Gabriel. A seaside cottage near the South Downs where she could care for Little Bek and copy her books to supplement the income he would give her. A cottage where VanCleve could visit, a sanctuary where Brother Gabriel never went. An Eden where the serpent never entered.

But the confessor was right. Brother Gabriel had a job to do. He would go to Paris, practice being apart from Anna. The only evidence he had gained was evidence that implicated Anna as a Hussite, but she was not remotely connected to Lord Cobham. Not that he would have betrayed her. He'd sooner betray himself. He was sure to uncover a source in Paris. Oldcastle had to get his copies somewhere.

And Brother Gabriel could perform his penance—at least in spirit. He would not touch her for a while. Brother Gabriel would deny his flesh to atone for VanCleve's sins. Or was it the other way around?

⚜

"He understands what you're saying. He doesn't want you to go."

Van Cleve picked the boy up.

"You're getting positively plump, you know that? You'll be a man soon. Look after Anna for me while I'm gone."

"An na, An na." The child's head wobbled an affirmative. VanCleve set the boy on the floor at his feet, then looked directly at Anna, who was avoiding his gaze.

"I will be back, Anna, your heart should tell you that. A fortnight. No more."

There was a small space between them. Neither attempted to close it.

"The heart sometimes tells the head what it wants to hear," she said.

She looked up at him then, and he could read the uncertainty, the trouble clouding her blue eyes, bunching the fine winged brows into little worried knots. How could VanCleve be expected to perform Brother Gabriel's penance? He leaned toward her, closing the gap between them. He could smell the scent of her, the fragrance of jasmine.

Brother Gabriel be damned. At least VanCleve would carry the taste of her with him.

"Then both your heart and your head can hear this." And he kissed her. But her response was not what it had been. She held something in reserve.

As they broke apart, Little Bek looked from one to the other, then grabbed hold of VanCleve's leg. Anna reached down and gently disengaged the boy's pale, thin fingers. They looked almost boneless, transparent, grasped in Anna's pink ones. Her voice was raspy with unshed tears and her tone with the boy less gentle than usual.

"Let him go," she said to the child.

Little Bek's eyes widened and he started to whimper, but he let go.

"A fortnight, Anna. I promise. Then I'll return and we will talk . . . we will come to some more permanent arrangement."

She said nothing, only nodded as she held open the door of her chamber for him to go. It creaked on its iron hinges, as if the heavy oaken door also protested his leaving. She did not look at him as he walked through it. He turned back, hoping for one last word. Instead she just stood there, waiting, clutching the hand of the child whose large eyes were like wide, opaque pools.

"One more thing, Anna. I don't want the English translation. It is far too dangerous an enterprise. It is a banned text. Do not have it in your possession. Burn what you have already done."

But she had already closed the door. He would burn it himself when he returned if she had not. Anna Bookman would have no evidence in her possession.

Brother Gabriel could go to the devil, if he had not already done so.

❧ ❧

Anna did not burn the Gospel of John. Not because she had not heard what VanCleve said. But she could no more burn the pages of truth than VanCleve could spit upon the crucifix. *In the beginning was the Word and the Word was God.*

The Word and the word. That was her legacy from Dĕdeček. And nobody could separate her from it. Not only did Anna not burn it, she finished copying. *I am the way, I am the door, I am the vine, I am the bread of life, I am the light of the world, I am the resurrection.* How could she burn this Word, this one book that Jan Hus from his pulpit in Betlémská kaple had called the heart of the gospel? So many times she had sat with her grandfather listening to John's six signs of Christ's divinity, listening as Jan Hus preached in the language of the people, watching the hundreds who listened with her.

When she had finished copying the gospel she looked at it and frowned. It was plain and unadorned except for one imperfect effort at the first capital. She could not reproduce the beautiful illuminated letters her grandfather had made. As a girl she had tried, but when her colors were not as pure as his, nor the lines as fluid, she had given up in frustration and contented herself with copying the words in the most careful, beautiful hand she could use. At least the words were pure and true, and she would be proud of her graceful lines.

The next day she went to the tanning yard to buy a leather cover. Heating a small stylus in the brazier, she carefully burned the title into the leather and then, beneath it, the words "copied for VanCleve by Anna Bookman." Then she wrapped it carefully in silk and put it in the bottom of the chest, next to the Wycliffe Bible, to await VanCleve's return.

At the beginning of the second week the first snow fell. Would that delay him? she wondered as she looked at the large flakes piling up against the leaded panes of glass. Was he warm? Was he safe? Was his business going well? What exactly was his business? He'd mentioned something once about the cloth trade. When she'd asked for more details, he'd said it was just buying and selling. Nothing very interesting. And he had changed the subject. But the smallest detail of VanCleve's life would have been interesting to

Anna. She wanted to know everything, but all she knew was that he had not spoken of marriage. "We'll make a more permanent arrangement," he'd said. And she'd been too ashamed to question him further.

There was no purchase in going to the square today, she thought, watching the color of the garden floor change from brown to white. Few would linger in the cold and freezing snow to buy a book. And Little Bek had started to sneeze. When she wiped the stream of mucus that flowed perpetually down the carved little snot path above his lips, she thought he felt warm. She dosed him with an infusion of elderflower and rosehip tea and put him to bed, watching anxiously until he nodded off.

Outside the snow piled up in drifts. He slept all through the long day and all night. Anna dozed too, wishing she had some work to do. She already had more inventory than she could sell. What she needed was commissioned work. Maybe she could find work in the Jewish quarter. She would ask at the stationer's shop. The monks and the guilds would not copy for the Jews, and there was always more book work there than the rabbis could do. She couldn't read the Hebrew, but her eye was good enough to copy the Hebrew letters. She'd make a sample to show the rabbi what she could do. She dozed off, the Hebrew letters dancing in her head like flames.

In the morning Little Bek was much better, his brow cool. She carried him to the window. He squealed with delight when he saw the patch of garden blanketed in a down coverlet of white.

"Snow," she said.

And to her delight he repeated, "Snow."

"Yes, yes, snow, snow." And she whirled him around the room.

He started to sing "snow, snow, snow" up and down the scale, pitching it high, then lower. She joined in singing it with him, dancing with the melody of it, until they formed a kind of polyphonic sound. She laughed and wished VanCleve were here to hear them, to join in the snow dance with them.

When she put the boy down, he reached for his crutches and, half hopping to the corner, pulled his hooded cloak from a peg and held it out to Anna.

"You want to go out?"

"Out." He nodded.

"But we can't. It's cold. *B-r-r-r,*" and she gave a mock shiver.

He burred his lips, forming spit bubbles on them as he mocked her.

"Out." He grinned, begging her with his eyes. Then started to sing the word up and down the scale he'd learned.

"It would be nice to have some hot soup," she said, thinking that all they had was the cold meat and cheese the landlord left outside the door. The old woman who cooked her pottage over an open fire might be in her little corner of the square. She would have a good business today just feeding the firewood vendors and gatherers. Something hot would be good for Little Bek, and best of all they could get out for a little while. The cozy little room was beginning to feel like a prison.

She bundled the boy into his wagon with an extra blanket until all she could see were his wide gray eyes.

"You look like a bunny," she said.

He made the *b-r-r-r* noise with his lips again, and grinned.

When they opened the door, a blast of wintry air greeted them and Anna immediately had second thoughts, but the boy laughed with delight. "Here, we'll put this between your knees," Anna said, placing beneath his blankets the lidded beaker that she kept warming on the brazier. They could empty out the hot water and bring back the hot soup in it, and it would keep the boy warm both going and coming.

Pushing against the snow piled against the threshold, they stepped out into a white world so pristine and pure that the beauty—or the sharp cold—brought tears to Anna's eyes. Foolish girl, she said to herself, reminding herself that like so many things it would not last, that underneath the snow dead leaves were decaying into a mass of slime, and when the snow at long last left, the mud and muck would be ankle deep. Nothing pure can stay, she thought. And wondered if that was true in Paradise.

She pulled hard to make the wagon's wooden wheels turn in the five inches of snow. A few flakes had started to drift down again. But in the distance at the corner of the square she could just make out the figure of the old woman bent over her cook fire, its smoke scenting the air. She looked back at Little Bek. His nose had started to run again, but so had hers, from the cold. He was holding on to the sides of the wagon for dear life as she tugged it through the snow, but he had a grin on his face. She couldn't feel her feet—or her face—anymore and her hand was frozen against the wooden handle of the wagon, but that look on his face was enough to keep her trudging.

At least when they returned to the warmth of their little chamber, they would be glad to see it. And there would be hot soup for supper.

Maybe VanCleve would return tomorrow. Maybe the snow and the cold had forced him to turn back. Two weeks, he had said.

And one week and three days were gone already.

TWENTY-TWO

In His love He clothes us, enfolds us and embraces us;
that tender love completely surrounds us, never to
leave us . . .

— JULIAN OF NORWICH,
REVELATIONS OF DIVINE LOVE

Reverend Mother, you said to call you at nones."

The voice beyond the thick oak door was soft and muffled and accompanied by a diffident knock.

"Thank you," the abbess called, then listened for the receding footfalls. A light tread. Probably one of the novices.

I should not have sent her away. Not without opening the door. Not without inviting her in and listening to the loneliness that always shadowed the young ones. I am mother to them now.

But she hated it when they called her "mother," she who was so unworthy of the title. Perhaps they were too near the age of that other girl who had once looked upon her as "mother." Perhaps there was too much pain of memory there.

The abbess knew she was regarded among the novices and younger sisters as formidable, both in tone and aspect. The tone she tried to change, making efforts to praise the sisters when praise was called for and scolding softly when they neglected their duties, as young girls—even young girls who are to be wed to Christ—were wont to do. But the aspect she could not change. The face veil would not be lifted. She would not bare her marred face even for these, her spiritual daughters. With the death of her old servant who had fled the fire with her, more than knowledge of the abbess's ruined face had passed. The last vestige of an abandoned life had died with the old cook of Blackingham Hall. Or so the abbess thought. But that was ten years gone and memories swirled within each shaft of autumn light shooting through her chamber window.

The Reverend Mother laid down her pen. Her hands trembled with fatigue. *Laborare est orare*. To work is to pray. And she had labored these thirty years. Pages of Julian's *Revelations of Divine Love* were spread out on the desk in front of her. These, thankfully, she did not have to copy in the tedious Latin or even translate into English because they were written in English, and thankfully also they were not contraband. Somehow, the holy woman of Norwich had maintained that fine balance between orthodoxy and heresy, clinging to the former while courting the latter.

Safe works such as these the abbess usually gave to the nuns whose loyalty she questioned—such as Sister Agatha. But Sister Agatha had been consigned to the kitchen garden for a spell and there was a commission for a copy of the work—a particularly fine copy. (The abbess sometimes marveled at the miracle of her steady hand despite her age. Surely a gift from God.) The abbey needed the money, and at this particular season in her soul, she needed the comforting words.

"All will be well," the anchoress of Norwich had written. "All will be well," the last words the abbess had copied, lay now beneath her quill. She prayed it would be so. *Lord, I know you are as close as my breath—and because of this veil my breath is very close. Let me know that all will be well.* But she could feel pressure building at her back, pressure for the abbey, pressure for those who dared dissent. And she feared for all who embraced the Lollard cause.

She had asked the novice to call her—sometimes she became lost in her work, especially when it was Julian's words she copied—because there was still the tedium of the duty roster to do: who will clean, and who will cook, and who will read at meals. Who will wash and who will scrub and who will tend the fields.

Laborare est orare.

But first, to rest her eyes, she stood up stiffly and went to the window that looked out over the cloisters. Its three-tiered fountain dropped water into the lavabo where the sisters gathered water for bathing. She did not allow them to wash in it, as was customary, but required them to dip water into basins lined up on a bench on the sunniest side of the cloister. Only on feast days and holy days were they allowed to dip their hands into the water, in a kind of ritual cleansing, after they'd already washed them.

It was not a large abbey. The fountain was an extravagance, chosen for its beauty and its clever engineering. A cistern behind it provided an almost endless supply of water. Like Grace, sometimes it trickled and sometimes it cascaded in a clear stream. Today it was scarcely a trickle; the autumn had been dry. But light gathered in the drops that overflowed into the smaller basins, so that each drop looked like a precious jewel. Soon they will become tiny frozen jewels, she thought. She dreaded the coming of winter, when the cloisters were shrouded in gray and even the fountain slept, dreaded too when her fingers ached too much to write. But she would not think of that. She would only be grateful for this moment, for the beauty of the brown leaf floating down into the light that hovered like an aura over the fountain.

She longed to sit in that light, to feel its rays on her ruined face. The dying autumn light always brought to the Reverend Mother more than the reminder of human mortality. Thin with remembered warmth, it evoked memories of the self she had long ago abandoned. In the glorious color of an English autumn, Kathryn had first loved Finn.

She turned away from the window and once more picked up the duty roster. With a determined sigh, she dipped the nib of her pen into the ink cup on her writing table and began to assign the daily tasks.

Laborare est orare.

～✢✤～

If to labor is to pray, then Jane Paul had spent all of her life in prayer. But now it was over. The old man was dead. Just this one last thing for Mistress Clare to do. One last vigil to sit, she thought as she washed the old man's body, careful still not to tear his skin, her touch made almost gentle by the memory of what he had once been. The Grim Reaper had crept in during the night. She'd heard nothing, and she slept lightly, listening always for his cough, his feeble call. Brother Francis had not even put up a struggle when the death angel came.

She washed his bony limbs, the fragile webbing between his fingers, his toes, then dipped her rag into the water and washed his shriveled private parts. He had not always been thus. He had first come to her in his prime. The girls had all made crude jests as they guessed what hung beneath his priests' robe, had all offered cheerfully to find out. But he'd been clear enough to the old woman who ran the brothel. He wanted a young girl, a virgin, and she would be his regular. He would not share, but he would pay well for sole use.

Even Jane, who had been no more than fourteen then, had smiled at this request and wondered which of the younger girls the mistress would try to pawn off on him. Margery and Alice were already simpering, straightening their spines, tugging at their low-cut gowns, trying to look prim. She could almost hear what was going on in their heads. *Here was steady income. A regular customer. And a friar—one whose wants would be more easily satisfied. One who would not be brutish—after all, he was a man of God. One who might even be grateful.*

She remembered the cramped little parlor on Bankside Street, as young Jane—that self long abandoned but living still in memory—intruded with the force of a dream.

Young Jane had almost laughed, thinking how foolish the women looked. Surely, even a priest could tell a seasoned whore from a maid. The old mistress must have known it too. She was scrunching up her eyes, furrowing her brow. Her large breast heaved like a bellows. Jane resumed her dusting—the mistress demanded that the parlor be kept straight, even though some of the girls' rooms were no better than pigstys.

Jane had come to the house two years past to char for the whores and the mistress of the house, because her mother had died and she had nowhere else to go.

"You have good teeth and pretty blond hair. They like the young ones. Have you started to bleed yet?" The mistress had looked her over, one arched brow raised in speculation.

"No, mistress." It wasn't a lie, not really, she thought. She had only bled once, and her mother had told her it would be every month. Sometimes she worried about it. Now she was glad. She was only twelve, but she knew what the mistress was getting at.

" 'Tis too bad. But this house has some standards. I'll not whore a child."

"Beggin' your pardon, ma'am, but I only want to char. I'm strong. I can carry water and sweep and cook a little. Me mum was sickly a long time."

Since then, the mistress had not mentioned it again. But all the same, Jane took care that she not see her bloody rags from the courses that had come regularly the last six months.

The mistress had clucked her tongue and shaken her head. "Sorry, Father, I'm afraid—"

Jane squeezed herself between her mistress and the door, trying to make herself invisible as usual. It was a tight squeeze. She bumped against the mistress, who turned around and seized her by the arm. The old woman's smile reached her eyes.

"I'm sorry, Father. I'm afraid I only have *one* girl to offer ye." Jane felt the imprint of the mistress's fingers gripping her arms, bruising her flesh, as she pushed Jane out to the black-cassocked priest. "She is just about to begin her training. I reckon ye'd be as good a teacher as any."

And that was how Jane Paul became a whore.

But not really a whore, she told herself. She'd wound up being a charwoman after all and as chaste as a nun. Brother Francis never touched her after she came to live with him. After he stole her son away. After she became Mistress Clare, a name she borrowed from the Poor Clares who had given her shelter when her mistress turned her out for her swollen belly, turned her out because she would not kill the second child in the womb. But her little girl had died anyway, and the Poor Clares who were kind to her had said it was God's will. That God took her little girl as payment for her sin. Would they have said that if they knew her child's father wore a Dominican robe? She had cried when her little girl was stillborn, but she didn't think it was the wrath of God. She thought it was a mercy.

"Jane Paul is dead," she'd said to Brother Francis, who took her in when she had to leave the shelter of the convent. They had made the bargain then. Her vow of silence in return for her place of service, and she had said, "From now on I will be called 'Mistress Clare.' "

"It matters not to me what you call yourself," he'd said, and he had never come to her again, though her body had yearned for just a touch, some human connection. As for him, she thought he'd found another, younger woman to give him physical release, but she never saw her nor knew her name.

As she sewed the old priest into his shroud, the needle pricked her thumb. It didn't even penetrate the callus, just stuck there until she pulled it out. She looked at the hands wielding the needle against the tough oiled serge. Once they had been pretty, but now they were the hands of a charwoman, red and rough. But from this day forward the only cooking and cleaning she would do would be for herself. And she would have to do it for herself. For Jane Paul had no family in this world.

Except for her son.

And she needed no promise to keep her from telling him his mother was so baseborn. (How rightly she had named him, this proud, beautiful creature—she trembled whenever she saw him to think that such a one had been nurtured in her womb.)

She was better off than most her age, she supposed. She thought of the little horde of silver groats and pennies she'd saved, thought about the little cottage by the sea with its tiny vegetable garden, payment for her secret. She would raise a few chickens for eggs and the occasional stew. She would make do.

The only part of the shroud left to close was over the old man's face. She lit a candle and held the flame in front of his lips to be sure. Not the slightest stir of air. Not even a flicker of life.

She bent and kissed him lightly on the lips. Never in all of her life had she kissed or been kissed by a man. Her lips lingered for a second, moved gently against his, just as she'd dreamed about in her youth, just as in her earliest memory she'd once seen her father kiss her mother.

The old priest's lips were cold.

Fumbling, she folded over the selvage edge of the cloth, then refolded it carefully to make a neat seam. He deserved this last thing—a well-sewn shroud. He had been a good enough priest, she supposed. He had important visitors. In the beginning. Before he got old. Before he was forgotten. When the visitors stopped coming, she used to make up excuses to spare his pride.

"Brother Francis, the bishop sends his good wishes."

"Brother Francis, there was an emissary from Canterbury to see you, but I told him you were sleeping."

This lie had earned her a stern scolding.

Another stab of the needle and this time it punctured the callus so that she felt it. He'd never beaten her or been rough with her. He had only ignored her. She was to him a lesser creature whose lot in life was ordained by God to serve His servant. If Brother Francis had noticed her misery, he would have felt no responsibility for it.

But he had been good to her son.

After the boy was old enough, he'd taken him away from Bankside Street. When he'd found how bright her Gabriel was, he had settled the boy's future and banned her from his presence, taking her in only after the boy went away. Well, she had kept her part of the bargain. Close enough at least to claim her due. But she would do this last thing for him.

And she would sit vigil by him in the chapel too. After she had gone to the abbot and gotten the promised deed to her cottage.

After she had summoned the boy to witness his father's burial.

TWENTY-THREE

A true lover is constantly and without intermission possessed by the thoughts of his beloved.
RULE XXX, *RULES OF COURTLY LOVE*

Good character alone makes any man worthy of love.
RULE XVIII, *RULES OF COURTLY LOVE*,
CAPELLANUS (12TH CENTURY)

December one. A fortnight had come and gone. Anna told herself VanCleve could be delayed by the weather. The snow had departed as quickly as it had come, leaving behind a muddy quagmire. Even the sturdiest coach would have difficulty navigating the roads. The weather warmed enough at midday for her to bundle Little Bek into his wagon and trudge to the market square. But in two days she'd only sold one pilgrim guide. There were few travelers on the Pilgrim's Way during winter. She would have to find another source of custom. Thank heavens the rent was paid until after Christmas. The landlord had informed her of that fact when she'd tried to pay him.

"Monsieur VanClef a payé le loyer pour le mois entier," and then he had handed her a rolled parchment with her name on it: "Anna Bookman, Rue de Saint Luc, Rheims, France." She waited, her mind itching with impatience,

as the portly little man smiled and patted Little Bek's head, pretended interest in the boy's new wagon, although Anna could feel him watching her out
of the corner of his eye. She waited impatiently beside the still-open door,
fingering the cord binding the parchment. Finally the landlord gave his
courtly little bow and bade her, *"Adieu, madame."*

In her excitement, she almost slammed the door in his face. Her fingers
trembled as she removed the cord and broke the seal, which in spite of the
poor traveling conditions was still intact.

"Dearest Anna," in VanCleve's fine cribbed handwriting. She could almost see his hands writing the words, envision his long fingers as they
guided the quill across the page, formed the breast of the *D*, a blot of ink
where he lingered on the pointy *A* of her name. *"Dearest Anna."* The words
sounded like a caress in her mind.

"As you can see from the weather, I am probably not going to make it
back to you within the time I had hoped." But he was coming back! He had
not gone back to his wife, to his other lover, to his life in Flanders! "In addi-
tion to the delay caused by the weather, upon my arrival in Paris, I registered
with the mercer's guild, where a message awaited me with some very bad
news that will require even more travel. My godfather has died and I am flying to his side to see that he is laid to rest with all due honor and to endow
masses for his soul. He was very old and very frail and his death was not unexpected. Yet I find myself strangely grieved. It is a great personal loss. I
wish I could seek comfort from your sweet face, your voice, your smile . . ."

Here the writing trailed off. A great personal loss, and he was not here for
her to comfort him as he had held her after Jetta's drowning. Not here for her
to kiss away his tears.

"Only the thought of you waiting for me brings me joy. It is my hope that
I shall not be much delayed. By the time you get this I shall probably already
have crossed the Channel."

Crossed the Channel? From Paris to Flanders?

"With this letter, I also sent the landlord enough money for the rent on
your room until I return. He seems an honest sort, but do not try to pay him
again. The temptation might prove too great. Give Little Bek a hug for me. I
dream of you each night, think of you each day, and will hold you in my
arms again, soon."

It was signed, tentatively, "VanCleve," as though the ink were fading.

That had been three days ago. She'd read the letter until the edge of the parchment was beginning to fray. She reread it now for reassurance as the gray December day seeped beneath the windowpane and chilled her, taunting her with its endless melancholy.

He is coming back, she told herself, holding the parchment tight against her breast. In lieu of the writer she would hold the writing.

"He has promised.

"This is just a delay." She said the words out loud to the boy. Whose wide gray eyes seemed to understand what she did not say.

···

Brother Gabriel leaned into the wind from the bow of *Le Petre de Dartmouth*. The Channel crossing was rough, especially down below, where few passengers huddled. His stomach churned, threatening. Even though there were few pilgrims this time of year—only necessary travelers plied the waters during the bleak midwinter months—still the stench of unwashed bodies was strong. The salt spray felt good against his face. It was as gritty as the reality that had abraded his spirit since he donned the Dominican garb.

Seabirds shrieked in the boat's wake, screaming for some scrap of refuse thrown overboard. Their raucous cries, incessant like harpies swooping and crying, added headache to his malady. He leaned into the wind.

"Feelin' a little peaked, are you, Father?"

Gabriel looked around. The voice must be addressing him. There was no one else in the bow. Yes, of course. Father. He was "Father." A woman of indeterminate age in a gray cloak and hood emerged from the seamless background of sky and water.

"I've a piddlin' bit of ginger in my pocket, if that w'ud help."

He could see her more clearly now that she had closed the distance between them. She was only a little beyond a girl, a girl with pretty eyes. He'd been vaguely aware when she came on board with an older woman, her mother probably. At an earlier time she might have provoked his thoughts to lascivious mischief—now all he noticed was her gentle manner. She only approached because of his black cassock. He doubted she would have made such a gesture to VanCleve.

"It's a bit dry and ugly," she said, offering him the gnarly root. "It carries better this way. Just a tiny bite will do—it's a mite peppery to the tongue."

"Thank you," he said, looking dubiously at the proffered root. One end looked as though it had already been chewed.

"Here." She whisked a little knife from inside her reticule and cut off a piece from the other end, then smiled as she waved the knife around. "For protection. We've come all the way from Boulogne. I've only had to use it once, to frighten away a cutpurse, until now."

She flashed him a smile, showing a complete set of nearly perfect teeth, good skin. He wondered why she had to travel without a man's protection. Such a passage was unsafe for women alone, even in pairs. Something about the sauciness of her voice reminded him of Anna, Anna who had come all the way from Bohemia alone.

He took the ginger root the girl offered him. "I'm feeling better," he said. "I'll save this for later."

"As you wish, Father."

The young woman's mother sat with the other passengers, huddled together in the center of the boat for warmth. From his position in the bow and through the fog and mist they looked like lumps, but he saw one lump turn toward him, then say something else to another beside her. There would be no need to watch out for her daughter, no need when she was with a priest, the woman would be thinking. He felt a little sting of guilt, and a newfound incredulity. How vulnerable they were—these sheep who trusted so completely in their black-robed Roman shepherds.

"Do you travel far, child?" he asked. The voice of a priest. The words of a priest. But not the heart.

"Just as far as Dover. My betrothed is to meet me there."

My betrothed. She said it so proudly. He tried to imagine Anna's lips forming those words, but Anna could never say those words, not for him.

A gull shrieked and swooped low over their heads, then settled for a moment on the railing of the boat before the force of the wind at its back fanned its tail feathers and lifted it off the rail. It went screaming into the wind. Van-Cleve is like that bird, he thought, resting on an uncertain perch, a stolen respite from the wind. The boat pitched forward. His stomach lurched again. Maybe he would need the ginger after all.

"Your betrothed is a lucky man," he said, thinking still of Anna. Thinking of VanCleve.

The girl blushed. "I'd better get back to my mother."

"God go with you, child."

The words. The voice. It was as though he watched this priest from a distance, as though the man who mouthed these ritual words had nothing whatever to do with him.

What advice would Brother Francis have for him? And then he remembered.

Brother Francis would for now and ever remain mute on this and all subjects. He would find no light to lead him there. To whom then would he confess his sins now? he wondered, remembering the cold, impersonal voice in the cathedral confessional.

He felt the gorge rise in his throat. But it had little to do with the roll and pitch of the small ship on the rough winter seas. He had never felt more in need of a confessor. The words of Psalm Six came into his head, the Penitential Psalm: "*Domine, ne in furore tuo arguas me* . . . O Lord, rebuke me not in thy indignation, nor chastise me in thy wrath. Have mercy on me, O Lord, for I am weak."

But without a confessor, how would he ever know his prayer was heard? He had not Anna's faith. There was no sign. The leaden sky surrounding him remained unchanged. The wind still spit sea spray into his face. The gulls still swooped and cried. The girl had joined the other formless masses in the middle of the ship.

He bit off a piece of the ginger root the girl had left him. It tasted bitter on his tongue.

※

On the first sunny day, Anna bundled up Little Bek and they walked to the stationer's shop.

Business was slow there as well. The stationer's wife seemed happier to see her as she walked through the door. She always spoke to Anna in English. She'd been a camp follower, one of the women who followed the English soldiers into France, but unlike most, this one had fared well, catching the eye of a French merchant. She'd been delighted to learn that Anna spoke English and had presumed an intimacy that Anna did not reciprocate.

"Pull the boy's cart on inside. That way you won't have to lift him."

But Little Bek had already gathered his crutches and was hauling himself out of the cart. It was all she could do to keep from helping him, but she recognized the stubborn look on his face. He wanted to show the stationer's wife that he was independent.

"My, he's growed big since last time I saw him."

Anna suppressed a smile as she watched the boy stretch himself even taller on his spindly legs. But it hurt her heart too. She knew how much it cost him to stand erect, to hold his head still. "Here, Bek"—she'd taken to calling him that, dropping the diminutive, because that was what he called himself. "Bek wants" or "Bek likes," he would say—"Come, Bek, you can sit here while we do business."

The stationer's wife favored them with her gap-toothed smile. "And it's glad enough for the business I am. It's been slow, what with the snow and then the rain."

Anna watched carefully as the boy twisted his body on the stool. "I'm afraid my custom won't help much. Just a couple of nibs and a bottle of squid ink." She counted out the farthings, looked at a stack of fine vellum.

"I can make you a good price."

"Perhaps later; my purse is thin right now. I thought I might find some business within the Jewish quarter. Can you direct me—"

The woman's gap-toothed smile snapped shut, her eyes squinting into little pinpoints. "The Jews! What would you be wanting with that lot?"

"My . . . husband often did work for them. They are a learned people and value beautiful books. And they pay well."

She gave Anna a hard look. "Well, you won't be getting any custom there. Haven't been any Jews in France since before I was born. The king had the good sense to banish them all."

"Banish?"

"They were lucky they weren't all herded into a synagogue and burned. That's what I've heard was done in other places. Not that I would hold with that, being a good Christian woman and all. It was enough to run them out."

Anna remembered the crowded settlement of Judenstadt, walled off from the rest of Prague. Remembered too how every year on Yom Kippur in the old/new synagogue, the Jews kept alive the memory of such a massacre in Prague. She bit back a sharp retort. It would not do for her to anger the only stationer within walking distance of her quarters. What good could her protest do, anyway?

The woman was studying her thoughtfully. "If it be Jewish books you're interested in, I have something to show you. Being a good Christian woman and all, I've not wanted to keep it, but it seemed a shame to burn it. I'll sell it to you cheap." As if Anna were not a good Christian woman.

She reached under the counter and dragged out a bundle wrapped in sackcloth. "Mind you, don't tell where you got it. I'll deny it with my last breath. That's part of the bargain." She cast a furtive glance at the window before unwrapping the bundle. "My lout of a husband bought it from a tinker—the fool didn't know what it was. He said the tinker's grandfather brought it back from the last crusade. I think it's some kind of Jewish black magic. But ain't it beautiful!"

Anna gasped. The book was bound in well-tooled leather, outlined with enameled crimson and gold leaf. There were a few holes in the finish of the leather, probably where gems, long since plundered and adorning the throat of some Knight Templar's lady or a rich Roman cleric, had been encrusted. Anna could read enough of the Hebrew letters to make out the title. שלמה הם פתח לחכמ ת. *The Key to the Wisdom of Solomon.*

Anna had heard of this book. The rabbi in Prague had once shown her a copy. And indeed it was a book of magic of sorts. But not black magic. Not witches' magic. A book of magic incantation for summoning angels. She ran her fingers over the gilded Hebrew letters of the title. Her mind cautioned her. Turn away. If it's dangerous for a citizen of the country, how much more so for a foreigner? Her mind flashed on Jetta emerging from the river, her body lifeless, her limp head thrown back over VanCleve's arms, her long gray hair trailing strings of water. She pushed the image aside.

"How much?" she asked.

The stationer's wife appeared to be calculating. Anna could almost hear what she was thinking. Here was a way to rid herself of the contraband book.

"For you, two gold florins."

A ransom indeed. She dared not spend her little hoard for it.

"My husband wants to burn it." The woman gave an exaggerated sigh. "Seems a pity."

"How about a trade? I have two copies of Christine de Pisan's *The Treasury of the City of Ladies* and three pilgrim guides. You should have no trouble selling those. I mean, if you were going to burn it anyway."

The woman made a great show of considering, biting into her bottom lip with her little saw teeth. "Well, there's the leather of the back cover. I could salvage that."

"Five books and one ducat for the leather."

"Done."

"I'll come back tomorrow."

The woman bundled the book back into its plain swaddling, handed it to Anna. "Go ahead. Take it now. I trust you. We are both good Christian women," she said, visibly relieved to be rid of it.

The woman worked quickly, wrapping the book in the prayer shawl that covered it, as though she were afraid Anna would reconsider. As she placed it beneath the blankets in Bek's wagon, Anna had another spasm of misgiving. Had she done the wrong thing? But they said the same thing about the Wycliffe Bible—that it was dangerous to own it. And no harm had ever come to her for having that. Again her mind betrayed her and she was transported back to the Vltava Bridge and Martin's skull gleaming on its stake. But Martin and the others had not died for possession of the Book. It was hubris that killed them. Dědeček had often warned his little group of dissidents against the kind of intellectual and philosophical arrogance that could undermine their truth and endanger lives. Anna did not have to shout her views in the marketplace. Ransoming the book was a good thing.

Somehow, she thought it was what Dědeček would have done.

TWENTY-FOUR

[L]et us leave celibacy for bishops . . . The holiest
kind of life is wedlock, purely and chastely observed.
—STATEMENT AGAINST CELIBACY BY
ERASMUS IN *ENCOMIUM MORIAE*

rother Gabriel was weary after his crossing. He'd had little sleep and less food since receiving the packet from Archbishop Arundel informing him of Brother Francis's death. But after the ship landed in Dover, he'd been suddenly impatient to return, though he knew there would be no friend to greet him in the old priest's quarters. Nonetheless, he had hired a horse and come straight to Battle Abbey in the heavy twilight and the cold mist that settled like a caul upon his skin. He didn't know what hour of the night it was when the abbey walls loomed before him. Only that it was late. A pale wedge of a rising moon within a veil of cloud lit the abbey grounds, reminding him of his last moonlit visit to the abbey, the last time he'd seen Brother Francis alive. He should never have stayed away so long, he chided himself. He'd known how frail the old priest was.

"Look sharp, lad," he shouted at the sleepy groom, who emerged rubbing his eyes as Gabriel rode through the gatehouse, unmanned now that the French raids had stopped. The abbey's numbers were too depleted to guard walls beyond which no enemy camped. Its population had never fully recovered from the pestilence that swept England during the last century.

"See that he gets a bag of oats. An ostler from Hastings will claim him tomorrow."

"Aye, Father." The horse whinnied as the boy led him away in the direction of the stable.

Oats for the horse maybe, but nothing for the rider, he thought, glancing at the darkened windows of the refectory, long since empty of the brothers who had eaten their silent supper. The kitchens too would be closed, the long deal tables scrubbed clean of every crumb.

Two bells.

The heart of the night. Anna and Bek would be sleeping in the little house in Rue de Saint Luc. At the sound of the peals the monks began their shuffling through the cloisters in answer to the matins summons. He would join them. He had neglected for far too long the Divine Office. Besides, only three weeks had passed since the prior's death. They were sure to still be chanting the Office of the Dead.

Brother Gabriel pulled his cowl low over his face, bowed his head, crossed his arms in the penitential posture, and joined the line heading into the chapel. He entered the familiar choir, his glance embracing the misericords where as a boy he'd traced the carvings with his fingers, impatiently waiting for the office to end. A few years later, as Brother Francis offered the mass, young Gabriel was thinking about the girl to whom he'd given his virginity. Thinking about carnal delights when he should have been thinking about the mystery celebrated before him. Carnal sins! Ah, there was mystery there as well.

Still thinking about his carnal sins—how heavily they weighed—he picked up the antiphonary, though he didn't need it. He knew all the words by heart. It had been a stern requirement of Brother Francis for his young protégé.

"*Dirige, Domine, Deus meus.*" He intoned the opening antiphon, joining his bass voice with the abbey choir.

Maybe after this he would be able to sleep. He had not slept well in many nights. He would take a cot in the monks' dormitory—surely no dreams of a red-haired woman would intrude upon that celibate company. Then tomorrow he would pay his last respects to the old prior and seek out the abbot to endow more masses for his soul.

After the mass, he followed the line back through the cloisters. At the corner of the quadrangle where it turned, he glanced over at the little enclosed cottage set apart. A shadow passed in front of the window. The shade of Brother Francis, resting ill? He rubbed gritty eyeballs and looked again. The silhouette was gone.

Mistress Clare. He had forgotten about her, would have thought her long gone by now. He wondered idly what she would do now that her job was finished. Wondered if she had family who would take her in.

But that was not his concern.

❧ ❧

The morning meal was simple: coarse bread, yeasty and crusty, still warm from the kitchen, and porridge—with a rasher of bacon reserved for the visiting priest, the quaestor who held the key to the treasury of grace. Gabriel was first in line, filling his wooden bowl, then settling down to the trestle board with the brothers who followed quickly behind him. The monks passed the bread down the line, each breaking off a piece and passing it with no word spoken into the stillness except for the Psalm reader, who intoned the lesson from the pulpit high above them.

Gabriel only half listened to the Penitential Psalms. It was a logical choice, part of the Office of the Dead, chosen like the mass to honor Brother Francis. The monotonous sound of the voice and the sound of swallowing—who knew that a couple dozen men all masticating under the rule of silence could be so noisy and so irritating to the senses?—was insufficient to distract Gabriel's mind from the residual stiffness of sleeping on the hard cot. Neither the quantity nor the quality of his sleep had left him refreshed. His hip ached in the joint. And no wonder.

He had dreamed again last night of Anna. This time she appeared in the guise of the angel who wrestled with Jacob at the foot of the golden stair. Like Jacob in his dream, Gabriel struggled with the winged creature, a fierce struggle worthy of a heavenly foe. Gabriel grasped and held the creature even as Jacob in the Book of Genesis had done, and the angel would have fled to Heaven up the celestial stair, had not Gabriel held on fast. But in the dream it was the priest and not the angel who was finally overcome, felled by the power of the beating wings that bruised his hip and sucked his breath away.

He'd tried to cry out in the dream, but his voice was locked—he still felt the constriction in his throat when he swallowed—until at last he lay beaten and still, his eyes closed, his body naked and cold, curled in upon itself like a child's. And yet the angel, not yet finished with him, hovered over him until he smelled its essence. Familiar, sweet. The smell of jasmine. Gabriel opened his eyes, looked into the creature's face.

Not the face of a male like the one Jacob wrestled, nor even some androgynous creature, as he'd always thought the angels to be, but a woman's face—Anna's face, with a nimbus of flaming hair burning with fire and yet not consumed, like Moses' burning bush. He could feel the heat of it against his skin. Felt it now, just remembering—remembering too, even in the cold and silent abbey refectorium, her perfect face. In her bright blue eyes, angel tears, shiny as diamonds, hovered at the corners, never spilling.

Gabriel wished at that moment with all his heart that Brother Francis were still alive to interpret his dream for him. Yet, some secret part of him, some perverse and secret self was glad that he would not have to suffer the reprimand.

Domine, ne in furore tuo arguas me . . . The words of the psalm floated down from overhead, penetrating Gabriel's remembered dream. *O Lord, rebuke me not in thy indignation, nor chastise me in thy wrath.*

A brother nudged him, urging him to take the bread. His throat swelled, threatening to refuse the spoonful of porridge he had just scooped into his mouth. He shook his head. The brother scowled and passed it across him, even as Gabriel straddled the bench and rushed from the room.

He opened the refectorium door to the withered kitchen garden, glad of the burst of cold air, glad to leave behind the brothers and their incessant gulping and swallowing, like pigs feeding at a trough. But gladder still to leave behind the voice and the psalm that begged mercy for the dead even as it mocked the sins of the living, David's plea for mercy for his sins, his carnal sin with Bathsheba not unlike Gabriel's own.

Domine, ne in furore tuo arguas me. Gabriel could still hear the chanting of the psalm. He stumbled toward the chapel. He could also still see the vision of the angel before him, the angel with a face like Anna's.

Brother Francis's body was interred in Saint Martin's chapel, the circular off-set to the left of the chancel. The flagstone of the floor had been lifted and the prior's body deposited, encased in its shroud, in the excavation nearest the altar of Saint Martin. This was a signal honor because after the grave—called by some "the flesh-eater"—had done its work, his bones would not be removed to the charnel house, but would remain in proximity to the saint. From this honored place, the old prior's soul could more easily progress through Purgatory. Most of the pilgrims who came to honor the saint would vouchsafe a prayer for the prior buried nearby. Spilled grace.

Morning light poured through the window that depicted Saint Martin wearing his half-cloak as he wrapped the other half about the arms of a ragged beggar. In the background the goose that was his emblem looked on with favor, his beak opened wide, proclaiming the humble saint's charity.

Gabriel knelt on the floor, ran his hand along the raw seam where the stones in the floor beside the altar had been replaced. Even in the dim light of the chapel interior he could see the mortar was fresh. He traced the newly carved letters of Brother Francis's name, rough-hewn but legible, in the headstone, then bent forward and pressed his lips against the cold stone. He felt a wave of remorse and longing as he tried to remember exactly what had been the last words he'd said to this man who had been like a father to him. Had he expressed affection? Had he expressed his gratitude? Even if he hadn't, the old man knew how much Gabriel loved him, didn't he?

"Your name was the last thing on his lips."

A woman's voice, familiar and yet not, nagged at the edge of recognition. He raised his head to see the speaker who stood in the door: a slender woman of late middle age and proud bearing, wearing a hooded cloak from which straggles of gray hair peeped.

Mistress Clare.

Probably come with some petty claim against the leavings of the old priest.

He tried to hide the irritation in his voice, irritation that she should in-trude upon his private grief. She had served Brother Francis faithfully. She was entitled to something, he supposed.

"I have come to grieve. I will attend you later," he said, not getting up from his kneeling position before the grave. Echoing off the stone of the chapel wall, his tone sounded hard-edged.

She was as still as the statue ensconced in the wall niche overhead. Only her lips moved. "I will not be here later. I have come to bid you farewell. I have waited since his burial for you."

Irritated by something in her tone, as though she had some claim upon his attention, he started to demand she leave him to grieve in solitude. Still, she was entitled to some modicum of courtesy for her pains. No doubt she would want some more tangible remuneration as well. For that he would re-fer her to the abbot—unless of course she'd already exhausted that resource. He struggled to his feet, feeling a cold pain in the core of his leg that started in his hip joint and shot down to the sole of his foot.

"A warm poultice will ease that pain," she said. "Brother Francis suffered from it also."

She said this last as though she drew some private satisfaction from his suffering. This surprised and puzzled him. She had ever been distant toward him, but he'd not thought her antipathy ran so deep.

"I have never felt it before. It is no doubt caused by the long ride from the shore."

"That or the weather," she said.

He sat down on the lone bench that was provided for the penitents at Saint Martin's chapel. A rainbow of light from the stained-glass window painted the other end of the bench.

"You may sit here, and we will talk about your claim," he said.

She sat beside him, her plain dun-colored dress suddenly colorful, her complexion rosy in the wash of the red tint from the window. He could see that in her youth, she must have been a pretty woman. It struck him that he knew very little about Mistress Clare, even though she had hovered for years in the background. He tried to remember when he'd first seen her. He'd been barely beyond the status of a green youth, fresh from his studies in Rome, and she had been there then. Brother Francis had simply introduced her as Mistress Clare, and she had disappeared into the shadows, as became her cus-tom whenever he visited.

"I have no *claims*." She said this a little indignantly, as though she found the very suggestion offensive.

"I waited to tell you how he died," she said, "and to assure you that your father's body was tended properly before he was laid to rest."

"That was kind of you," he said, feeling his way, still not sure what she wanted of him. He rubbed his leg to ease the pain that had only worsened when he sat down on the hard bench.

"Make yourself a warm hip bath and soak in it," she said. "That will help the pain."

"Thank you for that advice." And then searching for something to say to the woman, "Did he die peacefully?"

"He died in his sleep."

"I thought of him as a father, you know."

"And well you should. He was your father."

"Yes, my spiritual father. But more than that. He was really the only father I ever had."

"Yes, he was. That is why I stayed. To tell you. I thought you should know. As long as he was living, he forbade it."

He was thinking how well spoken she was for a common charwoman. None of the heavy Saxon accent one might expect in a woman of her class. She must have adopted the speech and vocabulary of the upper class she tended.

"Pardon me, please. My attention must be diverted by the pain in my leg." He rubbed the shank of his leg. "What were you saying about Brother Francis forbidding something?"

"He forbade me to tell you that he was your natural father."

A cloud passed over the sun outside and the rosy light grayed, turning her skin the color of the stone wall behind her.

Had he heard her right? For the briefest moment he wished it could be so. But no, the woman had merely picked up some gossip. She had not come to stay with Brother Francis until late in his life. She could not possibly know of what she spoke. She was merely repeating some devil's gossip she'd heard, probably to gain some advantage over him now that her livelihood was at an end.

"You are mistaken. He took me as a ward of the Church when I was about six years old." He could not bring himself to say his mother had been a whore. "I was an orphan."

"You were no orphan. You were his natural child. He took you from a brothel in Southwark. Took you away from your mother. Brought you here. Gave you an education."

"How dare you repeat such idle gossip? I—"

"Your mother used to visit you from time to time when you were very young. Then he sent her away. His plans for you did not include a mother of her class." She said this bitterly then added in a low voice, "Do you remember that? Do you remember her visits?"

Suddenly he was eight years old and his mother was kissing him good-bye. There were tears in her eyes. He could remember that, though he couldn't remember her face. But she had golden hair. One curl had escaped her cap, a cap of green velvet with a bit of lace tied at the chin. Its lace and her curls had brushed his cheek. He had not kissed her back.

"There was a scent she always wore . . ." He could hardly get breath enough to form the words. He wasn't sure he said them out loud.

"The attar of roses. It was her favorite."

"Her name was Jane. Jane Paul."

His throat was tight with shame and longing and a kind of anger. Anger at Brother Francis for the great lie, even though he knew it was for his own good, anger at her for revealing it now, and anger at that small boy who had sent his mother away that one last time without a kiss or even a good-bye.

"How do you know this?" he asked.

"One does not serve a man as long as I served your father and not learn everything about him. If you still doubt the truth of what I tell you, you have only to look in a mirror. Notice the little line that is beginning to run from your temple down your cheek to your chin. One day it will be a deep crease like his. The jut of your chin, that small dimple that forms on the left side of your smile, even that pain you have in your left leg—all are gifts from your father. Along, of course, with your fine mind and your strong body."

The rainbow of light had shifted. It no longer fell on her face. She sat with her hands cupping the caps of her knees, each hand a different color in the light from the window. She had long fingers, once graceful, now red and rough. But the shape reminded him of his mother's. He remembered her touch, light, warm. She'd once stroked his cheek with such hands, or was that the wishful dream of a child and not a memory at all?

No. It was all a lie, a trick. Next the woman would ask him to pay for silence. Then he would know it was all a sluttish, self-serving lie.

"My leg has never hurt before. I slept badly last night."

"You are about the age your father was when his began to hurt."

He never complained to me, Gabriel thought. And then he summoned a vision of Brother Francis rubbing his thigh. Another trick of memory, some suggestion put in his head? But his memory or his imagination conjured too the occasional grimace of pain, the infrequent times that his confessor walked with a limp.

She said it as though she read his mind. "His pain would come and go. It was subject to bad weather."

"His hair is . . . was dark, almost black."

"Your mother had blond hair."

That much also was true.

"Did you know my mother? Did you know Jane Paul?"

"I knew her once."

"Once? Where is she now?"

He waited for her answer, unaware that his breath did not come, wanting and yet not wanting to know.

She closed her eyes, as if the light hurt them, even though her face was in shadow.

"Jane Paul is dead," she said.

He breathed.

"Why are you telling me this now?"

"Because I was forbidden to tell you before."

"What good can come of my knowing?"

"I thought that you should know, lest the son repeat the sins of the father."

"Sin? You judge him, then?"

"God will judge him. He was not a bad man, I suppose. Perhaps he could have been a better man. He took a vow. He broke a vow. Your father valued high office more than he valued people. He has set you on the same path. I would have you know his faults before you set out to copy him; that is all. And to know that you were not the by-blow of some drunken lout in a London stew. Your mother was not a whore. Brother Francis took her when she was very young. She never knew another man. Perhaps—"

There was a movement in the chancel, a rapid shuffling of feet. A discreet clearing of the throat before he looked up to see the young novice.

"Begging your pardon, Father, but I have been sent to summon you. The archbishop is with the abbot and is asking for you."

She stood up. "I will be leaving now. I just wanted you to know, that's all. The knowledge may be instructive, may hold a mirror to your own path."

He stood too, so distracted by the summons—*I'm being called to give an accounting! Now of all times!*—that he scarcely saw her as she turned and walked away.

Only later, much later, would it occur to him that he should never have let her go without finding out where she went.

⁓⁂⁓

On Tuesday of the next week, Anna was again in her stall with Bek at her feet. The sun had come out, but the day was cold and windy. Few customers came by her little booth.

The old broth seller had warned her that the customers would not return until spring, when the pilgrims started to move from shrine to shrine. She had been right. Only she and Anna and one lone charcoal vendor braved the weather today. A few customers bought soup and charcoal. None bought books.

"Cold, An na. Bek cold," the child behind her whined. "Go."

It was hard to refute his logic when she'd not sold a single book all day.

She was taking down her awning, packing up her basket, when a man came by, a man of means judging from his furred mantle.

"Giving up so early?" he asked.

"You're English. It's nice to hear English," she said, strapping down the tent.

"Oh? You're English also?"

"No. That is—well, I've lived on the Continent all my life. My grandfather was English."

The man was about the age of her grandfather. He had kind eyes, and his beard was neatly trimmed. He thumbed one of Anna's guides.

"You write a good hand. Too bad you do not live in England. I'm a master scribe at the customs house in London. I could get you journeyman work during your slow season, though of course, being a woman, you'd not be a full member of the guild."

"Go. Cold." Bek's voice was adamant.

A woman had joined the scribe. She had her hands wrapped around a cup of hot soup. She held out the cup to her husband. He shook his head.

"This is my wife. She insisted on coming with me, said she'd never seen Paris. We're on our way home."

He laid the book down. Anna started to try to interest him in another and realized the futility of that. One didn't sell bread to a baker.

"I think she'll be glad to get back to London," he said. "She finds Rheims less desirable than Paris."

"We'll be leaving on Friday," the woman said, rolling her eyes. "And it can't come soon enough for me." She sipped her soup.

"Go! An na!"

Anna looked out over the empty square. She had not made a farthing in two weeks. Nor had she heard from VanCleve. He'd gone back to his wife or his other life. He'd probably forgotten all about his promise of a "more permanent arrangement." This might be her only chance.

"I'm going to England also," Anna said. "I was wondering . . . as I am a widow, would it be possible . . . that is, do you think my son and I could travel with you? I have money to pay for my passage. We would be no burden. It's just that traveling alone is dangerous for a woman and a child. I was hoping for a party of pilgrims, but . . ."

The man peered over her shoulder at Bek, whose shivers were becoming so violent his arms were flailing about. "Well . . . I don't know if—"

"Of course you may come with us," the woman said. "I'll be glad of the company. We will be leaving on the morrow. We will meet you here. If you still want to go, be ready."

"An na, go!"

Anna turned around to scold him. "Hush, Bek. We're going," she said, trying to keep the irritation from her voice. When she turned back to affirm her appointment the couple had already crossed the square. The woman waved back at her.

"On the morrow," Anna called.

The woman answered back, but Anna couldn't hear what she said. Apparently she was engaged in some kind of argument with her husband.

Well, she thought, *if they don't come back, what have I lost?*

TWENTY-FIVE

Old apple tree, old apple tree, We've come to wassail thee,
To bear and to bow apple enow,
Hats full, caps full, three bushel bags full,
Barn floors full and a little heap under the stairs.
—YULETIDE WASSAILING SONG

ood Christian though she considered herself, Lady Joan Cobham had no intention of denying herself the seasonal pleasure of the old ways. She saw no harm in lighting the Yule log and hanging the green. Every mantel of Cooling Castle was draped with yew and laurel, every doorpost garlanded with ivy and riband. A great Christmas bush of greens hung from the rafters in the great hall where the feasts would be held—the feasts and the Lollard meetings—permeating the air with the prickly scent of resin. But pride of place was given to the mistletoe that hung from every door lintel and twined itself with ribands around the four posts of the bed she shared with her husband.

Joan still believed somewhat in the magic of the pale little leaves with their bloodless berries. The old ones said they carried aphrodisiac powers. Not that she and John had ever had need for such. Until now. Of late John had been preoccupied, not his usual eager self, not since the meeting with the parchment maker. So Joan had tied the mistletoe around a wooden frame and embellished it with puffs of satin and velvet streamers to make a kissing bush. This she hung inside the canopy over her bed.

"Now do your stuff," she whispered, watching the little bush shiver as she fastened it overhead. She gave the streamer a little push for encouragement.

Sighing, she climbed down from the stool and smoothed her skirt, brushing off bits of fallen greenery. She had put a few Druid herbs in the kissing bush for goodly measure, sacred herbs that would ripen her womb to grow John's child: henbane and primrose and wolfsbane. She had her daughters from her first marriage and one son from her second but they were all grown up and gone. A pretty round-faced lass with a merry laugh and John's glinting eyes, tossing a bladder ball with her father in the garden or screwing her pretty mouth into a pout as she struggled over her clumsy child's embroidery, a little girl to grow into a gentle lady who would comfort her mother as she tiptoed into old age—that was the desire of Joan's heart.

But it had not happened. And with John's preoccupation with the Lollard cause there had been little opportunity of late. Fewer and fewer opportunities for fun of any kind. The wassailing, for example. What harm could there be in the mere lighting of bonfires, hitting the trees with sticks, or creating a loud ruckus with howls and blasts from a cow's horn while dancing around the most abundant tree?

But when she'd ordered two barrels of finest cider set aside for the wassailing to drink to the health of the guardians of the trees, John had frowned, his little pointy beard stabbing into the soft flesh of his second chin, tickling the skin of his third. He'd scratched it with the tip of his forefinger as he was wont to do when he was displeased.

"I'll take no part in it, wife. And—"

"But John. It is the custom. The servants expect it."

"And neither will you. If they wish to indulge, it will be on their souls. We will provide no cider for any drunken revelry connected with Druid worship of trees."

"Druid worship! Husband, it is but an empty, harmless ritual. Just a bit of celebration."

"Not to some. Too many still cling to the old ways. Mixing their Catholic ritual and their pagan rites in a hodgepodge of superstition that the Church winks at until it becomes inconvenient."

"The peasants work hard. Their lives are bleak. You would deprive them of a little revelry, husband? That is harsh."

"Invite them to one of the Lollard meetings. Serve them temperate cider, roast meats, and poppy seed cakes soaked in hippocras. I am not an ungenerous man. But we must teach them to be drunk with the Spirit of Christ. That kind of drunkenness does not lead to vomit and regret in the morning. It is decided. We will replace the old way with a new one. Replace, wife. Not add on."

She did not remind him that the servants and the apple trees as well as the earth in which they were rooted belonged to her. It would not have occurred to her. He was lord. His word the last.

Almost.

"Husband, I think you are in need of a purgative. And I shall blend it for you myself."

With that parting shot she had gone to the herb garden. A pinch of *Helleborus niger*—a tiny bit of the root from the Christmas rose. She foraged beneath its green-tinged, downcast blooms, the ugly winter-blasted jagged leaves, to pinch a bit of the root. A bit more. Her John was a big man. But maybe not that much. She didn't want to kill him. Just rid him of a little bile.

But now, judging from the sounds coming from the garderobe, the groans and squirts and rumblings, she surmised that she just might have misjudged the amount after all. Putting away her scissors and ribbons, she bustled off to the kitchen and was back within a span of minutes. John was still enthroned and the look of misery on his face piled on more remorse.

"Here, husband, drink this."

"Hair of the dog, wife? I've had enough of your elixirs for a while, I'll be thinking."

"Now, John," she said sheepishly, holding the small glass beaker with one hand, stroking the crown of his head with the other. "It is a tea made with fennel seed and peppermint. It will soothe your innards."

She lowered the wooden lid on the hole beside him and sat down, trying to ignore the smell. Fresh herbs for the floor after this. She made a mental note as she reached for the tussie mussie, the little bouquet of herbs hanging above the seat, their flowers dry and brittle now. She pressed it to her nose and breathed tentatively. Not much help there.

John drank the tea and gave a loud belch.

"I'm sorry, John. Mayhap I overdid the purgative just a bit."

"Mayhap," he grumbled wryly.

A tentative knock on the garderobe door, "Milady?"

"What is it?"

"Visitors, a cleric by name of Flemmynge. Says he is an emissary from the archbishop. Says he has an urgent message for Sir John."

John grunted. "Too bad for old Arundel if my bowels and my own good wife kill me before he gets his turn."

"You are only saying that to get back at me. It's wicked to tease about such things." But her heart skipped a beat.

Another squirt echoed down the hole that emptied through the sloping drain into the marsh between the castle and the sea. She lifted the flowered tussie mussie reflexively to her nose and sneezed heartily.

"Oh. Something offends my lady's delicate nose? Get out of here. Let me at least suffer this indignity in private."

"John—"

"Go on. I think this potion may be more efficacious than the last. Leave me in peace. Go get rid of Flemmynge."

She stood up reluctantly. But she didn't need to keep the archbishop's emissary cooling his heels too long. It wasn't prudent. "I'll be right back."

"And fetch me some more arse wipes." He handed her the empty glass. "Get several," he called after her. "And speaking of arse wipes, tell the archbishop's lackey that Sir John is indisposed and will wait on him another day."

"John! The servants!"

But she heard him mutter as she closed the door, "When the devil's balls get frostbite. That's when Sir John Oldcastle will give an audience to the archbishop's lackey."

She also heard his innards grumbling in agreement.

※

Joan had no more than got rid of Master Flemmynge and called for clean linen and fresh wash water to be placed in Sir John's chamber than the maid was back again with news that someone else was asking for Sir John.

"Whoever it is, just inquire about his business and send him away. Sir John is poorly. I need to tend to his needs now." Her tone was harsher than usual and she knew it, but she could not keep the irritation from her voice. It seemed as though some of John's bilious humors had infected her.

" 'Tis a *her*, milady, not a him."

"Him. Her. Whoever. I have more pressing needs."

"Aye, milady." The girl curtsied and left, but Joan could tell she was not happy with that answer. Bother. Joan had a good relationship with her maids; she worked hard to keep it thus. Their eyes and ears were important in such perilous times, their loyalty crucial. But she had more pressing matters to see to now. John's bowels had settled somewhat but not his mood. And she couldn't say she blamed him, she thought, as she rushed to his chamber through the adjoining door to her own to answer his querulous call.

"And shut the damned door! The draft is cold enough to shrivel the manhood of Zeus!"

Invoking a pagan deity, husband? How very impious of you! But she swallowed the retort, planted a placating smile on her face, and shut the door, drawing the heavy brocaded curtains across the leaded-glass window to shut out the draft.

"Here, my love." She took down his warmest tunic from a row of pegs, brushed its red fox lining brusquely. "Put this on. It'll warm you. I told cook to send you up some hot broth."

They both ignored the rumbling of his gut as though it rebelled against the promise of victuals.

"What did Flemmynge want?" he grunted as he pulled on his breeches.

She reached to help him with the front lacings, sensing that this was not the time to let her fingers wander playfully. She moved on to the lacings of his clean lawn shirt, which still smelled of the lye from the laundry. Her John might be a tad portly, but he was neatly turned out, his beard well trimmed, his clothes fashionable, and his linen immaculate. She'd noticed that Master Flemmynge's ballooning sleeves, though they were of the finest weave, had sauce stains around the cuffs, and she wondered how his wife could let him go about on church business in such a state.

"He said to tell you that there is to be a holy processional to Becket's shrine in Canterbury for the saint's day on December twenty-ninth. The archbishop requires of you a cadre of armed men, an honor guard in full Oldcastle livery, to stand along the processional route."

"By the saint whose moldy bones he kisses! I'll have no part of such a tawdry show." He shoved her gently. "Old Arundel knows that to have the livery of Sir John Oldcastle providing protection for such a show as the Romans put on with relics will be tantamount to a public endorsement of everything I preach against. I'll have no part in it. Get out of the way. I'll go tell him myself!"

She held out a restraining arm. " 'Twill do naught but add fuel to the fire, John, to anger him. He said Prince Harry will be in attendance, and he specifically asked for your men to line the processional."

"Hal?" He scratched his beard. "The feast of Thomas à Becket, the saint who was martyred because he provoked a king. Yes, I suppose he did." A bit of a smile then a chuckle. "Hal was ever one for laying down the gauntlet."

"John, this is no game with the two of you facing each other across a board. This is serious."

"Game or not. It makes no difference. I'll not do it. Is Flemmynge still here?"

"No, his feathers were ruffled that you refused to see him. He said he would not wait, that he's on his way to the abbey on business for the archbishop. I don't like that man. He quite puts on airs. Very officious in his demeanor. He said the archbishop has instructed him to make sure that the talents of the sisters are 'being employed for the glory of the Church and not some frivolous or heretical cause.' I didn't like the tone in his voice."

"Send a messenger to the abbey to warn the abbess of his coming. Flemmynge is sly, all right. More than once, I've heard him speak with praise of Wycliffe's teachings, and now that he's been appointed 'inquisitor' he's suddenly seeing heresy under every stone. Better still, I'll ride to the abbey myself. I'll warn the abbess and confront Arundel's toady myself."

"No, John, you're in no condition—I've already sent a messenger. The abbess is too clever to be outmaneuvered by the likes of—"

A knock at the door interrupted her.

"Yes?"

The maid's voice answered through the thick oaken door. "My lady, I have the victuals for Sir John."

She opened the door to receive the bowl of steaming broth and was about to close it again when the maid dropped a timid half-curtsy and continued.

"My lady, the woman I told you about. Beggin' your pardon, but I think you might want to see her. She's asking to see Sir John. Says it's a matter of the gravest importance regarding"—here the maid lowered her voice and Joan opened the door—"the Lollard cause."

"I told you Sir John is seeing no one."

"Please, milady, just you see her then. I can tell from her speech, she is a gentle woman, not one of the peasants. And she seems in much distress and almost faint with being tired. She says she will not leave without seeing Sir John. Says she has come all the way from Bohemia. Says she comes from—I can't remember the man's name. I think it was Finn. An illuminator of fine books or something for the university."

The maid looked up to the face of Sir John, who had joined his wife at the door, and added, "She has a child with her. He appears sick or crippled. She was pulling him in a kind of wagon bed."

"You say she is from Bohemia? Then she may have news of Jan Hus and the Lollard cause there. I will see her."

Joan sighed. The maid had guessed aright. She knew a woman with a sick child would not be turned away. And of course, John would not turn away any who shared his cause. "No. I will go down myself and meet her. I will bring her to you, if I think—" She turned her back to the maid and lowered her voice. "You are too trusting, John. Does it not occur to you that this woman could be a spy for Arundel?"

Turning back to the maid, she said, "Give the visitors food. I'll wait upon them presently."

Sir John was pulling on his beard. "She's from Finn the Illuminator. I know him by reputation. I should go to her at once."

"I am mistress here, John. Matters of hospitality are at my discretion. Don't worry. You will see this girl for yourself if I think she's who she says she is. But first eat your broth."

Joan closed the door and followed the maid downstairs to the castle kitchens, determined not to let her guard down. A woman and a child traveling all the way from Bohemia—that was somewhere in the heart of the Continent, she was sure—an unlikely tale, to say the least. She would hear her out, give her a few pence, and send her on her way.

TWENTY-SIX

*The River Ebro gives good water . . . its waters filled
with fish . . .
at Estella the bread is good, the wine excellent,
meat and fish abundant.*
—*LIBRI SANCTI JACOBI*, BOOK V
(12TH-CENTURY PILGRIM GUIDE)

nna was chilled to the bone. She sat on a three-legged stool next to the wide hearth and cradled her hands around the beaker of hot broth the cook had given her. She tasted it carefully. Cool enough to drink.

"Here," she said, handing it to Bek, who sat with his legs curled around the wooden chest in his small wagon. It had been a tight fit, but she had squeezed both boy and box into the narrow space without damage to either. And the box was lighter now. She'd sold the other books. All that was left was the Wycliffe Bible and the Hebrew book of spells hidden beneath a change of clothing for each of them. The Gospel of John she'd left with the landlord. "When Monsieur returns," she'd said, giving him both the book and a note explaining where she'd gone.

"Hold the broth carefully. It's hot," she warned.

The cook handed her another. Anna sipped it gratefully. They had ridden all day in the back of a dray cart from London to get here, and the fare to the farmer had taken her last ha'penny. She was almost numb with fatigue. Too numb to think what she would do if Sir John turned her away. But he would not. Would he? Her grandfather could not have misjudged him so. But the maid said Sir John was indisposed. What if he were too sick to see her? What if he were dead? Or gone mad? Or the servants wouldn't let her see him? She'd threatened the poor maid terribly, but that threat had drained her of her last spark of energy.

They should have stayed in London with the scribe and his wife. He'd offered her a job. But when she'd learned Sir John Oldcastle was only a few hours away, she knew she could not wait another day. *I'm here, Grandfather. I've kept my promise. The rest is up to God.* She leaned her head back against the wall.

"You look worn out," the cook said. He had a snaggle-toothed smile and a jolly manner. His face was red from the heat of the brick ovens that lined the wall. The warmth of the room made Anna drowsy. The morning's clouds had churned up a cold rain and dusk was coming on. Would he let them sleep on the floor beside the kitchen hearth? The stone flags would be hard, but Bek had his blanket and she her cloak. At least they would be out of the weather.

"Just sit awhile and warm yourself by the fire." He turned toward the great brick oven and withdrew a large metal tray with several loaves of bread. The smell made her mouth water.

"Would it be too much to ask for a slice of that for my son? We've come a long way. I don't have any money left to pay, but I'm sure you have some pots that need scrubbing."

He cut off a heel of the warm bread, spread it with sweet cream butter, and offered it to Bek, who looked at Anna for permission and only took it when she nodded her head at him. Then he cut off another slice and handed it to Anna. "Them hands don't look like they've done a heap of scrubbing!"

She looked down at her pale fingers wrapped around the mug of broth. Even the warmth of the broth had not brought color to them. "True enough," she said. "But I'm a fair scribe. Maybe you have a letter you need writing."

He laughed. "Me? No, I'm just cook's helper. Though cook might find something for you to do. You might could help him with inventorying the pantry. Do you cipher too?"

Trying not to gulp the bread, she reached out and wiped a bit of drool from Bek's mouth.

"What's wrong with the boy? He's not sickly, is he? If he is—"

Anna hastened to reassure the young man, whose good will seemed to be melting like the butter on the hot bread. "No. He's healthy. He's just had this affliction from birth."

"Well," he said grudgingly. "Even if he did have the ague or something even worse, milady wouldn't have me turn you out on a night like this."

Anna felt weak with relief.

"But I don't know if milady will see you or not."

"It's Sir John I've come to see," she reiterated. "I have a message for him, and I'm to give it to no other."

He laughed. "Beggin' your pardon, but at Cooling Castle ain't no woman will ever get to Sir John without first going through his wife. 'Specially one that looks like you." His cheeks seemed to redden even more.

"Where is the wench demanding to see Sir John?"

Anna looked up to see a plump, pretty woman, with eyes as amber as the honey silk she wore, bustling toward her. Anna stood up clumsily, her bread falling to the floor, and dropped an even clumsier curtsy. Her head felt light, as though she'd drunk too much mead.

"My lady, I have come from Bohemia with a message of importance for Sir John. If I may be—"

The curved archway lining the kitchen wall opposite the brick ovens began to crawl like snakes. Anna tried to shake her head to clear it. "My lady, if I—"

She heard Bek crying her name as she fell in a heap at Lady Joan Cobham's feet.

~⋇~

The abbess couldn't really say the exact moment that it happened—but no, she could if she really thought about it; it had been the day the priest came. She had taken one look at the handsome cleric with his Roman ways and known what he was about. After that, it had built steadily, this sense of foreboding, this anxiety that pressed against her chest, this certain knowledge that the activities of the abbey were becoming more and more perilous.

And not just for herself, but for the sisters in her care. For Sir John. For the Lollard cause they served. Even for the pardoner, blinded like Judas by his false allegiance.

The need to hide *the other*—as she now called the clandestine manuscripts even in her mind, not daring to speak the heretical Lollard name, not even calling it the English Bible—lest the snooping priest or others of his ilk pop in. The secrecy was wearing her down. The pardoner had a way of inserting himself into the most innocent-seeming conversation, lulling his prey into a slip of the tongue. The abbey had enjoyed a brief respite from his snooping these last three months. But last week Brother Gabriel had returned. And so had the pain in her head.

She shut her eyes against the flickering light of the candle flame in the gathering twilight. Thank God, this infirmity had lessened with the advancing years, though it still plagued her in nervous times. But the pain was no longer so pointed in one place. Perhaps it was God's way. Not to take away the suffering that strengthened her soul but just spread it out into her hands and back and ankles, because He knew that an old woman's heart could not take the pain in one foul dose inside her head.

She had begun the clandestine copying so many years ago, not knowing how the manuscripts would ever be distributed. Copying as much to assuage her loss as for the cause her copying served.

In the beginning she had copied only to ease her grief. A memorial to her heart's great loss of everything that mattered, an emptying out of her self through the strokes her pen made upon the calfskin. It was as though the blood drained from her heart into her hands and emptied into the quill.

Scratch, hiss . . . two sons lost . . .

Only the sounds of the pen penetrated the well of silence around her.

Scratch, hiss . . . a lover's loss, her heart's desire . . . the pretty little girl child more doll than real . . . scratch, hiss . . . into the great silence, the sound of her heart so faint she wasn't sure it beat at all.

But with the copying the Scriptures had seized her soul.

Scratch . . . hiss . . . In the beginning was the word.

The Word.

God had spoken creation into being. The word that separated man from animals. The gift of language, making men as gods, discerning good and evil. This ability to express one's thoughts, one's feelings, and then to use that word to talk about the Word made flesh. What higher cause could she serve? But high or low, she had no other cause.

The manuscripts had grown in number. First the Psalms of David, "The Lord is my Shepherd." Balm for her wounded heart. Then the beatitudes: "Blessed are the meek. Blessed are the poor." Then the blessed Crucifixion story and the stories of the Magdalene and the other women who supported Jesus, the first witnesses to his resurrection. (Why had no priest ever pointed that out?) The copies piled up as her body and her spirit healed at Saint Faith Priory, but she worried about the safety of the house that had taken her in should she be discovered.

And then one day Sir John had come to Saint Faith Priory and boldly commissioned a copy of the English Scriptures as though he were asking for no more than a common book of hours. She still remembered how he chortled the day she trusted him enough to deliver the stack hidden inside her chest. It was he who funded the breaking away into a smaller house, close by Cooling Castle, to serve Gravesend and Rochester, an abbey not powerful enough to invite suspicion, whose secret mission would be the copying of the English Scriptures and the Wycliffe texts.

The prioress at Saint Faith had given her blessing, even allowing Kathryn to take three of her best scribes, but Kathryn could tell that she was relieved to see the backs of them, these heretics she harbored in her bosom.

The little abbey at the back of nowhere—a tiny cluster of buildings: chapel, priory, scriptorium, cloister, and refectory—had been able to produce these contraband texts unmolested. Until now. But lately there was something in the air that called up to her senses the dreaded smell of burning pitch.

She feared the hounds of hell had caught again the scent.

The abbess put down her pen and stood to stretch her back and flex her hand, rubbing the knob of her distended knuckle. Maybe it was just the dreariness of the bleak midwinter that pressed upon her spirit and made her joints hurt. Maybe the priest was not a spy for the archbishop. Maybe it was just the rain and the heavy workload that made her knuckles ache and crooked the fingers in her right hand so that it was not steady against the parchment.

The rain, or the devil. Or both.

With the narrowing of daylight, it was harder to see. Even her uninjured eye was growing weaker. When she could no longer do the work, who would supply Sir John with the English Gospels for the Continent? Only one or two of the sisters could really be trusted. Sister Agatha had been a loss; though she'd been released from the kitchen duty and sent back to doing the work of a scribe, the abbess was careful to see that she was given only secular works to copy. Even more vigilance would be required now that the priest had returned.

She couldn't quite put her crooked finger on it, but there was something changed about him. For one thing, he looked tired, almost gaunt. And his eyes had lost some of their certainty. When she'd inquired if all was well with him, he'd said he was grieving over the loss of his father confessor. But he'd offered to hear the confessions of the sisters—a convenient enough method for spying out the conscience torn between orthodoxy and the Lollard heresy—though he'd confined himself to the guest quarters for the most part.

Once or twice she'd passed the chapel and heard him reciting the Office. She thought his voice sounded strained, heavy with some unconfessed sin of his own. Or maybe it was just his grief. She started once to tell him that now that his confessor was gone, he could say his prayers himself, confess directly to God. He'd no need of an intermediary. But she knew such an admonition would fall on deaf ears. Or maybe on ears listening for just such heresy. Besides, there was no dearth of confessors to give ear to his sins. The archbishop himself would hear the sins of such a rising star in the Curia.

But enough ruminating, she scolded herself. There was still light enough to work a little longer before the bell that summoned the sisters to vespers. As she crossed the room to get another candle, she gazed out the window that overlooked the quadrangle with its lovely fountain, a sight that always gave her peace.

No peace today.

Because sitting on a bench just inside the cloister was Sister Agatha, her body half in shadow, her doughy face highlighted by a fading sun, and she was talking to a strange man. He should not have been let into the cloister without the permission of the abbess. Unless of course it was a man of the Church. Another cleric on an errand of snooping. She had better don her veil and go down to stop this mischief. Uncanny how they always knew which one to seek out. Why couldn't it have been Matilde? Or even one of the novices, who were ignorant of the abbey's real mission.

But before she could get her veil adjusted, there was a knock at her chamber door.

"Mother, there's a messenger here from Cooling Castle. Says it's urgent. Shall I allow him in?"

Urgent. From the castle. Probably a warning. Too late, she thought as she closed the door behind her.

"I'm on my way to the cloister now. I'll see him directly. Give him refreshment and bid him wait."

Whatever wind Sister Agatha was blowing on whatever blaze needed to be stifled now.

By the time the abbess had made her way down to the cloister, the pair had been joined by a third. Brother Gabriel had likewise crossed the quadrangle, coming from the guesthouse, whose corner window also overlooked the fountain.

"Commissioner Flemmynge, an unexpected pleasure to see you out of Canterbury." Then, noticing the approach of the abbess, "Mother Superior, we have a visitor," he said.

The "we" did not go unnoticed by the abbess. How clever he was. The way he wormed his way in with just the suggestion of intimacy. One could almost pity a younger woman who felt the warmth of that charm. How uncircumspect to assign him as a confessor of nuns.

"And welcome, I'm sure. But I would ask the pair of you to retire to either the guesthouse or my office. This is, after all, a cloister for nuns. Vespers bells will be sounding soon. Your presence here would be an intrusion upon our prayers."

She gave Agatha a hard glance. The woman's face turned red and she dropped her head.

"I was just passing through on my way to the scriptorium, Mother." She'd only been released from kitchen duty last week.

"Then you'd best be about your business, Sister. I'm sure our visitors understand the call of duty. The poetry of Christine de Pisan awaits you."

"Yes, Mother." Her tone was more subdued than usual. Guilt perhaps at being caught out gossiping—or worse. Agatha's false sense of piety and general stupidity, for all her cleverness with a quill, could be easily manipulated into treachery. She nodded meaningfully at Agatha, who reluctantly began a slow passage across the quadrangle. The abbess could almost see her ears straining against the thin fabric of her wimple.

The stranger spoke first, his tone unctuous. "Forgive me, Mother. I did not mean to intrude. It is only that I have heard about the work in your scriptorium and sometime, when it would not be an 'intrusion,' would avail myself of the pleasure of an inspection. Canterbury is very interested in what you do here."

Sly words. A thinly veiled threat couched in the terms of flattery.

"The sisters do exemplary work," she said. "Their hagiographies are known throughout England. They even produced a *Life of Catherine of Siena* for His Excellency. We will be proud for you to see them. But I'm sure you can understand that an unannounced visit is a distraction from the sisters' daily routine of work and prayer. If perhaps you could give us some notice, we could entertain you better."

"It is not entertainment I seek, Mother, though your hospitality is generous, I am sure." He smirked.

Should she invite them into her study? Had she covered the work on her desk? She couldn't chance it. Perhaps a quick trip through the scriptorium to be rid of him. She would show him Sister Agatha's work station first— nothing damning there—giving Sister Matilde time to cover hers.

She continued, "You are welcome to visit the scriptorium, Commissioner Flemmynge. The sisters will be at vespers, of course."

Help came from an unexpected quarter.

Brother Gabriel put his hand upon the visiting cleric's shoulder in a friendly gesture. "The scriptorium is one of my favorite places in the abbey. But the light is fading. Perhaps you would be better to stay over in the guesthouse and begin your inspection tomorrow. When you can see the scribes at work. In the meantime, I'm sure the sisters would be honored to have you read the vespers Office. It is not often they have distinguished guests from Canterbury."

The abbess was so taken aback by Brother Gabriel's intervention that she almost failed to notice the visiting cleric preen at the finely delivered compliment. She was not surprised at the ease with which the pardoner handled the other—after all, he was slick-tongued; he had to be to sell empty pieces of paper with imagined significance—but she was startled by the conspiratorial wink he gave her as he guided the other away toward the chapel.

No two ways about it, she thought, as she headed toward the kitchen to meet the messenger from Cooling Castle who carried his belated warning. Brother Gabriel was a very dangerous man.

He's after bigger fish, she thought. He's not here to bring a few nuns up on charges of heresy. He's after Sir John.

· ϡ ͡·

"Here, just a whiff of this. I think she's coming around, John." The voice, a woman's voice, was low and musical.

For the second time in her life, Anna came back to consciousness in a place unlike any she had ever seen. But where the Romani *vardo* had conjured a vision of hell, this time she was sure she must be in paradise. The down mattress on which she lay was as soft as a cloud and her eyelids fluttered open to see a canopy of indigo sky strewn with a thousand flowers embroidered in crimson and gold. A small bush of greenery and crimson hung incongruously at its apex.

A sharp aroma of pine resin assailed her senses, accompanied a heartbeat later by the dusty odor of dried lavender so close to her nostrils it tickled her nose. She sneezed and looked up to see three faces like low-hung moons hovering between her own face and the indigo canopy. The heart-shaped, pleasant face of the woman was pretty in a faded way. Dark brown curls struggled free of an ecru lace cap framing apple cheeks and a large mouth. Another face was studded with sharp jet eyes beneath graying eyebrows that bunched in consternation. Two rounded chins were separated by a pointy little beard pulled by restless fingers.

Anna waved away the tussie mussie in front of her nose and struggled to sit up.

"Slowly now. Give your head a chance to clear," a woman's voice said, and the large mouth moved.

"Where am I?" Anna asked, her head slowly clearing, remembering before the words were out of her mouth the kitchen of Cooling Castle and her encounter with its lady.

"You are at Cooling Castle."

Cooling Castle. At last. Tears smarted behind her eyelids. The journey, the crossing with the seasickness she thought would never end. Cooling Castle. *I'm here, Dĕdeček. I've done what you said.*

"In Kent, England."

The words came out of the pursed little mouth working above the funny little mustache, viewed from Anna's vantage point, which was flat on her back, as upside down. The effect made her want to laugh with the humor of it, laugh with the relief that she was here at long last, and that this round white face hovering just above her must belong to Sir John Oldcastle. She smothered her exhaled laughter into a spasm of coughing.

"And ye be in milady's own bed!" the third face said—its mouth a perfect circle in the triangle of a young girl's face, the tone carrying the tiniest hint of outrage.

Anna became immediately aware of her disheveled appearance and stained travel clothes, noting with relief that at least they had removed her muddy cloak and boots before laying her on the bed. She tried to sit up.

The faces receded and a silk-clad arm, stronger than its shape suggested, whipped behind her back to support her.

The rest of the room came into focus: a small fire flickering, wall sconces already lit, the room bright enough even in the gathering gloom to make out the ornate tapestries insulating the walls from winter drafts. A large chest, heavy with oriental carvings, doubled as a sideboard. A chair and settle covered with silken cushions in bright hues was pulled close enough to the fire for the light to pick out their silken fringes. Green garlands of the season bedecked the mantel and the corner posts of the giant bed that held her.

"Where is Bek? He will be frightened without me. I must go to him." She tried to stand up.

"Rest a bit longer. I assure you, the child is being well taken care of." The woman nodded at the maid. "Go down to the kitchen and get the boy and bring him up." Then, she turned back to Anna. "And now," she said forthrightly, "I hope you are feeling strong and comfortable enough, ensconced as you are in my bedchamber, to tell me just what urgent business you might have with my husband."

TWENTY-SEVEN

In the abbey guesthouse Brother Gabriel picked at the roasted capon resting on the table between him and Commissioner Flemmynge. He watched with disgust as the cleric dragged his heavy pleated sleeve across the breast of the bird to disjoint a leg with greasy fingers, then offered this last joint halfheartedly to his mess mate. Brother Gabriel declined. He'd not much appetite of late. Not since he left Battle Abbey. Not since his visit with Mistress Clare.

"I'm glad we had this opportunity to visit," the visitor said between smacks. "The archbishop asked me to look in on you. He is concerned for your health since the passing of your father confessor."

Gabriel thought he denoted the slightest inflection of the word "father." Or was that just his imagination? Was he the last to know that he was the bastard child of Brother Francis? No, he was not the last to know. No one *knew*.

There was nothing to know because it was idle gossip invented in the mind of an embittered servant. The very thought of it called up the hard set of Mistress Clare's sharp little chin as she said the words. *"You are his natural child."*

Yet how could he be so sure it was a lie? He remembered the father's advice to him about his own carnal urges. The pain in his hip caused him to squirm in his chair.

"The death of Brother Francis was a great loss," Gabriel said finally. "He was more than my confessor. He was my *spiritual* father." He changed the subject. "Did you hear His Eminence voice concern regarding my well-being?"

"His exact words, I believe, were that he hated to see a man with such a promising career in the Church lose sight of his mission." Flemmynge licked his lips as though he were savoring more than the flavor of the bird.

"And did he pinpoint any specific dereliction of duty that might lead him to believe I was 'losing sight of my mission'?"

"Only that after considerable time and money spent in France, you have uncovered little evidence concerning Lord Cobham's sources for his heretical manuscripts."

No surprise here. The archbishop had told him as much already, and he had given the same reply he now gave to Flemmynge.

"I ruled out the French scribes by uncovering no source that could supply such a large number as Sir John would need for exportation to the Continent."

"Then all the more reason to look closer to home."

And that's why you've come, Gabriel thought. The condemnation of dead heretics like Wycliffe does not advance one's reputation like the burning of live ones.

Flemmynge swiped his bread through the drippings left under the bird's carcass, and when the juice dripped onto his lace collar, picked at it with a beringed finger.

"Have you done with the French sleuthing, then? Will you be going back?"

"I have no reason to return to France."

"Well, then. I suppose we will scour our own countryside to unearth the heretical scribes." He pulled a bit of sinew that had snagged between his teeth and wiped it on the cloth that covered the board between them. "And we might as well begin with this one on the morrow. If that fat old nun can be believed, we just might turn up a contraband text or two on this very spot. It would be a logical source, wouldn't it? Right here at Sir John's back door?"

Gabriel shook his head. "This abbey is too small. I don't deny that they may have produced an occasional English psalter on commission. But show me the scriptorium that has not. That's one of the reasons I came here, and I've found nothing of suspicion. But you can see for yourself on the morrow." Gabriel squirmed in his chair, trying to ease the pain in his hip. It ran down his left leg like a cord of fire.

"If they have not hidden them all. I don't trust a woman who hides her face behind a veil. And that one old nun said—"

"Sister Agatha? She's just looking for attention. I tell you, Flemmynge, there is nothing here. The abbess keeps her face veiled to hide scars from an old injury. Besides, in spite of her proud bearing, she's old. Too old to be running a heresy mill. The sisters are all devout. Leave them to their prayers and scribbles. Don't waste time chasing a rabbit down a hole."

"Then why did you come back here?"

"Because it is as close as I can get to Sir John without staying at Cooling Castle. And Lady Joan will not have me there. And if truth be told, after . . ."

He could not say "after he had seduced a woman and abandoned her"— and "abandoned" was the right word because he knew now he would never return to France. How selfish his dreams of VanCleve and his mistress had been! He would not follow in his father's footsteps and beget a bastard child upon an innocent woman. At least after that first time, he'd been wise enough to withdraw at the crucial moment. Nor would he deny her the true husband she would find in another, more deserving man.

"After Brother Francis's death I found it oddly comforting to be here among the sisters," he said, standing up. "Now, if you will excuse me." He nodded at the small cot in the corner. "I hope you sleep well. I shall seek my own rest."

Flemmynge frowned. "Not exactly the lap of luxury, is it?"

"No. But you'll find the bed linen clean and the mattress well aired. The abbess may be old, but she keeps a good house. We breakfast together after lauds and I will accompany you to the scriptorium, where you will see that all here is as it should be."

⌇⌇

Brother Gabriel wondered, as he spent yet another sleepless night tossing upon his cot, interrupted more than once with the self-discipline of his little corded whip—though it seemed the pain in his hip should have been discipline enough—why he had intervened, giving the abbess time to hide her texts, even lying to protect her. What spirit had possessed him? During his nocturnal prowlings, when all honest people slept, he had seen the candle glowing from her chamber window. He listened now to the familiar call of the bells to matins followed by the sounds of the sisters shuffling through the cloisters to recite their sleepy prayers in the cold chapel.

Still sleep did not come.

His head was filled with questions and yearnings for two women. Two faces painted themselves upon his closed eyelids: one framed with hair of gold, and one with hair of red. One as faded and ghostly as a long-ago memory, with no clear feature to mark a portrait. The other as clear as last night's troubled dreams, its eyes still lit with unshed tears. One a longing from the heart—the other a longing rooted in his soul.

At least one was safe in the little house in Rue de Saint Luc. In time she would forget about the merchant of Flanders.

And the other one—*"Jane Paul is dead,"* Mistress Clare had said. He could still see the bright glint of certainty in her eye when she pronounced it.

⌇⌇

"You are one of us. You are home at last," Sir John said when Anna told him of her long journey after the persecution in Prague, of her grandfather and her deathbed promise to him, of Martin's death—still calling him her husband. Anna had grown so accustomed to the lie of widowhood that she clung to it still.

"I knew your grandfather by reputation only, but that reputation said he served our Lord's cause well. You and your son will stay with us as long as you want, though I fear your grandfather may have overestimated England's tolerance for the cause."

Lady Joan frowned. "He is not the only one who may have overestimated it."

She had remained silent as Anna told her tale, her eyes fastened on Bek, who, having been brought to Anna, seemed content to sit on a pallet by the fire, his limbs twitching slightly, fingers drumming on the floor as he hummed softly to himself. Now she turned her searching gaze on Anna.

"Was your son born with this affliction?"

"He was not born to me. I . . . we took him in. He was abandoned." One lie was enough. Why tell another one?

"It is good that he was not born to you. He must be a heavy burden for a woman alone. You are to be commended for your charity."

"He is no burden. Caring for him gives me comfort. And since God gave him over to my care, he is as much my son as if he were born to me."

Lady Cobham's brow lifted. "I did not mean any offense. John says that I'm often too plainspoken. It is just that given your condition, you might worry more about the child you're carrying, if his brother—"

Her eyes widened, her glance darted from Anna to Sir John and back to Anna. Then she gave a little half-smile. "You don't know, do you? John, I think our young widow here doesn't know that her husband may have left her with more than his memory."

"I don't understand what you—a child?—no, that's impossible." But even as she said it Anna knew. It was not impossible. It was something she'd feared, pushed aside whenever the possibility crept into her mind, not knowing how to think about it. The fatigue she'd felt, the nausea on rising that lately did not go away, the courses that had not come for the last two months—she could see the signs copied out on the page from *The Sickness of Women*. But the manual had also said a woman's courses might be irregular during difficult times such as famine or hardship or even grief. She could at least lay claim to the last.

Thank God she had told them she was a widow. If they knew the truth, that she had lain with a man outside of marriage, might even now be growing his seed in her womb, might they have turned her away?

"When did you say your husband was killed?"

She did a quick calculation in her head. July. Six months. She would be showing hugely by now.

"In October," she lied again.

She and VanCleve had first been together in early November, in the little room in Rue de Saint Luc. Three months. She had not told them about the interlude in Rheims. They would believe that the journey that had really taken her six months could be made in three. She should be three months along by now. Scarcely two months from the first time she lay with him in truth. If it were true. Please, God, let it not be true for the sake of the child. Yet part of her wanted it to be true. Wanted it more than she had ever wanted anything in her life. And what a foolish thing that was.

"I fled Prague two weeks after he died," she said, telling herself that part at least was not a lie.

Sir John chuckled softly. He and Lady Joan exchanged glances.

Anna's mind still reeled from the hurried calculations. "I had hoped to earn my keep with my pen," she said. "I'm a good scribe. I've copied many a text in Latin and English and even Czech for my grandfather. I'm familiar with the Wycliffe texts. I can write some of them by heart."

"You are literate, then!"

"Even a little German and French. We copied for all kinds of people."

He whistled softly under his breath, exchanged glances with his wife.

"It seems, wife, that our Lord has sent us an answer to our prayers." He looked back at Anna. "Tomorrow, I will take you to a nearby abbey. You may be safer there than with us." He frowned, bunching up his eyebrows into bristling question marks. "The abbess there is a woman of the true faith. You will be safe there, and she will direct your work to the best advantage."

"Tomorrow! You'll do no such thing. She'll not go until she's rested. She's worn out with grief and worry and travel. Not to mention caring for that one." She gave Bek an awkward little smile of acknowledgment, embarrassed the way so many were in his presence, Anna thought. He grinned back warmly, his head bobbing like a flower in the wind.

"He understands what you're saying. He's not deaf. He likes you. He's grateful for your hospitality, as am I."

"Yes, well, I like him too," Lady Cobham said, so awkwardly that Anna almost laughed. Lady Cobham patted the boy's blond head as though he wore a crown of prickly holly. "I'm sure we will be great friends." She motioned for her husband to follow her. "Now. We are going to leave the two of you to rest. We shall talk again tomorrow. But you need not worry. You are home. And when you are strong enough, we will take you to the abbey. You will like the abbess. My husband assures me she is no less than a saint. And like you, she is a woman of learning."

Only after the pair left did Anna realize she was still in Lady Cobham's sumptuous chamber. Her kindness went deeper than her demeanor indicated. "Did you hear that, Bek? Lady Cobham said that we are home."

"Ome, ome, An na ome." Bek lay on his pallet in front of the hearth and chanted low and musically, like a lullaby, drugging Anna into sleep. But it didn't feel like home. Lord Cobham had said he would take them to the abbey. She wondered if she would be expected to call the abbess "mother." It was not a word that she had ever used.

❧

"Not today, John," Lady Joan would say each morning when Sir John poked his head into my lady's chamber, where the two women nibbled on honey cakes and talked about Anna's past. Lady Cobham was full of questions about Prague, about the Lollard movement there. She had been visibly alarmed when Anna told her how the students had been beheaded for burning the papal bull that granted the right to sell indulgences.

"Anna needs rest to recover from her journey. Besides, I'm enjoying some woman's company. Go on off and joust or hunt or do whatever else it is you do whenever you abandon me. And see that the boy is fed and has a companion."

Sir John pulled a long face, but bussed his wife on the cheek. Anna blushed to see the discreet little pinch he gave her bottom as his hand slid beneath her overskirt. Nor did she miss the easy looks that passed between them, conversing without words. Anna envied them this intimacy. Her mind betrayed her by replacing Sir John's round face with VanCleve's.

"I think 'tis time to take down that Druid bush, wife. Break your witches' spell, else how shall I ever leave?"

"It'll come down on Epiphany, husband. To do aught else would bring ill luck. Now off with you."

Anna blushed again. Lady Joan had explained to her the function of the little bunch of mistletoe hanging above the bed. After that first night, Anna had been relocated into another chamber, a pretty little room not far from this one. Close enough to hear the occasional giggle and moan when everyone else in the castle slept.

"It's just a maid's room. But it's comfortable. I want you close by."

So you can keep an eye on me, Anna thought. And then immediately felt guilty for thinking that Lady Cobham didn't altogether trust her. Perhaps it was just the memory of Lela that made her see jealousy in Lady Joan's heavy-lashed cat-eyes.

"Now, madam," Lady Joan said, when Sir John was finally gone, "let us find you clothes to wear for tonight's feast."

It was Twelfth Night, the feast of the Epiphany, and the boards had already been laid in the great hall, not only for the tenants of Cooling Castle but for visiting clergy and nobility as well. Anna didn't quite know what to expect. Lollard clergy or Roman clergy? Surely Sir John would not be bold enough to mix the two. And as for nobility, that was a concept totally foreign to her egalitarian upbringing.

The closest Anna and her grandfather ever came to entertaining dignitaries was the time Jan Hus joined them. But even though by that time the rector of Prague University was preaching to thousands of people each Sunday in Betlémská kaple, when he was in the parlor of the little town house, he was one of them. All equal in the little gathering in Old Town Square. If some, like Hus or Finn the Illuminator or Master Jerome, were more respected, it was because they had earned the respect.

Not like here. Anna didn't know the rules here, where some were born to rule and some not, some were the recipients of unearned homage while others more worthy paid that homage. Here, Anna felt a great social unease.

"My lady . . ." The words felt so unnatural on her lips. Why not just "Mistress Joan"? "If it is all the same to you, I would prefer not to attend the feast."

"You would prefer?"

Why did the corners of Lady Joan's mouth twitch as though Anna were a child or half-wit who had no right to state a preference?

"Well, it is not the same to me. I wish to show off my pretty ward—that's what I'll call you, my ward. That way you can sit on the dais above the salt. No one would dare question your rights. You will enjoy the protection of Sir John Oldcastle, Lord Cobham—" Then she added under her breath, "Though that protection may prove in the end to be less than an infallible shield."

Anna knew she was talking about the Lollard cause. Her grandfather, whom she had always thought the wisest man on earth, had been wrong about this one thing. England was no safer than Prague for the Lollard movement. Maybe even less so.

Joan pulled from out of the wooden chest a silk damask houppelande of a light cream color. She shook its long trained skirt vigorously. Little bits of lavender floated to the floor. She frowned, then discarded it in a heap. "No. Better this one, I think."

The overskirt was a rich green brocade. Joan dug deeper into the chest, pulling out a green velvet bodice with slashed sleeves and ribands.

"A tuck here and a nip there. Your bosom is smaller than mine and your bottom too. And maybe let down this hem—Hilda, fetch your needle and thread," she called to the servant. Then she set a horned headdress with a gauzy veil on Anna's head but, much to Anna's relief, discarded it in favor of a small metal coronet. "With all that hair, you don't need much more on your head. Where did you get all that red hair, anyway?"

"My grandfather said I inherited it from an uncle. Along with what he called a 'sometimes tempestuous nature.' " She could almost hear him saying it. The memory made her throat tighten with longing.

When the dress was fitted to Lady Joan's careful standards, Anna stood before the chamber pier glass feeling awkward and overdressed in so many layers of finery. Lady Joan, however, was obviously enjoying herself. She flopped onto a pile of cushions on the nearest bench and motioned for Anna to pirouette.

" 'Twill suffice," she said. Again, the corners of her mouth twitched with that irrepressible half-merry, half-mocking smile.

As Anna undid the lacings and stepped out of the heavy brocade houppelande, she felt the heat of Lady Joan's scrutiny.

"There's one more thing you need to do before you dress. Here." And she handed Anna a small cup, almost clear in color. Anna had never seen one like it outside an altar, more bowl than cup, with a wide mouth.

Anna peered into it quizzically.

"It's not for drinking. You pee into it."

Had she heard aright? "You mean—"

"Just go into the garderobe and make water into the cup. So we can see if you are going to keep that trim little waist of yours or no."

Anna felt herself blush. She had been feeling so much better—the sickness almost entirely gone, except on waking, she was sure, almost sure, please let it be so, she'd prayed daily, hourly, minute by minute, promising God she would live chastely the rest of her life.

"But I'm feeling in such good health . . ."

"Has the bleeding returned?"

"Well, no, but I've lost track of the right time."

Again Lady Joan's mouth twitched. "Take the cup."

"But how—"

"Did you ever hear of a piss prophet?"

"Someone who looks at urine to tell the future, perhaps?"

"Well, sort of, your future at least. Certain doctors claim to be able to tell from the smell, sight, even the taste, of a person's urine the condition of their bodies."

"You mean, you can tell—"

"Before my last son was born, a piss prophet looked at my urine and predicted that I was pregnant."

"But can we—can you read it?"

"I paid attention. I always pay attention." She took Anna's hand and wrapped it around the stem of the bowl. "Here. We'll see."

Anna took the little cup, thinking how like a chalice it looked, the large bowled cup that had become the symbol of the Lollard movement in Bohemia to signify the right of all penitents, not just priests, to take the cup of Christ's blood. She tried to push that image away, lest she desecrate the cup in her mind, knowing that it was just an image and images held no sanctification. Still, she blushed as she took it into the garderobe. She had scarier things to think about right now than the use and misuse of holy icons. Gilbert had said nothing about a pregnant woman's urine being different.

The task being accomplished, she handed the cup over to Lady Joan, who was careful not to spill its contents as she peered into it.

"You're not going to—"

"Taste it. No."

Anna waited, watching, feeling foolish as in her head she pleaded with heaven, calling up her oft-repeated vows of chastity.

Apparently, God was not in a bargaining mood today.

"Clear, pale lemon, running to off-white with a cloud on top," Lady Joan recited.

Anna forgot to breathe.

"It looks as though, my dear, your late husband did indeed leave you more than his memory."

TWENTY-EIGHT

[The lords and bishops] dined on the dais and daintily
fared
and many a trusty man below at the long tables.
Then forth came the first course with cracking of
trumpet
On which many bright banners bravely were hanging.
—FROM *SIR GAWAIN AND THE GREEN KNIGHT*
(14TH CENTURY)

y Twelfth Night Anna's sickness was replaced by a general
sense of well-being, both welcome and surprising—and a ravenous hunger.
She eyed the roast capon on the trencher she shared with Lady Joan. Her
mouth watered with anticipation as she attacked the bird with her knife,
though she was careful, even in her greed, not to get a drop of grease on her
borrowed finery. The morsel she slipped into her mouth was succulent and
tender. She closed her eyes, the better to savor it, then remembered that enthroned as she was, along with my lord and my lady and three other dignitaries upon the dais in front of the assembled company in the great hall, she
should show a bit more decorum in her appreciation of her food.

The feast was well attended by nobility and clergy. Archbishop something or other—Anna couldn't remember his name, only the sour look on

his face as she was presented to him and the quick way he turned away—a cleric by name of Flemmynge, and another bishop occupied the dais along with herself, Sir John, and Lady Joan. Closest to the dais was the knight's board. Thirty or so knights from Kent and Sussex and even Norwich, who had made the trip along rutted and muddy roads in the heart of winter to celebrate the Feast of the Epiphany in the great hall of Cooling Castle. They and their wives were arrayed like peacocks.

"John hates this," Lady Joan whispered from behind her hand. "He'd gladly trade his goblet of Gascony wine for a pot of ale with yon yeomen at the end of the hall."

Anna looked down at the far end of the hall to the cluster of families making merry. They did indeed look to be having a good time. A quick pang of memory reminded her of the gatherings in the little town house in Prague.

"Then why doesn't he sit with them?"

Lady Joan put down her knife and turned the full force of her gaze on Anna as if she had said something too stupid to be believed.

"My dear, Sir John is a nobleman. He sits in Parliament. He has certain . . . responsibilities. He can't sit with commoners when nobility is present."

She said the word "commoners" as though the word carried fleas upon its back.

"But I'm a commoner, and you are sitting with me." She couldn't resist this at least, though it was said more by way of obtaining information than complaint.

Lady Joan heaved an exaggerated sigh. "No, my dear. I'm not sitting with you. You are sitting with me. At my invitation. And that's a very different thing."

Anna bit back a retort. She would save her tongue for tasting the apple tartlet nesting beside the roast pork that the carver was placing on their trencher. The smell alone was heaven-sent. Heaven's scent. Anna picked up her knife again.

When she could hold no more, she breathed deeply, inhaling air overheated with the many charcoal braziers lining the boards and with the heat of so many bodies. The lacings of her bodice were too tight, and no wonder, she thought, eyeing the scanty remains of the roast pork.

"My lady, I'm quite full. May I send the rest of this apple tartlet to Bek?"

"Bek has his own apple tartlet."

"I didn't know," Anna answered, embarrassed lest she had given offense. And then, only making it worse, she added, "I noticed that the fare is humbler down the boards. I just thought—"

"Bek's dinner is the same as the knights enjoy. Except for the wine, of course. He has milk to drink. You might remember, Anna, even though you're eating for two, when the babe is gone, you'll still carry his baggage on your hips, so best to leave off when you've had enough. Don't worry. It'll not go to waste. We have beggars enough at our back door—especially on a feast day."

Joan turned her head to whisper in her husband's ear. He chuckled.

They're laughing at my ignorance, Anna thought, but there was no malice in their laughter. Strange as her environment was, she felt that she was at least among friends.

Her belly full, she turned her attention to the snatches of conversation around her. On the other side of Sir John was Bishop Henry Beaufort. Lady Joan had whispered to her that he was a favorite uncle of the king's and probably would have been appointed chancellor had he not been born on the wrong side of the blanket.

"He and the archbishop are enemies. It should be interesting to watch the sparks if, in spite of his low birth, Beaufort gains ascendancy at court."

Sir John appeared in earnest conversation with Beaufort, but Anna could not make out what was being said. Though she couldn't help noticing how carefully Lady Joan was listening.

"I always pay attention," she'd said. And here was proof. Judging from the furrows on her brow and the straight set of her mouth—no amused twitching now—she was not pleased with what she heard.

On Anna's right the old archbishop and Flemmynge ignored her, immersed as they were in their own discussions.

Apparently they found the entertainment lacking.

"What do you expect from a professed Lollard, except dullness," the younger cleric said as he dusted crumbs from the breast of his ornate tunic. His full sleeves had sopped enough dripping from his trencher to grease a griddle.

He made no effort to lower his voice, trusting perhaps to the cover of the noise in the great hall, or thinking that Anna's opinion of their discourse was so insignificant that it did not matter if she heard.

"Not even a lord of misrule, or a lone jongleur. Not even a strolling musician."

The archbishop grunted. "If 'twere a strolling troubadour, he'd like as not be playing Lollard hymns. But don't make the mistake of thinking Sir John dull. He's shrewd enough to know his enemies. He only invited me because I saw him at the hunt at Colcut Manor last week and pressed him for an invitation."

Flemmynge gave a knowing grin and nodded. "Since I met him at Rochester Abbey, my invitation was likewise obligatory."

"Well, between the pair of us we've frighted off our prey. Cobham will have no Lollard preachers here. Sir John is not that bold. Odd that the abbess is not in attendance with her benefactor."

"I'm told she never leaves the abbey."

"A contemplative?"

"No. Not as such. The abbey is an enclosure of scribes. She seems to have some sort of affliction that keeps her from going about in company. I've only seen her once—"

He lowered his voice, actually glancing in Anna's direction. She nibbled at the bite of blancmange, feigning disinterest in their conversation.

"She wears a thin black veil over her headdress and wimple that completely hides her face."

They were talking about the woman whom Anna would call "mother." Her mind pulled into itself until the voices receded to meaningless chatter. She felt keenly her social isolation on the dais and wondered if she would ever again find that sense of belonging she'd had as a child. She looked out over the crowd at the grand ladies seated with their noble husbands. She felt no kinship with them either, except for perhaps the one or two who were clearly with child beneath the layers of satin and velvet and fur that covered their swollen bellies.

When would she begin to show? A quiver of anticipation crawled up her spine at the thought of it. How could she feel this little thrill, this guilty pleasure, whenever she thought of the tiny child growing inside of her? Whenever her mind conjured the image of her boy child—for she could not think of the child growing inside her as other than male—it was a blond boy child with VanCleve's intelligent eyes and wide brow that she saw. And she loved him already. Loved him as she had loved his father. Loved him as she still loved his father, for she knew that if VanCleve could have come back to her he would have.

Not for the first time she wondered if he might be dead, or if some ill fortune had overtaken him. Or possibly even grief at the loss he mentioned in his last letter. She didn't want to think that he might have another life or even a wife in Flanders, though it had crossed her mind more than once. No, she would not believe that. He had loved her. Of that she was sure. That was why she'd left a note with the little innkeeper telling him where she was.

Would she have waited if she had known about the child? No. It was better that she was here. She had promised her grandfather she would come to England. She could not wait for a man who might never return.

"Sir John's trying to influence the throne through Beaufort," Flemmynge said on her right.

" 'Twill do him no good. Beaufort will never be chancellor."

"But he's the prince's favorite."

"No matter. A bastard will never wear the great seal of England as long as I am archbishop! Not even John of Gaunt's bastard."

The word "bastard" intruded abruptly.

But her son would never be called "bastard." The world would think, even the child would think, his father dead—and she would tell him how his father, Martin, a scholar at the university, died defending the true faith.

The weight of the anticipation of so much lying lay against her heart, as leaden as the too large meal she'd just consumed.

The carver came and removed the used trencher, replacing it with a fresh one. But Anna had lost her appetite for whatever followed. Not just her stomach, but her bladder, as well, felt overfull. She was just about to ask Lady Joan if she could be excused when her ladyship tapped Anna on the shoulder.

"You are probably needing some relief from too great a crowd of men. I know I am," she said, and taking Anna by the hand, led her down from the dais toward one of the three arched entrances to the hall. They paused briefly at the knights' table while Lady Joan made pleasant inquiries regarding their guests' health. "My lady, you look well. My lord, how nice to see you. Did you find the viands to your liking?"

The pressure in Anna's bladder grew as the courtesies were exchanged, and she tried to make appropriate responses to each introduction, aware that all in turn were making their own assessments of her importance, her place in the noble household, how much courtesy they should show her. Anna would have told them bluntly, had they been bold enough to ask with their tongues and not their eyes, that she had no place in this noble household.

Lady Joan moved on to the clerics' board. Lesser churchmen, not noble born. Here there were several empty seats. Lollards whom Lady Joan had said were warned away when the archbishop invited himself.

"Prior Timothy." Lady Joan turned her attention to a tall thin man of severe demeanor. "I had hoped to see Brother Gabriel. I wanted to introduce him to my ward."

This Brother Gabriel must be in sympathy with the Lollard movement, Anna thought idly, thinking how she wished they would hurry lest her bladder burst.

"He's the father confessor at the abbey, a friar and a pardoner," Lady Joan explained to her. "One with papal approval. A favored position indeed. I thought you might like to meet him outside the confessional." Then she offered that enigmatic little half-smile, her mouth twitching like a cat's.

No Lollard sympathizer then. A pardoner! One of Rome's sanctioned predators. She'd not be likely to meet him in the confessional either. But Lady Joan knew that. It was her way of mocking both pardoner and prior without giving obvious insult.

Her irony was, of course, lost on the prior. "Brother Gabriel was taken ill. Shortly after the feast commenced. It was just as you were approaching the dais in procession. Most unusual. He turned quite pale, then murmured something about feeling ill and bolted for the door. When he didn't return I went after him, but he was nowhere in sight."

"Probably just a touch of the ague. I'll send an inquiry to the abbey tomorrow."

But Anna hardly heard this last. She was already through the archway and headed for the first-floor garderobe that served the great hall.

TWENTY-NINE

*Though you have pocketfuls of pardons . . . Though
you be found in the fraternity of all the four orders.
Though you have double indulgences . . . I set your
patents and your pardons at the worth of a peascod!*
—WILLIAM LANGLAND IN
PIERS PLOWMAN'S PROTEST (14TH CENTURY)

he abbess had grown so accustomed to viewing faces through
her thin black veil that all humankind bore to her a striking similarity in col-
oring and complexion. But even seen through the fine webbing of her veil,
there was something different about the young woman standing in front of
her desk.

"Abbess, I have brought you a gift." Sir John put his hand across the
shoulders of the girl and gently drew her forward. "This is Anna Bookman.
She came from Prague, where she worked with her husband, who was martyred for the same cause we serve. And she has bravely made her way to us
seeking refuge and employment."

It was the hair. That was what was different. Almost without thinking,
the abbess lifted her veil to get a better look at the young woman. She had
only known one other with hair like that. The abbess stood up to acknowledge the introduction. The girl was as tall as she. They stood eye to eye with

only the desk separating them. The abbess fingered the quill in her scarred left hand to keep it from reaching up of its own volition to stroke the copper-colored curls. A bit of lace merely threatened their confinement. The girl reached up and straightened the kerchief in a reflexive movement.

"Refuge, certainly," the abbess said. "And welcome, but how employment in the company of nuns who do everything for themselves, including the meanest chores?"

The girl's blue-eyed gaze remained open and unwavering, with the merest flicker of astonishment when the abbess lifted the veil to reveal her scarred face. She did not turn away self-consciously, as others did on those rare occasions when Kathryn lifted her veil. Even Sir John looked at some fixed point over her shoulder as he spoke. To alleviate his discomfort, she lowered her veil. Sir John's gaze returned to her face.

"Anna is a fine scribe. She copied the Scriptures with her husband. She can translate the Latin into both English and Czech. She worked with the followers of Jan Hus at the university in Prague."

The abbess had heard of Hus. She knew that Lollardy had swelled to a great force in Bohemia under his leadership and fiery preaching. She knew too that Prague was the ultimate destination for many of the English copies of Wycliffe's teachings that the abbey produced. If indeed the girl could translate directly into Czech, here would be a step removed. A godsend indeed.

"Is she aware of the danger?" It did not occur to the abbess that the girl might be a spy. She had that much faith in Sir John. "Is she aware that such transcriptions are illegal and carry the harshest punishments?"

"She is well aware. Her husband died because of it and she was put out of her home. She has endured much hardship just to get here. It was her husband's last instruction to her."

The girl's eyes wavered. She glanced down, appeared to be studying her hands, made anxious no doubt by the memory of it.

"Is this true, Mistress Bookman?"

"Yes." She breathed deeply and looked up. "It is true. I am a scribe, and I will willingly translate the Scriptures for you. It is also true that I share your belief that the Holy Word of God should be available to all who can read it in their own tongue." The girl's eyes were a startling shade of blue.

"Well, then, Mistress Bookman, you are indeed welcome and—"

"Please call me Anna."

"And you may call me 'Mother.' "

The girl swallowed hard and nodded. "Yes . . . Mother." She hardly said it above a whisper, then added, "Thank you for taking us in."

"Us?"

Sir John cleared his throat. "There is something else. There is another, a boy. He is afflicted. But if the abbey cannot accommodate him, we can . . ."

"How old is the boy?" She addressed this to the young woman.

"He may be as young as six or as old as eight years. I don't know for sure. He was abandoned because of his affliction." Anna tugged again on the bit of lace, tucked a curl inside it.

"And you care for him alone?"

"Yes . . . Mother . . . There was another, but she is dead."

"Then here you will have help, and he will find others among the sisters who will love him."

For the first time since the interview began, the lines in the girl's face relaxed, though the abbess noticed her shoulders remained rigid.

"There is something else," she said. "There is to be another."

"Another?"

The girl put her arm over her belly in a shielding movement.

"Oh. I see," the abbess said.

"It happened before . . . before Martin was killed."

The abbess looked at Sir John, whose gaze seemed once again fixed on some fascinating spot on the wall behind her. His face was bright red.

"Well, Sir John. It would seem that you have brought us not one but three gifts this day. You may leave Anna with me where we will see her settled in this very night. And after we have had a chance to get to know each other—by tomorrow, I think, will be enough time—you can bring the boy to us. If that is convenient, of course."

Sir John smiled broadly, his third chin paling to a faint pink.

"It will be convenient. Young Bek and I will attend you tomorrow. I left him playing with a tin whistle, as happy as a pig in mud." Then he gave a courtly bow and turned on his heel.

"I think Sir John is glad to be rid of this women's talk." The abbess laughed. "Now sit. I'll ring for refreshment, and you and I can become acquainted. Then I'll see you settled into your quarters. I'm afraid the guesthouse is taken with a sometime-resident cleric, but there are two rooms behind the refectorium, small but bigger than the nuns' cells. They will accommodate you and your children comfortably."

From the chapel tower, a bell tolled monotonously. "That is the call to prayer. The sisters will be occupied. I'll fetch some bread and butter and warm cider for us myself. You just rest."

When she returned shortly with a crockery pitcher, the girl's head was thrown back against the high-backed chair. Her eyes were closed and the smallest snore indicated the even rhythm of her breathing. She had removed the kerchief and still clutched it in her hand. Her bright hair spilled down her shoulders, but it was the way one curl drifted across her high forehead that made Kathryn's heart clutch. Strange how one thing, the smallest thing, like the color of a person's hair, could evoke an old memory from a life forgotten. You are a foolish, sentimental old woman, she scolded herself. Still, she reached up and swept the curl away from the girl's closed eyelid.

A coal shifted in the small grate that warmed the mother superior's office, sending a shower of sparks up the chimney. The girl never even broke her rhythm of breathing. The abbess remembered, though it was so long ago it was almost as though it had happened to another, the fatigue that had stalked her during her own pregnancy. She had been about the same age as this girl—late for a first child—when she'd borne her twin sons. Sighing, Kathryn covered the girl with the woolen shawl draped over her own chair and lit the tallow drip on her desk. Who knew how long Anna would sleep?

She picked up her pen. She could at least copy a few lines before the daylight faded altogether. Something about the sleeping girl made the creeping evening shadows seem less lonely. She felt an unexplainable lightness in her soul.

☙

Anna felt at home in the snug confines of her abbey rooms. The next day, Sir John brought Bek, as promised, and the two of them fit quite comfortably beside their own small hearth. The day after that, a cold rain settled in, sealing the abbey into its own little gray world.

Nights, Anna slept well, lulled by the rain dripping from the eaves, and each day she ate ravenously from the abbey kitchen's simple but nourishing food: heavy soups made with boiled barley and marrow bone and root vegetables, too dried and shriveled to eat any other way, and always accompanied by plenty of fresh bread and cream from the small herd of milk cows the sisters tended.

In the scriptorium Anna was assigned a desk with two inkwells, one for red and one for iron gall black—these were always miraculously filled each morning—and a high stool next to a kindly older nun named Sister Matilde. The sixteen scribes sat four abreast, separated by an aisle running down a long rectangular room and then crossed by another aisle. Their desks were positioned deliberately, Anna supposed, far enough apart to stop gossip, and given the nature of the abbey's work, far enough apart also to deter wandering eyes. Anna's desk was the last one, next to the west window to gain the late light. Sister Matilde's desk abutted the aisle. Anna noticed that several of the desks were empty. The abbess had explained that many of the scribes did kitchen and garden duty also. But Anna noticed that her desk and Sister Matilde's desk, along with four or five others, were rarely empty.

"We must be discreet, dear," Sister Matilde had said, handing Anna a half-copied bifolium, a folded sheet of calfskin making two pages. Several of these bifolia would make a quire; several quires could be sewn together to make a book. This bifolium was a poem by Christine de Pisan to place on top of her real work whenever visitors entered the scriptorium. On the stand above her desk, which held the slim text of John Wycliffe's sermons that she was copying and translating into the Czech language, was also a book by Christine de Pisan.

Sister Matilde pantomimed for her, sliding one sheet behind the other, as she said, "Even some of the sisters are unaware of *everything* we copy." She nodded meaningfully toward the other end of the scriptorium, where a large nun with a scowling expression watched.

But Anna did not have to do her sleight-of-hand tricks that week. Sister Agatha did not stop by her desk to chatter with the newest scribe, though she cast a few inquisitive and baleful glances in Anna's direction whenever she sailed her wide hips down the aisle.

No visitors came to the abbey. The winter rains and fog kept travelers close to their own hearths. Anna's days were spent doing the work she loved. Even Bek had found a vocation of his own. He tolerated the gentler clang of the chapel bells calling the sisters to prayer and trailed to chapel eagerly after them. They chanted the Divine Office accompanied by the high, thin notes of his little tin whistle. At first the sisters had ignored him, then tolerated him, finally accepting him into their world. Some acknowledged him with a wink and a smile whenever they passed the cushion at the foot of Anna's stool, where he sat practicing his music. Sister Matilde had assured Anna she didn't mind his playing, and Anna was glad. His soft breath made the whistle notes light and fluid, like the wind chimes made from cockleshells that Anna remembered from her little courtyard in Prague.

The chapel bells clanged now, three bells calling the sisters to nones, the last of "the little hours" in the heart of the afternoon. The sisters put down their quills as if on cue and rose, some stretching discreetly, some stifling yawns, grateful no doubt for the respite from the tedium of copying. The boy struggled to his feet, drawing himself up hand over hand on one leg of Anna's stool and holding on to Sister Matilde's hand for support. They joined the processional. Sister Matilde always brought up the rear because of Bek's affliction, but Anna considered it no less than a miracle that the boy could walk at all without the help of the handmade crutch VanCleve had fashioned for him. His legs still jerked and wobbled, but at least they supported him.

The scriptorium emptied out, leaving Anna alone, excluded from the obligation of the Divine Offices. Oddly, this exclusion did not pain her as had her exclusion from the Gypsy women, if exclusion it could be said to be. Her participation would have probably been welcomed by the sisters, but she had no desire to chant the prayer ritual. Still, she felt in some sense tied to these women in common cause, and even to their prayers, though she preferred to say hers alone, a personal, private prayer of thanks to God that she and Bek had found a home at last.

Her grandfather had been right to send her here. She should have come sooner. But no. She would not regret the time in Rheims. How could she? Not with the memory of VanCleve's arms around her. A memory that might have to sustain her forever here in this company of women. And how could she regret their "sinful dalliance," as others would call it, with the knowledge that his son grew inside her, a son she already loved? But still her conscience pricked. She wondered what Mother Superior would say if she knew the truth about Anna's child.

Anna looked out the window to the cloister walk and beyond to the three-tiered fountain, where raindrops plopped like tears into the still pools below.

Quiet pools like the reservoir of tears inside her that filled up the empty places in her heart. Tears for Martin, for her grandfather, for VanCleve, who had abandoned her. But not all tears of bitterness. Tears of hope too. Van-Cleve had left her with this secret part of him that fostered charity in her, charity enough to think that someday he would return to the little house in Rue de Saint Luc as he had always intended. Finding her gone, he would come searching for her. The landlord would give him the Gospel of John and the note, telling him where she had gone. That thought warmed her. That and how pleased her grandfather would be that she had kept her promise and was carrying on the work to which he'd given his life.

The sisters—and Bek—would be returning soon. The room would fill up again with the whispering of nibs on parchment, the scraping of penknives against the cured flesh of the calfskin, and the plaintive notes of Bek's chanting. (He no longer chanted "An na" but now words from the prayers: the *kyrie eleison* and *Je su Je su*.)

She should go to the privy before the sisters returned. These days her bladder's demands seemed to follow the frequency of the Divine Hours. She did not like to leave Bek unattended, lest they think she took advantage. She pulled on the hooded mantle hanging on the peg beside her stool and rummaged around to find the French poem, which she placed carefully on top, leaving her quill on the last unfinished word as though she had stopped mid-sentence to step away from her writing table. Then she laid the book of poems on Wycliffe's text before heading for the necessarium behind the priory.

She pulled her hood up to cover her hair and closed the door behind her. No need to latch it. The sisters never latched it when they went to prayers. And who would come out on a day such as this to nose among an innocent abbey filled with women?

·—⊰❧⊱—·

Brother Gabriel sat gratefully in front of the small hearth in the guesthouse and rubbed his calf, grimacing at the tender spot. The ride back to the abbey from Canterbury in the rain had not helped. What was it Mistress Clare had said about the pain in Brother Francis's leg? It bothered him when it rained? The pain shot from Gabriel's hip to his ankle in a string of fire. He went to the little wooden cupboard and took out a flask he'd procured from an apothecary in London, poured from it into his hand, and gingerly massaged his leg, releasing the fragrance of peppermint into the air.

This was a pain surely sent from the devil to punish God's anointed. Or sent by God Himself perhaps, to punish His anointed? It was the same punishment that had come upon Brother Francis in midlife. After he'd had carnal knowledge of a virgin. After he'd stolen her child from her and sent her away.

"Your mother was not a whore. She was a virgin when Brother Francis first knew her." He could still hear the condemnation in Mistress Clare's voice, the inflection on the word "knew" leaving little room for any misunderstanding that such "knowledge" was in a biblical sense. At least Brother Gabriel had thought Anna a widow when he'd first made love to her. VanCleve, on the other hand, really did not care. And yet the latter's intent toward Anna was much purer than the former's. How naïve VanCleve had been in the purity of that intent. How false Brother Gabriel. Where did one begin and the other end? And was this pain in his leg sent by God or the devil? Or was it merely something one man had inherited from his father? *The fathers eat sour grapes and the children's teeth are set on edge.* The sins of the father.

He put down the bottle of peppermint oil and stood up gingerly, wincing when his foot accepted his full weight. VanCleve might be gone, but Anna Bookman lingered in the thoughts of Brother Gabriel. He was besotted with the woman, powerless to discipline his thoughts, like some poor victim from Greek lore. He saw his enchantress everywhere: her image hung on his closed eyelids like a beautiful tapestry; her visage lay upon the faces of painted saints; the corona of her bright hair shimmered in goblets of still wine. Two weeks ago, his imagination had conjured her in the personage of Cobham's ward ensconced upon the dais beside Lady Joan. Dear Lord, what a fool he'd made of himself. He'd been so overcome with emotion, he'd been almost too weak-kneed to stand even the next day when he was called upon to accompany the archbishop back to Canterbury.

That trip to Canterbury alone had been enough to aggravate the pain in his leg. The three of them, Brother Gabriel, Commissioner Flemmynge, and Archbishop Arundel, in the intimate space of the heavily draped carriage, as Flemmynge the sycophant sallied forth on the evils of the heretics. Gabriel had closed his eyes and leaned his head back against the wooden panel of the carriage, hoping his companions would think him asleep. But who could sleep with Anna there, standing in the doorway of the little town house in Rheims, as he had last seen her, her eyes bright with unshed tears?

"Flemmynge thinks we should concentrate on the abbey."

In the pause that followed he realized the archbishop was addressing him. He opened his eyes.

"I beg your pardon, Your Excellency."

"I said we should concentrate on the abbey. Have you searched the abbey?" The archbishop's words rose and fell with the motion of the carriage as it rocked back and forth on the rutted winter roads.

"I've been in the scriptorium many times when the sisters were copying. The last time with Flemmynge himself." He looked directly at the bishop, who was sitting on the carriage seat next to the archbishop, the better to whisper behind his hand, Gabriel thought.

"Then perhaps you need to search it when it is empty," Arundel said archly.

Flemmynge smirked.

The archbishop continued. "Oldcastle will be summoned to give an account of his actions during the occasion of the Feast of the Blessed Saint Thomas à Becket."

"Why? What did he do?" Gabriel asked.

The crescent-shaped creases framing Archbishop Arundel's face deepened. "Prince Harry ordered him to provide a guard to line the processional route for the holy cross."

"Did he refuse?" Gabriel asked.

"Worse. As the processional cross passed, each of Sir John's armored and liveried vassals turned their backs on the holy cross that carried the image of Our Blessed Lord."

Brother Gabriel drew in a sharp breath. That was a bold move even for Sir John. And a reckless one. An open challenge, not just to the church but to the king who ordered him to serve at the processional. One had to admire the man's courage. Or deplore his foolishness.

Flemmynge disturbed the smirk on his lips to comment. "Prince Harry is not pleased. Oldcastle is being summoned the day before Candlemas to answer for his blasphemy."

Candlemas. Well timed to draw out Sir John's heretical tendency. The blessing of the candles was just one of the many rituals the Lollards despised.

"Did you tell Sir John of the impending summons as you accepted his hospitality?" Gabriel asked. He could not keep the sarcasm from his voice.

The archbishop registered it with a belch and a frown before commenting. "No. Best to let him think he got away with it. While we gather more evidence. You are to return to the abbey by the end of the week—that will give you time to offer indulgences at Canterbury to those brave pilgrims hardy enough to venture forth in this weather. When you return, make a thorough search of the scriptorium, and this time do it when the nuns are not present. You will have two weeks before the summons to come up with more evidence."

Two weeks, the archbishop had said. Starting today.

When the abbey bells tolled nones, Gabriel returned the liniment to the cupboard and carefully pulled his boot over his tender calf. Then he pulled up his hood and slipped out the door of the guesthouse. Nones was a shorter office than some, but the scriptorium was sure to be deserted for the next fifteen minutes or so. There would be time to make a start.

※

When Anna returned from the necessarium, the nuns were already beginning to exit the chapel in one long line, threading the cloister like a black silk cord. Cutting diagonally across the quadrangle courtyard, she opened the door on the end closest to her writing table and was surprised to see that she was not the first to return. At the other end of the long, rectangular room, a figure hovered over one of the slanted desks.

The dim light of a winter afternoon had already cast the eastern end of the scriptorium into shadow, but it was easy enough to see that the head bent over Sister Agatha's desk wore a hooded cowl and not a wimple. She was about to hail the visitor when, probably startled by the blast of cold air ushered in by Anna's opening of the door, he slipped out of the door on the opposite end that led into the refectorium and not the cloister walk.

The "sometime resident friar" the abbess had mentioned? But what was he doing at Sister Agatha's desk and why did he bolt like a frightened hare down a hole? Probably nothing. But she would mention it to Mother next time she saw her. Blowing on her frozen fingers for warmth, Anna settled on her stool, put her frozen foot on the welcoming, warm bricks—which like the inkwells seemed to be miraculously replenished several times a day. She positioned the outside sheet of the quire containing pages one and two beneath the weighted cords to hold them in place, took up her pen knife for scraping mistakes in one hand, her quill in the other, and began to work. She looked up only long enough to smile at Bek as he settled at her feet.

The nosy friar slipped as easily from her mind as he had slid from the scriptorium.

***

Brother Gabriel waited two days before making another attempt to search, certain that the young postulant—it was not one of the regular sisters; he could tell by her dress—had reported his snooping to the abbess. He should never have tried to search the scriptorium during "the little hours"; he should have known there was not enough time.

His heart was simply not in it, Brother Gabriel thought. That was why he was making such a bad spy. Lately, he'd come to wonder why the people he most admired seemed to be on the other side. Sir John, for instance. One surely had to admit the man had the courage of his convictions. And the abbess. There was something about her spirit that made him want to bathe his wounded soul in it. And then of course there had been Anna, who despised the very notion of grace dispensed by priests and friars and pardoners. They didn't understand the frailty of the human spirit: that's what Brother Francis would have said. They didn't understand how one soul had not the strength or the purity to meet God without the crutch of God's divinely ordained.

The keys to the kingdom did not belong to anyone who claimed them. He knew that in his heart. And yet something in his spirit sided with the heretics, or at least was beginning to understand how they could come to their heretical notions.

When a summons from the abbess did not come, he concluded that it might be safe to try again, but he would wait until vespers. The nuns had their last meal of the day afterward. That would insure him sufficient time for a thorough search.

But what would he do if he found something? That was the next question.

He would report them, of course. What else could a loyal son of the Church do?

At the sound of the vespers bells, he listened until the last footfall faded, then he lit a small lamp and went out into the cloister. He would have all the time he needed. The windows of the scriptorium were already dark. The sisters would not be back tonight.

Anna would wonder later what might have happened if she had not ignored the flame flickering in the scriptorium windows, lighting first in one, then the other, like some ghostly firefly in the middle of winter. Probably one of the sisters back from vespers filling the inkwells in preparation for tomorrow's work, collecting the finished work, she told herself, and then she put it from her mind. She and Bek had been invited to take their evening meal with the abbess in her quarters. She had come to treasure these intimate moments with the abbess. She did not want to be late.

THIRTY

In his chamber at Westminster Abbey, Prince Harry was finishing the musical composition to be performed at his father's funeral. The doctors of medicine had pronounced it a matter of days, perhaps only hours. Henry Bolingbroke, King Henry IV, had been stricken while at prayer in Westminster Abbey's Jerusalem Chamber. He was now unable to speak or even to move. He took no food. No water. He would not last long. Prince Harry, who had been summoned to his father's side, would be crowned immediately upon the king's death. Indeed, Harry had already tried on the royal diadem.

It did not fit ill.

Harry had written the music down on two pages, each page with carefully drawn neumes, signs above each syllable of text, to show whether the melody would go up or down, and not just one melody but two, two polyphonic sounds to be sung in counterpoint.

First, he would send for the archbishop, who also kept the death watch, to solicit his approval. Then, he would send the music out to be copied for distribution to the court musicians. With the melody humming in his head, he considered. How to sign it? Henry V? Prince Harry? No, some signature for his music alone. He picked up the pen and with a flourish signed, "Roy Henry." It looked good on the page.

⚜

Prince Harry was playing one melody on his lute, while guiding Lord Beaufort to play the other, when the archbishop answered the summons.

"No, Excellency, not yet," Harry said as Arundel rushed into his chamber. "No word from His Royal Majesty yet. I've summoned you on another matter. Attune your ears to listen to your prince's composition." Harry nodded at Beaufort to begin. "Psalm Twenty-three. It is to be sung at my father's funeral. Though not to the sound of the dirge. I'm not partial to dirges." He plucked the first notes of the second melody.

The archbishop frowned. His demeanor never changed during the playing of the lutes. When the last note died away, there was silence in the room.

"Well? What say ye?" Harry was unable to keep the impatience from his voice.

"Your Highness, it is a tune . . . worthy of a monarch's passing. I've no doubt it would be rendered more so if Your Grace had a less inept accompanist. But when Your Highness has time, I have matters of graver importance to discuss." The archbishop gave the merest hint of a bow, took a step backward. "I shall return when Your Grace is alone."

Irritated at the archbishop's disdain for one he preferred—as well as for his lack of musical taste—Harry answered sharply, "Excellency, prithee, proceed with your 'grave matters.' We have no secrets from our uncle."

Now you have something to frown about, Harry thought, and then reminded himself that he was not king yet and Arundel could be a powerful enemy. He nodded at Beaufort apologetically. "Attend us, uncle, after you have had your dinner."

Beaufort, ignoring Arundel as though he were not even in the room, bowed deeply. "As Your Highness commands." He backed out of the room.

"Now, Excellency, you have our sole attention."

"It concerns Lord Cobham, Your Grace. Candlemas has passed. Lord Cobham has ignored your summons to appear at Leeds to answer for his heresy."

"The roads are scarcely passable with the flooding."

"Neither has he sent a messenger to show cause for his delay," the archbishop retorted.

"If Sir John could not get through, how then could we expect a messenger to?" Harry could not keep the irritation from his voice.

The archbishop merely nodded, conceding the point reluctantly. "There is more, Your Grace."

More? How could there be more than the deliberate disobedience of a subject to his lord? "Say it, then, before it burns your lips, so eager are you to have your prince's friend hauled before you in chains."

"Brother Gabriel has searched the abbey scriptorium, which is under the patronage of Lord Cobham, and he has found damning evidence indeed."

"What kind of evidence?"

"The sisters are copying the banned texts."

"You mean the English Scriptures?"

"Not only the Scriptures, Your Grace, but translating and copying the very words of the heretic Wycliffe." He reached into the voluminous skirt of his red wool cloak and withdrew a slim quire of parchment, handed it to Harry. The words were written in a fine hand in a language he couldn't understand. But he recognized the name John Wycliffe in the header.

"How came ye by this? How do we know it is not a forgery?"

"Forgery, Your Grace? Surely you do not accuse Holy Church—"

"I accuse no one. I merely seek the truth of the matter."

"Brother Gabriel brought this evidence himself. He braved the flooded roads to serve his church and his king. And there is more. An English Bible such as the ones the Lollards carry has been found in Paternoster Row. It contained a bill of sale to Sir John Oldcastle."

There was no way to put the man off, so Harry decided to offer him a sop. "Ask Brother Gabriel to attend us."

"Brother Gabriel is gone. He had matters of personal importance to attend. I gave him leave to pursue them as a reward for his courage. But he will be available to testify at the trial."

"Trial! Your Excellency, be warned that you do not rush to judgment untimely. We do not wish to put an abbey of nuns on trial as our first sovereign act."

"The nuns will be used only to bring in Lord Cobham. We need only frighten them into confessing—"

"Leave the papers, the book with the bill of sale with us. We will study whether or no they have any significance."

"But Your Grace, surely—"

"You may leave us now, Excellency, to contemplate this 'evidence.' "

"As you wish, Your Grace."

After he left, Harry picked up the lute and began to strum his melody. It sounded like a dirge after all, he thought.

᠁

His mission finished, Brother Gabriel had made up his mind to go in search of Mistress Clare. He wanted to confront her with reasoning unclouded by grief. He wanted to look her in the eye and hear her repeat her charge that Brother Francis had been his sire. Mistress Clare had said Jane Paul was dead, but maybe he could uncover the circumstances under which she died, discover if she had other children—he might be brother or uncle. This new thought was startling, but oddly pleasing. And if it was true that Jane Paul was dead, he could lay some token on her grave, put her ghost to rest. He could do that for the sweet-faced woman who had cried when he had not hugged her back.

The archbishop had made inquiries for him. Through the abbey Mistress Clare had purchased a small cottage near Appledore in Romney Marsh, where property was cheap. She had probably retired there after Brother Francis's death. Brother Gabriel was determined to go there immediately to seek her out.

And afterward? Afterward, he would cross the Channel. He needed to see Anna one more time, needed to tell her—tell her what? The truth . . . if he could but find the courage. He owed her that, at least. He had promised her VanCleve would return. If VanCleve could not, then Brother Gabriel should explain.

But there was one more thing he had to do before he could confront his own demons. When he got to Wrotham his horse turned north toward Gravesend and not southeast toward Romney Marsh. Back toward Rochester. Back toward the abbey.

He would warn the abbess that she would soon be called to answer for the evidence he'd given against her. She would no doubt warn Sir John. But where was it written that they did not have the right to defend themselves? Sir John was a powerful enough man to petition the king to proceed with dignity, not to terrorize an abbey full of nuns—most of whom were probably innocent—with ham-handed searches and threats of torture and burning.

After all, Brother Gabriel had done his job, and done it well. The archbishop had been pleased, called him a loyal son of the Church, praise that left him feeling more damned than blessed. There was something about the whole procedure not to his liking. Wasn't loyalty to the Church the same as loyalty to Christ? Brother Francis would have said so. But he'd seen a few such inquiries. He knew how confessions were gained. There was little that was Christ-like about the procedure. Little justice and less mercy.

Just thinking about the damning evidence he'd uncovered, the Wycliffe tracts already translated into Czech tucked innocently beneath the French poem by Christine de Pisan, made him dig his heels into his horse's side. The rain had started again, and there was only an hour or two left of daylight. Best to hire a coach and driver in Wrotham to take him to Rochester.

His leg began to ache as he contemplated the ride across the hard-washed roads. His head ached too, thinking about the encounter that was only a few hours away.

Anna tapped at the abbess's door, hesitant to disturb her.

"Yes?" The voice was impatient, weary, accompanied by a shuffling of paper.

"It's Anna. The sisters were all busy. I've brought your dinner. Shall I leave it outside the door?"

"Anna. No." The voice lifted. "Don't leave it. Come in."

Lifting the latch with her left hand, Anna balanced the small tray of bread, cheese, a pitcher of warm cider, and boiled beef tongue with her right. The sisters ate meat only when they were ailing, and Mother Superior had been pale and easily tired of late. The sister in charge of the infirmary had prescribed meat to build her up. Mother Superior, who was sitting behind the desk, lowered her veil as Anna entered. Anna set the food on the corner of the desk not covered by pens and quills and parchment, and turned to go.

"Wait. Don't leave. Sit with me and tell me how young Bek likes his new lute."

"If I stay, will you lift your veil so that you can take your food while it is fresh from the kitchen?"

Anna was appalled at her own boldness. She felt herself blushing.

Mother Superior laughed. "You bargain like a guild merchant," she said as she moved her chair back from the window that overlooked her desk—just a bit, enough to paint her face in shadow. She lifted the veil and draped it back.

"You probably think me vain," she said. "I only wear it to protect others—and myself a little. The veil stops their embarrassment and their questions."

"I do not think you vain. I think you beautiful and brave and kind and—"

The abbess held up her hand in a gesture that said "enough." Anna felt her face grow hotter still.

"It's just that I am grateful, Mother."

"I am grateful as well, Anna. Grateful that our Lord has seen fit to provide us with a scribe of exemplary talent and industriousness. And a young musician." She cut the beef tongue in half and laid a piece on a slice of bread, then handed it to Anna. "Eat it for the sake of the babe you carry inside you. I should have thought of it sooner. I shall instruct the kitchen that you are to have red meat once a week and an egg a day. We want your little one to have strong bones."

The salty, heavy texture of the beef brought back memories. Her grandfather had always insisted there be meat upon his table—at least once a week—meat he'd shared with the students from the university. *They come for the food for their bodies,* he'd said. *They return for the food for their souls.*

If the abbess noticed tears pooling in Anna's eyes, tears prompted by her memories of Prague, she did not remark upon it. They chewed in companionable silence for a while.

"Has Bek learned to play a melody on his new lute?" she asked between bites.

"Yes." Anna swallowed, daintily licked a spot of grease from her fingers. "Thank you, Mother, for providing him with the lute. He would thank you if he could. He has such difficulty getting his words out."

"I wasn't sure he could discipline his fingers enough to pluck the strings."

"It is amazing. It is the music that pushes him past what his body would do. He's already coaxing melody from the instrument." Anna laughed. "And it has a mellower sound than the tin whistle."

The abbess smiled at the sound of Anna's laughter. It was a sound that surprised Anna too. Laughter was a sensation she had not enjoyed for a very long time. The abbess did that for her. It was as though she lived in a pool of tranquillity, and all who were in her company received a kind of baptism in that pool. She wondered what Dĕdeček would have thought of her. It would have been fun to watch the two of them together—two strong wills united in the same goal. They would have been a formidable force.

Once or twice Anna had tried to connive a meeting with some kind widow or well-favored spinster, but her grandfather had always got his back up. "I have loved two women in that way. That's enough for any sane man." His blue eyes had hardened into glass, and Anna had known not to probe further.

The sound of splashing as the abbess poured more cider into Anna's cup brought her back from her reverie.

"I'm sorry, Mother. I should be the one serving you."

"We all must serve each other, Anna." She returned the pitcher to the tray. "I worry that the inherent danger of the work we are doing makes you anxious. Are you sleeping well?"

"Very well, thank you, Mother. It is work I love, and I am not afraid." Anna was about to say that she had faced such danger before, that she'd had a remarkable role model to show her courage, when there was a knock at the door.

"Mother, it is the friar. I told him you were at dinner and not to be disturbed, but he insists on seeing you now. He says it is urgent."

Anna, recognizing Sister Matilde's voice through the heavy oaken door, rose and gathered up the remains of the dinner.

"No, Anna, stay. It's the resident friar I told you about. I'd like you to meet him. He's a pardoner. Maybe even an honest one. I'm not sure. You can help me decide."

The abbess lowered her veil just as the door opened to Sister Matilde. Trailing behind her was a Roman cleric, his cowl and cassock dripping water onto the floor rushes. Anna receded a few steps, turned her back to place the tray on the chest on the other side of the room. She remained there to give the newcomer her chair across from the abbess's desk and herself time to compose her features in such a way as not to show her natural animosity toward the pardoner.

"I am sorry for the intrusion, Abbess, but I have come on an errand of mercy."

The timbre of the voice startled Anna.

"You need to know that a warrant may soon be issued for Sir John's arrest on charges of heresy."

Anna was so distracted by the voice itself, that at first the full import of the words did not sink into her understanding. So like VanCleve's voice, she thought, and yet different too, very different in tone, very authoritarian.

"This warrant will be obtained based on evidence gained in your scriptorium. No doubt you or some of the sisters will be questioned, even asked to testify against Lord Cobham."

The abbess did not respond immediately. The room seemed to hold its breath. Or was it just Anna's breath that would not come? When the abbess finally answered, her tone was cold as steel and just as hard-edged.

"Evidence gained by whose hand?" she asked.

The friar's tone did not waver. "Gained and given up by mine own hand, in the service of the Church. But damning as the evidence is, if you prepare a proper defense and with my recommendation, the abbey will probably get off with an admonition. The most hurtful document was found at the west end of the scriptorium, the desk nearest the window."

What the friar was saying had finally registered with Anna. The candle flickering in the window, the friar she'd caught snooping! Why had she been so negligent? Why, when she had missed the finished text of the Czech translation, had she assumed that it had already been gathered up by the person who filled the inkwells? Why had she not been vigilant?

"Why are you warning me? Such a warning seems to fall outside your loyalty to the Church," the abbess said from behind Anna.

"I am warning you because I know you to be a dedicated servant of our Lord. This abbey can be a valuable tool for His service. It has merely fallen under wrongful patronage. Nothing can be gained if the abbey is closed and you are imprisoned."

There was some exasperation in his tone. Had the man expected gratitude?

"Give up for interrogation the nun who sits at that desk and plead ignorance of any conspiracy to provide English and Czech Scripture to the Lollards."

Anna felt faint. Her hand shook, knocking the cider pitcher from the tray. It clattered to the floor with a startling crash. Anna clutched the edge of the chest for support, felt herself about to topple like an overblown seed head on a stripling stalk.

The voice that answered the priest's demand was resolute.

"I will not identify the sister who sits at that desk. You may go back and tell your archbishop that whatever culpability falls upon the abbey rests with its abbess alone. While I await his summons, I shall be strengthened by the Paraclete and the sure knowledge that I am in His will. You see, Brother Gabriel, I too have my loyalties."

So calm were her tone and demeanor, she might have been discussing the cancellation of an order for diluted ink or inferior parchment.

"But I apologize for one thing, Brother Gabriel. It seems my manners are remiss. Anna, I would like you to meet the sometime-resident friar I told you about. The guesthouse will be soon available after all. It seems the friar's work here is done."

It was a wonder frost did not form on her lips as the words exited her mouth.

Anna turned around and stumbled forward. She gave a little half-curtsy, a mere nod to acknowledge the introduction.

"Anna is a widow from the Continent, a guest of the abbey. She and her son will be with us only until the weather clears and she can complete her pilgrimage."

The cassocked figure stepped forward and Anna looked full into his face for the first time.

Her first thought, born of some great reservoir of longing deep inside her, was that VanCleve had come for her at last. But no. Given the conversation that had just transpired, it could not be VanCleve. Perhaps his evil twin then.

In a halting movement, the friar reached up and drew back his hood, revealing his eyes. His eyes betrayed him.

The quivering in her voice betrayed her. "Brother Gabriel and I are well acquainted, Mother. We met in Rheims."

The color drained from his face. "You are mistaken . . . that is . . . I'm sure we've never met. I've not been in Rheims—"

"I would not likely forget such a meeting, Brother. I remember all my customers. You once purchased a book from me." Her voice was hardly above a whisper. "You paid exceeding well, though had I known your true occupation, I might have considered the coin to be as counterfeit as your wares."

He just stood there for the longest moment with his mouth open, as though words would not come. But his eyes were eloquent. She could read the struggle in his soul, but she stiffened herself against any compassion for him. Bitterness welled up inside her. In that moment she despised him.

"What kind of book did he buy, Anna?" the abbess asked. Incredulity and a struggle for understanding overlaid her question.

"He bought an English translation of a gospel, Mother. I fear he is no honest pardoner after all, but a spy for Rome."

He held out his hand like a supplicant. "Anna, Mother Superior, there—"

"Now, if you will excuse me," Anna said, "I'll leave Brother Gabriel to explain to you as he wishes. If you want me, I shall be at my desk." Here she looked at Gabriel, directly into VanCleve's eyes. "It is the desk closest to the window at the western end of the scriptorium."

THIRTY-ONE

God, I have lost my lover, he who loved me so, hand-
  some and fair.
'Twas such an oath I had from him . . .
And where is now the young squire gone
Who begged me ever, night and day?
And now I am all alone . . .
  —FROM *THE PRETTY FRUITS OF LOVE*
  (12TH-CENTURY FRENCH POEM)

hen the message came, Lady Cobham was inventorying the pantry, making sure there would be enough stores to get them through until the summer harvest. With so much rain, some of the rye was moldy. She gave orders to feed it to the hogs. Some fed it to the peasant class, but not Joan. She'd seen too many serfs with mind sickness—hallucinations and wild ramblings—from eating moldy rye. The barrel of ground wheat flour infested with weevils—that she would pour out in plain sight so that the beggar women could come and scoop it off the ground. She knew they would pick out the bugs and make it into bread for their children. The very thought of it disgusted her, but she knew when early spring stores got low and there was little flour even in the almshouses, the infested flour might help keep some peasant child alive.

"Don't pour it directly on the ground. Just set the barrel by the kitchen door. It'll be empty soon enough," she told the butler.

She moved to another of the dozen barrels lined up along the wall, picked out a few of the weevils herself, crushed them between her fingers, frowning in disgust.

"This one too," she said. At this rate she'd be picking out weevils from Sir John's bread.

"Milady, this came from the abbey. The messenger said it was urgent."

Joan wiped her hands on her apron and broke the seal on the folded parchment. A quick scan of the contents—just a few lines in a fine feminine hand, "The hawk should fly west, the nest is clean. Make all haste."

She recognized the seal from the abbey. The message was clear enough.

"Tell Sir John I need to see him in his chamber. He may be in the stables. He has a sick mare."

Now she had more to worry about than diminishing winter stores.

❧

"I want to go with you," his pretty wife said as Sir John stuffed books and smallclothes into a bag. Flames leaped in the fireplace as he added crumpled paper to the fire. It burned quickly. Just one of the reasons—that and the price—that they preferred paper to parchment for the contraband texts. The Gospels he could not bring himself to burn—only the Wycliffe tracts—but he could not carry them all. And he would not leave them here. It was too dangerous for Joan.

"No, my love, I can move faster alone." He stopped to scribble some words on a paper in a bold, wild scrawl. "You are to show them this when they come to search. It says that I have abandoned you because you would not join my cause. Play the injured wife."

"I am the injured wife. You are abandoning me for a mistress with whom I cannot compete. Your piety comes between us, sir."

Her pretty little pout that she'd so often used against him, that pout he could not resist, crumpled. Big tears slid down her cheeks. He took a deep breath, steeling himself not to take her in his arms. If he did he might never leave.

"That's the pose," he said, trying to keep his tone light. "Pull that face when they question you. When this blows over, when the king comes round,

I'll send for you. If Harry were king, I'd answer the charge now, but Boling-broke lingers and Hal is a fearful pup treading Arundel's heels. I'm abandoning you to protect you."

"I don't want to be protected. I want to go with you."

"If any of the poor priests come, turn them away. There could be spies among them."

Rip. Tear. The flame in the fireplace flared again. Such a pity. But no time to think of that now. Survival was more important.

"Tell them Sir John has fled to Wales and they are no longer welcome here."

Great drops of sweat lined his forehead. One drop trickled down it. He wiped it away with his elbow.

"You are abandoning them too? Abandoning their cause!" Her eyes were round with astonishment and bright with unshed tears.

"Of course not. The leaders among them know where I've gone."

"What about the abbey?"

"You are to continue in your patronage of the abbey, but tell the abbess to translate only Latin Gospels and secular works in English. She has already burned the rest—'the nest is clean.' When Prince Harry is king in truth, then he can be reasoned with."

To his surprise she did not argue further. He paused and stared at her, his beautiful, passionate wife—so much more than he deserved. Jesu, how he loved her. How it hurt to leave.

"How can I get in touch with you?"

"Send letters to my holding in Herefordshire Castle. I'll get them as I'm able. Write nothing incriminating, only news of yourself and Cooling Castle. With angry words. I'll read endearments in your recriminations and answer as I'm able, begging your forgiveness for abandoning you, haranguing you for your orthodoxy."

He cupped her chin with his hand. "Each word, each smear upon the page, will speak silently of my love."

He drew her to him and kissed her, crushing her to his chest so tightly he could hear the pounding of her heart.

"I'm taking your mare. The hunter is winded and my mare is almost ready to drop her foal." He held her out, wiped a tear from her eye. "Her foal will be a sign. I'll be back afore the foal can bear your round little rump on his back." He tried to laugh but choked on the effort. He kissed her again, then peeling her arms from around his neck, tried to recover his man's emotions.

She followed him out the door, into the courtyard, where her mare waited, bridled and ready. The groom handed him the reins as he mounted, then withdrew. John leaned down from his saddle, kissed the top of his Joan's head, said low into her ear, "It'll be fine. You'll see. Just a short separation. They say the king is at death's door."

She merely nodded her downcast head in tight little jerks.

He straightened himself in the saddle, pulled on the reins of his horse, and trotted off, leaving her standing in the courtyard. Behind him, he thought he heard her sniffle. He did not look back.

～⚹⚹～

The ostler carried the news to the watcher at the keep. It was the heart of the night. The watcher roused the steward, the steward the chamberlain. It was the chamberlain who decided not to wake his lady. The news would keep till morn, the news that Sir John's favorite mare had died. The foal was stillborn.

～⚹⚹～

Anna lay awake in her narrow bed, the sound of her intermittent, stifled sobs mixing with the little snuffling snores from Bek in the next room. Just lately he'd felt secure enough to sleep somewhere other than at her feet. She was glad because tonight she needed to be alone. She'd started to cry with the compline bells. When the bells called matins, she was still awake, and still crying.

It was almost a relief when the summons she dreaded finally came.

A gentle knock at the door. A soft voice. One of the novices.

"Mistress Bookman?" The voice was scarcely above a whisper in the darkened hallway outside her chamber. "The abbess bids you attend her."

Anna got up too heavily—the weight of the pardoner's child in her womb? The shattered fragments of a foolish woman's fantasy? Or dread? Even in Prague they'd heard about the tactics the Inquisition used to solicit confessions of heresy. And Anna had seen firsthand the vengeful wrath of an angry bishop. She tried to push the images of the Vltava River bridge away.

The abbess had clearly intended to protect her and then she, foolish, stupid girl with too much arrogance, too much pride, had blurted out her culpability before the cleric. Thinking to hurt him. Thinking to hurt VanCleve. More stupidity! Going over it again and again in her head, remembering how he'd questioned her about the book; information was what he'd wanted from her all along! Even as he'd whispered love into her ear. Even as he'd released his seed inside her.

VanCleve. A friar! Cloth merchant from Flanders—such a cunning, malicious liar could only have been spawned by the devil. No seller of cloth. A seller of purloined grace, taking money from the poor and ignorant for that which was given freely by the Savior's blood! *Brother* Gabriel. *Father* Gabriel. She hated him. But she hated herself more. What would her grandfather say if he knew she carried a pardoner's child in her womb? For the first time since his death, Anna was glad that he was not here. Glad he would never know.

But the abbess would have to know. Maybe she already knew. Maybe she had read it in Anna's face. Would she continue to protect her if she knew the child was not her "husband"'s but that of a monk? A sin on either side of orthodoxy.

Another knock. "Mistress Bookman?"

"Yes, I'm coming." Anna moved to the door. The scrape of wood on stone echoed in the night as she opened the door a small crack—just enough to make herself heard but not seen in the glow of the candle the girl carried. "Tell her I'll be right there."

"Begging your pardon, mistress, but the abbess bade me wait to guide you. She said you might stumble in the darkness."

"Very well," Anna said. "Give me a minute to dress."

Stumble? Or run away? Had the abbess mistaken the horror in her face for fear? Had she decided to give her up to save the other sisters? Was that why she was being summoned in the middle of the night? Who could blame her? Her first loyalty would be to protect her abbey. That was only right.

Anna threw cold water on her face, thought about throwing her cloak on over her shift for the sake of speed, then thought better of it. They might have come for her already. If she was going to gaol she did not intend to go in her shift. She took another moment to bind her unruly hair into a knot at the nape of her neck. The novice waiting in the hall would be getting cold.

"Just one more moment," she called softly. She gathered up her cloak, stuffing a comb into the pocket along with a handkerchief, then tiptoed in to peek at Bek. He was sleeping soundly, clutching his tin whistle in his sleep. His lute lay on a chair beside his bed. Within reach. If she did not return, he would grieve. But the sisters would take care of him, she knew. At least he had his music.

⁓ ⁓

"You may leave us now," the abbess said to the novice. "You may return to your bed." She nodded to Anna. "Come sit by the hearth. You're shivering."

The girl was in such distress that the abbess feared for the child she carried. She gathered the shawl from her own chair and spread it around Anna's shoulders, noticing in the firelight how the girl's red-rimmed eyes searched the shadows.

"We are alone. You need not be afraid. I will do everything I can to protect you, in spite of the fact that you practically told the friar you were copying the contraband texts. You are no more guilty than the rest of us, but by your confession you implicate all of us."

"That was foolish, I know." Anna's voice was small.

"Very foolish because it puts not only you but your unborn child in danger. And you do not strike me as a foolish woman."

Anna said nothing. The midnight shadows danced on the walls with the movement of the flames. The abbess lit the oil lamp on her desk to make the room appear less sinister. She moved her chair closer to where Anna hunched in a little pile of misery. She reached out and took the girl's hands in her own.

"Is there something you want to tell me, Anna? About your previous association with Brother Gabriel?"

The girl closed her eyes, but one tear escaped anyway. Her hands trembled. She shook her head as if to say she could not speak.

"You said you met him in Rheims. And though he denied it to your face, he admitted after you left that he knew you—rather well, I think. He was quite distressed, Anna. He kept saying over and over that there was a misunderstanding, and that he needed to talk to you. I sent him away. I hope that was the right thing to do."

"I hope never to see him again."

The bitterness in her voice disturbed the abbess. She knew if such anger turned inward it would fester like proud flesh. It might even mark the child she carried. It was plain that there was more here than philosophical differences. She had never been one to pry into other people's secrets, but this went beyond personal factors. There were implications here for the abbey. The priest had been visibly shaken by seeing Anna.

"What was he doing in Rheims, Anna? Do you know?"

"Spying!" She almost spit the word into the flames. "He was spying for the Church. He posed as a merchant, prancing around in his fine silk garments, buying gifts for Little Bek, pretending to offer friendship, when all he was really trying to do was spread a net to trap Lollard scribes and copyists."

"Did he find any?"

She looked up, her eyes gleaming. "Just one." She put her hands on her belly. "Maybe two. Did you tell him about the baby?" Her voice trembled.

"No. Of course not, I—Anna, did he offer you more than friendship?"

"He is the father of my child." And Anna began to sob so deeply that it was several minutes before the abbess could calm her enough for Anna to tell the story: how she'd fled Prague under threat of persecution, alone and friendless; how she'd traveled with the Roma pilgrims to Rheims. How there in the shadow of the great Notre Dame Cathedral, she'd met a merchant named VanCleve, a man who'd offered her shelter and said he loved her.

Only much later, long after the first light of dawn had come and the sisters had shuffled off to prime and Anna's exhaustion had driven her to sleep, did the abbess stop to remember how very similar this conversation had been to one she'd had many years ago when she'd held another unwed mother in her arms and tried to give her comfort. But that memory belonged to another life and had no purpose here—no purpose except to remind her of the time she'd sent another man away.

The shock, the pain in Brother Gabriel's eyes: it hurt to see it. Had Finn had that same look in his eyes when the prioress had sent him away? But she couldn't think about that now. That had been another lifetime. It no longer mattered. In this lifetime, she had her abbey to protect. She'd best get at it. The archbishop's soldiers would come soon. They would find the scriptorium and the nuns' quarters swept clean. Not a crumb of heresy anywhere.

Please, God, let it be so.

From her little cottage outside Appledore village, Mistress Clare leaned on her broom and paused in the sharp, cold air to look out over Romney Marsh. In the distance she could hear the booming call of the bittern hidden in the reeds. Some might have thought her vista lonely. She merely found it peaceful. Loneliness was an enemy she'd long ago faced down. At least here she had to serve none but herself.

The cottage suited her. It was snug enough with its own round fire pit and stone hearth, its roof well thatched with reed. She could hardly wait for spring to till the little patch of withered herbs beside the stoop. She'd made her last payment from Brother Francis's legacy and still had a little horde left—enough to see her through if she supplemented it with the sale of eggs in the village. She blessed the parsimony that had at long last bought her freedom from servitude.

Her cottage faced east and from her front stoop she could see Romney Marsh and beyond to the busy seaport in the distance. To her south the river Rother wound its way through the marshlands. And just to her north beyond her little patch of garden, she could make out the steeple on the village church.

On clear days like this she could sometimes see the laborers working on the steeple. The locals had told her about the violent history of Appledore when she'd secured the cottage with her first payment—years ago. For centuries the seaport had been a favorite for warring ships. First the Danes, and lately the French; raiding, pillaging, and burning. That was why she'd got the place so cheap—that and its lonely aspect. During the Peasants' Rebellion of '81, even Appledore's stone chapel had been pillaged and burned, along with Horne's Place, the village manor house. But William Horne had got his revenge. He'd been one of the commissioners appointed to put down the rebellion. He'd been well rewarded for his loyalty, his great farmhouse and its fortifications rebuilt during the intervening years with money from the bishops. And now his heirs were at work on the chapel.

The locals had told her something else too. Yesterday, the village provost informed her that a cleric had been inquiring about her. "I told him naught, but if he comes nosing around again, shall I tell him?" Her heart was racing as she gave him her permission.

The bell from the chapel rang out. She liked the sound. Shading her eyes from the bright glare of sun, she turned in the direction of the bell, squinted into the distance. A sharp north wind lifted her kerchief. She shivered and, rubbing her hands together, went back inside. No sign of a horse and rider picking his way down the lane that led from the village to her cottage.

But he would come.

The provost had said he seemed very anxious. She'd best go in and punch up the fire, put out a simple supper. Just in case. Her boy would be cold after his long ride.

⁓⋇⋇⁓

Brother Gabriel wondered as his horse picked its way through the marsh what demon had driven him to this godforsaken place. The only sign of life was a curl of smoke from the cottage on the headland. He kept his eyes fastened on it as though it were a beacon of hope though he had no rational explanation for what drove him to seek out the old woman who lived there. What possible succor could she offer? She'd never even shown him any warmth.

In the distance an abandoned flat-bottomed boat slapped against the pebble shore. That's me, he thought. Rudderless, adrift. The abbess had sent him packing, refusing even to let him speak to Anna, even though he'd begged and confessed to her more than he should have. She'd not been unkind, merely firm. But he was glad he could not see her eyes behind the veil, could not read the condemnation there. He'd thought to stop at Cooling Castle to warn Sir John, but had urged his horse on by the gatehouse, lacking the courage to face the man he'd betrayed. Surely the abbess would warn him. The last thing Brother Gabriel wanted to do in his current state of mind was to be called to testify against Sir John.

"Well done," the archbishop had said. Were those the same words the high priest once said to Judas Iscariot? Where he once would have preened at such laudatory words, now they turned his heart to lead. He could not quit Lambeth Palace fast enough.

He looked back at the curl of smoke. *Mistress Clare can tell you who you are,* a small voice inside his head said. Any port in a storm. There, perhaps, he could gain perspective. For Brother Gabriel no longer knew where his loyalties lay.

But worst of all, he'd betrayed Anna. Anna. He could almost hear the devil's laughter.

❧

Mistress Clare was sitting beside her blazing hearth, waiting, the table already laid with a simple meal, as it had been for the two nights since her conversation with the provost. Yet, when the knock came, she started with the quickness of a deer.

So. He'd come at last. Just as she'd hoped he would.

It had taken him longer than she thought, but that had given her time to make up her mind. He was in trouble. Why else would he have come looking for her? If he'd let it alone, she would have left him to the future he'd chosen. But he had not. She was his mother, and she was entitled to tell him so. She was entitled to give him comfort. She'd kept her bargain. Now he'd come looking for Jane Paul. And he would find her.

THIRTY-TWO

rchbishop Arundel jerked his sable-lined hood over his forehead. The March wind kept pushing it back, exposing the thin skin of his bald pate to the cold. Finally! Cooling Castle was in sight and not a minute too soon. A cold mist was rising or settling. Hard to tell which. But he could see the keep and crenellated tower rising on the marshy headland like a great white ghost.

He belched heavily, feeling the sourness burn his throat as he spurred his horse and tried to keep up with the king's soldiers, who seemed disinclined to slow their pace to accommodate the archbishop. He should have stayed back at Lambeth Palace. He was not a well man. The learned doctor from the university who had kept him cooling his heels in an anteroom like any commoner had not helped one whit! His only contribution, besides smelling the bishop's urine—with an unmistakable look of disgust on his face—had been to discourse on the imbalance of black bile in his humors and turn him over to a barber surgeon to bleed him. And for this the learned doctor had charged his archbishop the exorbitant sum of seventy-five pounds—and delayed their departure for Rochester. The noxious herbal prescription he'd scrawled only added to the sourness in the back of the patient's throat.

But no matter how ill his health, the archbishop's duty to his Church mandated he be present when the search was made. Besides, if he had stayed behind in his warm bed, he would have been denied the delectable satisfaction of seeing this nemesis of Holy Church squirm, of hearing the sergeant read the search warrant signed by the very man Oldcastle had been smugly hiding behind. One day soon he would obtain a royal warrant for his arrest and see Lord Cobham clapped in irons—if he lived long enough!

Breathing heavily, the archbishop brought up the rear as the party of six armed soldiers presented its demands to the warden at the gatehouse.

The sergeant unfurled the parchment. The newly minted seal of Henry V gleamed richly. The bells of London were still tolling Bolingbroke's death when the archbishop brought the summons to the king. It was no accident that Arundel had maneuvered things to make this one of Prince Henry's first official, if reluctant, acts as king. Best to let the young pup know from the beginning who really held the reins of power.

"We've a warrant to search and summons Sir John Oldcastle, Lord Cobham, by order of Henry the Fifth, Sovereign King of all England," the sergeant intoned. "We demand that he surrender his person to the archbishop's authority for questioning on matters touching heresy."

The aging warden at the gate seemed unimpressed. He stepped out into the courtyard and, scratching his head, picked out a louse and impaled it upon his thumbnail. Then he coughed and let loose a string of spittle through the empty space vacated by a missing tooth. The spittle landed on the hoof of the sergeant's horse. The beast skittered sideways, shivering his haunches in protest.

"His lordship's 'person' beint here," the warden said.

"Where is he, then?" asked the sergeant, irritation in his voice. But not as much irritation as Arundel felt. All this way for nothing.

"Don't know. His lordship don't usually tell me his *itinerary*." The fellow cleared his throat and spit again, this time just missing the furred edge of the bishop's cloak. "Beg yer pardon, Excellency. A touch of the lung rot, I reckon."

The mist was thickening to a real rain. Arundel felt the chill of it to his marrow. This was not the scenario he'd imagined when he'd dragged himself from his sickbed.

"Call Lady Cobham, then," he said to the warden.

The wretched little warden dared to look him in the eye. "Can't do that neither," he said. "She beint here."

"Is she with Lord Cobham?"

"Nay. She's gone off to visit her daughter. Matter of fact, nobody left here 'cept me and a few crofters. She took the house servants with her."

"Where does Lady Cobham's daughter live?"

"Don't know."

The sergeant looked at Arundel as if asking what he should do now. Arundel pointed to the ring of keys hanging from the warden's belt.

"Open up the castle."

The old gatekeeper fumbled at his belt, removed the keys slowly. "I'm not sure—"

"On order of the king, warden. Surrender the keys. Now!"

He handed the keys to the archbishop, who pitched them to the sergeant. "Open it up. I mean to search every devil blasted corner of this hellhole."

⁘

Darkness had fallen by the time the search was completed. The archbishop had watched, giving orders as he hunched beside the lackluster fire he'd ordered lit in Oldcastle's chamber. It was a peat fire. And it burned as bilious as he felt.

The search rendered nothing but a pile of letters left out in plain sight, obviously contrived by Cobham to protect his wife from prosecution. The prey had slipped the snare. This time. But the archbishop had the search warrant with Henry's signature. Soon he would have an arrest warrant. He could wait. But not too long, the black bile in his throat reminded him. Not too long or the next archbishop would be the one who caught the fox for whom he'd set the trap.

"Go down to the cellar and bring up some of Cobham's wine. I'm chilled through. But be prepared to ride at first light. We'll quarter here tonight. Tomorrow we search the abbey."

⚜

For three days the abbess had been expecting them. On the third day the office of prime had been sung and she had settled in to work on a book of hours when the archbishop and the soldiers appeared at her door. There was no need to cover the Latin text.

She had a moment of compassion for the old man the novice ushered in. He looked wan and frail. But the band of soldiers accompanying him and the harsh, dismissive tone with which he addressed her soon erased that.

"Mother Superior, it has come to our attention that your abbey may be harboring copyists within your bosom who transcribe heretical texts for Lord Cobham and the Lollards. I have come to search your scriptorium and the abbey's private quarters."

No mention of a warrant. She could not demand one. The abbey, its lands, even the clothes the sisters wore on their backs, belonged to the Church. Only a cardinal or the pope himself had greater jurisdiction.

"As you wish, Your Excellency. But it is early in the day and you appear to have ridden far. Would you care to break your fast before you begin? You and your men could be served in the refectory. All the sisters are at work."

"This is not a social call, abbess. But a small bowl of gruel, unseasoned and dusted with pulverized almonds, would not be unwelcome." He grimaced. "Doctor's orders. I shall eat it here while the soldiers conduct their search."

"The gruel we can manage easily enough." His skin looked gray, even accounting for the veil through which she viewed him. "The almonds, I'm less sure of. We are a modest abbey, not given to luxuries such as the bishops enjoy at Lambeth." She smiled, hoping to soften the implied criticism.

He appeared to take no notice of either the words or the smile.

She nodded toward the novice, who slid silently from the room on her way to the kitchen. On her way too to give the alarm. Though Kathryn knew if all the nuns' quarters had not already been purged, it was too late.

"If you are going to search private quarters, may I gather the nuns in the chapel? The sisters would find the presence of the men disturbing."

He nodded his assent. "Better if they are all assembled in one place. I can question them there."

Question them? God forgive her, if she had endangered them without just cause. But the cause was just. She knew it in her heart. And she would do everything she could to protect them. Most of them were innocent of any knowledge of the contraband texts. This would surely show. The others were strong women. She had prepared them, even practiced with them what to say. All except Agatha. And Agatha she'd assigned to infirmary duty, hoping the men would not venture there for fear of contagion. She had given orders that the nun on duty in the infirmary would not answer any bells.

"Have the bell ringer call the sisters to convocation," she said to the novice, who returned with the bowl of gruel and, curtsying, placed it in front of the archbishop. "Three short rings."

"Yes, Mother." The girl looked at her with fear in her eyes.

Kathryn patted her on the shoulder. "Don't be anxious, little one. We are innocent of any wrongdoing. This is but a formality. When the archbishop finds nothing here but a cloister of devout nuns serving their Lord, he will go and leave us in peace to our prayers."

"It is my understanding that you are more than a contemplative order, Mother," said the archbishop. "That you do more than pray."

"We make no secret of our other work. We support ourselves through the copying of texts. I'm sure you will visit our scriptorium."

"Search there first," he said to the sergeant, who was looking ill at ease. It was obvious that he lacked the archbishop's enthusiasm for this task.

"Please wait for the bells," Kathryn said.

And as if on cue, they rang out—three short peals. They were quickly followed by the shuffling of feet through the cloisters. The abbess could hear a difference in the procession. The even rhythm was broken. There was excitement, even urgency in the hurried slapping and scraping of leather along the pavement. (The sisters would not shed their leather-soled stockings until May Day.) There was even whispering. They were seldom called to unscheduled convocation. The last time was when they were threatened with an outbreak of bloody flux.

The archbishop put down his spoon and nodded at the sergeant.

The abbess rose and took down her ring of keys from the peg above her desk. "I will open the scriptorium for you," she said. And she left with the soldiers, leaving the archbishop to rifle through the papers on her desk. He would find none anywhere else. Her closet was as clean as an abandoned bird's nest.

⁓ ⁊ ⁌⁓

Anna answered the summons too, assuring Bek that there was nothing to worry about. The sisters were not going to be chanting the hours. Yes, he was coming too. Come on. Hurry. No. He did not need his lute or his whistle. Just leave them in the scriptorium beside the desk. No need either to hide the papers she was working on. The only thing on her desk besides a book of poems by Christine de Pisan was a new musical composition she was copying for Bek. By some miracle he seemed to be able to follow the strange little markings above the words, even if he could not read the words themselves.

Her heart was pounding as she filed into the chapel with the others. This was VanCleve's fault. Why did she still think of him by that name? By any name? It was all his fault. And hers for falling prey to him.

The sisters huddled in little groups, whispering. Many of them were completely baffled. When Mother Superior came in, the sisters ceased their whispering, waited for her to address them.

"Sisters, there is no cause for alarm. I've called you together because we've been invaded by a small company of male visitors in the company of Thomas Arundel, Archbishop of Canterbury. I thought to spare you their prying eyes. They will be conducting a routine inspection of the abbey, after which His Excellency may have some questions for some of us. Answer any question put to you as honestly as you can, remembering that our first loyalty is to Christ, whom we serve, and then His Church. I'm sure the archbishop will not bring the men into the chapel."

Anna marveled at how calm her manner was.

Sister Matilde's gaze met hers and was followed by a nod and a reassuring smile.

"Will the men be going through our personal things?" one of the young oblates asked in a tremulous voice.

The abbess smiled. "Don't worry, Sister Teresa. They merely want to see what manner of work we do. They have no interest in your clean shift or the hairbrush and small mirror you may have hidden under your mattress."

Small chuckles. And sighs. The tension lightened somewhat.

"Now, may I suggest that we put this unscheduled convocation to good use. Sister Mary, you may lead us in a psalm."

They chanted every psalm they knew before the archbishop entered the chapel. Anna tried not to look at him. She did not want her gaze to call attention to herself, but from downcast eyes she took the measure of the man. He was of stern, unpleasant aspect, as she had suspected he would be. But she had not suspected that his personage would be so unimposing. He huddled in the pulpit, scarcely discernible from the carved figures of the rood screen behind him, as he addressed the sisters, who seemed to be holding their collective breath.

"Good afternoon."

The wooden figure had a voice. It was thin and light for a man.

A few of the nuns mumbled back the greeting. By this time it was afternoon. They had been enclosed here for hours, it seemed to Anna. Her stomach was beginning to growl. She gave a discreet little cough to cover the sound. The archbishop looked at her and frowned. Of course, she could not hope to blend in. If her grumbling stomach had not betrayed her, her dress would have. She and Bek were the only souls present not in nuns' garb. And beside her, Bek, his muscles stressed beyond all discipline by so long a time, began to jerk, calling more attention to them.

"I bring you greetings from Canterbury. And I have come to warn you of a concern that your archbishop has regarding the Lollard heresy that spreads like a pestilence across Christendom. This infection has spread to your very doorstep and may have even crossed your own cloistered threshold."

He paused for this to settle. One or two of the nuns gasped.

"Your patron and neighbor, Sir John Oldcastle, Lord Cobham, is suspected of spreading this heresy through transcribed texts."

He paused for the gasps of surprise he expected. He was not disappointed.

"If any among you knows of such copying, has been asked to copy a text by the heretic John Wycliffe or an English translation of the Holy Scriptures, which has been declared by Church Council and the law of the land to be a profane text, the possession of which is punishable by death—" Here he paused again to let this sink in. "Then now is the time for you to step forth and confess it."

The light washing through the grisaille glass from the chapel window lent a sickly gray glow to his face. "If you confess now, an amnesty may be granted you and your abbey on the grounds that, being innocent of any knowledge that such activity was heresy, you were only the tool of others."

Surely that pounding in her ears was not her own heart. Or was that the sound of all the hearts around her beating as one? She scanned the crowd for Sister Agatha. Mercifully, she was not present! Mother Superior's face was inscrutable behind her veil, but her demeanor was as calm as though the archbishop were delivering a familiar homily.

He waited for a long moment.

"Who will be the first to step forward to protect your abbey?"

The nuns all gazed at the floor, none daring even to raise their eyes.

"Very well, then. You should know that evidence has been given. Though we found nothing in our search today, contraband texts have been confiscated." The sickly gray color of his face prompted a feeling of nausea in her. "Who sits at the desk closest to the window on the western end of the scriptorium?"

Anna heard rushing in her ears. She thought she was going to faint.

"We rotate the seats," the abbess said.

"Then you will surrender the rotation schedule."

"I have no such schedule. We do not keep them. We scrape them at the end of each week to write anew on the parchment."

The archbishop's gray face showed a little color for the first time since he'd begun.

"Abbess, I warn you. We can hold you responsible for what your nuns copy. I have but to give the words and the sergeant will take you into custody to be tried before an ecclesiastical court for heresy. If you are convicted, your abbey will be closed and the sisters dispersed." He turned to face the sisters. "Is this what you want for your abbess and your fellow sisters?"

Anna stood up. The abbess was too old. She would never survive the questioning. And Anna owed her too much to let her bear the brunt for all of them. Better one of them should suffer. Beside her Little Bek made a gurgling sound in protest, as though he could read her mind. She could feel all eyes directed on her, all the upturned faces now washed too in the gray-green light from the window.

"I sit at the desk by the window on the western end of the scriptorium," she said.

He looked surprised. "You are not one of the sisters."

The abbess stood up also, turned to face Anna and spoke loud enough for all to hear. "Your Excellency. Anna is not one of us. She is a guest. A widow from abroad that we took in. She will be leaving soon. She copies the poetry of Christine de Pisan to pay for her keep and that of her afflicted son, who sits at her feet. She is a good scribe, but she does not have a vocation and would have no interest in theology. She only copies whatever we give her."

"Abbess, we are impressed with your charity and protective manner toward the stranger in your gates." His tone dripped sarcasm. He turned his gaze on Anna.

"Madam, from whence came you?"

"My home was in Prague, Bohemia."

He smiled as though that answer gave him great satisfaction. "Prague. The home of Jan Hus! A hotbed of heresy."

Anna hated that she had given cause for his gloating.

"Madam, I shall not ask you if you have copied the Scriptures in English. You have admitted to sitting in the seat where the heretical texts were confiscated. Indeed, I really don't care if you have copied them. My question for you, madam, is what is your relationship with Sir John Oldcastle?"

There was no sound in the room. Not even Little Bek moved.

"He is a kind man who took me in when I was in distress and delivered me and my son to the abbey for refuge."

"A careful answer, madam, but not a wise one. Sergeant," he called to the man waiting outside the chapel, "we will search this woman's quarters again in her presence and in the presence of the abbess."

Then he turned to the congregation of nuns. "Go back to your labors," he said gruffly, making the sign of the cross. *"Laborare est orare."*

THIRTY-THREE

*The estate of the pope has no peer, an emperor is next
him everywhere and a king is correspondent, a high
    cardinal
next in dignity . . . then a prince, an archbishop is his
    equal . . .*
    —FROM *OFFICES IN A NOBLE HOUSEHOLD*
    (15TH CENTURY)

hat proof do you have that what you say is true?"

It sounded cold, but it was all Gabriel could think to say to the stranger who had just served him dried apple tartlet with cinnamon. Under calmer circumstances it might have occurred to him to wonder how she had come by such an expensive spice or if she had saved the little horde against just such an occasion. But his distress was too great to think of such things now.

The story Mistress Clare had just told him undercut the very foundations of everything he believed. That he had been divinely chosen, God's anointed. That Brother Francis had been his savior and Holy Church his refuge. For if what this woman said was true, he was not only the bastard child of a profligate priest but both he and his mother had been cruelly exploited to satisfy the lusts, whims, and ambition of the man Gabriel had thought carried the very heart of Christ in his bosom. No. There had to be another answer.

Gabriel had never witnessed any spiritual or emotional or physical intimacy between Brother Francis and the woman he called Mistress Clare. Indeed, on more than one occasion, Brother Francis had referred to her service to him as an act of charity on his part. What was more, this reserved, cold woman bore no resemblance to the pretty, affectionate woman he remembered. How could he—how could they have lived thus if what she said was true?

She got up from the table, bent to coax the miserly fire in the grate. "He has made your heart cold, I fear," she said with a sadness that touched him. "The proof you seek is locked inside you."

"I'm sorry. It is just that you are so different from—"

"In the brothel on Bankside Street—" As she poked at the fire, a tiny orange flame danced to reward her efforts. She turned to look at him, her gaze guarded, inscrutable, as he remembered it. "Do you remember anything about Bankside Street?"

He saw again the little parlor with its grime-streaked window, the stairway to the hell above—*"I'll be Jane, Father, if ye're partial to Janes."* He nodded for Mistress Clare to go on.

She put down the iron poker and moved to the small glazed window—her one luxury, she had told him proudly when she'd first showed him her tidy cottage—and looked out over the marshy wasteland. "You and I lived on the second floor with the others. There was a small wardrobe in our room. Whenever . . . whenever . . ." She took a deep breath. Apparently the memory was as painful for her as him. "He always insisted I lock you in the wardrobe before his arrival."

Her voice was so low he had to strain to pick out her words. "You hated being shut up like that. You said it was too dark. But I never locked it even though he said to. I never had to. You were such a good boy. You never came out until he'd gone. But sometimes I could hear you crying."

She made a fluttering motion in the air with her hand, a long slim hand with well-formed bones in spite of the roughened skin. It was a gesture of futility. And a familiar one. She'd made just that gesture the day she hugged him, and he had turned away, truculent at being embraced, angry that she came so seldom, angry that she was pregnant. It had been the last time he'd ever seen her. Brother Francis had said she'd abandoned him.

The air seemed close in the little cottage, stifling, the smell of cinnamon and apples mixing with the smoke from the fire, cloying. He'd asked for proof. This was his proof. Or was it? Jane Paul could have confided in her.

Mistress Clare continued to stare out the window with her back to him. The fluttering hand wiped at eyes he couldn't see. There was the slightest movement of her shoulders.

"He didn't want me to see him, then? Was that why he told you to lock me up?" Gabriel asked.

She turned to look at him, her face a mirror of the bitterness in her heart. "He didn't want to see you! He took no interest in you. He did not want to be reminded of your existence. Until one day he came in the morning and saw you playing in the room downstairs. You used to play in front of the window on sunny days." Her face softened. "You had a small stuffed horse. He saw you playing and saw what a handsome boy you were. And how clever. You made up games with the horse. Elaborate games where you did the voices. I saw him watching you. 'That is your son,' I said. I wanted him to love you. What a stupid, silly girl I was!

"When he said he was going to take you away, I actually felt relief! I wanted so much more for you, Gabriel. I gave you that name, you know. Whenever the light hit your hair you looked like an angel."

The taciturn woman whom he'd never heard speak more than a sentence or two seemed to be a fountain of words. He wished he could turn it off. Too many words banging in his skull. He needed to think, but she talked on.

"At first, after he took you away, he let me visit you, though infrequently. I watched him turn you into a younger version of himself. Jane Paul died a little bit every day."

Gabriel found his voice. "You quit coming to see me at the abbey. Why did you stop coming?" Half afraid to hear the answer. Even as a boy he'd regretted the hateful way he'd pulled away, feared that she'd felt his childish resentment and taken it for rejection.

"He forbade me to."

"And you accepted that?"

"Not at first. I argued. Then I pleaded. By that time I was carrying his second child. He said I was not worthy to be your mother. Said Holy Church would be the only mother you needed. He called me a whore. Though I'd never lain with another man. You need to know your mother was not a whore. I was as faithful to him as though he were my husband. But he said that I would shame you with my presence."

"What about the second child? Do I have a brother or a sister?"

She smiled a bitter, twisted smile. "It was a perfect girl child. Stillborn."

"How did you come to live with him?"

"He took me in out of charity, as he often reminded me. He was not a bad man—just a blind one. A victim of his own ambition. I had nowhere else to go. I promised him that you would not know that I was your mother and that I would not try to see you."

Gabriel tried to remember the first time he had seen Mistress Clare. Brother Francis had always visited him in the Dominican abbey. He'd never visited Brother Francis until long after he'd returned from his studies in Rome. He remembered how carefully she'd watched him then. He'd thought it was because she didn't like him.

She turned back to stare out the window. The ebbing light picked out the bubbles in the bits of glass between the leaden seams. She was a figure in silhouette. An unknown woman, a featureless stranger. She was his mother.

He said softly to the back of that silhouette—or to himself, "It was my father who was the whore."

All a lie. Every bit of it. Gabriel had not been called of God. He'd been called by his father and not to the service of Christ, but to the service of vain ecclesiastical ambition. And now his father carried the rags of that ambition with him into Purgatory.

And what had the son done in the service of that ambition?

The son had delivered a righteous man to the authorities and hurled the woman he loved headlong into danger. If the father was in Purgatory, the son was in Hell. He heard sobbing in the room and realized it was his own. The silhouette moved away from the window and came toward him.

He felt the cool touch of his mother's hands on his face.

≈≈

There weren't a lot of places to search in the one small room and tiny anteroom shared by Bek and Anna: two small cots, their blankets neatly cornered, a narrow corner cupboard, gleaming starkly against the bare whitewashed walls, a washstand with basin and pitcher. Four wooden pegs stuck out of the wall on either side of the washstand. On these hung Anna's two other garments, one cinnabar colored, one pale gray, both gifts from Lady Cobham, as was the squirrel-lined cloak hanging beside them.

The other hook held an extra shirt and breeches and a woolen doublet for Bek. The soldiers had already emptied Bek's little box, spilling out his tin whistle onto the rush-strewn floor. She was glad she'd sent him with Sister Matilde and he was not here to see. She seethed, biting the inside of her lip, saying nothing, as the sergeant rubbed the fine English wool of her cloak between his dirty hands.

"Naught here, Your Excellency." Only the sergeant searched the room—in the presence of the abbess, the archbishop, and Anna, the three of them standing so close Anna could almost see the pupils of Mother's eyes through the thin gauze of her veil. From outside she heard the murmurs and husky laughter of the soldiers, waiting.

"What's in that?" The archbishop swallowed a belch as he pointed to a carved wooden chest at the foot of her cot.

Before Anna could answer, the abbess, who had remained as still as a statue, interrupted. "Your Excellency, do you think it seemly for your men to go through a woman's undergarments?"

"Well, you do it then."

The sergeant stepped back. The abbess knelt and opened the chest. One by one, she took out Anna's linen shifts and chemises and, rising, laid them out in neat stacks on the cot. When she had finished, the only thing left at the bottom of the stack was a necklace of some sort.

"What's that?" the archbishop asked.

"It's my cross. It belonged to my mother. It's a family heirloom."

"Then why aren't you wearing it?" he asked archly. "Is it because like the Lollards you find the wearing and use of such icons mere 'superstition'?"

He stroked his own gold pectoral cross. Its gems glittered with pearls and rubies even in the dim light of the oiled parchment that served for window glass.

"The silver chain is broken, and I had not the wherewithal to fix it."

The abbess bent down to pick it up, but the archbishop was already scooping up the necklace and examining it carefully. He merely shrugged and laid it in a tangle on the pile of linen. He looked long and hard at the chest, his eyes squinting and his mouth skewed to one side.

He jerked his head in the direction of the chest, speaking to the sergeant. "Pick it up," he said. "And turn it over. I've a notion something else is in there."

The sergeant picked up the chest and, turning it over, laid it on the cot. He examined it carefully. "Sounds solid," he said, pecking on it.

"As indeed it would," Arundel said, "if it were filled with something solid—say something like, I don't know, bricks . . ." He shot a sly look at Anna, the look of a fox sniffing his prey. "Or maybe . . . books?"

He bent down and ran his heavily beringed fingers along its carvings, pausing on two carved roses at the corner. He pressed with his thumbs on the centers and a lid flew open. The archbishop's smile spread to his eyes.

Anna remained perfectly still. She would not give him the satisfaction of showing fear.

"How very clever," he said. And then peering into the chest, "What have we here?"

"I am a scribe," Anna said. "These are my own books. I put them there to keep them safe."

"Take them out so that we may examine these volumes by which our scribe sets such store. She hides them away as though they were some secret treasure when most among her class display their wealth."

The sergeant lifted out the two books and laid them side by side on the bed, next to her clean shifts—first the smaller, plain codex, the one with the leather binding whose jewels had been removed, then the larger one, the Wycliffe Bible. The archbishop pushed the sergeant aside and opened the larger book to the exquisitely colored and patterned carpet page—the only adornment of the text—the carpet page Finn the Illuminator had colored so lovingly. *"This is our Bible, Anna. It will be yours when I am gone. And after—well, someday you will pass it on to your children."*

But the archbishop wasn't looking at the beautiful carpet page. Anna followed his gaze as it settled on the title page. He recoiled as though he'd seen a viper.

He read aloud in a voice raspy with hatred: " 'The Holy Bible: A translation of the Holy Scripture into the Language of England.' "

"Oh, Anna," the abbess said, her breathy voice filled with disappointment.

In trying to protect the abbess, Anna had handed the archbishop the very evidence he'd been searching for. Had she not confessed, the books, the evidence he sought, might never have been found.

"These are mine own books. The abbess knows nothing about them. They have been here with me in this chest as you found them since I arrived here. They were not unpacked until just now."

The archbishop appeared not even to hear her. He turned the pages of the Bible. Anna wanted to scream at him to get his bony, shriveled, ring-encrusted fingers off them. He was not fit to touch the pages so lovingly copied. The room started to tilt around her. Mother appeared at her side, her arms around her for support.

"Here, Anna, sit before you fall." She guided Anna to the chair.

"It is well she should sit to hear what I have to say," the archbishop said. "Madam, have you ever heard of a law called *De haeretico comburendo*?"

Anna heard the abbess gasp, felt Mother's arms grow rigid around her.

"Surely, Excellency, that would not apply to a stranger and a woman who could know nothing of our English law. Surely, merely to own a book would not carry so harsh a penalty, especially when the book is a family heirloom and Mistress Bookman could not have known the mere owning of the book was illegal?"

He waved her words away as though he were swatting at a gnat, acknowledging them only with a grunted comment. "Ignorance of the law is no excuse, else every churl and liar in the land would claim ignorance. As to her being a stranger to our shores, the laws and beliefs of Holy Church are universal." He bent slightly—he was not a tall man—putting his face so close to Anna's, she could smell his foul breath. "Madam, the *De haeretico comburendo* can be translated "On the Burning of Heretics" and it says that the mere possession of an English Bible is enough to procure for the sinner a sentence of death."

"Excellency!" Mother gasped. "Please. Show the mercy our Lord would have you show. This girl is innocent. And you should know you threaten not one life when you threaten hers, but two. Mistress Bookman is carrying a child."

"Bring me that other book," he instructed the sergeant, who was looking at the smaller volume with a look of puzzlement on his face.

"'Tis some strange language. Not English. Not the tongue of Holy Church." He held it out to the archbishop, who snatched it from his hand.

"It is Hebrew. I cannot read it, but I've seen this devil's scratching before." He thumbed through it, turned it sideways, then up and down. "Hmm," he said. His eyes narrowed to tiny slits. "It seems, Sergeant, we may have caught ourselves more than a heretic. We may have caught ourselves a witch as well."

"Faites flottez la sorcière!" Anna could hear the words ringing in her ears, could see the lifeless body of Jetta being pulled from the river. *"Faites flottez la sorcière!"*

She felt the leek soup she'd had at nuncheon rise in her throat. She tried to swallow it and gagged. Mother cupped her hands in front of Anna. "Here, Anna. It is all right."

Anna threw up into the hands of the abbess, then put her head on her knees.

She heard water splashing into the basin. It sounded far away, like Mother's voice. "It is only a book." Anna could hear her washing her hands, then she handed Anna a wet cloth to wipe her face.

"Only a book, Abbess! It is a book of Jewish spells. A book for summoning angels." He pointed to a diagram of a six-pointed star.

"But Anna is a dealer in books. She might have bought it for the parchment alone."

"Then we will question her. If she is innocent her innocence will manifest itself to her interrogators."

"Archbishop Arundel, have some compassion," Mother pleaded. "What about the child?"

"She can have it in the tower. When the child is born it will be given to a monastery. At least, that's one soul that will be saved."

Anna jumped to her feet. The room swirled. She fastened her gaze on the oil lamp mounted above the cupboard. The swirling stopped. The lamp centered. But the fury that she had bitten back as they rummaged through her personal belongings and desecrated her holy book seized her reason. She stood face-to-face with the archbishop, smelling his sweat, his rotten teeth, the stench of his stagnated soul.

She could feel Mother's breath in her ear, hear her whisper, "Be calm, Anna. Think of the baby. All will be well."

I *am* thinking of the babe, she thought. I have nothing left to think of but the babe. How can I be calm when my thoughts are a jumble of red and violet rage? She threw her head back and laughed, a wild, hysterical laugh that became a scream and bounced back from the walls, frightening even her.

The archbishop took a step back. "She is possessed."

The spasm was over and in its wake Anna was suddenly calm. She felt spent.

Her next words were quiet and low. "You try to take my child, old man, and I'll see you in Hell."

She scarcely heard the sergeant behind her step forward. She stood wooden and staring at the archbishop, who would not return her gaze. The sergeant seized her hands and began to bind them together at the wrists with a leather thong.

"Not so tightly," the abbess protested, her voice firm enough that Anna felt a slackening in the leather binding. "It will be all right, Anna. All will be well. We will pray for you and the babe," she said as she drew Anna's cloak around her, fastening it beneath her chin.

"Mother, do you really think anyone will be listening?" Anna said.

"Of course, Anna. He always listens. Do not lose your faith. You must have your faith to get you through. All will be well!"

All will be well—the phrase from Julian of Norwich that the abbess always quoted to the sisters. How often had she heard that same phrase on her grandfather's lips? And where was he now? No, Anna doubted that all would be well. But she would not say so. Let the abbess keep her faith. She would need it. Perhaps she, like Finn the Illuminator, could have enough for both of them.

The sergeant steadied her as she climbed clumsily onto the palfrey they provided. "I'm sorry, Mother," she said, but she didn't look at her. She kept her gaze on the ermine edging of the archbishop's cloak. Once white, now a dirty gray, it trailed behind him in the mud.

~※~

From the bell tower, Bek saw Anna leave with the men. He knew it was Anna by the color of her dress. But she would be back. Anna would not leave without telling him.

He had not gone to Sister Matilde as Anna had told him. Instead he had dragged his splindly legs up the stairs to the chapel belfry. He didn't want to sit with the nuns in the scriptorium. Didn't want to wait for Matilde to help him up the wooden steps. What if the bells started without him? He had his crutch. It was not the first time he'd gone to the belfry alone, though Sister Matilde scolded him for it, said he would get splinters in his legs from the wooden steps. Sister Agatha said he would tear his leggings. But his arms were strong. With the help of his crutch, he didn't have to crawl.

Anna had first taken him to see the bells. She had shown him how he could make them sing. Or how he could hush them. "To tame the beast," she'd said. And it had worked—as long as he was there, in the belfry, when the tolling began. But sometimes, the nuns would come to the bell tower without him. He was too slow, some said. But if he was already there, even Sister Agatha would let him pull the cord that made the bell chime.

He huddled in a corner of the belfry to wait, pulling his jerkin around him against the morning chill, watching the sundial in the center. One of the sisters would be here soon, and she would let him ring the bell for terce.

He waited.

A gust of wind stirred the frayed edges of the bell rope. Bek shivered. He sang to himself. Anna would return soon. She would not leave him. An na An na. The shadow crept across the top right hand of the dial. Past terce.

A wren flew into a nest high in the rafters. Still nobody came. They had forgotten about the bells. One of the young ones whose job it was. But she would not likely forget the next one. Someone would come to ring the bells for sext. He would wait.

He took the three stones out of a little leather pouch tied round his jerkin and tapped them on the floor. One-two-three, three-two-one, two-one-three. Tap. Tap.

The wren flew out of her nest, scolding him, showering straw onto the shoulder of the tallest bell.

The shadow crept toward sext. Somebody would come. Somebody would notice the bells were quiet and they'd skipped the "little hours." They would never forget the bells.

Three bells. Sitting in their squat frames. The big, long one was the hardest to pull. Its hinges were stiff with age and misuse. The nuns never pulled on it. His arms were strong. He could pull it, if they'd let him. The newer bells, the *nola* for the choir and the *squilla* for the refectory, were newer, shorter, and easier to pull. Each bell had a different voice so the nuns would know what each bell meant. But Bek did not call them by their names. He gave each a number. The heavy, long bell he called number one. The medium bell, the *nola,* he called number two. And the third, the *squilla* with the wide mouth, was number three.

One. Two. Three. Tap. Tap. Tap.

The shadow on the sundial crept toward three marks. Time to ring the number three bell. By the sun. By his stomach too.

But the shadow crept past sext and nobody came to ring the bells.

Bek squinted, studying the peaked roof of the bell tower, in deep shadow now. He counted the black blotches on its girders. Bats, Anna had said. Four bats.

Why did nobody come to get him? Anna was gone. Were the nuns all gone too? Not a soul had stirred for hours in the cloister below. The only movement in the garden below was the shimmering fountain.

They were all asleep, he thought. He would ring the bells. He would ring all the bells. That would wake them. He worked out the pattern in his head. Number one, first. Then the *nola,* number two. Then the *squilla,* number three.

He ran the number sequences in his head. Three-two-one, one-two-three, two-three-one, one-three-two, and on and on and on. If he had four bells he could go on forever!

He pulled on the frayed rope for the long, narrow bell. It barely budged on its stiff hinge. He pushed on the bell with both his hands and, lifting his body off the floor, freed the bell in a little half-swing. It creaked on its hinge. Enough to move the clapper. One more time and the bell rang out in a half-tone. Then full tone. One. Two. Three . . . The bell tower reverberated with the sound of it. The glorious, glad sound of it. The bells, bells, bells . . . And down below the nuns all ran from the chapel, where they'd been keeping vigil at the altar, looked up at the bell tower, shouting and pointing.

"It's Little Bek," the old one shouted. "We've forgotten Little Bek. Sister Matilde, go up and get him before he wakes the dead."

Little Bek heard Sister Matilde climbing the stairs. He looked down at what looked to his fuzzy eyes like a flock of large black birds. There was not a colorful bird among them.

But Anna would not leave him.

"Take the prisoner on to London, but hire a cart and driver for her," the archbishop had said when they paused in High Street. "Send her horse back to the abbey."

That's me they are talking about, Anna thought incredulously. I am the prisoner. But she was grateful for the cart at least. London was a hard day's ride on horseback. Hard for a woman. Harder still for the child in her womb.

"I'm stopping here at the cathedral to pay the Bishop of Rochester a courtesy call. He needs to know about the suspicion that has fallen on his diocese. Though I doubt it'll be news to him."

The sergeant reached up to help her down from her horse. "Drop the prisoner off at Newgate Prison, Excellency?"

The archbishop scowled at Anna. "No. Though Newgate is what the hellcat deserves. Out of respect for the abbess, take her on to the White Tower. Newgate's no place for a woman of learning. No place for a woman with child either."

But there was no compassion in his voice. Was the White Tower a better place, then? Was she to be accorded some measure of civility?

The archbishop's fine white steed snorted impatiently, the bells on its elaborate silver harness tinkling in the morning air. The archbishop steered the horse toward Boley Hill, toward the great cathedral, leaving the sergeant and two other men to make up the little prison party. The back of the cart was heaped with hogsheads. Anna sat on the floor of the wagon on a fur pelt provided by the driver. The driver of the cart whipped the reins and whistled to the pair of horses that pulled the wagon.

"What's the White Tower?" Anna shouted at the driver above the clopping of the horses.

"It's London's royal palace," he threw back over his shoulder.

"A royal palace?"

The sergeant laughed. "It'll not likely be the royal apartments for the likes of you, mistress. More likely it'll be the dungeons for you."

Anna knew all about dungeons. There'd been one at the *hrad*, the castle on the hill above the river Vltava. She'd heard of people who went in there and were never heard from again. She'd come all this way to end up in a dungeon, charged with heresy—and worse. At least Martin's death had been swift.

"Don't worry that pretty red head of yours about being lonely. Ye'll have plenty of company. His Excellency says they'll probably have to build a tower at Lambeth to house all the Lollards he's planning to catch in his net."

She closed her eyes against the March wind that slapped her face and made her eyes water. The jostling of the wagon along the rutted road caused pain in the small of her back. She leaned back against one of the hogsheads. The metal rim bit into her shoulder. But at least it gave her some support.

The sergeant trotting along beside her was laughing with his men, paying her scant attention. The driver whipped the horses, urging them to speed up. What if she flung herself beneath the horses, beneath the wagon wheels? At least she would deprive the archbishop and his minions of their sport. She was going to die anyway. She knew how this was going to end.

No, you don't, Anna. Only God knows how it's going to end. Put your trust in Him. Think of your baby. All will be well.

But those were her grandfather's words. Not hers. She had not his faith. Or his courage.

They stopped at a roadside inn for food. Anna wasn't hungry, but her bladder was full to bursting.

"The privy's out back." The driver nodded to her unasked question.

The sergeant untied the leather binding on her wrists. "We'll be watching you from the window, mistress. Don't even think of running."

She looked down the road, where late afternoon was already clumping the trees into threatening shadows. Safer here than there. At least the sergeant would protect her from rogues. He would want to deliver his goods unharmed.

After lingering in the privy as long as she dared, preferring even the noisome odor to the company of the rough men inside the inn, she entered the smoke-filled common room. The sergeant's men paid her no notice. She sat down beside the driver and scanned the room for a friendly face. There was no woman, not even a barmaid to whom she might appeal.

"Eat up, mistress," the driver said as he stripped the flesh from a chicken bone. "I'd take advantage if I was you."

"I have no money," Anna said.

He laughed. "What'll they do if you can't pay—put you in gaol?"

Anna smiled in spite of herself. "I'm not hungry anyway," she said. Then she thought of her baby. She'd eaten nothing all day. "Bread and cheese, please."

"That'll be twopence," the tavernkeeper said, putting down her food.

"He'll pay," she said, nodding in the direction of the sergeant.

The driver winked at her with approval as she took a bite. But unable to swallow more than a bit of the bread, she tore off a notice posted on a nail above the table and, seeing it was fairly clean, hastily wrapped up the rest of the food and slipped it into her pocket. Who knew when she would eat again?

"Best be going," the driver said, "if you want to make London by nightfall."

The sergeant paid the innkeeper and to Anna's relief did not quibble over the bill. He even offered his hand to her to help her into the wagon, where she settled more comfortably, now that she had at least stretched her legs and relieved herself. But the heavy twilight brought such a feeling of despair that for one brief moment she felt her heart pounding in her ears the way it had the day her grandfather had died. *Calm down, Anna. All will be well. Trust Him.* She could hear his voice so clearly that she reached out her hand to touch him. But it encountered only the splintered wood of the large beer barrel.

Heavy dusk had already fallen when they entered the city. Lights were twinkling in the windows of the houses high on London Bridge.

"That there be the White Tower, mistress," the driver said, pointing off to the right. The river lay on their left. She could no longer see it, but she could smell the brine in the brackish water where the sea backed into it. Downstream, she could make out a large boat, illumined against the darkness. Who could afford so many candles? she wondered. And how did they stay warm? She was shivering beneath her woolen mantle, hunkering behind the casks to shelter from the wind. She looked in the direction the driver pointed. A great curtain wall enclosed several towers more gray than white. High in some of the towers she thought she saw a candle or two, mere flickers in the tall shadows. From the barge on the river, laughter drifted in, accompanied by music, the strings of harp and lute.

"That'll be the new king's barge coming in. His Majesty likes to take the dandies of the court out on the river. Some say he fancies himself a musician."

"Go on around to the quayside entrance," the sergeant said sharply. "We'll go in through Traitor's Gate."

An ominous name. An ominous sight, Anna thought as she looked up at the large iron gates with their steps leading down to the river.

"Hey ho, warder," the sergeant called. "I've a prisoner for ye, sent from His Excellency Thomas Arundel, Archbishop of Canterbury."

The gates opened with a groan and a creak.

The driver whipped his reluctant horse to enter. Anna shivered with a foreboding that had nothing to do with the chilly March wind.

From the river drifted the sound of laughter, followed by the high-pitched melody of a pipe.

"Welcome to Tower Prison," the warder said, as he reached up to help Anna down from the cart.

THIRTY-FOUR

The money was indeed the thing that killed the Jews. If they had been poor and if the feudal lords had not been in debt to them, they would not have been burnt. After the wealth was divided . . . some gave their share . . . to the Church on the advice of their confessor.

—FROM *THE CREMATION OF THE STRASBOURG JEWRY*, JACOB VON KÖNIGSHOFEN

n the third day, Brother Gabriel came to the abbey at first light, exhausted, almost incoherent, begging to be admitted to the mother superior's private chamber. The abbess was exhausted too. She had not slept for two nights. Her thoughts were haunted with what might be happening to the young woman she'd sheltered and then embroiled in their dangerous enterprise. But this time, unlike that time so many years gone, it was not her fault. The girl had not only volunteered to do the copying, she had turned herself in.

But none of that mattered. Whenever she closed her eyes, Kathryn saw only Anna's face as they had led her away.

Anna's face and yet not Anna's face at all.

Now Friar Gabriel was pacing back and forth in her chamber. In the emerging light of a gray dawn seeping through the windows, she could see his robes were disheveled and marked with the stains of the road. Dark smudges outlined his eyes.

"It is not my place to judge you, Father. That is for one much higher than I." The abbess felt great compassion for him, she could not help it. "How did you hear?" she asked.

"There was a notice posted on the door of a church in Appledore. Her name was on the list of people arrested for questioning. In connection with the search for Sir John."

She exhaled heavily. "Lambeth Palace wasted no time," she said. "The copyists have been busy, the messengers swift."

"The archbishop is dedicated to bringing down Lord Cobham. He considers it his legacy to stamp out the Lollards, to free the Church from heresy. I fear he will deal harshly with Anna to make her implicate the abbey."

Deal harshly? Was he so oblivious to the abuses committed in the name of God by his own Church?

"If they can prove the abbey has been providing Sir John with contraband texts, then they have a tight case against him." He whirled around, his tone almost confrontational. "I warned you. Why did you not destroy the writings?"

Her compassion counseled patience for the accusation in his voice.

"I did. She brought the documents with her. I fear you have not heard the worst. Not only did she have a Wycliffe Bible hidden in her linen chest, but she also had some kind of book of Jewish spells." She paused. "The word 'witchcraft' was mentioned."

"Holy Mother of God!" He beat his fist on the oaken surface of her clean, uncluttered desk, punctuating his words. "She is a stupid, willful girl. I warned her when we were together in France."

He did know. And therein lay his anger. A charge of witchcraft gave greater license for torture. When the devil was the enemy, what did it matter how much pain the body felt if the soul could be saved?

"You are a man of influence, Father. You have the archbishop's ear. Can you not intercede on her behalf?"

He laughed. It was a sad, bitter laugh. "You are naïve, Abbess. This is

Arundel's mission in life. He has the power, and he has the will to destroy any and all who threaten his Church. And he will do it."

"Then there is one other thing you should know. And the knowing of it may buy her a little time. It may also make a difference to you as you decide where your loyalties lie."

He straightened up, rubbing the heel of his hand where it would probably bear a bruise.

"Anna is with child," she said.

His skin took on the gray hue of the creeping dawn. It was hard to watch a man's face dissolve. Better to do it all at once. Just rip away what was left of the mask and see if there was a man behind it.

"It is your child, Father. Five months gone. She has already felt it move in her womb."

He did not deny it. Nor did he confirm it. He just stood there like a man who had been slapped, his eyes stunned, his expression melting into disbelief.

How can this be a surprise to you? she thought. *How could this not have occurred to you? Did you not notice the fullness of her figure when you saw her here? Did your lust consume you so when you spilled your seed inside her that you did not think of this? Or did you just not care? And you dare to call me naïve.* She wanted to say it out loud, but what good would it do now to heap such guilt upon him? The world had enough of guilt.

She turned her back on him. To look at him now would be wrong, like intruding on his most basic private moment. The room bore the chill of early morning. She could smell the damp in the ashes, mingled with the mossy, moist smell of the earth in early spring. Outside, the bulbs in the cloister garden would be swelling, quickening in the ground, forming into life, like the child in Anna's womb.

"I will go to the king," he said. "Bolingbroke lies a corpse at Westminster. The new king is a friend of Sir John's. That is the only way." His voice sounded small, unsure, propped up by the sheer resolve of his will.

But at least, she thought, he has a plan. That gave her hope.

She turned to face him and lifted her veil, wanting him to see her eyes when she said what she was going to say. He appeared not to even notice the scarred left side of her face. "Do you realize, Brother Gabriel, what it means for a son of the Holy Roman Church to align himself with the king against the archbishop?"

His gaze met hers unflinchingly. "It means the end of my advancement in the Church." Then he added, in a tone she could only describe as filled with discovery, something akin to wonder even, as though he were just now coming to realize some truth, "And that no longer matters to me."

"It might mean more than the end of your advancement, or even of your Dominican habit. If the archbishop discovers your alliance with Anna, he will say that she bewitched you. You may be subjected to his soul-saving devices as well."

But he seemed not to even register her words. As if now that he'd found his purpose, he'd found his courage too, and could not be bothered with things like personal danger. She could see his mind already racing. That gave her more hope.

"They took the books as evidence, I'm assuming," he said. "Arundel is nothing if not thorough. What else did they take? Do you know if they found anything else incriminating?"

"The abbey was clean. Thanks to the warning of a friend—whose name I have forgotten. An old woman's memory, you know." She smiled and he smiled back weakly, a new fellowship between them. Then she added, "They took what was on Anna's desk in the scriptorium. Nothing incriminating. A book of poetry. Some music she was copying for Bek."

A new concern crossed his face. "How is Bek? He was very attached to Anna. Is he all right?"

She liked that he asked after the boy. Rome had not robbed him of his compassion. "Sister Matilde looks after him. They have developed a bond of sorts. She is teaching him to ring the chapel bells."

"The chapel bells! But he hates the sound of bells."

She felt the pull of her scarred face as she smiled. It was good to think of these small successes. "Whatever things are lovely, think on these things," the Apostle Paul had written in his letter to the Philippians. Good advice for troubled times.

"He doesn't hate them if he can control them. He composes the changes for them and Sister Matilde helps him write them down. Of course, he still chants Anna's name at bedtime. His version of compline prayer or a lullaby that helps him sleep."

"Give him a message for me when he wakes up? Tell him VanCleve has returned. Tell him VanCleve has gone to bring back Anna."

"Will you rest before you go?"

"I cannot rest, Mother. Not until I've seen her. Not until I've asked for her forgiveness."

"Then go with God," she said.

The bells for prime chimed out, not just one monotonous bell tone but a cacophony of glorious sound, startling in its energy.

"Those are Bek's bells," she said. "He has a different melody for every office—if melody such joyous clamoring can be called—some mathematical sequence he keeps in his head."

Gabriel smiled. "That alone is proof enough of miracles, Mother. Now pray for another."

As he rode away, Kathryn joined the processional to the chapel. April third. The Feast of Irene, the fourth-century maiden who was burned for reading the Holy Scriptures. How ironic, Kathryn thought. No. That was just fatigue infecting her mind with such troublesome thoughts. All would be well. Brother Gabriel would find the girl. He would use his influence to see that she was safe. Henry IV was dead. The old order had passed. Please, God, let the new king be more tolerant of the cause.

Exhausted, the abbess fell asleep halfway through the office.

⁓✠⁓

"Mother, the office has ended." It was the novice who attended Kathryn, shaking her gently to waken her.

"Yes, yes, of course," she said and then murmured the last line of the Te Deum, grateful for the veil, hoping the girl would think her consumed by contemplation and not fatigue. Stiff with sitting so long in the same position, she took the young hand offered her. As they exited the chapel, she felt the sudden warmth of sunlight on her face.

She paused. "I think I'll linger here to meditate a little longer." And then she thought of the day's chores that lay ahead. "Maybe not," she said and sighed.

They were just outside the door of the little room where Anna had stayed. The horror of that situation came settling back on her. "I'm going to pack a small chest for Anna, then perhaps we can find someone to take it for us . . ." But even as she said it she was thinking, *Who?* There was no one left at Cooling Castle—not with Sir John and Lady Joan both fled. If only she could get a message to Anna. Some reassurance. Clothes. Some money even. She'd heard that prisoners had to pay for their own food. The girl had been taken away with nothing but the clothes on her back. She didn't even know where they'd taken her. Godspeed, Brother Gabriel, she prayed. Godspeed.

In the meantime, she would write a letter of inquiry to the archbishop's office demanding to know of Anna's whereabouts. After all, she was an abbess and a friend of Sir John Oldcastle's, who was a friend of the king's. Surely someone in that office would respond! Unless they were themselves too afraid of the taint of heresy.

It had been three days since they'd taken Anna away. Little Bek had moved in with Sister Matilde—her cell was closest to the bell tower—and Anna's room had a musty, unused smell. Kathryn unhooked the oiled parchment from the window to let in the fresh air. She took down Anna's two dresses, folded them carefully, and put them in the bottom of the chest. These would need to be let out soon. She would add a needle and some thread to the chest. Perhaps the needlework would take Anna's mind off the misery.

If there was enough light to do needlework. She took three precious candles from her store.

The contents of the chest still lay strewn across the bed just as the archbishop's men had left them. She folded two clean chemises and added them to the pile, then tucked in a bar of sweet-smelling soap and a clean linen rag from beside the washstand. And Anna's hairbrush. She smiled at the memory of that wild chaos of curls and added a small net snood.

A beam of sunlight fell across the bed, snagging a shard of light on the silver necklace. Kathryn picked it up. She would have the chain repaired and send it also. Anna had said it was a family heirloom. It would give her comfort to have it close to her.

It was an unusual necklace. There was something a little different about the cross. She'd seen someone else with one like it, something about the way the pearls were placed. She closed her eyes—she really needed to get herself some kind of tonic to balance her humors, to stir up her old blood. Clutching the necklace in her fist, she fingered the tiny filigreed crossarms with their random scattering of pearls. No. Not random at all. But cleverly designed. A hidden star. A six-pointed star!

Kathryn sat down heavily on the bed. She studied the cross, prodding old memories left too long to lie. And what memory offered up was an image of that same cross around the slender neck of a young woman with raven hair and striking eyes and skin like cream. Nothing like the girl Anna. Anna with her hair as bright as . . . as bright as Alfred's had been! And eyes as blue as Colin's. And smooth white skin like Colin's. Kathryn's sweat bloomed on her forehead, even in the coolness of the little chamber. She saw herself trying to coax a squirming little girl with bright curls and milk-white skin into a fur jacket. Her old heart ached with the memory of it.

No. This was reaching far beyond the bounds of reason to fulfill some buried wish. That child had been called Jasmine.

"I gave her a Christian name. After our Lord's mother," the old midwife had said. *"We named her Anna,"* she told Finn. Anna who was fired with a temper inherited from her uncle. Anna with the cool clear eyes of her father. Anna who spoke so lovingly of her beloved old grandfather.

Finn. The grandfather for whom Anna grieved.

Finn, the love of Kathryn's life, and the man she had betrayed.

Her old heart fluttered like some wild bird. A sharp pain in her chest traveled down her arm. She tried to get up, to call out, but her legs folded under her.

"Mother, are you all right?" It was Sister Matilde bending over her.

The abbess heard the sister calling her name but had not the breath to respond. All her thoughts, all her energy were directed toward fathoming the answer that pricked her mind.

"Go to the apothecary. Ask the sister for some foxglove," Matilde shouted to the other sisters who were gathering.

Jasmine! It was Jasmine whom the archbishop had taken away to prison, Jasmine, the child whom Kathryn had coddled and loved and been comforted by when she had no other. No. God was not some cruel jester. He would not send her the child only to take her away. To take her away as her grandfather had once been taken away in shackles from Kathryn.

She felt the squeezing in her chest. Struggled to get her breath. Struggled to calm her old heart. She could not die now. Not now. Not when Jasmine needed her.

She owed that much at least to Finn.

Lady Joan paid the messenger and greedily tore into the packet of letters, ignoring the pleas of her two-year-old grandson, who tried to climb her skirts. She had taken him into the courtyard to give her daughter, Lady Brooke, some respite from the child's incessant whining. They all spoiled him mercilessly because her last child had been stillborn and the one before had died of a fever at fifteen months. "In a minute, poppet."

"Up. Up." He held out his chubby arms and pumped his fists. She sat down on the low stone wall surrounding the courtyard, and heaved him into her lap. With the other hand, she held her letter into the sunlight to read it.

Her John was safe at Herefordshire, unmolested! Thank God and all the saints!

Her eyes scanned the page hungrily. He had answered the ecclesiastical summons with a written statement of his beliefs disputing the sale of indulgences, the confession of priests, and insisting that only doctrine founded in Holy Scripture to be the truth of the gospel.

How else, good wife, I argued, can a man (or woman) know that truth unless they be allowed to read and interpret the words of our Lord for themselves? Must they put their faith in greedy priests and unholy friars, who would sell them that which God in His word offers freely to all mankind?

But her eyes quickly scanned John's theological treatise searching for the words she longed to hear. And there they were. Not even in code, but said boldly—he must surely think the storm had passed.

I fully expect excommunication will be the worst Arundel can offer, and since my Christ and not some Antichrist pope holds the keys to the true Kingdom of Heaven, I do not fear such. As for you, my love, your lands have ever been under interdiction, so it is probably safe enough for you to return. Without royal writ—because of the act we pushed through Parliament—the archbishop has no power to harass us further. I will bide here awhile to let old Arundel's fire burn out. Henry IV is dead and the crown has passed to Harry. It is my hope that he will prove more tolerant

for the soldiers' bond we once shared. Before ere long we can return to our
"normal pursuits."

How much faith he put in comradeship!

In the betwixt time, good wife, return to Cooling Castle and call upon
our friends and advise them to be circumspect and wait patiently for my
return. I shall hold you in my arms ere long, though I may have to come
to you under cover of night until the lay of the land is clearer, but when
was the nighttime anything but friend to us?

Standing up, she shifted the child from her lap to her hip and strode into
the hall.

"Bridget," she called to her maid. "Pack my traveling chest. We are going
home!"

A sennight later, Sir John lay with his wife in the high curtained bed in the
lord's chamber at Cooling Castle. The room was chilly in the predawn because the chamber fires were not yet lit. She had not called for coals at bedtime. She and John between them created enough warmth.

"It's good to be home, sweet wife. But I cannot tarry. I must be on my
way before the cock crows. As long as I am within Arundel's diocese, I am
subject to the archbishop's authority here and too easily found."

"Are you so sure, then, my lord, that your friendship with the new king
can stand such a test? Arundel will not give up easily."

She had not told him at first, not wanting to break the glad spell of their
reunion. He'd other things on his mind that pushed aside the urgency of political and religious matters. But he would have to know.

Her head lay in the crook of his arm. She felt his lips brush the crown of
her head.

"Did you check in on the abbess? Is all well there?" he asked.

As if he'd read her mind.

"The abbess has been very ill. But they say she's better now. Twice I've
taken her coltsfoot infused in honey and mince conserve. The last time she
seemed stronger. We passed an hour together in the spring sunshine, watch-

ing the first green shoots of spring. Though she talked but little. I could not tell behind the veil, but the way her head nodded I think she dozed. Once she woke to ask me if I knew her granddaughter. When I pressed her for more information, she laughed weakly and said that she'd been dreaming. That was all."

"Well, she has plenty of time to take a rest. There will be no more copying for a spell, I fear. I thought Arundel would search the abbey."

"He did."

"But he found nothing, right? The nest was clean. She'd burned everything, right?"

"I'm afraid not quite everything." She hated telling him, she knew he'd been fond of the girl. Would feel responsible for having placed her in harm's way—as did she.

"The young widow from Prague. They found a Wycliffe Bible in her possession. And another book as well—a book of Jewish spells. They arrested her, John. Took her to Lambeth Palace for questioning."

He swore under his breath. Outside, they heard the first crow of the cock. "There's my signal, good wife," he said, getting up and reaching for his breeches, which he'd flung across a chair in his haste. "I'll go to Harry. I'll demand the girl be released."

How like him, to take action first, without thinking it through. Straight on and damn the consequences! That had earned him an award of valor on the battlefield. But this fight was not so straightforward.

"Husband, think! Arundel means to question her to gain evidence against you. He'll use the witchcraft charge to pressure her. What girl could withstand the threat of burning? If you go to the king in her behalf, you but abet his case against both you and her."

"But we cannot leave her to—"

"Brother Gabriel has gone to petition the king."

"Brother Gabriel!"

"There's much that's come to light, my love, during your absence. But it grows light and you must be away." She got up from the bed, wrapping the bed linens around her to protect her goosefleshed skin. "I will tell you all later. Just know that Brother Gabriel is doing all at court that can be done to secure her release."

"But I thought—"

"Shh. You hear that? The servants are stirring. You must be away before they even know you are here. Gossip spreads quickly."

She kissed him good-bye, and only minutes later as the first gray light appeared at the window, Bridget tapped at her door.

"Milady, I've brought coals for your fire."

"Come in," she said, snuggling back into bed. The covers were still warm from his body.

As Bridget stirred the fire, Joan heard the fast clip-clopping of a horse, its footfalls rapidly fading.

THIRTY-FIVE

Who therefore resists the ruling power, resists the
ordinance of God, . . . For it is not the ruler's own act
when his will is turned to cruelty against his subjects,
but it is rather the dispensation of God . . .
—FROM *THE NATURE OF A TRUE PRINCE*
BY JOHN OF SALISBURY

wo archery slits set high in the wall in Anna's tower chamber
testified to the castle's many-purposed use. Each morning she stood on the
stone base betwixt floor and wall to see the world outside. Sometimes, in the
thin afternoon sunlight, girls in colorful gowns and court dandies clad in
fur-trimmed tunics and silk stockings played at bowls in the green expanse
below. This morning her fingers encountered frost on the stone lip as she
grasped it to pull herself up while balancing on her tiptoes. The green below
was empty and blanketed with a hoarfrost. The only movement came from
the black-winged ravens swirling and diving in the morning air. It was a
frozen, silent world. Even the Westminster bells had finally stopped. They
had tolled incessantly for the first two days.

"The king is dead, long live Prince Harry," the old warder who fed her
once a day had growled in answer to her question. That first day she'd had

only scant bread and a little water, but she'd not complained and had thanked him graciously, knowing he was her only link to the outside. Such restraint had cost her much—her tongue was sore with biting—but her courtesy and seeming meekness had paid off. The next day the quantity, if not the quality, had improved, and yesterday she'd been given an egg with her bread. Today, he'd brought a gray sliver of boiled mutton and two chunks of bread. She'd saved one for later.

The arches in her feet hurt and the woodsmoke curling from the castle's many chimneys stung her eyes. She stepped down gingerly from the stone base, careful lest she lose her balance and injure her babe. She had no fire by which to huddle, but she had discovered that one wall of her chamber abutted another with a fireplace and some warmth leaked through the stone. She had pulled her pallet up against that wall. She sat down on it now, her back supported by the almost-warm stone, and pulled her cloak tight about her. She closed her eyes and wondered how she could get through the day. One could only sleep so much before the dreams intruded.

After some time—she had no measure of counting the hours, except for the streaks of light that crept across the stone floor from the two narrow windows—she heard the lock scrape in her door.

"It seems ye are not friendless, mistress. This came fer ye. A heavy box to be lugging up these stairs."

Anna almost cried when she saw her traveling chest. At least she was not forgotten. She fell upon the chest as soon as the old man departed, muttering complaints under his breath. She fingered the oak, inhaling its aroma. Clean clothes. She smothered her face in the clean, sweet-smelling linen. *I would sell my soul for a bath,* she thought and then realized she could still hear the warder's slow shuffle outside in the hallway.

She pounded on the door and shouted. "Please, master chamberlain, I know it would be trouble, and you've been so kind to me already, but if you could just provide me with a small basin of water for washing . . ."

Moments later, the metal covering on the narrow window in the door grated open. His wizened face appeared—or at least the stubble-covered part of it. She saw his mouth working, heard him mutter more imprecations under his breath, something about high-handed airs, before his face disappeared.

She returned to her pallet, easing her increased bulk down gingerly and rubbing her arms for warmth. She could smell the fear and sweat on the chemise that she had worn for days. But she could not bring herself to put on a clean one without washing. She considered the small beaker of drinking water. But she was hard put to keep her thirst at bay as it was. At least she had the soap and the rag. She was thinking that the next time it rained she would wet the rag in the rain that collected on the floor beneath the archer's slit, when she heard her door unlock.

A pitcher and a washbasin appeared and then the door slammed shut again.

Anna washed herself and was just putting on her clean chemise when she heard the lock grate again. She threw her cloak around her, not wanting the old warder to see her thus. But it was an old woman. "I've come to empty yer slops," she said and picked up the foul-smelling chamber pot in the corner.

That at least answers one concern, Anna thought.

"Tuesdays and Saturdays," the old woman hissed through the spaces where her teeth should have been.

That answered another.

"Could I trouble you to leave the little window in the door open, good woman? It would make the air a little less foul."

The crone studied her a moment, a sly look in her eyes, then answered. "Aye, I'll do that fer ye, missy. And I'll take that dirty chemise to the castle laundry."

Anna shivered, thinking that if the old woman wanted her filthy shift, she must be more desperate than she. Or maybe there really was a castle laundry where the castle's mountains of dirty linen were scrubbed and boiled. Either way, Anna would probably not see her shift again.

"I hope yer not a heavy bleeder, it'll make both our lives harder," she said as she flung the soiled shift over her shoulder and backed out of the door holding the chamber pot in both hands.

Seconds later she was back. She'd probably done no more than hurl the contents from a convenient window.

"Thank you for emptying that for me, and you needn't worry. I won't bleed," Anna assured her. Not regularly, at least, remembering what Gilbert the Englishman had said about breakthrough bleeding. "I am with child."

"Oh. Well. That be yer good fortune, then, missy. That'll buy ye a few weeks"—she eyed Anna speculatively—"mayhap even a few months."

She said it so casually she might have been talking about bartering for grain.

"Visitors to this chamber don't usually stay long." And then a look of sympathy crossed her face. "I'll bring ye a pillow fer yer back. Left by a fancy gentleman on t'other end. It was the headsman's ax instead of the hangman's rope for him. 'Twere nobility. Most here are. Rest go to Newgate or the Clink." Then, as if considering that this might not have been the most comforting thing she could say, she sought to make amends. "I'll bring ye fresh water for bathing on Tuesdays and Saturdays too—usually I get a few pence for the extra burden, but never mind. I can tell ye probably haven't a groat to yer name. Else ye'd have a few more comforts in this hellhole." She gave Anna the benefit of her toothless smile. "I'll do it for the wee one in yer belly."

After she had gone, Anna sat for a long time, her hands on her rounded belly, which strained against the too-tight chemise, thinking about the "wee one in her belly." A scalding tear slid down her cheek.

Don't start bawling, Anna. She eyed the chest on the floor. *It could be worse. You are not without friends.*

She picked up the brush and, wincing, dragged it through the tangled mass of hair.

❧

"The war with France, my liege. It is a drain on the treasury. And there's the matter of the Lollards. Arundel wants—"

Harry answered his new Lord Chancellor abruptly. "Arundel is not the king."

"With all respect, Your Majesty, neither are you until the Archbishop of Canterbury places the crown on your head and gives you the blessing of Rome."

"Odd that you should make the archbishop's argument for him. You know he's already angry with me because I have made you chancellor." That should remind Beaufort of his place.

"I am aware of that, my liege. And though it pains me to think my appointment might prove troublesome, I can assure you that my loyal service to you will more than balance the scales. Indeed, to show my loyalty to you, I do make his argument in this one part. You know the Lollards preach against the sale of the papal indulgences. I would point out to Your Majesty that the loss of the revenues from the sale of those indulgences would further impoverish your treasury, already drained by the French wars."

Harry knew the truth of that. "And they also preach against the pilgrimages that do much to help the treasury," he said.

"Exactly so, Your Majesty! It is true. If tomorrow all the holy shrines should disappear, the pilgrims quit their traveling, the badge sellers would have no custom, nor the alehouses and the inns—what then would happen to England's economy? It may be holy, my liege, but it is still commerce."

Harry shifted, restless in his great high-backed chair. "Yes, yes, I know that, uncle, but he wants an arrest warrant for Sir John. For all the gossip, we are not talking about some slack-gutted buffoon, but a noble lord of courage who has served England well and honorably."

"Sir John leaves you no choice. You read the statement he sent in answer to the ecclesiastical summons. It was a blatant declaration of heresy!"

Harry laughed in spite of himself. "You have to admit, uncle, he has the balls of a bull."

"Well, Arundel would make a bullock of him. There are witnesses. One awaits her interrogation even now within these very walls. Do you doubt she will give evidence of whatever her interrogators press her for? It is not Sir John's courage that is the issue, Your Majesty. It is his orthodoxy and his loyalty to his king. I urge you to put aside the luxury of friendship and consider signing the arrest warrant."

"And what of my loyalty to a friend?"

"You owe him no more than you can give. You do not owe him England. A king has no friends. His loyalty must lie with his kingdom."

"You make the matter of a little unorthodox religion sound so grave. Just because a few people want to read the Bible for themselves and choose to interpret it differently?"

"It *is* grave. Whenever Lollardy has been preached there have been uprisings. The commoners feel empowered by the reading of the Word for themselves. They no longer rely on the Church. They say they answer only to Christ himself. Not to the archbishop." He paused to weight his next words with meaning. "Or to the king."

"But doesn't the Bible tell them the king rules by divine right and must be obeyed?"

"I have not read it for myself, my liege, but apparently it does not."

"But this is Sir John Oldcastle, Lord Cobham! Not some rabble-rousing priest! God's wounds, uncle, he has a seat in Parliament!"

The chancellor sighed. "Sign the warrant, Your Majesty. Let him be brought in. Perhaps you can persuade him to recant out of the bond you share. If he does not, then it is he who breaks that bond and not you."

A timid knock offered a welcome interruption.

The chamberlain opened the door, bowing at the waist, "Your Highness, the armorer is here. You said to tell you, and there's another, a Brother Gabriel, who says he would speak with you on an urgent matter."

"A cleric, you say?"

"Yes, Your Majesty. He said to tell you by way of introduction that he was on the council at Lambeth Palace on the problem of heresy."

Harry frowned. Here was probably more piling on. Best to get it over with. "Send them both in," he said. "We'll hear the priest whilst the armorer measures us."

"A new suit, Your Majesty?" Beaufort smiled.

"Aye, and I pray it does not weigh as heavily as the crown."

THIRTY-SIX

nna had been in Tower Prison five days and nobody had come to question her or charge her formally. Were her tormentors waiting so that her own fears could work against her? Or had they forgotten about her? At night her dreams were haunted by nightmare images. Women screamed and writhed as fires were lit beneath them. Disembodied heads dripped blood— her own and Martin's. On poles. On the Vltava Bridge. Black ravens, instead of gulls, circling.

Every morning she thought, *Today will be the day,* and prayed for courage not to endanger Sir John and the abbess. Every night she thought, *Tonight. They will come in the night like the soldiers in Gethsemane, terror flickering in their torchlight, to drag me down the winding stairs.*

Another day was drawing to a close and still she waited.

She was sitting on her pallet, the headless nobleman's fine silk pillow at her aching back. The perpetual gloom of the chamber deepened. Through the indigo slit high above, the first evening star had appeared. The day had been warmer and the breeze created between the open window in the door and the archer's slit had made the air less foul. The light from one precious candle kept the night from intruding untimely, but it was insufficient for her task.

And not only the light, but the level of her skill. The tedious picking out of the seams and restitching was bloodier work than the failed embroidery of the pilgrim badges. She'd abandoned that project, but she could ill afford to abandon this one, else she would have to shred her shift to give some ease for her growing child. The high-waisted dresses would serve but not the narrow undergarment. The easing of the seams would buy her but a few weeks.

"A few weeks," the old woman had said. *Please, God. In the name of Holy Jesu, our Lord and Savior, let that be enough. Do not let my child be born in this foul nest,* she prayed. Praying was what she did when she was not stabbing at the linen and pricking her thumbs. Or when she *was* stabbing at the linen and pricking her thumbs. Praying and reciting from memory the verses that she'd so often copied. She couldn't really say they gave much comfort—comfort was elusive in such a place—but she had to admit she could not bear the stench and discomfort and icy hot fear without them.

She'd worked out long, elaborate prayers in her head, translating them from Latin, to English, to Czech—*which language, God, will please you most? Or is it as my grandfather said, that you can read my heart and have no need of language? Well, if you can read my heart, Lord, you know it's broken in any language, and I'm in need of such a miracle as only you can give.*

And then she remembered Jetta. No angel had come in answer to that prayer—unless Anna was supposed to have been the angel, Anna who hesitated, trembling with fear, on the bank of the river while Jetta sank beneath the rippling water. The memory shamed her. *If you've chosen an earthly angel to do your bidding, please, Lord, choose better this time. Do not let him be as craven as I.* And then she always added, *If not for me, Lord, then for the innocent life within me.*

She punctuated her stitching with her prayers—or her prayers with her stitching. Her conversations with God had grown so familiar, sometimes she talked aloud to Him as though he sat on the bed beside her. Sometimes she screamed at Him, to ask Him, *Why?* At other times she whimpered to Him, wanting only to curl up in His love. *"Come unto me all you that are weak and heavy laden and I will give you rest."*

"That's me, Lord. That's me. Anna. I'm here. I'm heavy laden. And I'm waiting." And she would cry to Him, "Abba, Father," as she shivered on her straw mattress.

Was that what the apostle Paul meant when he said to pray unceasingly? Or would He consider such familiarity profane? She had a fleeting image of the nuns at prayer, the rituals of the office. What if her grandfather had it all wrong? What if God was offended by her simple language? Considered her prayer in this fetid stinking place to be unworthy? Then she remembered Gethsemane. In his most urgent hour Christ had not gone to the temple to pray.

But look what happened to him, the devil whispered in her head.

She felt the child move inside her body. Her breath caught in her throat with a little heart leap of unexpected joy, as it had each time she felt the stirring inside her womb. She put her hands on her belly to comfort him. "Shh, little one, all will be well." The movement ceased, and she tried to calm her thoughts by envisioning his tiny body curled inside her, lest her child, like God, listen to her heart and not her words.

She was at the end of the seam. She bent her head to bite the thread in twain. The door creaked on its hinge.

"Is it Saturday?" she asked, not looking up. "I hope I'm last on your rounds, so we can talk. I felt the babe move—"

"Nay. 'Tis only Thursday. I've brought you a visitor, missy."

The black skirt of her visitor's cassock where it met the floor reminded her of the ravens roosting on the crenellated towers. The ravens of her dreams. "I have no need of a priest." She lifted her head to confront the intruder.

He stood outside the candle glow, his cowl pulled up, leaving his face in shadow. Like the pictures she'd seen of the Grim Reaper. Was that why he was here? To confess her before her ordeal? Was it beginning? She put her hands on her belly, instinctively, protectively.

"You may leave us now, good wife," her visitor said in his cleric's authoritarian tone.

She recognized the timbre of the voice!

Her heart hammered. "No! Don't leave him here with me. I told you I have no need of a priest!"

"I'll be at the end of the hall, Father. Just holler when ye want to leave." The old woman shut the door behind her.

He stepped forward and pulled back his cowl.

"Anna, please. Don't be afraid," he pleaded. "I've come to help you!" He stepped into the little circle of candlelight and reached out to take her hand.

She dropped the linen to the floor, recoiling from his touch. "Don't touch me! You have helped me enough!"

He dropped his hand. "I can believe that you are a witch," he said softly. "How completely you have cast your spell on me."

"Well, then, Father, abracadabra! I release you," she hissed at him, waving her hands in the air in a ridiculous caricature. "If I were a witch, I would have turned you into the vile creature that you are. What? A toad? No, a serpent! A serpent with a forked tongue who sheds his skin as easily as he lies."

He sat down beside her, put his head in his hands. She recoiled. Then he raised his head and said, not looking at her but staring at his hands, speaking to his hands, "But that's the trouble, Anna. You cannot release me. You are in my blood and bone and sinew. My soul is infected with you. Only God can release me. And he has not."

She heard the bitterness in her laughter and would have stopped it if she could. "How prettily you speak, Brother Gabriel, to woo a maid who is no longer a maid, made so by your own sly deceit. First I am a witch and now a pestilence. Look about you, Brother, Father—whatever ecclesiastical title you prefer. Smell the fetid air I breathe. Feel the chill of these hard, gritty walls. This is your doing. You have betrayed me for your Church! I hope it brought you the reward you seek!"

He did not answer her anger. He didn't even raise his voice but said simply, "The abbess told me you were with child."

"That is your doing too." The words fell like stones into the stillness, but they were said quietly, her shrewish fury spent. "Go away. I told you I have no need of a priest. You are but a false priest, anyway. You broke your vows of celibacy. And you sell that which is not yours to sell. You sell the very mercy that our Lord gives freely to all who ask. So go peddle your grace somewhere else. I have no coin to pay."

"I have given it up," he said.

"Given it up? But you still wear the habit. You still carry the indulgences." She pointed to the black silk pouch hanging at his waist, the pouch that carried the receipts of remission.

"Only to gain entrance here. Only to gain admittance to the king, where I have this day gone to beg for your release."

She felt both dizzy with hope and a great weight of dread that it could only be a false hope, if it came from him. As false as his paper pardons. Turning her back on him, she looked out at the narrow slit of sky that had deepened to a royal blue, like a great illuminated *I* carved into the stone wall. *I* for illegitimate, like the child that had quickened in her womb.

"My son will not be born a bastard," he said to her back. "Neither will he become a pawn of the Church."

There was a bitterness in his tone she'd never heard before. What had he to be bitter about?

"The king has taken your case under advisement. I'm to return to him tomorrow or the next day for his answer. I should still be wearing the cloth. If he refuses clemency, I will need to maintain it to gain access to you. If he sets you free, I shall renounce my vocation and marry with you. We will go away. Perhaps back to Rheims, where we were happy."

She could not breathe. Dare she trust him? What if it were naught but an evil trick? He'd betrayed her once. She turned around to try to read some truth in his eyes. He reached for her hand. His touch burned like a brand. She snatched it away.

"And if he does not set me free? And even if he does, you should know, Brother Gabriel, my forgiveness cannot be as cheaply bought as that remission which you carry in your papal pouch. You will never touch me again of my own free will."

He withdrew his hand. His gaze met hers, even, unwavering. "So be it, then. If that be my penance, I shall serve it. I will never touch you again without your consent." He got up and walked toward the door, called out through the window grill, "Warder, bring us a small brazier. It's freezing in here."

The warder returned momentarily, carrying a bucket of live coals.

"There be a small fire pit and a flue for drawing smoke built into that wall," the old man said, gesturing toward the right base of the wall against which Anna had rested her back. He opened a little grate and shoveled the live coals in, then probed them to life with a stick.

"We are not quite finished here," Gabriel said in his cleric's voice. "I will call you."

Anna said nothing. The baby moved inside her. The old man shuffled away, leaving the door slightly ajar. Gabriel closed it all the way, but there was no sound of scraping metal, no key turning in the lock. So much authority his clerical robes invested in him, she thought. Would he give up such status, such power for another human being? Selflessness was not a characteristic for which the powerful clergy was noted.

The child was restless. He kicked inside her. In spite of herself she laughed with the pleasure of it.

"Your child hears your voice and moves. Would you like to touch it?"

"Have I your consent then?" It was VanCleve's eyes that looked back at her. Just for an instant, then quickly replaced by the colder, more discerning look of Brother Gabriel.

"Only to lay your hands upon him for a blessing, Brother Gabriel."

He shook his head and turned away. "I'm not worthy to bless him."

Was that it? Or did he not care to bless him? Either way, the thought saddened her. Surprised her too—that she could feel compassion for a despised Roman prelate.

He opened the pouch and removed the indulgences and, kneeling beside the little brazier, fed one to the flames.

"What are you doing?" She felt panic rising inside her. "No, you cannot—"

Martin had died for this very thing! For the burning of papal indulgences.

"Don't do it. Not for me. I would not have you— Don't renounce your faith for me. I would not renounce mine for you."

"Then perhaps your faith is stronger." He fed another to the flames. "Or your love weaker," he said, throwing a fistful into the fire. He didn't look at her as he said the next words, low but loud enough for her to hear, "Herewith, Anna Bookman of Prague, I, Gabriel, plight thee my troth."

The fire leaped up, blue at its core. He consigned the last bit of paper to the flames and the pouch followed after. The fire coughed and hissed, almost choking on the velvet cloth.

"No! Don't do this!" She knelt beside him and would have snatched the papal pouch away, but he restrained her. She was crying, tears running down, collecting salty in the corners of her mouth. She closed her eyes against the vision that formed upon her eyelids. Three poles on Vltava Bridge. But this time it would not be Martin's dark curls on the center pole. She felt the warmth of the fire against her cheek, smelled the acrid smoke from the burning cloth, but she did not get up. She was conscious of his great black shadow looming over her.

"Anna," he said, his voice low, soft, filled with emotion, but she could not move. "Anna, do not be afraid. I have every hope that the king can be persuaded to release you. He has asked the archbishop to see the evidence. I told him that I could not remember from which desk I took the banned texts. I will not give evidence against you. I said I thought the abbey only copied the occasional heretical text, perhaps unknowingly, for some Lollard customer. The abbess is determined to protect you too. I petitioned the king that you be pardoned for the books found in your possession. Anna? Won't you look at me?"

But she could not. Fear paralyzed her. Fear that she would see the eyes of VanCleve when he'd left her in Rheims, promising to return.

Finally, she heard the whisper of his hem against the floor. Felt his shadow move away. When she opened her eyes, the door was closing behind him. She was alone in the room.

It had all been some fear-wrought vision, she told herself.

But the charred coals chewed on the remains of the velvet pouch, breaking the chill in the stone chamber.

She tried to conjure the vision of herself and VanCleve, happy in the little house in Rue de Saint Luc. But it would not come. That memory was forever gone, like words scraped clean on a used parchment.

⁓ ⁓ ⁓

Harry positioned himself in his chair, steeling himself against the confrontation that was to come with the morning council. He knew the Dominican preacher had waited outside his chamber for the last two weeks for an answer to his petition. But the king had a lot on his mind—the dauphin in France uppermost. Henry V, King of England—and France. He liked the sound of it. Some among his advisers counseled pursuits of peace. Others war. Harry listened to both, but he leaned toward war. Battle, not diplomacy, was his forte.

Then there was the matter of Sir John. Harry had gone through all the evidence. Sir John's own words damned him. The man verily called himself a heretic! Harry would have no choice but to sign the arrest warrant Arundel wanted. No choice if he wanted Arundel's blessing. And without the blessing of the Archbishop of Canterbury, how could he govern? Henry V, King of England—and France—would be an empty dream. But he would not put the friar off any longer. Why was the man so interested in the girl anyway? There was a story there—but he had no interest in it. Harry was a warrior, not a lover.

He had not much interest in the girl either. Indeed, he was about to cede the girl to the archbishop when he'd come across a pleasant piece of evidence that weighed heavily in her favor.

Harry loosened the strings on his ermine-edged robe. The day promised to be brighter. Already the sun checkered the floor at his feet with diamond panes of light.

"Lord Chamberlain, we are ready. Has the archbishop arrived?"

"Aye, Your Majesty. He waits without. As does His Grace, the Lord High Chancellor Beaufort. And the friar."

"And the girl? Has she been summoned?"

"Aye, Your Majesty. She awaits in the anteroom with the Lord High Constable."

"Then you may send them in."

If he could get this business disposed of in a timely fashion, then he could take a turn with his lute in the garden before dinner.

⚹

When the constable ushered her into the throne room of the royal apartments, Anna searched the room for Brother Gabriel. There. He stood just below the king's chair, between the archbishop and another richly dressed nobleman who wore a great gold necklace about his neck. The constable nudged her forward.

She dropped what she supposed was a curtsy, not understanding the protocol for a prisoner. She felt a sharp poke in her ribs.

"This is the King of England, missy, not some piddlin' knight. On your knees," he hissed.

"Mistress, you do not assume the supplicant's position?" the king said to her.

She was surprised at how young he looked despite his severe monklike haircut. Younger than she by some years. She blushed. "If it pleases Your Majesty, I am with child, and it is difficult for me to kneel. But I will try to do as Your Majesty orders me to do."

"You may stand." He motioned for her to approach. The few steps seemed a great distance.

He said nothing. The silence was heavy in the room. Her eyelid began to twitch. A sunbeam infused a cloud of smoke from the perpetual fire, turning it blue. She looked up at the king from beneath lowered eyelashes. He seemed to be thinking about something else entirely, not gazing at her but following the blue sunbeam to the blaze of sunshine that was its source. A broken robin's egg lay on the lip of the window. A cloud passed over the sun and the blue sunbeam vanished.

"Who is the father of your child, mistress? He should be here to lend support and plead your case."

She glanced first at Brother Gabriel, then at the archbishop, who gazed back at her smugly.

"The woman is charged with witchcraft, Your Majesty. Her child, whoever his father is, was probably misbegotten under a devil's moon in a coven circle of naked crones."

What a vile imagination the old man has, Anna thought. And this is the man who would lead English souls to Paradise?

The king smiled. "Is this true, madam? Did you hold congress with the devil beneath a full moon?" There was just the slightest hint of mockery in his voice. The chancellor smiled. The archbishop frowned. Brother Gabriel said, "Your Majesty—"

No, you will not say it. You will not endanger yourself for me. I will take nothing from you.

"The father of my child was a man I met in France. He bought a book from me, then seduced me and abandoned me. I have not seen him since."

That was no lie. The man she knew in France had only existed in her imagination. And how can one see one who lives only in imagination? She kept her eyes fastened on the tapestry hanging behind the throne. A stag had been pierced by a huntsman's arrow and lay dying in a circle of hounds. The sudden insight into the stag's plight made her eyelids smart with unshed tears.

"Never fear, Your Majesty. Whatever the witch's fate, her child will be baptized a Christian, if we have to cut it from her womb to do so. His soul will be nourished by the monks to undo whatever evil seed wrought him."

There was such vehemence in his voice. *He really believes this*, she thought. *He really believes I am evil.*

"Your Majesty, if I may speak in my own behalf?" Her voice echoed back thinly, small and frightened, from the gabled rafters.

"Please, mistress. As there seems to be no one here to speak for you."

"Your Majesty—" There was pleading in Brother Gabriel's voice.

The king motioned him to silence. "We have heard your opinion already, priest. Please continue, madam."

"I am innocent. I am a seller of books. The book of spells found with my belongings, I purchased at a stationer's in France. Its bindings and parchment are valuable commodities to a scribe and a bookseller. I do not know what it says. I cannot read Hebrew."

"And what of the charge of heresy? Why did you have the English Bible in your possession?"

"It belonged to my grandfather. He is dead. It is all I have left of him." She thought of Saint Peter denying Christ before the Roman soldiers' campfire. She thought of her grandfather and his courage. She gazed fully at Arundel, challenging him with her directness. "I read it often. I find great comfort in the words of our Lord."

The old man gasped. "See, Your Majesty. Find one heretic, find a nest. She can lead us to others. Let her be interrogated. At least the charge of heresy—"

The king raised his hand.

"Madam, are you aware that heretics are either burned or branded? With a hot iron? On even such a lovely face as yours? The letter *H* burned into your flesh would be a considerable blemish."

The friar—she could only allow herself to think of him thus—stepped forward, opened his mouth. Again the king held up a restraining hand.

"Have you ever read the Holy Scriptures for yourself, Your Majesty?" Anna asked quietly.

"Insolence! She should be whipped for her insolence, sire!"

The king swatted at the air above his head as though he were swatting a gnat. "Our Latin is . . . insufficient," he said.

"Just so, Your Majesty. That is why it has been translated for you. For you and all who would read it. You might find much there to guide you. Advice from the king of all kings to England's king. You might also find that much the Church tells you is scriptural truth is not there at all."

The archbishop gasped again and this time was seized by a spasm of coughing.

Anna continued. "Things like the doctrine of Purgatory and the sale of indulgences, and—"

"Enough!" The king sighed. "Why is it that all you heretics are so intent on your own destruction? You leave me no choice, madam. While we conclude that there is not enough evidence to charge you with witchcraft—no witnesses have assembled here to speak against you—we must concur with the learned archbishop that the charge of heresy stands. Your own words convict you."

The archbishop bowed so low, he seemed about to topple.

Brother Gabriel stepped forward. "Please, Your Majesty, I beg you consider—"

"But," the king said. "We are coming upon Holy Week. The week when our Lord and Savior, Jesus Christ, was crucified and rose again for the sins of mankind. In the spirit of the celebration of grace, we offer you an Easter pardon, Anna of Prague. You will return in the custody of Brother Gabriel to the abbey at Rochester, where you will repent your sins and study the true doctrine of the faith under his tutelage."

"Your Majesty, I most rigorously urge you to reconsider. You are making a grave error." Arundel sputtered between coughs. "You are sending her back to the very source of the heresy. May I remind Your Majesty that your coronation is imminent."

The king's next words made no sense to Anna, some private struggle between the king and the archbishop.

"Don't threaten us, Archbishop. Do not push your king too far. England has one martyred archbishop at whose shrine to worship. You will have your writ of arrest for Lord Cobham, but do not ask me to help you trap him. You will not use this woman toward that end."

At those words even the chancellor looked grave.

"Before you go, I would have a word with you, Anna Bookman. I wish to ask you about a piece of music you have copied." He smiled. "We would like to meet the young man who plays our music. I understand he is your ward."

Anna's confusion must have shown on her face.

The king fumbled among the papers in front of him. He held up the paper she had been copying the day she was arrested. "The music composition signed 'Roy Henry.' It would give us great pleasure to hear him play our music. With your permission, he may someday play at court."

It took a moment for this to sink in, then Anna laughed in spite of herself. It was not Brother Gabriel who had secured her release, after all. Nor all her brave rhetoric! It was Bek! The king had simply been flattered that her half-wit son could play his music. And then she just as quickly sobered to think what a mad world she lived in when her fate hung on such a whim as that.

"We all serve at Your Majesty's pleasure," she said. And with that she was handed off to Brother Gabriel.

THIRTY-SEVEN

nna and Brother Gabriel barely spoke on the long journey
back to Rochester. He hired a horse litter for her and rode his horse beside
the covered litter. Two of the king's armed guards rode ahead to ensure protection. Few vagabonds or outlaws would accost a party carrying the king's
banner at its front. The monk—she was determined to think of him thus;
how else to guard her heart?—was as careful with her as though he were a
knight and she his lady from some chivalric romance, providing her with
warm blankets and a cushion for her back, stopping frequently to let her
stretch her legs. But he was no knight. And she no lady.

Still, how different this journey was from the journey up. And all because
she'd copied the king's music for Bek. They stopped at the same alehouse,

but this time Brother Gabriel spread a cloth in the April sunshine outside the inn yard lest the rude company offend her.

"I thank you, Friar Gabriel, for your intervention with the king in my behalf." She had not formally thanked him and she supposed he deserved that much at least. "And for your courtesy," she added as he spread their picnic.

She regretted the coldness in her tone when she saw the hurt in his eyes. She was reminded of the wounded stag hanging above the king's head. She wondered if he too remembered the little picnic in Rue de Saint Luc.

"No longer think of me by that name, Anna. This black habit is no more than a disguise I must wear until we can go away."

"You are no wool merchant. VanCleve is not your name. How else should I think of you?"

"Think of me as Gabriel. The father of your child. Your husband. Soon to be."

It was Friday, so their few vegetables were augmented with a bit of pickled herring.

"Where in the Bible, Friar, does it say the faithful should eat fish on Fridays? Oh, I forgot. You have not read the whole of the Bible. So you would not know. But I can tell you, Friar Gabriel, it does not."

He just looked at her. She saw again the wounded stag. She wished she could cut out her tongue.

They finished the meal in silence and in silence recommenced their journey. She heard Gabriel tell the postilion to make haste, even his cleric's voice unusually curt. They reached the abbey a little after nightfall.

As she prepared with relief to disembark, he reached up and offered his hand to help her down. Instead she clung to the side of the cart as her feet fumbled for the footstool provided by the postilion.

Sister Matilde rushed out to greet her, wrapping her in a welcome embrace.

"Oh, Anna. We have been so worried! I shall wake the abbess. She has not been well. But she will want to know."

"No, Sister. Wait until the morrow. Soon enough. Oh, it is good to be home." Ready tears sprang to her eyes.

She turned to bid Gabriel good night, to thank him more sincerely for his part in her homecoming, but he was already gone.

"Brother Gabriel must have been tired from his journey," Sister Matilde said. "He is usually not so unfriendly."

"He has a lot on his mind," Anna said. "Being a lackey for the archbishop is hard work."

⚜

The next morning, Anna was awakened by the sound of bells. What a joyful sound—albeit a little startling at prime—and the cacophony seemed to go on forever. It took her a moment to realize she was back in her room at the abbey, where last night Bek had greeted her with a great flailing of arms, his face wreathed in affectionate smiles. An na An na. But now he was gone.

By the time she was dressed and had braided her hair into one long rope, the nuns had already shuffled off to prime. She was wondering where Bek had got to so early when he poked his head through the door. "Bek's bells!" he announced proudly. "An na like?"

It took her a minute to realize what he was talking about. "You rang the bells?" He rewarded her with his big sloppy grin. She reached out and gathered him to her. "Anna likes."

"Anna fat," he said, touching her stomach.

"Yes, Anna fat." She laughed. She held him out at arm's length. "You saved Anna, Bek. With your music. You are my angel."

"Angel?" The word came out slowly and a bit slurred.

She looked at his large head and cloudy eyes that always seemed to wiggle a bit in their sockets, at his twitching limbs, and thought what an unlikely angel he was. "Someday I will explain it to you," she said. "When I have reasoned it out for myself."

After they had broken their fast together in the refectory, Anna feeding him to keep both herself and him from being splattered with porridge, she went in search of Mother, surprised to see the strong, vital woman still in her bed. The squeeze she gave Anna's hand was not hearty.

"Brother Gabriel promised he would bring you back to us, and I see he has."

"Mother, are you ill?"

"Just the illness of the old, Anna. Some of my parts are wearing out. My heart flutters like a caged bird, and I grow faint."

But her smile was still warm and filled with light. And the soft skin of her cheeks retained their roses. One cheek at least. She did not wear the veil, but the white linen wimple that wrapped her face partially obscured the injured side.

"The learned doctor that the bishop sent says that I should rest. But I would prefer to do it in the garden, where my spirit can be cheered by the snowdrops and the Lenten rose."

"Maybe we can take a turn there later in the afternoon," Anna said. "When it is warmer."

"Sit beside me, Anna." She patted the edge of the cot. "I want to hear about your adventure. Were you badly frightened? Do you think any harm has come to the child?"

"Both the child and I are well, Mother. Though I was frightened nearly to death. But I took great comfort in the clothes you sent me because I knew that I was not forgotten. And I took much comfort from my knowledge of the Scriptures. I am more sure than ever that every man should read—"

"And Brother Gabriel? Did he come to see you? He appeared to be in great turmoil when he heard of your arrest. Vowed to do whatever he could to see that you were freed." She still held to Anna's hand, gave it another light squeeze. "I told him, Anna, about the child. He owns that it is his. He says he will renounce his calling and marry you."

Embarrassed, Anna did not let her gaze meet Mother's. It settled on the cross above Mother's bed. She'd never noticed before, but it looked as though it had suffered damage and been restored. The figure of the Christ was misshapen, and one corner of the wood was badly charred. Odd that she should put it in such a place of honor when everything else about the abbey, all its furnishings, were of the best quality.

"He told me the same," Anna said. "But I do not know if I can trust him."

"He seemed sincere. But that is for you to know. You must pray for discernment. Let your heart guide you. Your heart and your child's need."

She sighed and lay back on the pillow.

"You need to rest, Mother, as the doctor says. I will come back in the afternoon and we will sit together in the garden. What would you have me do in the meantime?"

"Do not go to the scriptorium. Someone may be watching. The sisters are only copying Latin Scriptures and English poetry. But your very presence might bring more suspicion."

"The king has signed a warrant for Sir John's arrest," Anna said.

"I am not surprised. All the more reason we must not copy the Lollard texts for a season."

Anna released Mother's hand and smoothed her brow, then bent to kiss it.

"One more thing, before you go, Anna. What was your grandfather's name? What did he do for a living?"

That seemed a strange question for a sick woman with so little breath to spare.

"He was an illuminator of great reputation and talent, Mother. His name was Finn."

The abbess closed her eyes and took a ragged breath, but she said nothing. Anna wasn't even sure she heard. She moved toward the door as quietly as she could.

"Come back this afternoon, Jasmine. We'll sit in the colonnade in the sunlight, and we'll talk about Finn the Illuminator."

Jasmine! Had the abbess called her "Jasmine"? *"My little Jasmine flower,"* her grandfather used to call her. No. She had probably misunderstood. The abbess's voice was breathy and low.

Anna started to ask her, but she appeared to be sleeping. Anna walked softly to the door, lest she disturb her, and headed for the kitchens. She had a sudden craving for milk curds mixed with honey.

～✤～

Good Friday. The cotters at Cobham Hall brought their token gifts of eggs to the great kitchen. Lady Joan accepted them graciously, giving them hot cross buns in return. After pronouncing an Easter blessing upon the household of each giver, she invited them to an Easter mass "in celebration of our risen Lord" to be held in the chapel on Sunday. The mass would be followed with a feast in the great hall: a lamb stew cooked with spring onions for the yeomen and lamb shank bone stewed with the dried remains of last year's root vegetables for the villeins. And there would be another Easter miracle—the very eggs they'd offered to their lord as gifts returned to them in the form of custards, puddings, and caudle, and, best of all, simnel cake, decorated with marzipan balls, twelve, one for each apostle.

Lady Joan had found a Lollard priest, one she knew could be trusted, to say the mass. The Easter service was not noised abroad as it might have been before Sir John became a fugitive. And even though Lord Cobham might return for Eastertide, he would be served Holy Communion in secret. The lord of Cobham Castle would not be present at the Easter sunrise mass to be celebrated facing the sea—facing east.

But he would certainly be present at the secret ceremony following and at its attendant celebration. So this Saturday morning, Lady Joan hummed as she, like any other good wife with her skirts hiked to her girdle and her chestnut hair bound in a scrap of cloth, wielded her straw broom against the spiderwebs in the corners of the chapel rafters. She'd already had the floor swept in the hall and ordered fresh rushes to be put down. And she'd hired a piper and a lutist. There would be dancing after. These were grim times. They deserved a bit of celebration, she thought, as she laid the altar with candles and a purple cloth. John was coming home! There was going to be a wedding!

She'd laughed out loud when Brother Gabriel had come to her with the request. "The Lollards will get your soul yet, Brother—the Lollards or the devil." And then she'd sobered and told him in the most honest way she could, "You know this goes beyond the loss of your vocation. Arundel will take your renouncing of your vows as a personal affront. He will be your enemy. Unless, of course, you mean to keep your marriage secret, as many do. A clandestine marriage he could probably give a nod and a wink."

"I cannot keep it secret, your ladyship. At least not for long. I mean to give her child my name."

She did not question him, did not say what she'd long suspected, that Anna was not a widow. "Take care. Lest this child inherit your enemies along with your name." She did not say "your child," though she had her suspicions there as well.

"I know. I've already thought of that. I'll have to wear this habit a few more weeks. But I want to put Anna's mind at rest."

"The priest can be relied upon to be discreet."

At least the girl's wedding would be merry. Joan was going to see to it. She'd decorated the chapel with apple blossoms banked below the altar and behind, spilling their lace and fragrance from every windowsill. Anna deserved this at least, after all she'd suffered. Mayhap this Easter morn would mark the beginning of better times, Lady Joan thought, as she thrust her straw broom above the altar where a spider dangled from a silken thread. She swatted it to the floor and crushed it with her heel.

The cloister garden carried the scent of lily of the valley growing wild across the quadrangle. Holy Virgin's tears, the sisters called them. Anna sat with the abbess in a sunny corner of the colonnade enjoying the sunshine and the fresh sweet scent of them. They listened in companionable silence to the splashing of the water in the fountain.

"Mother, are you warm enough?"

Maybe this was not such a good idea, Anna thought, and said as much, but the abbess had insisted. She looked very frail and no longer wore the veil. Since her weakness, as she called it, the scars didn't seem to matter to her. One silver-gray hair had escaped her wimple and a light wind blew it into the corner of her eye. Anna reached up to brush it away. Her fingers gently touched the scar. It felt smooth and soft, but firmer than the velvet, looser skin of her cheek.

An inchworm fell from the apostle's beard carved in the column capital and landed in Mother's lap. Anna picked it up and quickly flung it away. "Go measure somewhere else," she said.

The abbess smiled. "We are all measured for our shrouds sooner or later, Anna. Besides, that's just a silly superstition."

"I know, Mother. But in your case, I wish it to be later."

The inchworm resumed its arched posture and measured the apostle's stone cape instead.

"Tell me about Finn the Illuminator, Anna. Tell me about your grandfather."

"He was a wonderful man. A man of talent and wisdom and compassion. A man not given to easy laughter, but when he did laugh, it seemed the whole world was happier." Then she realized how childish that might sound. "Well, at least my world. I always wanted to please him."

"Was he easily pleased?"

"Not always. He had very high standards. He liked things to be . . . perfect."

"That must have been hard for you."

"Sometimes. But it was useful too." She could hear the defensiveness in her tone.

"You loved him very much."

"He was everything to me. I never knew my mother or my father."

The inchworm had disappeared inside a wrinkle in the apostle's stone cape.

"Why did he never marry? I mean, such a paragon must have been much in demand." Only gentle sarcasm in her tone. Anna loved her wit.

"When I was much younger I remember they were always after him. Friends from the university were forever pressing him to meet some widowed sister, or maiden aunt, or cousin, telling him I needed the influence of another female. Once I asked him why he always put them off. He said he'd loved two women, and they'd both left him with a broken heart. And then he laughed and said one woman per household was enough. Of course, I was hardly more than a child, but he always made me want to be older, wiser, the woman of the house."

The abbess nodded, smiling, seeming oddly pleased at those words.

"Did he have an easy life?"

"By most standards. We were comfortable in our little town house. He had friends and he had his work. He was also very committed to spreading Wycliffe's teachings, more so year by year. That seemed enough for him. Most of the time. Sometimes a brooding sadness would come over him, but it never lasted long. I guess he worked himself out of it."

The abbess nodded as though she understood fully. *It's a sign of her great compassion that she can take such an interest in someone else's life,* Anna thought. *It's probably because they shared the same cause.*

The abbess looked down and picked at the edge of her wimple with her long fingers. *They look so frail, the bones no stronger than dried winter twigs.*

"And his death? Was that easy too?"

Surprised, Anna found that talking about him thus gave her some comfort. Her grief was no longer raw. She no longer felt as though she had lost him, because he was still with her, his image leaping into her mind whenever she called it.

"He suffered only a little pain. He died in his sleep."

"Only a little pain and then to die in your sleep. Life's final blessing for a life well lived." The abbess sighed and closed her eyes.

She's thinking of her own death, Anna thought.

"He must have felt great hurt at leaving you behind," the abbess said, still not opening her eyes.

"He did. He made me promise that I would come here. He trusted Sir John. He'd been working with him in the Lollard cause for the last few years. When the persecution started in Prague, he thought I would be safe here with Sir John. He had no way of knowing."

"No, I don't suppose he did." Her voice sounded weary beyond all revival.

"Mother, are you ready to go in? Is the breeze too much?"

"No. Anna. I'm just gathering my strength to tell you what I have to tell you."

Anna felt a clutch of fear, like something slipping inside her. *She's going to send me away,* Anna thought. *Like Mistress Kremensky, she's going to say it is not safe for the other sisters for me to be here. Her compassion makes it hard. I should not make her say it. I should tell her I will leave. But where? Oh, Holy Jesu, where?*

"Mother, I think—"

The abbess shook her head. "Shh, Anna, let me tell you what I have to say."

The inchworm had gained an expanse of the apostle's robe. He lost his hold and dropped to the ground and began again. The abbess fumbled in the little pouch that hung at her waist and withdrew something, held it out to Anna.

"I had your necklace fixed," she said, pressing it into Anna's hand, "and now I want to tell you its history. Have you ever noticed how the little pearls at the center of the cross make a six-pointed star?" She traced them with her fingernail.

Anna squinted at the necklace. She could see it! As clear as day, now that it was pointed out to her. She'd only ever seen the cross. Not noticed the star at all. But she recognized it for what it was.

"It looks like . . . it's the star of Judah," she said.

"You know it, then. Your grandfather told you."

"I know it because he worked for the Jews in Judenstadt. He illuminated beautiful manuscripts for them. I delivered them to the rabbi there."

"Your grandfather never told you, then? About the necklace?"

"Only that it belonged to my mother and her mother before her. It was my grandfather's wedding gift to my grandmother Rebekka. I never noticed the star before. I'm sure he would have told me if I'd asked."

The abbess frowned. "I'm surprised Finn never told you. It was cowardly of him. But it was his love for you that made him craven."

"Told me what? He was the bravest man I—"

"You had two grandmothers, Anna. Your grandmother Rebekka was a Jewess."

Rebekka. Not a Christian name. Why had she never wondered at that? Her grandmother a Jewess! But how could such a thing be? Her grandfather would have told her. Wouldn't he?

She saw again the cramped quarters of Judenstadt, the humiliation heaped upon the Jewish people even in Prague, one of the last refuges left to them in all of Christendom, remembered how she'd pitied them and how glad she was that she had not been born one of them. How God must have laughed at her!

Now she understood the odd affinity her grandfather had for the Jews when others in Prague shunned them. She was too stunned to wonder how the abbess could have this private knowledge of her, too stunned to think of aught but what it might mean.

"Then I am a Jewess too? And my babe—"

"No, Anna. You are a Christian. If you choose to be. You were baptized a Christian. You were raised a Christian. But you should know. It is your choice. Two grandmothers, Anna. I am Kathryn. I am your other grand-mother."

She reached out as if to take Anna's hand but only let it hover and then withdrew it.

"You? You are Kathryn?" No, Anna thought, she must have misunder-stood what the abbess said. "You can't be Kathryn. At least not that Kathryn. She died in a fire in the great revolt. My grandfather would not have lied . . ."

The abbess did not look at Anna; her eyes looked down at her hands folded in her lap, her only sign of distress the twisting of her habit between her fingers.

"His was not the lie," she said. "He thought I died. I deceived him and it was not the first time I deceived him, I fear. But I have paid for that deception many times over." She paused, looked up at Anna, her gaze direct. "It was the only way, Anna. He would not have left if he knew I lived, and if he'd stayed, his life would have been over. The bishop who held him prisoner would never have let him go, and I was too ill to go with him. I knew his only chance, your only chance, was to escape to the Continent."

"But how did you know?"

"I knew there was a connection between you and me from the beginning. I thought it was the cause we shared. Until I recognized the necklace."

In the stillness of the garden, neither spoke while Anna's mind whirled with questions—and a little resentment too, when she remembered her grandfather's lifelong grief for this woman. Then, finally, in a voice so low Anna had to bend down to hear, the abbess began to speak again—about Anna's mother, Rose, and Finn the Illuminator and a woman named Kathryn of Blackingham who loved them both. "I loved your mother like a daughter," she said. "And I grieved for years her loss—and yours."

By the time the abbess had finished her story, her hands were trembling and Anna was fighting back tears of regret for both Finn and Kathryn. The inchworm had once again made its way onto the hem of the abbess's habit. Anna smashed it with the toe of her shoe.

"Do not be so angry, dear. You cannot kill death. Some of us even see him as our friend. You'll know what I mean someday when you are as tired as I. I know you have questions, but I think I'd like to rest now. Help me back inside."

Anna helped her up carefully, walked with her to her chamber door, helped her onto her bed. "Grandmother," Anna said—the words did not at all feel strange on her lips—"I wish my grandfather could see how beautiful you are." And she kissed the scarred temple gently, feeling its tautness against her lips.

The abbess patted Anna's hand. "We'll talk later. When you've had time to think about what I've told you. Brother Gabriel was asking for you earlier. I told him you'd be in the chapel this afternoon. He could seek you there. He has his faults, Anna, but I believe him to be a good man. He may yet be redeemed, with the help of the Lord and a good woman."

Anna laughed in spite of herself. But the laughter quickly faded. She wasn't at all sure, for she had seen the chameleon change his skin.

She went first to her room to wipe the red from her eyes. Then she went to the chapel. But not to see Brother Gabriel, she told herself. She wanted to confront another. So many questions. And where better to invoke the Spirit than in one of the places he was reputed by some to reside?

THIRTY-EIGHT

. . . beguile a woman with words;
To give her troth but lightly
For nothing but to lie by her;
With that guile thou makest her assent,
And bringest you both to cumberment.
—ROBERT MANNING IN *HANDLYNG SYNNE*

rother Gabriel did not come to the chapel, though Anna lingered there until vespers. *Stupid girl, to even expect it!* But she had too much to think about to deal with him. Even the anxiety that the mere mention of his name engendered in her could not temper her joy. She was not alone. She had a grandmother. An abbess. A woman of prestige and some power. But, caution argued, a woman also under suspicion because of her association with Sir John. A woman so sick and frail that she might die in her sleep.

You should never have sent him away, Grandmother. She muttered the words under her breath like a prayer. How different would all our lives have been. The very thought of it grieved her like a fresh loss. But who could really know? *Think of the good the two did separately for the cause, Anna. Think of the books they have copied, the souls they have reached.*

When the violent bells tolled vespers and the nuns shuffled to their chanted prayers, Anna slipped from the chapel and crossed the dusky garden to her small quarters. She stopped outside Mother's—Grandmother's—door and listened. There was no sound. Softly she opened it and peeped in. The abbess lay as still as a statue upon her bed. A statue or a corpse. *Please, no, Holy Jesu. Not when I've just found her.* Then she saw the slightest movement of the old woman's chest, and, relieved, tiptoed from the threshold, closing the door gently behind her.

She glanced in the direction of the guest quarters. That door was also closed. His chamber looked vacant, its lone glazed window like a giant cyclops's eye gleaming darkly. She'd known better than to trust him, so why did her heart freeze a little at the thought he'd abandoned her yet again?

Had he not meant the words he'd said in the tower room? Had it all been a trick? Why was she surprised? Or had her adder's tongue stripped from him a faint resolve? Easily turned away, then, for all his determined rhetoric and protestations of love. The burning of the indulgences was all for show. He'd probably already replaced them. Come to think about it, she'd never really seen what was written on the paper anyway.

Or had he been frightened away because the abbess had told him that his betrothed had a drop of Jewish blood in her veins? *Then you are not the man my grandfather was,* she thought. *And I will have no less.*

She had removed her dress—these seams too would have to be let out soon in spite of the high-waisted fashion. She was standing in her shift when a gentle knock came. Her heart gave a little thump. But he would not come to her chamber. It would not be seemly.

"Mistress Anna." It was the young novice. "I have a bundle for you."

"Who sent it? Do you know?" Anna asked, taking the bundle from her.

"No. A young page brought it from the castle."

Lady Joan had been so kind to her. She would know Anna was rapidly outgrowing her clothes. In spite of the great weight of worry she had about Sir John, she'd remembered Anna's need.

Anna hurriedly spread out the dress on her cot. And yes, it was considerably fuller, even in the bodice. It was of an exquisite royal-blue damask with ribands of a darker blue and slashed sleeves inset with white cream satin. It was the most beautiful dress Anna had ever seen.

Generous indeed! But not at all what she needed. Where would she ever wear such a fine garment as this? It was not a dress for a humble scrivener—not even for the wife of a defrocked cleric, she thought bitterly.

Wrapped inside it was a garland woven with love knots of cream satin and lily of the valley and dried pink roses. It was a garland such as a bride would wear.

She lifted the garland gently, removed her caplet, and placed it on her head. A note drifted to the floor. She picked it up, read the words feverishly.

Anna of Prague, accept this dress and wear it to the chapel on Easter morn, the day of our Lord's resurrection, the day when everything is made new and the world redeemed. After the Easter mass, I will meet you at the chapel steps, and before Lady Cobham and assembled witnesses and a priest I'm sure you will approve, I will make you wife. Your wearing of this dress will constitute your consent. My heart longs to see you in it. Whatever our future holds, we will face it together and will welcome our child into the world together. In time I shall regain the trust you no longer have in me.

The note was signed with a bold stroke, "Gabriel."

She took off her cap and, placing the wreath on her head, held a candle in front of the glazed window to try to discern her reflection in the candle glow. The woman that stared back at her didn't look at all like a Jewess, she thought. Her eyes were blue, and her red head was crowned with a garland of flowers. *I look like a bride, a Christian bride.* But the candle glow picked out the pearls in the cross at her throat. Now that she knew it was there, she would never look at the cross again without seeing the star.

She sat down on her bed and picked up Gabriel's letter. Read it again. And yet again. She didn't know what to make of it either. Was it all a sham? Some new trick from a Roman spy to catch her out? She could not believe that of him. Did not want to believe that of him. But could anything good ever come out of that Roman nest of false religion and greed? She'd not thought so. Might it be that he was as confused as she? Just as desperate? Just as lonely? Could it be that there was more of VanCleve in him than Dominican friar? "Tell me what to do, Dĕdeček." But no ghostly presence appeared to give her comfort.

Thinking that she was glad Bek was not here to hear her crying, she lay back across the bed and sobbed into her pillow. The flowery garland was knocked awry. One of its fragile roses shattered, scattering its dried petals on the floor in a pile of faded pink dust.

꽃무늬

Brother Gabriel returned to the abbey after dark, stabled his horse, and walked across the quadrangle. No light emanated from Anna's room. He'd intended to return before nightfall, to encounter her in the chapel and press her for an answer, but the Lollard priest delayed him. It took some trouble to convince the man that Gabriel was not just another lust-filled, corrupt friar out to deceive some simpleminded girl into a clandestine marriage and then abandon her.

For two hours he'd listened as the man interrogated him. The irony did not escape him. How the tables had turned! A Dominican friar of the order that had led the Inquisition and routed out heretics for centuries now being called to defend his faith before a lay priest. And he could not. Using Wycliffe's very words, brick by brick, the Lollard had dismantled the structure of theology that Gabriel had spent his young life learning, outlining the abuses of the clergy: the selling of that which should be free, the emphasis on prilgrimage and holy relics, the denial of the sacramental cup to any but the ordained "worthy." Who among the friars and priests he'd known was worthy? Not the archbishop, who plotted the entrapment of a good man, not Father Francis, whose whole life had been a lie, and not Father Gabriel, certainly. No one was worthy—all were made worthy by the blood of Christ.

It was a good thing that he'd sent the dress provided by Lady Cobham on ahead. He had offered to pay her but was relieved when she refused, saying it was her gift. What funds did he have with which to purchase his bride a dress? Despite its great wealth, the Dominican rule allowed for no individual ownership. Though all the "impoverished" priests slept on down pillows and rode fine horses and drank French wine, they owned nothing. Every farthing Gabriel used, every morsel he put in his mouth—all belonged to the Order. He was bound by the rule of the beggar. Everything belonged to the institution he was renouncing. It would not be easy to break from that kind of bondage.

The import of what he was doing pressed on his chest like a weight. He could scarcely breathe. How was he going to feed a wife and child—two children, for was Bek not like Anna's own child? He'd expressed this fear to Lady Joan, along with his gratitude when she offered the dress.

"You are a learned man, Gabriel. As is your bride. You will find a way—without selling your soul!"

She was the first to call him "Gabriel" aside from Mistress Clare, aside from his mother. Even Anna, after she'd seen him burn the indulgences and heard him announce his intent to renounce his calling and marry her, had still called him "Brother" with a sneer in her voice.

Would she come on the morrow? Would she be there in her bridal attire?

He removed his black habit and scapular, his fine white tunic, and folding them neatly, put them in a chest. He took the priest's vestments from his cupboard, raised the amice and stole to his lips, and, folding them reverently, laid them on top. It was over. The next time he wore them it would be as a disguise.

Disguise came easily to him, Anna had said. Was she right? What truly lay beneath his skin? Was there a man with beliefs and courage and honor inside? Or was the man merely no more than an actor in a mummer's play who took the form and mouthed the words his costume suggested? As a youth, when he'd lived in the insular world of the monastery, he'd taken their beliefs and thought them his own. But faith, unlike silver spoons and precious books, was not something a man could inherit. In the crucible of life, such faith crumbled to ash as easily as his paper indulgences.

How could Anna's faith be so strong? And what about that Lollard priest who lectured him—and even Lord and Lady Cobham and the old abbess? Where did they find the moral courage to challenge the ordained authority of centuries of received wisom?

In the bottom of the chest lay the hair shirt and the "discipline." He picked up the little whip, slapped it across his open palm. Such was the discipline of his mind that he hardly felt the sting of it. But it raised a welt inside his hand, reminding him of the legions of pilgrims, the flagellants who had no money to pay for penance, who marched barefoot through the towns beating their backs until they bled while women rushed to collect their blood and smear it on their own faces because someone had told them it was holy.

He flung the whip across the room. It made a hissing noise as it landed among the rushes, a coiled strip of braided leather with little bits of bone for fangs. Where in the Bible did it say that Christ and the apostles ever mutilated their own bodies? Had not others done that for them? Were there not always others to do that for the man or woman who sought the narrower path?

He could quote whole pages of Latin catechism, could read the ancient philosophers in Greek, but he could not summon one verse of Christ's words to give him comfort. He had preached of hellfire and damnation and offered purchased grace to those poor lost souls who struggled in the slime of their own sin and the sins of others. He had not preached a personal God. And now he had great need of one. Great need of a presence who walked with a man like a friend, a Holy Spirit that truly comforted—not some magical Latin incantation or pious litany or piece of paper with the pope's seal adorning it. Did such a being even exist? And if it did, how was he to find it?

He lay down across his bed and closed his eyes. Either Anna would come—or some grudging part of her would come to him—on the morrow, or she would not. Either way, he would not go back as he was. Easter morn would be for Gabriel, son of Jane Paul of Southwark, a new beginning.

※

Midmorning found Father Gabriel waiting alone in the small chapel at Cobham Castle, still pondering what he had done, what he was about to do. But he was not alone for long.

"Were you at the sunrise service?" Lady Joan asked, entering, her arms laden with yet more apple blossom branches and a garment of some sort. She placed the branches on the purple cloth beside the chalice and the candlesticks. "I did not see you, but then I hardly knew you just now. Those leggings, that simple doublet, you blended well with the crowd."

"I am looking for the simple man inside me," Gabriel said.

"But this is your wedding day! Don't let it be too simple. Here." She held out the garment to him. "I've brought you this surcoat. It's one of John's. The seamstress tucked it in last night," she said.

He shrugged his shoulders into it. She smoothed its ermine fringe and stepped back with a speculative gaze. "It still hangs a bit loose but fit enough for a bridegroom."

"I thank you, Lady Cobham. Aside from the clerical robes, these leggings and tunic purchased last night are the only clothes I have."

"Well they become you, sir. Better than the black habit."

The light faded as a silhouette appeared in the open door. Gabriel looked up to see an angel standing in the door, an angel with a great mass of curls, loose and flowing free down her back and shoulders. Her head was covered with a gossamer veil held in place with the little wreath of flowers. She was wearing the dress of blue brocade.

As long as I live, never let me forget this vision of her, Lord.

It was the first English prayer Gabriel had ever said. He was surprised at how easily it formed itself in his thoughts.

⟣⟢

"I'm sorry. I thought the chapel would be empty—" Anna squinted into the shadows.

"Anna, you look beautiful!"

Anna recognized Lady Cobham's voice, but she was with someone else—in the dim interior it was hard to see—a yeoman perhaps. Even the Lollard priests wore habits.

"I was afraid you wouldn't come."

It was VanCleve's voice. Or Brother Gabriel's. Neither. Or both.

Her eyes adjusted to the light. He was in layman's dress.

"It is hard enough to make one's way in the world. My child will not enter it carrying the shame of bastardy."

"Our child, Anna."

"I must go and see that preparations are ready for the bride ale," Lady Cobham muttered. Before Anna could protest, she had bustled out the door.

"So," Anna said into the awkward silence, "your costume leads me to think the archbishop has not been invited." She hadn't meant it to sound as hateful as it did.

"Our marriage must be a secret for now, to protect you and the babe from the enemies I will make with this action. But our vows will be witnessed by Lord Cobham's crofters and retinue. There will be a nuptial mass. A Lollard priest has agreed to marry us. You will find such a vow binding."

"But will you?"

"My vow is to you before God and our witnesses."

She moved closer, into the chapel interior, so that she could see his face. "Well said, but Bro—Gabriel, there is something I must tell you, though the knowing of it may make you take back that troth which you plighted in ignorance. But to keep it from you would be less than honorable. Better our child should be a bastard than have a mother who is without honor." She was startled to hear how much that little speech sounded like something her grandfather might have said.

Her hand went to the cross around her neck. She fingered it carefully, feeling for the points of the star. Did she trust him enough to tell him? His order had long persecuted the Jews. The very fact of her Jewish blood could be enough to gain her expulsion from England. From the only home she had. But how could she marry him with such a secret on her conscience? It would be hypocritical when she had berated him for his own deceit. She almost wished the abbess had not told her.

"My grandmother was a Jewess," she said.

She watched his face for the telling frown, the bunched brow. But all she saw was the merest flicker of an eyelid. His gaze remained steadfast, direct, honest.

"My mother was a whore," he said. "My father a corrupt friar even by my own Church standards. What have they to do with us?"

"They have much to do with us," she answered quietly. His ready response had stripped the bitterness from her reply. "We must understand from whence we came in order to know where we are going."

"You will tell our child, then? That he has Jewish blood?"

Suddenly she saw again the little Jewish boy outside the walls of Judenstadt, his silly little hat, his tears. She heard too the taunts of the other children. "I . . . I don't know. It is a hard thing to know."

"We will decide together," he said.

Together. How she longed to believe in those words.

"I can read your face," he said. "You do not trust me. But I would beg you to remember that my disguise was not the only one, Anna. You were no widow. It was a maiden's virtue I took that night in our little love nest in Rue de Saint Luc."

She started to explain, but he held up his hand. "I understand there is much that must pass between us before there can be trust. As I promised, I will not claim the marriage debt from you nor will I pay it until such trust returns between us."

The scent of the apple blossoms perfumed the tiny chapel. She sat down on the lone bench beside him.

"I have no dowry," she said.

He laughed. "And I no dower to offer you, except what resides in heart and hand and head. I bring nothing to our marriage but the clothes on my back—and they were purchased by that Church which you despise."

Outside, voices gathered and called to them.

He led her outside onto the gray stone steps of the chapel, where the wedding vows were to be said before they reentered the chapel to celebrate their first mass as man and wife. The Lollard priest was waiting there with Lady Joan and Lord Cobham. The abbess was there, leaning on Sir John's arm, wearing her thin black veil. Anna could not see her eyes. Only a small crowd of local peasants and laborers had gathered—most were at the Eastertide mystery plays being put on by the guildhall in Rochester.

The priest cleared his throat.

"Have the banns been published?"

Lady Cobham spoke up. "There was no need. The bride is a stranger to these parts. Father, you may proceed."

The Lollard looked as though he might challenge her, then thought better of it. "Then are there any assembled here who know of any impediment to the marriage?"

Not even a murmur.

"I can see the couple is of age," the priest said. "Do you swear that you are not within the forbidden degree of consanguinity?"

Gabriel said, "We so swear, Father."

"Do you consent freely to this marriage, then, Anna of Prague?"

"I do." Anna nodded.

"Do you, Gabriel, the friar's son, enter into this holy bond of matrimony with Anna of Prague of your own free will?"

At the mention of Gabriel as a friar's son, a murmur drifted around the fringe of cotters and servants gathered to watch. A knowing smirk appeared on some few faces, as if to say, "Another one."

"I do," Gabriel said.

"Then join right hands. Gabriel, have you a ring as token of your pledge?"

Gabriel took the ring—also provided by Lady Cobham. "Here, you will need a ring," she'd said, as if it were a little thing and handed him the silver band set with garnets. He handed it now to the priest, who held it up and then placed it in turn on the first three of Anna's fingers, intoning, "In the name of the Father, the Son, and the Holy Ghost," letting it finally rest on the trembling third finger of her left hand.

Then the priest delivered a small homily on the sanctity of marriage, but Anna could not quiet her mind long enough to listen to his words. She could only wonder at how she had come to be standing here, with a child growing in her belly, pledging herself to a stranger who represented everything her grandfather had taught her to disdain.

She wished she could see her grandmother's face behind the veil. But since the abbess had made no move to stop her, didn't that argue for consent? Didn't her presence bespeak her approval?

Gabriel held her hand lightly. But she could feel the sweat on his palm and found it strangely endearing. She looked up to read his expression, but he was not looking at his bride. He was looking at the priest, actually listening to his homily.

And then it was over and they were moving inside the flower-bedecked chapel to kneel before the altar and take their first Communion as husband and wife. When the priest offered not only the host but the cup to Anna, Gabriel looked surprised, opened his mouth to speak, and Anna feared that he would object. She knew the Roman Church did not give the cup to laity. Only the priests were allowed to partake of the wine. It had been a bone of great contention in Prague. But her bridegroom closed his mouth and remained silent as she drank the blood of Christ.

At the conclusion of the mass, the priest passed the kiss of peace to Gabriel, touching his lips to Gabriel's cheek. Gabriel passed it to his bride. Anna could scarcely feel the brush of his lips on hers, so lightly was it transferred.

THIRTY-NINE

he bride ale was almost finished. Anna and Gabriel sat without touching each other, not on a dais in the great hall, but at the head of the small but festive board in the solar. She'd read of great men, royals and such, where bride and bridegroom had never met before their wedding day. I am marrying a stranger, she thought, as much a stranger as if we'd never met in Rheims.

Lord Cobham toasted the health of all assembled: the yeomen and retainers attached to his estate, his own "fair bride of a few happy years," the abbess, who honored them with her presence, and lastly, the bride and groom. With each toast his jocularity increased and Anna's too rapid heartbeat quieted a little. A piper piped a pretty tune and then a fiddler played a love song. Its plaintive notes reminded her of the Gypsy fiddles, and she wondered where Bera and Lela were, if they'd ever made it to Spain.

She stole a glance at her new husband when she thought he wasn't looking. Only one thing about him looked familiar. He wore a flat suede cap to cover his tonsure, and his blond hair curled beneath it just the same way it had curled around VanCleve's red silk hat.

The wine was good and the food tasty. There were the usual Easter subtleties—confections in the shape of crosses and eggs—and a small bride and groom made of marzipan standing on tiny chapel steps made of cake. And there were gifts. The abbess, pleading fatigue, left early but presented the couple with a purse of gold florins before she departed. A child's wooden cradle from the lord and lady came with a blessing that "they should fill it well and often."

Anna felt herself blush. "This is for our child, Gabriel," she whispered in her husband's ear. "It is beautiful."

"Yes. It is." But Gabriel appeared to address the company at large more than his bride. He did not tag the blessing of the cradle as a more enthusiastic bridegroom would surely have done.

She made no other attempt to gain his ear and felt only relief when the feast was ended and they departed for the abbey. Since it was only a short distance from castle to abbey, Anna rode in front of Gabriel. She held her body stiffly so as not to lean against him overmuch, wishing that the horse would walk less sedately, but knowing that Gabriel walked it slowly for the sake of the child.

No raucous wedding party followed them to the bridal chamber. When they reached the abbey, the sun had already set and that shadow-drenched loneliness that heralds the night had descended.

He walked her to her chamber door and, with a stiff little bow, said in a strained voice, "I will not see you on the morrow. I must go to Lambeth Palace. The archbishop has summoned his council to consider the problem of Lord Cobham."

She could feel her temper rising, the bridle slipping from her tongue. "But surely you—"

"The archbishop must not know of my decision. If I am to save Lord Cobham from the fire, he must think me still committed to stamping out heresy."

"He is the true heretic. It is he who presents a false salvation. He who takes that which is pure and whole and simple and twists it to enrich himself and that devil's institution which he serves."

He just stared at her. "Anna, beware. Your tongue can not only destroy yourself but your husband as well. And if that does not move you to silence, then have a care for our child—else this will all have been for nothing."

Her husband. How strange to hear him describe himself thus.

He did not look at her but over her shoulder. His lips formed a faint smile. A goodly sight! She realized she had not seen him smile all day.

"I see Lord Cobham's gift has already arrived." He pointed to the cradle beside Anna's bed.

"His horse was faster than yours."

"Perhaps his burden less precious."

He is talking about the child, she thought.

He held out his hand as though he were going to clasp hers, but let his drop listlessly to his side. "I bid you farewell, wife. I will return as soon as I can. Take care while I am gone."

She knew he meant that she should guard more than her own good health. He reached again for her hand. She did not offer it. Tomorrow he would don his black friar's habit and he would leave her. She did not know what that meant.

"Godspeed, then, husband."

She watched him walk away. She noticed again how the fine blond hair curled below his brown suede hat.

It was not the first time he'd left her thus, promising to return.

❦

On May Day, the morris dancers came to the abbey yard. Anna took Bek outside to watch them dance around the maypole. She envied their lithe bodies.

She felt heavy now. And always tired. And she was worried about her grandmother, who hardly ever left her bed except when Anna took her to the gardens to watch the bees and the butterflies and the new spring flowers.

"You will hear from him soon, Anna. He is a good man. It's not easy being caught between two worlds."

When the abbess wasn't dozing in the sunshine, she told Anna stories about her mother, Rose, and her father, Colin. Stories Anna was always hungry for. "You got your religious zeal from your father," the abbess said. "And that quick temper and red hair—well, you got that from your uncle Alfred."

These memories seemed to console the abbess as much as Anna.

"And my mother, what did I get from her?"

"Grace and beauty and a lineage that goes back to our Lord."

"You do not hate the Jews, then, Grandmother?"

"My Lord was a Jew. How can I hate the Jews?"

"In Prague once on an Easter Sunday, they shut them all up in a synagogue and set it on fire. Three thousand of them died." Anna had heard that story many times, but this was the first time she envisioned it. She could hear the cries all around her as the smoke billowed, saw in her mind the flames, smelled the smoke and fear. Anna put her hand protectively around her belly. "Some of them were children," she said.

But the abbess had not heard her. She was sleeping in the sun.

⁓⊱⊰⁓

In June a short message came from her husband. Or so the letter was signed. She didn't feel as though she had a husband. It was cryptic and short.

> *I fear my disguise is wearing thin. My absence would cause questions here and my presence there pose a danger for you. You are safe at the abbey. Give my regards to the abbess. I have been in touch with our mutual friend to apprise him of the danger he is in. I may go to him ere I come there.*

It was signed "your husband."

Oddly enough, she drew some comfort from the coldness of the letter. For when he had spoken words of love to her he had willingly abandoned her. Perhaps duty and not love would drive such a man as he. Though duty kept a cold hearth.

As did resentment, she reminded herself.

⁓⊱⊰⁓

In mid-July Anna went into labor. *Twenty pains or so!* she thought after six hours' labor. What did Gilbert the Englishman know? And then she remembered how easily Lela had given birth to her son.

"She is old for a first bairn," the midwife said, clucking her tongue. "It's hard for the older ones."

Sister Matilde held Anna's hand and mopped her brow, lifting her heavy hair that dripped with sweat. She felt the cooling breeze on her neck, then braced herself for the next wave of pain. "Pay her no attention, Anna. Just think about the babe. Think about holding your infant in your arms."

Twelve hours later, wan and depleted, Anna held her son in her arms.

"He's a fine lad," the midwife said, preening as though she were responsible. As though Anna had not done all the work.

"Where's his father? Shall I call a priest from the village to baptize him, or will you take him to chapel on the morrow?" she asked.

"We will take care of it ourselves," Anna whispered, not taking her eyes off her son.

"Mother will baptize him," Anna said when the midwife had gone. "She has strength enough to dip a child in a baptismal font." She knew Sister Matilde would not protest. The sisters even celebrated the mass themselves when no priest was around.

"What do you wish him to be called, Anna?" The abbess had appeared in the door of the chamber while the midwife was cleaning up.

"His name is Finn. Finn, Gabriel's son."

The abbess smiled. She was not wearing the veil. The smile spread to her eyes.

❦

Gabriel's son was six weeks old when he first saw him.

"She's in the kitchen garden with the wee one, Brother," the novice who answered the abbey gate told him.

She was sitting in the shade of a pear tree, her blouse unhooked, the babe at her breast. Her head rested against the trunk of the tree and her eyes were shut. The expression on her face was that of a woman lost in a pleasant dream. At her knee was the basket of pears she'd been picking, their skins rose-brushed like the skin of Anna's white shoulders and neck. The heat of the afternoon pressed the fragrance of overripe fruit into the air. The only noise was the drone of a bee that hovered over the basket and the little tiny sucking sounds his son made. The vision left him almost light-headed. Here at last was Eve. Here Eden.

He felt a surge of desire and with great effort tore his gaze away from her full cleavage and fastened it instead on the bald pate of his son. His son!

Greedy little sprite. He made a little gurgling noise in his throat. Gabriel laughed.

Anna opened her eyes. Her face tightened.

"You've come, then, finally. To see what it is you've, what we've, wrought. It has been four months since you promised to be my husband."

"I have kept my promise."

She looked as though she did not know how to reply to this.

"I mean, I have been faithful to you. And I am here, at last. May I hold him?"

"You need not ask permission. He is your son. I'm glad you are in your husband clothes. He might spit up on your fine black habit."

Not Eden after all.

He held out his arms, accepted the child carefully in the crook of his arm. He'd baptized many an infant. Yet this one felt different. This one was as much a part of his arm as if it had grown there. The child screwed up his mouth as if to cry, and then closed his eyes and went to sleep. Gabriel brushed a bit of milky white from the corners of his mouth, tried not to stare as Anna fumbled at the thin fabric of her bodice to close it.

"I shall not have much use for the habit in the future, at any rate," he said, giving the child his finger to suck on, wondering if the sensation was more intense against Anna's pink full nipple. Setting that thought deliberately aside, he said, "The archbishop is growing impatient. He suspects my gathering of further evidence is a pretense. I've been buying time for you and the babe to grow strong enough to leave."

"But . . . but where will we go? How shall we live? Does he know of the marriage?"

"No, he does not. Not yet. But he suspects that I have betrayed my calling. Sir John has been arrested, and I tried to warn him. When that failed, I argued for him, even went to the king on his behalf. I will be called to testify at his trial, and I mean to testify in favor of him. If the archbishop finds out about you, then you and my son will be in danger. He might even try to use you as a lever to make me testify against Sir John. I'm going to take you to a safe place. I'll take you to my mother's cottage in Appledore. If I survive the trial, I'll come for you. If I don't, you and—what did you name him?"

If I survive the trial! "Finn. Gabrielson. After my grandfather," was all she said.

He brushed the downy head of the child, the soft spot in his skull reminding him of his son's vulnerability. "You gave him my name too."

"That was the reason I married you, remember? To give him your name," she said, then added, "I did not like 'Friarson.'"

"Neither do I," he said.

"But what about Mother? What about Bek? Are they safe here?"

"I don't think Arundel will bother with the abbey again. There is not enough evidence. As for Bek? Well, he has the patronage of the king. You can bring him, if you want, but if he is happier here—well, you and he decide."

"But this is my home. I cannot leave—"

"You must leave, Anna. And you must do it now!"

"Now, Gabriel? You think you can just—"

"Now, Anna. For the child. Not for me. For him. If Arundel finds out he is my child, he may wind up in some monastery, raised with that religion you call false, raised like me. Is that what you want for him?"

"Let me tell the abbess good-bye," she said. Then looking at him with tears in her eyes, she added, "Gabriel, did you know that the abbess is my own true grandmother?"

"But you said your grandmother was a Jewess." He whispered the word, lest even the pear trees have ears.

"I had two," she said. "Kathryn of Blackingham was my other grandmother. My father died in the Lollard cause. So, you see, I have a long heritage of heresy."

She reached for the child and gathered him back into her arms. Then she turned and went through the abbey kitchens, leaving him to contemplate his empty Eden.

FORTV

he king had not slept well. The day had finally come he'd been dreading for a sennight—September 23, the year of our Lord 1413. That was the date on the Royal Writ. The date by which Sir John Oldcastle, Lord Cobham, was to surrender himself to the king's guards.

As Harry watched anxiously from the chamber window, part of him secretly hoped that his old friend would evade arrest, just as he'd circumvented the archbishop's search warrant. But an order to surrender, signed by the king's own hand, how could he evade that?

The Lord High Chamberlain entered the room, followed by an usher carrying a heavy tray. "A rasher of bacon and some poached pears, Your Majesty, just as you requested." They laid the board close to the hearth, for the chill of morning still clung to the castle walls.

"There is a merchant seeking redress and that same Dominican friar and a—"

"Send them all away. We are not taking petitions today," Harry said.

He chewed halfheartedly on a piece of bacon while the chamberlain warmed his linen by the fire, and then he waved the whole away. Above the clatter of the usher's clearing away, Harry heard the creaking of the portcullis and rushed to the window. Just a few carters with the daily delivery of goods.

"We are to be informed immediately of any noble visitors," he said to the chamberlain.

"Yes, Your Majesty." He held out the king's doublet. "Shall I bring your harp?"

Harry shook his head. He was not in the mood. "Some writing materials, perhaps," he said as the chamberlain helped him lace his boots.

At midday, the chamberlain and usher returned with another tray.

Harry flung down his pen and scowled at the lines of poetry he'd crossed out. He raised the cloth on the tray and looked askance at the eel broth and fish pastie. "It is not Friday. Take this away and bring a veal pie and some pea soup."

The chamberlain motioned for the cupbearer. "You heard the king," he said gruffly, handing him the tray. "The Lord High Chancellor is without, Your Majesty."

Harry sighed. "Send him in."

Beaufort bowed his way into the room and they talked of taxes and campaigns against the French.

"Your Majesty seems distracted today," Beaufort observed when they had finished.

"Has Lord Cobham surrendered?"

Beaufort frowned. "No, he has not. You will be informed, Your Grace."

They shared a flagon of hippocras, then his uncle left, muttering under his breath.

Harry heard the portcullis groan again. Again he went to the window. He could see the Thames and the whole of London spread out beyond the wharf. Only a drover with a few cattle headed for the castle butchery crossed the dry moat into the castle. Their hoofbeats clattered on the wooden drawbridge. There would be a loin of beef on the morrow, he thought idly.

He sent for his lute, but the muse was still not in attendance.

[386]

When he looked again, the portcullis was open, but the entry was deserted.

In the afternoon, Beaufort came again with some papers for him to sign.

"Still no word, uncle?"

"You will be informed, Your Grace," the chancellor repeated in his long-suffering tone. He gathered his papers and left, still muttering under his breath.

Harry considered calling for the falconer to take his peregrine hawk out on this glorious September day, but Sir John might come while he was gone. He slumped in his chair, noodling in his head how best to go after his knight if he did not surrender. The Welsh marches were the place to start, but there were a million hidey-holes where Merry Jack could hide, and he knew them all.

Dread descended on him with the encroaching afternoon shadows.

At sunset he heard a commotion from outside, the trumpeting of a herald's horn. From the window he saw that a small crowd had gathered on the green, pointing and shouting excitedly into the distance.

Riders. Fifty or sixty, helmeted and armored, galloped in a cloud of dust across the drawbridge and through the curtain gate. A surprise attack! Surely not, with so few in number. Harry surveyed the horizon—no war machines creaking from the west, no cadre of archers descending from the east. No barges on the Thames. He was doing a quick count of his guards on duty—there should be at least six hundred, but he'd sent some to Calais—when he saw a herald carrying the familiar colors come into view.

Gules and cross argent. A silver cross emblazoned on a red background.

The pennant fluttered arrogantly in the breeze.

So. Cobham had come after all, with armed retainers, though hardly the hundred with which he had previously offered to defend his faith in trial by combat. Henry V was going down the same road as Henry IV—he was going to have to do battle with his own nobles. God's blood! He'd known it would come to this. And of all his barons, for it to be Sir John who took up arms against him! He cursed Arundel under his breath.

"Close the portcullis!" the constable shouted as the riders thundered up. "Sound the alarm!"

A yeoman scuttled off to the bell tower.

Harry recognized the figure of Sir John in the lead, just behind the herald. The portcullis started to creak and groan, but the machinery was too slow. The mounted riders would be inside the courtyard in seconds, up the stairs and in the king's chamber in minutes.

But just at the moment when he should have led his riders in, Sir John reined in his horse, took off his helmet, and tucked it under his arm. He looked up, shielding his eyes from the sun's reflection off the curtain wall, and appeared to be searching the windows of the White Tower for the king's apartment. Then he lifted his sword arm—and saluted.

Damn you, Jack! This is not some game. 'Tis the stake for you if you lose this time.

"Hold the portcullis. 'Tis the king's man," the constable shouted.

No, you fool, it's a trick. But before he could shout a warning to the constable, Oldcastle turned and signaled his retainers to withdraw. Harry watched with grudging respect and a great measure of relief as his knight handed his sword to the constable and rode on through the portcullis alone.

Harry laughed out loud. The gesture was so like Merry Jack, proclaiming, *This is a courtesy, to save you the trouble and embarrassment of coming after me.* Sir John would know a challenge from one of the king's nobles this early in his reign would be a hard draught to swallow.

But the smile soon faded. Tomorrow would be the trial. Harry had seen Arundel's evidence, and it did not look good for Sir John.

⚜

At first light, Gabriel donned his priest's robe for the last time and left his Lambeth quarters for Blackfriars. In the blackness that comes just before dawn, he'd prayed his Gethsemane prayer, but he knew this cup would not pass until he'd sipped from it. He only hoped he did not have to drink it up.

He steered his horse though East Cheap and was headed up High Street to Ludgate Hill when he saw the prison cart. His throat closed as he recognized its lone occupant. Sir John! Transported to his trial for heresy in an open hurdle, paraded through the streets like a common criminal. Gabriel had not expected such ignominious treatment for a nobleman. But, he reminded himself, this was how Arundel treated his enemies, and he might soon be numbered among them.

At this time of the morning, most of the churlish element were still abed. Only one, stumbling home from a tavern, yelled to nobody in particular, " 'Twill be a hangin' tonight." Then he started to singsong drunkenly, "Hangin' tonight, hangin' tonight." The good honest yeomen who were about at this time of the morning gave the drunk a wide berth as he wove his way among the ditches, finally falling into one.

Gabriel paused to let the hurdle pass. Sir John looked directly at him, the expression on his face registering first surprise, then disappointment. Gabriel wanted to shout out some encouragement, to reassure him that the black-frocked friar before him was no Judas. But this was not the time, not here in the public street.

The hurdle rattled past. Gabriel's mount snorted and tossed his head, jangling the silver bells of his harness. Flinching beneath Sir John's accusatory gaze, Gabriel looked away to avoid witnessing Sir John's humiliation. He need not have worried. The old knight wore his humiliation like steel armor, his stance as proud and defiant as though it were he who rode the noble steed and Gabriel the prisoner's cart. Gabriel turned his horse away, steering it to an alternate route up Ludgate Hill.

A few minutes later, he entered Blackfriars Hall and took his seat to the right of the council, opposite Sir John, who stood in the dock bound between sergeant and beadle. It was dim in the great hall after the bright September sun. Gabriel squinted as he scanned the crowd—mostly clerics and a few courtiers, curiosity seekers—for the king. Henry V had been Gabriel's last hope. Ever since the news of Sir John's arrest warrant, Gabriel had been trying to get to the king. But he'd been refused an audience again and again. Only Henry Beaufort, the chancellor, was present to represent the crown.

Three judges sat on a dais at one end of the hall. The one immediately on the left wore a Dominican habit. Gabriel recognized the prior of Blackfriars, who had been present at Gabriel's own ordination. The cleric on the right, almost hidden in his elaborate dagged sleeves, he recognized as well. Commissioner Flemmynge, reveling in this plum assignment, proof of his growing favor with Arundel.

A rigged court, to be sure, but for all their ecclesiastical power, they could not stray too far from English justice if they expected the crown to carry out any sentence of execution. They could not do the burning themselves. *Ecclesia non novit sanguinem.* The Church does not shed blood. Easy enough to get around that little nuisance. Since Pope Lucius III in 1184, the Church courts had been handing over their condemned to the secular authorities. But they would need powerful witnesses to persuade a reluctant king. Gabriel felt the burden of his responsibility bearing down on him. Christ had not had a wife and child when he submitted to God's will. What of Anna and their son?

In the middle sat Thomas Arundel, archbishop of Canterbury, a gloating expression on the sour face that floated like a pale oval above his furred cape and glittering pectoral cross. Arundel's voice was as thin as his beard. "Do you know why you've been summoned before this ecclesiastical court, Lord Cobham?"

Sir John's voice was deep and resonant. "I have some notion. And it's not a charge worth answering, except that my king requested me to do so. I am a loyal subject, else I'd not have taken the time. I've more important matters to see to and holier meetings to attend."

The crowd murmured, some few tittering. These would have cheered, Gabriel felt sure, had they dared.

Arundel sputtered. "Take care, sir, that you do not lean too heavily on your former association with the king. His Majesty will not hold your contempt for this court and for your Church in light regard." He unfurled a scroll and intoned, "You are charged with disseminating the heretical sermons of John Wycliffe, holding Lollard meetings, and transporting and disseminating the banned English translations of the Bible both in England and abroad."

"Have you any witnesses to prove this charge?" Sir John asked, looking straight at Brother Gabriel as Christ must have looked at Judas at the Last Supper.

"A profane English text of the Holy Scriptures was found in Paternoster Row. It contained a bill of sale made out to you. Do you wish to tell us where you procured such a text?"

Gabriel felt the words like a slap. He had not known of this evidence, which was enough to seal the man's fate. It would be pure foolishness, he told himself, to sacrifice his safety and Anna's and Finn's for a man already condemned.

"I have no knowledge of which book you speak," Lord Cobham answered. "I buy books from many sources. My household values books."

Gabriel blessed the man's courage. He was protecting the abbess, protecting Anna too.

Arundel smiled. "A recalcitrant memory sometimes may be prodded to be more . . . fruitful."

More whisperings.

The archbishop continued. "There is one present in this court who will give testimony that you entertained large assemblies of Lollard heretics where Wycliffe's sermons were read, that you further desecrated the mass by the reading of profane English Scriptures and denied publicly the miracle of the Eucharist. Brother Gabriel, please tell us what you observed at Cooling Castle."

This was it. The telling time. Gabriel felt light-headed as he stood up and stepped forward. What manner of man was he? How far would he go in the service of truth? How much would he give up? He wasn't sure what words would come out as he opened his mouth.

"I . . . I observed . . . both Lord and Lady Cobham to . . . to run a good and noble house, Your Excellency," he said, in a voice loud enough for all to hear. "Exemplary of that Christian hospitality for which Lord and Lady Cobham are well known."

Arundel looked irritated.

"Yes, yes, Friar Gabriel. But it is not his hospitality that is in question."

It seemed Gabriel had made his choice. If choice he'd ever had.

"I misunderstood, Your Excellency," Gabriel said, keeping his tone even. "I thought his hospitality was exactly the question. You say he is charged with harboring Lollard priests. I never saw anyone turned away from Cooling Castle."

"You saw Lollard priests, then?"

"I saw many priests. I myself was often entertained at Lord Cobham's table, as I believe Your Excellency has been on occasion."

"Do not mock this court, Friar. I warn you." He raised his voice a notch and asked deliberately, slowly, "Have you ever witnessed a gathering of Lollard priests saying a Lollard mass and reading the English Scriptures in the presence of Lord Cobham?"

Gabriel heard the words as though they originated somewhere outside his head. *All you have to do, Gabriel, is tell the truth. It is as simple as that.*

He answered, surprised to hear that his voice did not waver. "I have not, Your Excellency. Any evidence that I might give in that regard would be rumor. And I'm sure the ecclesiastical court would not convict a nobleman of the realm on rumor."

Arundel looked apoplectic.

A broad grin broke out on Sir John's face.

"Brother Gabriel, have you ever seen a copy of a Wycliffe translation of the Bible at Cooling Castle?" Arundel asked, his high-pitched voice increasingly shrill.

Ah! Not simple after all. For here is a truth that works against justice.

Gabriel opened his mouth, unsure of what to say, wondering how to serve both truth and justice. "I—"

"Of course he has, Your Excellency," Lord Cobham thundered. "I make no attempt to hide it. The Wycliffe Bible rests on a table in my solar, alongside a Latin Vulgate translation, so that all may read our Lord's words. You do not need to quiz this brother. I will give you my confession of faith. I have nothing to hide."

His answer filled Gabriel with both alarm and gratitude.

Sir John continued. "I believe that salvation comes through Christ alone without intermediaries."

Arundel squirmed. This was good Catholic doctrine so far as it went.

"A careful answer, Sir John. But is it not true that you deny the miracle of the mass and the necessity of the confessional?"

More murmurings among the assembled onlookers.

"I do not deny the miracle of the mass." He paused, as if weighing the cost of truth in his own scales, then thrust out his chin and said in a voice bold enough for those outside the hall to hear, "I deny that the bread becomes the literal body of Christ in the mouth. I deny that the blood becomes the literal blood. They are symbolic of the sacrifice of our Lord. The miracle of the mass lies not in bits of flesh and blood, not in the baker's and the vintner's art, but in the saving grace of our Lord Jesus Christ."

Arundel smiled and settled back in his chair.

"And the confessional?"

"A priest is merely a facilitator of confession. Every man and every woman can make his own confession to Jesus Christ without benefit of a priest."

Arundel's smile broadened. "And the Holy Father? The sacred relics? It is widely reported that you turned your back on the cross at the Easter processional." Arundel's whine had dropped almost to a whisper.

It was as though the whole room held its breath.

Gabriel closed his eyes and waited for the inevitable.

"I believe that to put hope, faith, or trust in images is the great sin of idolatry. I declare any pope who sanctions the sale of relics and pardons to be the Antichrist. Such practices serve nothing for the granting of grace to unwitting sinners. They only serve to swell the purse of unscrupulous pardoners and the Roman treasury while duping sinners into hell." And then he repeated loudly, lest any in the hall had not heard, "I declare any pope who sanctions the selling of Christ's mercy to be the Antichrist."

The onlookers gasped in one long collective intake of breath, followed by a few shouts of "Heretic, burn the heretic," from the pardoners and friars. A few, having heard enough, began to edge toward the doors. Anxiety stirred the air in the hall, but Sir John seemed strangely calm. Gabriel envied him that calm, for he was suddenly seized with fear and the sure knowledge that his own arrest was imminent, to be followed by torture until he confessed to heresy.

He looked around the room for a way out.

Arundel was no longer smiling and was pale with rage. He banged his gavel upon the table. "Your own words condemn you as a heretic, Lord Cobham. We have no need of any other testimony." He conferred briefly with the other two. "If you confess and submit, we shall give you absolution."

Now was Gabriel's only chance for escape—while Arundel was so distracted by white-hot anger he could think of nothing but lighting the fire beneath his enemy. Some of the Blackfriars in the crowd had surged forward. Gabriel moved toward the edge of the crowd, then pulled up his cowl and looked back.

The morning light streaming through the windows fell in a strip across Sir John's face. He looked like some saint from an illuminated text as he raised his hands, which were bound in front of him, to shield his eyes.

"I will not confess to you," he said. "I confess all my many sins only to God. You may condemn my body, but you cannot harm my soul."

Arundel was no longer smiling.

"Then, my Lord Cobham, we have no choice but to condemn you for heresy and hand you over to the king's men for execution. May that God, with whom you claim such familiarity, have mercy on your soul." He banged his gavel again.

It was the moment for which those assembled had been waiting. In the general hubbub that followed, Gabriel made his escape though the archway leading to the refectory, thinking of Anna and their son, and the fury he'd unleashed on all their heads.

⊱⊰

Every day Anna watched the lane between Appledore and her mother-in-law's cottage. And every day it was the same; no one came down the path from the village. Anna thought how bleak it would be to spend the winter here, but Mistress Clare seemed not to consider it so. Although her demeanor was somber, sometimes Anna heard her humming as she went about her chores. Today the lane was fog-wrapped. Gray sky and sea melded together until it was hard to tell if the sky swallowed up the sea or the sea the sky. It was all one great void.

"You must be patient," Mistress Clare said.

Anna could not think of her as Gabriel's mother. The only similarity she saw was in her beautiful hands, well formed and shapely in spite of the reddened and chapped skin. Anna had first noticed VanCleve's hands the day he'd carried Little Bek on his shoulder, his well-shaped hands clasping the boy's skinny knees.

"It is hard," Anna said. "Not knowing."

"He will come," the taciturn old woman said.

There was a hard, determined strength in Mistress Clare's eyes. It was a look that reminded Anna of Brother Gabriel. She'd only once seen that look in VanCleve's eyes—the day they'd argued about the indulgences.

The babe woke and started to cry. He hushed when Anna tipped the cradle, the cradle that had been a gift from Sir John and Lady Joan.

I should never have let him bring me here, she thought, to this windswept headland. I should have stayed behind with Mother and Bek. At least there, she would have had news.

"I'm going into the village," she said, wrapping a shawl around her and bending to lift the sleeping child.

"I will watch him," the woman said.

"Thank you." Anna smoothed his blanket, tucked it more tightly around him, thinking how small he looked, how fragile. "I won't be long."

It was only a couple of furlongs to the village. She stopped at the first shop, the chandler's, and bought some tallow dips. "What news from London?" she asked as though it did not matter. "What news from the new king's court?" As though she were only some goodwife in search of gossip.

"The price of beeswax just went up. A new tax for the new king's French wars," the chandler grumbled. He handed her the tallow dips. "Some pilgrims passed through here yesterday from Canterbury. Said the archbishop was putting Sir John Oldcastle on trial for heresy. A bad business, that. He'll likely burn afore it's all over."

Anna saw in her mind her child sleeping peacefully in his cradle, the cradle Sir John had given him, as though he lay in a world not gone mad with fierce and angry men who used the Word of God as an excuse to kill and maim.

"Was he the only one?" she asked, thinking too of the abbey and Lady Joan. Thinking of her husband.

"Only one?"

"Arrested." She paid for the candles.

"As far as it be told, 'twere no other but him."

The chandler looked at her quizzically. "Beint you living with the old woman in the cottage on the headland?"

"Yes. My name is Anna."

"There was a messenger in fancy livery asking for you not an hour gone."

Anna's breath caught in her throat. "What were his colors?"

The chandler scratched his head. "Red and something . . . silver . . . I think."

Cooling Castle's colors were red and silver. But he'd not been sure of the silver. Her mind raced to try to think if she remembered the archbishop's colors. "Did you tell him where to find me?"

"I did. I'm surprised you didn't pass him on the way."

She would have noticed a rider on horseback on the lonely path through the marsh. Even in the fog, wouldn't she? What if it were some spy for the archbishop? *"If the archbishop finds out about you, you and my son will be in danger."*

She didn't even bid adieu to the chandler, but bolted out the door.

Her heart was hammering in her chest as she pulled her shawl tightly and started home. The little cottage glowed like a beacon in the dense fog. She bent her back against a north wind and headed toward that beacon.

As she neared, she could make out the outline of a horse tethered to a sapling. She picked up her skirts and ran, not breathing, until she was close enough to see the red and silver of the Cobham livery.

Shivering with cold and relief, she reminded herself that it could still be a trap, but as she entered she recognized the familiar figure of the Cobhams' gatekeeper. He was bending over the cradle, making clicking noises to the tiny occupant. Mistress Clare hovered, watchful as a mother robin. He stood up and handed Anna a rolled parchment with the abbey seal.

"It's from one of the nuns, mistress. She bade me wait for an answer."

Anna hastily broke the seal and scanned Sister Matilde's familiar script.

"It's my grandmother," she said to Mistress Clare. "She is very ill. She's asking for me."

"Then you should go to her."

"But how can I? I can't take him; it's too dangerous. And he has to nurse."

Her breasts felt full after just her brief absence.

"No, he doesn't. There are other ways. I can hold a cup of honey and barley water to his mouth."

"I don't know, I've never—"

"He'll get enough. We fed my baby brother that way, when my mother was too sick to nurse him. He lived to be a hearty man, hearty enough to go to sea at sixteen. I never heard from him after that." She looked directly at the messenger. "Will you take her to the abbey?"

"That's why I waited."

"Will you bring her back here, when her visit is done?"

"Aye. Not much doing at the castle these days with Lady Joan away again."

"I don't know—"

The infant stirred and started to whimper. Anna reached to pick him up. Mistress Clare placed her hand on Anna's arm to stop her. "No. Let him get hungry first. I'll put the barley on to boil and show you we can do it so you can go with an easy mind."

Two hours later, Anna watched in amazement as her two-month-old child drank his fill from the honeyed water held to his lips. For his next feeding she gave him her breasts, more for her relief than his.

The next morning she left at first light with the gatekeeper of Cooling Castle.

"If I'm not back when Gabriel comes, and if there is danger, tell him to flee with our child to safety. He should not come after me. I will return unless—"

Mistress Clare nodded soberly, showing she understood. "We will keep him safe," she said.

FORTY-ONE

Of what profit is a good knight? . . . I tell you that
without good knights, the king is like a man who has
neither feet nor hands.
 —Díaz De Gámez in *The Chivalric Ideal*
 (15th century)

he fool!" Harry paced the floor in his chamber. Beaufort had just brought the news that Sir John had confessed. "I warned him! What does he expect from me?"

A gust of wind rattled the glass in the window and caused the candles to flicker in the wheel chandelier hanging from the rafters. Shadows danced.

"It would be my thinking, Your Grace, that he expects a royal pardon."

"Then he expects too much. He knows the game. I have not been anointed yet. To go against Arundel would be regicide—and suicide."

Beaufort looked grave. "Lord Cobham's retainers might come to his defense, and he is popular with the peasant class. Even that friar who was sent to spy on him would not give evidence against him." He added under his breath, "I would not want to be in his boots right now either."

"So I am to begin my reign like my father before me, with insurrection among my own nobles?" Harry stopped in his pacing. "What do you recommend, uncle? Give me the benefit of your wisdom."

Now it was Beaufort's turn to pace.

"I've given it much thought, Your Grace. There is no politic response. You either incur the wrath of the archbishop, whom you need to crown you to lend legitimacy to your reign, or you risk civil war with your nobles."

He bent down to poke at the fire sputtering in the grate, a ploy merely to gain time, Harry knew. Beaufort was a strategist. That was why he was chancellor, not due to nepotism as some had dared suggest.

"Exactly so," Harry said. "But you forget one thing else. What loyalty friend owes to friend."

"Ah, sire, but loyalty is a door that opens both ways. In going against you, has not Lord Cobham already betrayed that friendship? Are you bound to honor a bond already broken?"

Harry said nothing. But in his thoughts he was arm wrestling with Merry Jack across a tavern table, with Mistress Quickly and Bardolph and Pistol cheering on their favorites. He could almost smell the sweat and spilled beer of the common room.

Beaufort cleared his throat, clearing the memory from Harry's mind as well.

"This is my advice, Your Majesty. You do not pardon him. But you defer his execution for forty days, pleading that such an extension is warranted for a knight of the realm. You say that you will try to reason with him, persuade him to recant. This will irritate Arundel, but it will not be sufficient cause to make him delay your coronation—especially if at the end of the forty days he knows he will get the burning he wants."

"But how can he know it?"

Beaufort's gaze did not waver when he answered. "Because everyone who was at that trial knows. Sir John Oldcastle will not recant. For good or ill, he considers himself pledged to a lord greater than Your Majesty, and he is prepared to die for it."

"Then, of what good is—"

"It will buy you time. And who knows what may come in time? Besides, you will not have his death on your conscience. You will have done what you can do. Mercy becomes a monarch."

Harry thought for a long moment. Another gust of wind, fiercer than the last, rattled the window. He sat down at his desk, took out a quill and a parchment, and handed both to Beaufort.

"Write here, uncle, what you think I should say to the archbishop in this regard. I will sign it. Send it by one of my messengers. Arundel should not think it comes from you."

After the chancellor had written the message, Harry scrawled in his best hand across the bottom: "His Royal Majesty, Henry V, King of England." Then he stamped the hot wax with the royal seal and handed it back to his uncle.

"One more thing, Chancellor. See if you can find that friar. We would talk with him."

"I shall try, Your Grace, but it may not be easy. If I were he, I'd be long gone before the sun rises on another day."

⚜

Gabriel shed the Dominican habit to reveal the simple hose and doublet he'd worn on his wedding day. He pulled the hood low over his brow. If he could avoid the archbishop by blending in with the other visitors in Blackfriars Priory, he could read the lay of the land and make his escape. Perhaps Sir John's too. But the chancellor's men collared him outside the priory. He started to make a run for it.

Then he reconsidered.

There were two of them, both bearing sidearms and requesting his presence at court with all due speed. Best not have both the king and the archbishop on his tail. After all, the king was reputed to be a friend to Sir John, and he had proven a valuable ally to Gabriel once before.

As he followed the men into the palace apartment, however, it occurred to him that it might be a trick. Arundel was not the kind of man to leave a betrayal unpunished. He might even be using the king to bait a trap. But when Gabriel was ushered into the king's private chamber, and not the presence room, he found King Henry alone. The king signaled for the soldiers to leave. Gabriel made the required obeisance.

"We see you have abandoned your habit, Friar."

"I find that I am unsuited for the demands of a monk, Your Majesty."

The king smiled. "It would please us if you would put your habit back on, Brother Gabriel." He held out Gabriel's abandoned habit.

So it was a trap, then. This boy king was Arundel's stooge after all.

"For one last benediction?" the king asked. "As a favor to your sovereign. And then you may fade away with your pretty wife into lay obscurity."

"My wife?" Gabriel stammered, wondering if Arundel already knew also. But the marriage he would have stomached. He'd looked the other way for greater sins; it was Gabriel's testimony or lack of it that would bring down the archbishop's anger. The king seemed to find the fact of his marriage amusing.

"Ah, what else but love could make a man with your destiny give it all up? You would hardly be the first."

"Could not a man simply be called to a sounder doctrine?" Gabriel felt his face grow hot, the ever-present curse of a fair complexion.

The king frowned. "I see Sir John has made himself a convert."

Gabriel thought it best to neither confirm nor deny this.

"Do not confess it. We've heard of one too many confessions to heresy this day. I'm asking you to don your habit once more. I care not for your reasons; I have reasons of my own, reasons that have more to do with friendship than theology. And that, Brother Gabriel, puts us on the same side. On this day, at least."

And then he told Gabriel of his plan to free Sir John. Gabriel almost laughed aloud at the simple audacity of it.

❧

"You call this thin broth and stale bread supper? How does a man get some real food here?" Sir John was shouting at the warder of the Lion's Tower when the old man unlocked the heavy door and ushered in the visitor. Sir John saw only the black habit.

"By the bones of Saint Peter, man. I don't need some bloodsucking priest. If I'm to last another forty days, I need bread and meat and ale. Even a condemned man needs nourishment or there won't be anything to burn."

Then he recognized the brother. "I didn't expect—"

"Leave us," Brother Gabriel said to the warder. "Lord Cobham will make his confession in private."

"You don't happen to have a joint of beef inside those sleeves, I suppose," Sir John said when the door clanged shut.

"Better. I've brought you news," his visitor whispered.

"Unless it's a pardon from the king or news from my lady wife, I'd just as soon have a piece of beef, if it's all the same."

The friar shook his head and put his finger to his lips. He should know better than anybody, Sir John thought, that the archbishop had spies everywhere.

"I've come to give you an opportunity to recant and to tell you that if you do not, your lady has endowed a chantry for your soul." The friar said it loud enough for his voice to carry outside the heavy oak door.

John knew that was a lie. Joan would never pay a priest to say masses for her dead husband. So what was the man's purpose here? Why was a friar who'd broken faith with his archbishop still hanging around? Unless that too was some trick of Arundel's to lull the prisoner into false security so that he would give testimony against others. Joan had often accused him of being simple when it came to divining the motives of others. He had too much a tendency to take a man at his word.

"I'll not recant. You're wasting your breath, preacher."

Friar Gabriel began to intone loudly. *"De profundis . . ."*

Sir John started to protest. Father Gabriel shook his head. He leaned down and said more softly, but never breaking cadence, "A parchment maker from Smithfield bade me give you his regards and say that he wishes you good health."

"I don't know—"

"Requiem eternam . . . Master Fisher . . . *Domini . . ."* First loud, then soft, following a rhythm. "William Fisher. Bade me tell you . . . *Et lux perpetua . . .* that some hides are worth more trouble than others."

The king! It was a message from Harry.

"Tell Master Fisher to give me his good wishes in person," Sir John hissed.

"He says that he may not be able to get away from his duties, but he will do what he can . . . *Gloria Patria. . . .* You are to be ready."

Before Sir John could respond, the priest called out, "Warder, we're finished here."

The key grated in the lock almost immediately. "Fetch this man something else to eat. He'll not last forty days at this rate, and the king has ordered that he be given forty days. His Majesty would be displeased to know you ill-treated one of his nobles. I have other visits to make in the White Tower and wish to call upon Sir John after his devotions are complete. Just leave the key in the lock, and I shall return it to you."

The friar followed the warder out the door, and the key was left as instructed.

Sir John scarcely had time to consider what the message meant, and just what he could do to be ready, when the key turned in the lock again.

No cassocked priest this time.

He recognized his visitor immediately.

"Master Fisher, you've come to offer sympathy, I suppose. Though it is pardon for which I beg."

"Beg? The proud Lord Cobham?"

John felt a flush of anger. "Very well. I do not beg favor from my king. I press payment against an old debt from a comrade-at-arms."

"Then we must hurry," Harry said. He drew from out of his shirt a black habit and pitched it at Sir John. "Put it on. The archbishop thinks his king has just left the presence chamber to take a piss."

John felt himself grinning. "Like old times, eh, Hal?"

Master Fisher did not return his grin. "The sport has gone, Jack. This is a dangerous game you're playing."

"And the brother that wore this robe?" asked Sir John, struggling to make the robe go over his large frame. "Is he hiding somewhere naked?"

"He's already on his way to meet his wife, wearing the simple breeches and doublet of a man of much humbler ambition."

"Ah." Sir John pulled the cowl over his head. "That is good. She's a good lass. She deserves an honest husband. Besides, I'd hate to have his death on my conscience."

"I understand that sentiment, my lord. But there are some deaths we cannot prevent. You will be wise to remember that in the future. There are some loyalties greater than friendship."

"I could not agree more, Your Grace." He wasn't smiling either.

～✖～

When Master William Fisher and a Dominican priest stepped into an empty hallway and down the stairs of Tower Prison, the lackey at the gate paid scant attention. "G'day to ye, Brother," he called, never noticing how much the tall, lanky friar who had entered less than an hour ago had grown both in girth and stature.

◦≈ ≈◦

The king, the chancellor, and the archbishop were talking of coronation matters when the messenger entered the room. Arundel left and came back quickly. His face was the color of old ash. He darted a hostile glance at Beaufort, then whispered in the king's ear.

"What do you mean, he has escaped?" the king blurted out in feigned outrage to the frowning archbishop. He noted the look of satisfaction on his chancellor's face. Beaufort was no Lollard lover, but anything that put the archbishop in his place was bound to gratify.

"How? When?" The exhilaration of the game was such that Harry could scarcely keep the smile from his face. He wished for a moment that Sir John were here to share the satisfaction. But if all had gone as planned, Sir John was already down High Street, headed for Wales, still wearing the habit of a Dominican friar. "Did he have help?"

The archbishop looked as though he were delivering a hard stool into the piss pot. "It seems a parchment maker from Smithfield conspired with a viper in our very midst. A certain Brother Gabriel, whom I trusted."

"Tsk, tsk," Beaufort smirked. "Another monk gone bad. My, my, Archbishop, can you not keep your troops in line?"

"May I remind you, my lord Beaufort, that you were bishop before you were chancellor? And bishop you might one day be again. And I might someday have cause to say the same to you."

"Lads, lads. Don't fight," the king clucked. "We will put out the hue and cry against Lord Cobham on the morrow. Maybe the exchequer can find enough for a reward. For now let us continue with our plans. England needs its king to be anointed."

The strain still showed in the archbishop's face. But all he said was a grudging, "As you wish, Your Grace. I suppose tomorrow will be soon enough. He'll not get far."

◦≈ ≈◦

Gabriel made Hastings by first light. It lay a few miles southwest of Appledore. He stopped just long enough for one last visit to the abbey at Saint Martin's.

He stood in the chapel and looked down at the spot in the floor where Father Francis was buried. And felt nothing but regret. Everything he'd thought he believed in lay buried there, rotting, like the flesh beneath those stones. What had begun as a wrenching pain twisting inside him had settled into a great numbing void.

Gabriel was no longer sure about the Dominicans—or the Lollards. He wasn't sure whether the pope was the true descendent of Saint Peter or whether he was the Antichrist, whether pardon came from the the father in Rome or the Father in Heaven. He wasn't sure if God preferred prayers in Latin or Czech or English. He wasn't sure if the wine turned to blood in the mouth or only in the heart.

He didn't know if any of it, the dogma, mattered at all.

But he knew that someday, when his son stood over his father's grave, he did not want him to feel this emptiness. And he knew something else. He knew that God did hear prayers—in any language. How could he believe otherwise? Even though he had abandoned his Church, he'd felt the Paraclete, the true Spirit, with him in these last days, like a wind at his back, giving him courage, nudging, beckoning him in directions he might not have gone. *Pastor Dominus est.* The Lord must be my shepherd now, he thought, now that I have no other.

On his way out, he stopped in the prior's office. "There is a horse in the stable that belongs to the archbishop. See that it is delivered to Canterbury," he said to the secretary there.

The brother looked as though he were struggling with recognition. "Is there any message, yeoman . . . ?"

How much we are defined by our costume, Gabriel thought.

"You may tell the archbishop that Friar Gabriel is returning his property. He no longer has any use for it."

The monk was still staring with his mouth open in recognition when Gabriel left.

He caught a ride with a carter headed toward Appledore—to his mother and Anna and their son. He didn't relax until he could smell the sea. A fine

September sun was burning off the fog. There was a ship rocking in the harbor waves. He didn't know its destination. He didn't need to. Tomorrow or the next day or next week, whenever or wherever it set sail, Gabriel and Anna and baby Finn would be on it. God—and Anna—willing.

FORTY-TWO

istress Clare bent over her grandson's cradle, bundling
him for the hundredth time. He was bent on kicking off his blankets in spite
of the chill in the room. The smoke from the peat fire had clogged his breathing, so she had tamped down the brazier and moved the cook fire outside.

The room darkened as a shadow filled the doorway. She turned to see
Gabriel's tall silhouette, stooping beneath the low lintel. He crossed the
threshold, pausing just inside the door. He looked haggard, his face drawn
and covered with the stubble of a beard.

"Where is Anna?" He pointed to the cradle, concern rasping the edges of
his voice. "Why is it so cold in here? Is he well?"

"Your son thrives. He is hardy like his father."

In spite of her assurance to Anna, Mistress Clare was relieved that
Gabriel had returned, relieved not because she had feared his intent but be-

cause she knew the terrible power he must stand against. She wanted to hug him to her. But too much distance lay between them. What if he pulled away? She could not bear that rejection more than once in a lifetime.

"He breathes better without the smoke from the fire. He is bundled tightly and I keep warm bricks beneath his cradle."

"You? Where is Anna?" His voice rose.

"She has gone back to the abbey to—"

"The abbey! You mean she has abandoned him? She would not. I know she would not. I've seen her—"

"Of course she has not abandoned him, Gabriel. Calm yourself. The abbess, her grandmother, is very ill. Maybe dying. Lord Cobham's gate-keeper came for Anna. I told her to go."

He scrubbed his face with his palms in a gesture of frustration. "How could you do that? It may be a trap. You don't understand." He paced in a circle—like a desperate animal in a too small cage. "I have betrayed the archbishop—if he knows she is my wife, he'll use her to get to me by—"

Mistress Clare spoke in deliberate, measured tones to calm him. "Anna is aware of the danger. She will be careful. She had to go, else she would live with regret her whole life. I know what it's like to live with regret." Then she added, because she'd promised she would, "She said to tell you not to come after her, that if she does not return, you are to take the child and flee to the Continent."

But he was already out the door and headed down the path toward Apple-dore. She called him back.

"Wait. You'll need money to hire a horse," she said, plundering once again her small horde.

He thrust the coins into his pocket and wrapped his arms around her. "Take care of yourself. Take care of my son. I have made some powerful enemies this day. If I don't return, you may have another son to raise."

She held him out at arm's length, locked her gaze with his. "Don't you worry about him. I lost one son to the church. I'll not lose another."

※

Anna did not weep when Sister Matilde met her with the news.

It was just before dawn. They had made the whole journey dawn to dawn, stopping only long enough to rest the horses. At Headcorn Manor the old gatekeeper borrowed a second horse for Anna so they could move faster. They'd stopped again in Maidstone for refreshment, but Anna had eaten only one bite before the food clogged in her throat.

For all their hurrying, they had not arrived early enough.

"I'm sorry, Anna. Mother died last night," the sister said, her eyes glittering with unshed tears. "She died very peacefully. She just smiled and closed her eyes as though she were seeing some wonderful heavenly dream."

"I want to see her," Anna said.

"She is laid out in the chapel. Some of the sisters are sitting vigil. You need to rest first. To ride so far, so recently after giving birth—Anna, you must rest."

"I will rest after I have seen her," Anna said quietly.

"Very well, then." When they entered the chapel, Sister Matilde motioned for the sisters to leave. "We'll be right outside," she said as they shuffled across the floor.

The chapel was lit only with the flickering candles at each end of Kathryn's bier and a few torchlights along the wall. The candle flames danced as Anna approached the bier. The smell of incense, cloying and sweet, failed to mask the smell of death and threatened to overcome her. She felt dizzy, but fastened her attention on the face in front of her.

Anna still did not weep.

She stood mutely at the altar, numb of mind and body, staring at the woman who had so lately entered her life and yet had always been a part of it. She is beautiful laid out in her snow-white linen habit, Anna thought. No wonder my grandfather loved her so. Her wimple was pulled forward, framing the perfect oval of her face, almost hiding the scarred cheek, and the fine smooth line of her brow, even the few lines around her mouth, looked as though they were carved in alabaster. She looked like a statue of some venerated saint to whom the pilgrims prayed. She is my grandmother, Anna thought. Where are my tears? She was all I had. She loved me. She deserves my tears.

She stood there for a long time in the flickering candlelight, her body so stiff she felt she could not move, her engorged breasts heavy and aching. From outside she heard shuffling and the murmuring voices of the sisters, a bell tolling the little hours.

She loosened the lacings of her bodice. Her shirt was damp, and she worried that her child might be hungry, worried too that her milk might dry up before she could return to him. The silver cross hanging around her neck had fallen inside her tight cleavage. It pricked her breast. She unfastened the clasp, and as the necklace fell into her hand, she remembered the day her grandfather had given it to her, passing it down from her grandmother Rebekka and her mother, Rose. She remembered too how Kathryn had repaired it for her. It had been the key that brought them together.

With trembling hands she raised the little filigreed cross to her lips and placed it in Kathryn's clasped hands. The silver cruciform gleamed against her scarred left hand, the tiny pearls of its star glowing creamy against the marble whiteness.

"When you see Finn the Illuminator, give him this," Anna said softly. "Then he will know I kept my promise."

The rushlights danced in their sentinel sconces. Anna's footfalls whispered against the flagstones in the silent chapel as she walked away from Kathryn's body lying cold and still as the stone on which it rested.

And still she did not cry.

❦

Anna was standing alone over Kathryn's grave when Gabriel came for her.

It was evensong of the next day and the last shovelful of dirt had been heaped upon the coffin. The faint voices of the sisters singing the vespers mass for Kathryn echoed from the choir. In the gathering dusk, she mistook the approaching man for the grave-digger who had finished setting the cross in place, the charred cross from above Mother's desk. Anna had insisted they use it as a marker. Sister Agatha had protested the melted, disfigured crucifix. "You can't even tell it is a man," she harrumphed. But Anna had been firm. She knew the story of that cross. "It guarded her in life. It should guard her in death. The next abbess will have no use for it, anyway."

"Anna," he said.

Her body stiffened at the low, sad sound of her name in Gabriel's voice, urgent, pleading, yet still carrying the vestiges of clerical authority. "I'm sorry," he said. "I know you are grieving. But you must come back with me. You are not safe here and our child needs you."

The heart that she'd thought frozen gave a little jerk. She turned to face him. "Have you seen him?"

"He is all right, Anna. He is well cared for."

"Your mother is a good woman. Our child is safe with her."

A frown twisted the fine line of his mouth into a scowl. She wanted to reach up and straighten it with her fingers.

"Yes, she is a good woman," he said. "But a child needs a mother."

"I do not need that reminder, Gabriel, when I'm standing over the grave of the only woman I ever called 'mother' and that so lately come." She swallowed hard, surprised by a sob clotting in her throat.

From the shadowy stand of yew trees bordering the graveyard came the mournful call of a turtledove to its mate.

"Anna—" He reached out his hand to her, but she pulled her shawl tighter, drawing into herself, unable to take his hand.

"What news of Sir John?" she asked.

"He was condemned to death."

"Gabriel, no. Please, God, no." The words blended with the murmuring of the yew branches, as though they too were praying for Sir John.

His hand rested on the hem of her shawl. "You can take some comfort. He has escaped and is safe away."

"Where?"

"Wales, probably. I do not know. I do not want to know." He did not look at her as he answered. His fingers worried the fringe of the shawl, brushing against her skin.

His touch sent warmth surging through her and yet she shivered, remembering the predatory look in Arundel's eye the day he'd come to arrest her, remembering too the nobleman whose cushion she was given in the prison. His noble estate had not saved him either. Hugging herself more tightly, she withdrew from Gabriel as if to deny her body the comfort of his touch, lashing out instead in anger.

"What was your part, *Brother* Gabriel? Did you testify against him? Did you help the archbishop condemn a good man to death for daring to spread the gospel of the same Lord you profess to serve?"

She held her breath, sorry for the coldness of her tone, sorry too that she had raised her voice in rancor here, beside her grandmother's grave. She was not even sure how she wanted him to answer. If he said yes, that he had testified against Sir John, then he would have betrayed her once again. If he said no, then it would mean that his life was worth less than the instruments of torture they would use on him. Her life as well. And the life of their son.

"I testified for him, Anna. I helped him to escape. With that action I may have condemned us all."

She bent away from him, toward Kathryn's grave, feeling hot tears sting her eyelids. It was the answer she most wanted, and most dreaded.

"I am a hunted man, Anna, as long as Arundel lives. If I stay here, my life and yours, our son's, even my mother's, will be in danger. I mean to be on the next ship out. I don't know if I will ever be able to return. The archbishop—if he learns of our marriage, and he may already know—will think I've abandoned you as I've abandoned my other vows. You will be safe. He'll have no further use for you. You and our son can stay at Appledore for a season. Then maybe you can return home to the abbey."

"Then the archbishop would be right about one thing, wouldn't he? Isn't that exactly what you are doing? Abandoning me? It wouldn't be the first time, would it, Gabriel?"

Return home to the abbey! Without Kathryn, what was there for her here? Even Sir John and Lady Joan would be gone, in hiding, or worse. Grief surged over her, bringing with it a blackness she hadn't felt since that day on the bridge when she'd fallen into the water. But here there was no river to receive her, only raw earth. Her knees sank into the damp mound of Kathryn's grave.

A light rain had started to fall. It was as though the sky had labored all day, piling up its doleful clouds, gathering its tears to release them now in concert with Anna's—a torrential flood of tears, running down her face with the rain. A great tearing sob racked her body, and another, and then she could not stop. She beat upon the mounded earth with her fists, clutching the soil in her hands, mingling great handfuls with her tears, smearing it on her hands, her arms, even her face, tasting the grit of it on her lips, smelling the heavy clay.

Gabriel's voice called her name over and over as though from a great distance. She was conscious that he was kneeling beside her, his knees mired in the mud, wrapping his arms around her, pleading in his voice.

"Don't, Anna. Don't. Please. The abbess would not have wanted you to make yourself mad with grief. Such a life as hers deserves a celebration."

But Anna was grieving all of them: Finn and Martin and Jetta and Kathryn and Jerome and even the headless nobleman and more—Sir John and all the ones still to come. All that death had claimed from her and would claim from her. Why did Death not take her too? Let her melt into the grave and join the body there.

But it was not death's breath she felt on her neck. It was Gabriel's—warm and quivering, whispering words in her ear like that first night when Van-Cleve had held her after Jetta's death.

"Shh. Come away, Anna. Out of the rain. Our child needs you."

VanCleve's voice. No, not VanCleve's voice. Gabriel's voice. Gabriel's arms like bands holding her together. Her husband's arms. She could feel his beating heart.

"I love you," he said. "I have loved you since the first day I saw you, standing in the marketplace in Rheims. You have come so far. You must not give in to this despair. If not for me, for Finn. For that faith you claim."

Finn? Which Finn did he mean? Was he talking about the old man sleeping in Týn Churchyard? Or the baby, slumbering in his cradle, hidden like the infant Moses, in Romney Marsh?

A flash of lightning split the clouds. Anna looked into that glowing heat and saw Death astride his pale horse, galloping toward them across the sky, his scythe upraised like the pictures carved in the cathedral doors. Beneath his hooded cowl, she thought she saw Arundel's face, the flesh falling away to the bone. She felt her knees sinking deeper into the grave.

Gabriel's arms, his voice, tugged at her. "Finn needs you, Anna. He needs his mother. I need you."

A sob turned in her throat and erupted in wild, hysterical laughter. She raised her fists toward the image of that Grim Reaper who stalks all souls. *Did you hear that, old man? You have not taken it all from me. My husband is beside me, my husband who loves me, and our son sleeps in his cradle. The joke is on you. There are two Finns. They will meet someday underneath heaven's great gold canopy of light—all the Finns and Kathryns and Rebekkas and Martins and Jans that you have harvested with your dull blade. And where will you be then? Rotting in that Purgatory conjured by your own imagination, and no one will be left to pray your sorry soul to heaven.*

With a sound like the crashing at the world's end, lightning ripped the sky again, blinding her. The pale horse reared up on its hind legs, sawing at the clouds, its rider falling to the ground like Satan hurled from heaven. Death—the dreaded enemy transformed to a pile of rag and bone. In that moment of startling clarity and melting rage, Anna might have pitied Death, pitied even the old archbishop—if she'd had strength enough to feel.

The lightning ceased.

The thunder rolled low and far away. The clouds blended to a wall of gray.

Anna's sobs, like the thunder, subsided.

Gabriel half lifted, half dragged her away from the grave to the shelter of the lych-gate. He took off his doublet and put it around her. He held her. They sat together on the bench where Kathryn's coffin had rested only hours gone, listening to the rain drip from the eaves of the peaked roof.

When she had gained a modicum of composure, Gabriel said, still holding her, "We should not linger here, Anna. I'll take you back to Appledore. You and the babe can come with me or not. You married me to save our child from shame. But only you can make a husband of me. It is your choice."

She pulled away. He stood up and wiped the mud from her face with his sleeve.

"After all that you have given up, Gabriel, you would say that?" Her voice was husky. It hurt to talk.

"I have given up nothing, Anna. I told myself the day I saw you standing in your bookstall that God had put you there for me to save."

In the pause that followed, the dove called again to its mate, a lonely cooing sound. Anna wondered if Kathryn's spirit heard it too.

"But it was the other way around," Gabriel said softly. "God in His mercy put you there to save me. The only real thing in my life—the only thing I'm sure about—is my love for you and our child." He pointed to the new-made grave. "I saw more of Christ in her than I ever saw in my black-robed brothers."

"You're wearing your husband clothes," she said at the mention of the black robes.

She considered him carefully as though seeing him for the first time—this weary yeoman, leaning against the portal of the lych-gate, mud on his breeches, his wet shirtsleeves clinging to his skin. What would she have thought of him if she'd met this Gabriel first? Would she have loved him? Looking at him now, his stooped shoulders, the pain in his eyes—how much courage it must have taken to reexamine all that he thought he believed, to watch it all crumble beneath him. There was something of Van-Cleve in him. Something of the Dominican friar. He was both and he was neither, something better, nobler. She thought of Finn the Illuminator and his beloved Rebekka. How he had spurned his noble estate to marry a Jewess.

"It was a mercy for me too," she said. "I have no other home except the one you and I and Finn will make together."

She looked hard into his face, trying to discern what he was thinking. She thought she saw relief in the easing of the tight muscles around his mouth, the little half-sigh he allowed.

"Anna, are you sure? Are you sure that's what you want to do? You could stay with my mother. You and the child would be safe. I am not abandoning you. I shall send you what sustenance I can."

"Do you not want us, then, Gabriel? Is that what you are saying?"

"No! By my troth, I swear it. I want you with me. I want him. It is my heart's only desire. But your safety——"

Safety. Kathryn had sent Anna's grandfather away for his safety, letting him think she was dead. She had given him up because she loved him. Was that what Gabriel was doing? Her grandfather had grieved that loss all his life. Kathryn and Finn had accomplished much apart, but how much more might they have done together? And how much joy had they lost?

"There is no safety but what God in His mercy freely grants us." She took his hands in hers and drew them to her heart. "I am your wife, Gabriel. Whatever we face, we face together, trusting to that same mercy that brought us together."

"Then you can forgive VanCleve's deceit?"

"If you can forgive Anna's bitterness."

A ghost of VanCleve's old grin softened his next words. "A sharp-tongued wife can be an asset for a scribe, I suppose—and yours is sharp enough to point the toughest quills."

" 'Tis very well, then, Master Scribe, that you think so, because you've likely not heard the last of it." She kissed him lightly on his lips, her next words soft and low. "We will learn forgiveness and trust together."

He was about to return the kiss when Anna stopped him. She pointed to Sister Matilde, who, heedless of the misting rain, was heading for them as fast as her wide-hipped body would allow. "Anna, thank God I found you before he did," she said breathlessly. "You have to leave. At once! Sister Agatha sent me to warn you."

"Sister Agatha!"

Matilde shook her head. "Don't second-guess a gift. Just take it and be grateful. The Lord works in mysterious ways. Master Flemmynge is in the visitor's room. He is here to pay his respects, or so he says. He does not need to find you here." She looked directly at Gabriel, making no mention of his strange appearance. "Or you either."

"Can't I at least say good-bye to Bek?"

"There's no time. There's a limit to how long Sister Agatha can stall the cleric. Her talents are not large. Bek is happy here. If he sees you now, it will only make him miss you more." She had an arm around each of them and was guiding them back into the rain. "Lord Cobham's servant will meet you at the Rochester Cross with fresh horses. When you are well away, Gabriel, see that she rests."

Anna held out her arms to hug her but remembered her muddy clothes and drew back. "Sister Matilde . . . you have been like a sister in the truest sense to me . . ."

"Off with both of you before you set me to crying. And Godspeed to—"

Sister Agatha's strident voice interrupted, carrying from the open door of the chapel. "Master Flemmynge, it is kind of you to want to see Mother's grave even in the rain, though I think you'll find that everyone is gone." Loud even for Sister Agatha.

Matilde thrust a bundle at Anna. "Here are some dry clothes and a bit of food. Don't go back through the cloisters. Leave from here." Then she hugged Anna, not seeming to care about the mud that transferred itself to her clean white linen.

Sister Agatha was still standing in the doorway, completely blocking Flemmynge's view. She heard him grumble something and Sister Agatha stepped aside to let him peer into the empty graveyard. Without even a glance at the lych-gate, he stepped back inside, out of the rain, lest he spoil his fine garments. Agatha shut the door.

As they left the abbey behind, Anna looked back. Candlelight glowed in the windows of the abbey chapel, where the sisters would be finishing their evening prayers. *This is the last time I will see it,* she thought, trying to carve it in her memory.

Her gaze moved to gather in one last look at Kathryn's grave. In the misting rain and shadow of the trees, she could just make out the outline of the cross where the persistent dove still called to its mate. Loneliness and loss welled up afresh. She could not leave like this. Where would they go? What would they do? What if Gabriel tired of her and regretted all he had given up?

Then from out of the highest branch of a bordering yew another dove sailed low and fast and settled beside its mate on the cross arm.

"Look, Gabriel," she said. "There is a pair."

It is a sign—she thought, but did not say, lest the learned friar think her silly. A sign that Finn and Kathryn are together at last. *I will take it for a sign of blessing.* She felt her spirit lighten.

"That is as it should be," he said, reaching for her hand. "But we must hurry, Anna. Lest the archbishop's lackey discover us."

"Do not worry, husband; he has no interest in two ordinary pilgrims seeking only God's mercy."

EPILOGUE

31 December, the year of our Lord 1417

My dearest Anna,

How wonderful to hear your news of the birth of your twin daughters, Rebekka and Kathryn. I only wish that Mother had lived long enough to know her namesake. Though I am glad she did not live to hear the sad tidings I must impart to you now. We received news yesterday that Sir John has given his life for that cause in which he believed. It was reported to us that he died bravely and many were converted by his noble example. I fear that his death marks but the beginning here in England.

It is worse in Bohemia, where, after the burning of Jan Hus, civil war has broken out. I pray that you and Gabriel and Finn, and his two little sisters, have found a refuge there in Paris from the persecutions to come, and that you will not return to Bohemia. Since Gabriel has been admitted to the guild as a master scribe, I must conclude that you are prospering. You mention the Bible readings in your home. Please be careful.

Sister Agatha is abbess now. We do not do the good work we once did. Now we copy only those works approved by Archbishop Chichele. He persecutes the Lollards with even more vigor than did Archbishop Arundel.

And the king is with him in that effort. But with Sister Agatha as abbess, we need never worry about heretical books in our scriptorium.

Concerning books, King Henry returned your books to the abbey in person, saying that it was his understanding that your use for them was not sectarian in any way. I am sending them with this letter. Mother Agatha would not have them here anyway.

You asked about Bek and Lady Joan. Sir John was captured in Wales. Lady Joan was not with him. Cooling Castle is deserted and we have had no word from its lady. I have heard she is with her daughter, Lady Brooke. I pray that it is true and that there she can find solace for her grief.

You need not worry so about Bek. He has grown tall in your absence, and although he will never be strong in body, he is strong in spirit. He writes music for our choir. He misses you, but he seems happy. He is always singing—when he is not ringing the bells. One day, the king called upon him—yes, the king. It was the day His Majesty returned your books. It was quite something to see them together—Bek huddled with the king, instructing His Majesty's fingers on the correct placement on the strings of a harp. Bek seemed to think himself an equal with the king and the king seemed not to mind. I saw a deep sadness in His Majesty. They say he is bitter at Sir John's plot against him. I know few details of that supposed plot or of Sir John's execution, and I would not burden you if I did.

I must return to my duties, Anna. Without Sir John's patronage we are hard-pressed to earn our way. Godspeed be with you. I will leave you with the words from Julian of Norwich that Mother so often quoted: All will be well.

Your loving Sister,
Matilde

AUTHOR'S NOTE

fter the Peasants' Revolt of 1381, the Church in England attempted to stamp out the dissent sparked by the teachings of the Oxford cleric John Wycliffe, a movement which came to be known as Lollardy. While the bishops succeeded in driving the movement underground, they could not stop it from traveling abroad, especially after Richard II, who was king of England during Wycliffe's time, married a woman from the noble house of Bohemia. Queen Anne was more receptive to Wycliffe's ideas, and because of the new relationship between the royal houses of Bohemia (now known as the Czech Republic) and England, a student exchange program between Oxford and Charles University in Prague brought Wycliffe's radical ideas to Bohemia. There they flourished under the preaching of Jan Hus. By the early fifteenth century, the seeds of Lollardy were once again sprouting in England and presenting a direct challenge to the authority of both the established Church and the king.

Henry V, who reigned from 1413 to 1422, is probably best known for his defeat of the French at the Battle of Agincourt during England's Hundred

Years' War with France. Thanks to William Shakespeare, who used him as the original prototype for the scurrilous Falstaff, Sir John Oldcastle is remembered primarily for his early friendship with the young Prince Harry before he became king. The two served together in battle and became, according to Shakespeare, good drinking buddies; but Lord Brooke, the master of entertainment at the Court of King James, thought Shakespeare took too many liberties with his honored ancestor. Not wanting to offend such an important member of his patron's court, Shakespeare wrote a disclaimer and changed the name of the jocular but cowardly Sir John to Falstaff.

There was nothing cowardly about Sir John Oldcastle. History records that he died bravely. Some say he died a Christian martyr, others a traitor. After Henry V, driven by archbishops Arundel and Chichele, grew ruthless in his persecution of the Lollards, Sir John was charged with plotting to seize the king at Eltham during a Twelfth Night celebration and form a commonwealth that would allow for religious dissent. When that effort was aborted, several other insurrections and plots followed—all laid at Oldcastle's doorstep. A reward of one thousand pounds was put on his head. He was wounded and captured in Wales and brought to London in a horse litter. There he was summarily condemned without trial, on the basis of the previous conviction, when he had escaped execution with the help of a parchment maker by name of William Fisher.

To flesh out the characters of both Henry V and Sir John, I drew not only from the historical record but from Shakespeare's characterization of these figures. To my knowledge, there is no historical evidence or even conjecture that William Fisher and Henry V were one and the same, although history does point to the king's reluctance to execute his old friend. History also records that on December 14, 1417, Sir John Oldcastle was taken to Saint Giles Field beside the Tower, where he was drawn (stomach cut open) and hanged (for being a traitor) over a slow fire, where he was burned to death (for heresy).

The Lollard persecutions continued until the Reformation. Many men and women were tortured and executed for religious dissent, including Jan Hus in Bohemia. Unfortunately, such religious intolerance did not end with the Reformation.